Hortense Mancini, Duchesse de Mazarin.

From an Engraving by G. Valck, after the picture by Sir Peter Lely.

FIVE FAIR SISTERS

AN ITALIAN EPISODE AT THE COURT OF LOUIS XIV

BY

H. NOEL WILLIAMS

AUTHOR OF

"MADAME RÉCAMIER AND HER FRIENDS," "MADAME DE POMPADOUR,"
"MADAME DE MONTESPAN," "MADAME DU BARRY,"
"QUEENS OF THE FRENCH STAGE,"
"LATER QUEENS OF THE FRENCH STAGE," ETC.

WITH PHOTOGRAVURE PLATE AND
SIXTEEN OTHER ILLUSTRATIONS

LONDON
HUTCHINSON & CO.
PATERNOSTER ROW
1906

TO

MY WIFE

LIST OF ILLUSTRATIONS

HORTENSE MANCINI, DUCHESSE DE MAZARIN *Frontispiece* (*Photogravure*)
From an engraving after the painting by Sir Peter Lely.

TO FACE PAGE

CARDINAL MAZARIN 10
From an engraving after the painting by Mignard.

ARMAND DE BOURBON, PRINCE DE CONTI 38
From an engraving by Frosne.

ANNE MARIE MARTINOZZI, PRINCESS DE CONTI 40
From an engraving after the painting by Beaubrun.

LAURE MANCINI, DUCHESSE DE MERCŒUR 58
From a contemporary print.

LOUIS XIV 72
From an engraving after the drawing by Wallerant Vaillant.

MARIE MANCINI 110
From an engraving after the painting by Sir Peter Lely.

ANNE OF AUSTRIA, QUEEN OF FRANCE 158
From an engraving after the painting by Mignard.

PRINCE CHARLES (AFTER CHARLES V) OF LORRAINE . . . 200
From an engraving by Nanteuil.

MARIA THERESA, QUEEN OF FRANCE 220
From an engraving after the painting by Beaubrun.

LORENZO ONOFRIO COLONNA, PRINCIPE DI PALLIANO, GRAND
CONSTABLE OF THE KINGDOM OF NAPLES 238
From an engraving after the drawing by Giacomo Bichi

MARIANNE MANCINI, DUCHESSE DE BOUILLON 254
From a contemporary print.

ARMAND DE LA PORTE, DUC DE MAZARIN ET DE LA MEILLERAYE . 268
From an engraving after the painting by Mignard.

MARIE MANCINI COLONNA, PRINCIPESSA DI PALLIANO . . 310
From the painting by Mignard.

CHARLES EMMANUEL II, DUKE OF SAVOY 330
From an engraving by G. Vallet.

MARIE LOUISE D'ORLEANS, QUEEN OF SPAIN . . . 352
From an engraving by L. Armessin.

OLYMPE MANCINI, COMTESSE DE SOISSONS 384
From a contemporary print.

FIVE FAIR SISTERS

CHAPTER I

Mazarin and his family—Hostile criticism provoked by his promotion of his brother Michele—His sisters, Signora Martinozzi and Signora Mancini, and their children—The Cardinal determines to bring his nephews and nieces to France—Arrival of Anne-Marie Martinozzi and Laure, Olympe, and Paul Mancini—Their reception at Court—Prediction of Madame de Villeroi—Kindness of Anne of Austria to the little girls—Question of the relations between the Queen-Mother and Mazarin considered.

FOR five years after he had succeeded Richelieu as chief Minister, in May 1643, Mazarin remained an isolated man. He had no relations in France, and, with a single exception, he brought none of his kinsfolk from Italy to share his prosperity. Madame de Motteville tells us that he was wont to declare that the beautiful Italian works of art with which his hôtel was filled were the only relatives he desired to have with him.

The exception referred to was his younger brother, Michele Mazarini, a Jacobin monk at Rome, to further whose interests he did not hesitate to use the diplomacy and power of France, since, not content with appointing him Archbishop of Aix, he intimidated the Pope into making him a cardinal. He soon had reason to regret his misplaced kindness. The new cardinal differed strangely from his brother. Giulio—or Jules, to give him the Gallicized form of his name—was

B

"affable, insinuating, and a charming companion";[1]
Michele, rough, headstrong, and brutal. So far from
being grateful for the favours bestowed upon him, he
treated the all-powerful Minister with the utmost
familiarity, and was accustomed to speak of him
behind his back with undisguised contempt. He had,
indeed, respect for no one, not even for the Queen-
Mother, and in a short time contrived to render himself so generally detested that, in order to get rid of
him, Mazarin sent him as Viceroy to Catalonia, an
appointment which gave rise to much scandal. Michele,
however, whether from incapacity or some other cause,
only held the post a few months and then returned to
Rome, where he soon afterwards died, a victim of
debauchery, if Gui-Patin is to be believed.

Nothing which Mazarin had hitherto done had excited
such hostile criticism as his efforts on behalf of this
unworthy brother, and the failure of the experiment
discouraged any desire on his part to bring the elder
members of his family to France. But the younger
members seemed possible elements of strength. Before
Mazarin left Rome, as the Pope's vice-legate to France,
in 1634, he had established his two sisters in excellent
marriages. The elder had married Girolamo Martinozzi; the younger, Hieronyma by name, Lorenzo
Mancini, a Roman baron. Of Martinozzi, little is
known, save that he is said to have been of noble
descent. But the Mancini were undoubtedly an old
family, who could trace their ancestry back to the
fourteenth century, though whether they had ever
been quite so illustrious as the Duchesse de Mazarin
(Hortense Mancini) tells us in her " Mémoires " is open
to question.

[1] Maréchal de Gramont, "Mémoires."

Signora Martinozzi, now a widow, had two daughters
—Anne-Marie and Laure. Signora Mancini had been
blessed with ten children, of whom eight—three sons,
Paul, Philippe, and Alphonse, and five daughters,
Laure, Olympe, Marie, Hortense, and Marianne—were
still living.[1]

In 1647, finding himself firmly established in the
Queen-Mother's affections, and apparently firmly established in power, Mazarin resolved to make a fresh
experiment towards transplanting his family to France,
and accordingly demanded from Signora Martinozzi
her eldest daughter, and from Signora Mancini two
of her daughters, the eldest, and her son Paul. These
children were from seven to thirteen years of age.
Although invited to journey to a foreign land, to which
their mothers were not bidden, there was no hesitation
in sending them to the brilliant lot which awaited the
adopted children and probable heirs of the great
Minister, and in September they arrived at Fontainebleau, in charge of the Duchesse de Noailles, who had
been despatched to Rome with a numerous suite to escort
them to France, just as if they had been Princes and
Princesses of the Blood.

"On 11 September (1647)," says Madame de Motteville, "we saw arrive from Italy three nieces of
Cardinal Mazarin and a nephew. Two Mancini sisters
and the nephew were the children of the youngest sister
of his Eminence, the third niece was a Martinozzi,
daughter of the Minister's eldest sister. The eldest
of the little Mancini (Laure) was a pleasing brunette,
with a handsome face, about twelve or thirteen years
of age. The second, also a brunette (Olympe), had

[1] We have adopted the Gallicized form of the Christian names of
these children, as it is by them that they are known to fame.

a long face and pointed chin. Her eyes were small, but lively, and it might be expected that, when fifteen years of age, she would have some charm. According to the rules of beauty, it was impossible to grant her any, save that of having dimples in her cheeks. Mlle. Martinozzi was blonde; her features were beautiful, and she had much sweetness in her eyes; and had we been astrologers enough to divine in her face the prospects of her fortune, as we did those of her beauty, we should have known that she was destined to high rank. The last two were of the same age; we were told about nine or ten years old."

The little strangers were met at Fontainebleau by Madame de Nogent, who brought them to Paris and conducted them to Anne of Austria's apartments in the Palais-Royal. The Cardinal was with the Queen when they arrived, but he took scarcely any notice of his young relatives, and almost immediately retired to his own apartments, on the plea of fatigue.[1] The Queen,

---

[1] Pending the completion of the Palais-Mazarin, in the Rue Neuve des Petits-Champs, Mazarin occupied a suite of apartments in the *basse-cour* of the Palais-Royal, opening on to the Rue des Bons-Enfants, which enabled him to have constant access to the Queen, whose apartments were situated in the right wing of the Cour des Proues, the only part of the Palais-Royal, it may be remarked, which still retains some traces of its primitive ornamentation. These apartments had been left in an unfinished state by Richelieu, but they had been completed by order of the Queen, who had added an oratory, a bath-room, and a gallery. It was in this gallery, which connected the apartments of the Queen with those of the Cardinal, that the meetings of the Council were usually held, and it was here that, on 18 January 1650, took place the arrest of the three princes—Condé, Conti, and Longueville.

At the time when he became chief Minister, Mazarin occupied the Hôtel de Clèves, situated in the Rue du Louvre, called also the Rue de l'Oratoire. This hotel, which was demolished in 1758, had been erected for Catherine de Clèves, widow of Henri, Duc de Guise, assassinated at Blois in 1588. After the discovery of the Duc de Beaufort's plot against his life, in September 1643, the Cardinal, feeling that he was no longer in security at the Hôtel de Clèves, vacated it for

however, greeted them very kindly, thought them pretty, "and all the time the children spent in her presence was employed in remarking on their appearance." After her Majesty had dismissed them, they were taken to the Cardinal, "who did not appear to care much for them ; on the contrary, he jested about those who were silly enough to show them attentions. But, despite this scorn, he certainly had great designs based on these little girls. His indifference about them was all pure comedy ; and by this we may judge that it is not only on the comic stage that good pieces are played."[1]

The following day, the nieces were again brought to the Queen, who received them as kindly as before, and "kept them some minutes near her to examine them." Their uncle was again present, but, as on the previous day, affected hardly to notice them. After this they were shown to the Court, and the time-serving courtiers, undeceived by the Cardinal's seeming indifference, crowded so eagerly round the new arrivals that there seemed some danger of them being suffocated by the press, and vied with one another in extolling their beauty, their charming manners, and their intelligence, "which they credited them with on sight." "See those little girls," remarked the wife of Maréchal de Villeroi to Gaston d'Orléans, the King's uncle, "who are now not rich ; they will soon have fine châteaux, large incomes, splendid jewels, beautiful silver, and perhaps great dignities. . . ." The maréchale was a true prophet. It was evident that the first families

the apartments in the Palais-Royal, or Palais-Cardinal as it was then called, which had been bequeathed by Richelieu to the late king, and whither the whole Court removed from the Louvre, a few weeks later. —Amédée Renée, " Les Nièces de Mazarin."

[1] Madame de Motteville, "Mémoires."

of the realm would be ready to dispute the hand of the Cardinal's nieces, and that he would have only to choose amongst the wealthiest, the most powerful, and the most illustrious, to efface, by brilliant alliances, his own humble origin and establish his power on a sure foundation.

The three girls were at first installed at the Hôtel de Clèves, in charge of Madame de Sénéce, formerly *gouvernante* to the young king ; while Paul Mancini was sent to be educated by the Jesuits at their college at Clermont, where he was allotted the room formerly occupied by the Prince de Conti, and treated in all respects as if he were a Prince of the Blood. Soon, at the instance of the Queen, the nieces were transferred to the Palais-Royal, to be brought up with Louis XIV and his younger brother, the little Duc d'Anjou ; but the Queen herself instructed them in religion, frequently taking them with her to benefit by the saintly conversation of the nuns of Val-de-Grâce, and treating them with the same tenderness as her own children.

There is, perhaps, no stronger proof of Anne's devotion to Mazarin than the manner in which she occupied herself with these girls ; and here it may not be out of place to devote some little space to a question which, though it has been discussed *ad nauseam* by French writers, seems to us to have hardly received satisfactory treatment from English and American historians : the relations between the Queen-Mother and the Cardinal.

At the accession of Louis XIV (14 May 1643), Mazarin's position in France was a most precarious one. Surrounded as he was by powerful enemies eager to undo the work of Richelieu, and regarded by the bulk of the nation with dislike and suspicion, on account of his foreign birth, he quickly perceived that his sole chance of making head against the forces arrayed against him lay in securing the unequivocal favour of the Queen-Mother, and to this end all his energies were forthwith directed.

Anne of Austria had then just passed her fortieth year. She was very devout, but also very coquettish, in a romantic and strictly decorous way, attaching great importance to high-flown compliments, languishing looks, and delicate little attentions. Had Richelieu condescended to such means to conciliate her, it is possible that he might have gained as much influence over her as Mazarin subsequently enjoyed. But the great Cardinal was "*pédant en amour*," to borrow the expression of Anne's confidante, Madame de Chevreuse, an unforgivable fault in her Majesty's eyes.

Mazarin profited by his predecessor's failure. He pretended to be madly in love, and yet overwhelmed by the sense of his own unworthiness. He had nothing, he said, but his devotion to plead for him ; he was more lowly than the grass before his goddess. His handsome face, his charming manners, the superiority of his intellect, his unswerving devotion to her interests and those of her infant son, all combined to flatter the *amour propre* of the Queen. He succeeded, and succeeded beyond his most sanguine expectations.

Yet, his success was not immediate. He had to overcome not only indifference, but a feeling well-nigh amounting to aversion on the part of Anne, who had long regarded him merely as the creature of Richelieu, and for some weeks his fate trembled in the balance. His *Carnets*, which reveal to us the inmost workings of this subtle mind, show that in the summer of 1643 he himself was doubtful as to the issue, for he complains of Anne's dissimulation, and that her entire confidence was not given him. By September, however, that distrust is dispelled. "I should no longer doubt," he writes, "since the Queen, in an excess of goodness, has told me that nothing can take from me the part which she has graciously given me."

What that part was has, as we have said elsewhere, been much debated. According to a curious anecdote, which Brienne relates in his "Mémoires," Anne herself protested that the Cardinal's attraction for her was of a purely intellectual order.

One day, Madame de Brienne, the wife of the secretary, was in the Queen's oratory, when Anne entered, her beads in her hand, plunged in a profound reverie. "Let us pray together," said she; "we shall be the better heard." As they rose from their devotions, Madame de Brienne craved permission to speak to the Queen, in regard to her Majesty's relations with the Cardinal. Anne consented, and was accordingly informed of all that malicious tongues were saying. The Queen blushed, and tears filled her eyes. "Why have you not told me this before?" said she. "I confess that I am attached to him—I can even say tenderly; but my affection does not go so far as love, or, if it does, I am not aware of it. My senses have no part; only my mind is charmed by the beauty of his intellect. If this is wrong, I will renounce it before God and the saints. I will speak to him no more, save of the affairs of State, and check him when he speaks of anything else." Madame de Brienne then asked the Queen to swear on some relics of the saints which were in the oratory, that "she would never abandon what she had promised God," a request with which her Majesty complied readily enough. "God's goodness," said the pious confidante, "will soon make your innocence known."

"Anne, however, had taken oaths before," observes Mazarin's able American biographer, Mr. J. B. Perkins, "and the remembrance of Val-de-Grâce makes us doubtful whether simple admiration for beauty of mind could have withstood the shock of circumstance and survived the lapse of years."[1]

However that may be, the tone of the Queen's letters to the Cardinal is strangely inconsistent with her protestations to Madame de Brienne. During Mazarin's second exile, in 1652, Anne concludes one of her letters to him with this passionate cry : " 15 [the Queen] is a thousand times ≇ [yours] until the last sigh. Adieu, I can write no more, and he [Mazarin] knows why."[2] And again, some months later, when the Cardinal was with the army, she writes : "I cannot but tell you that I think the sight of those one loves is not unpleasant, even if it be but for a few hours. I fear that your fondness for the army will be greater than all others. Still, I pray you to believe me that I shall be always what I should be, come what will."

The years bring no change in the warmth of these epistles. "Your letter," she writes, in June, 1660, "has given me great joy. If I had believed that one of my letters would have thus pleased you, I would have

---

[1] "France under Richelieu and Mazarin."

[2] In their private correspondence, the Queen and Mazarin employed certain signs or ciphers, of which the key exists. The numbers 16, 22, and 24 indicate the Queen; the numbers 15, 26, and 46 indicate Mazarin. The Queen is likewise designated under the names of *Séraphim* and *Ange*, and Mazarin under those of *le Ciel* and *la Mer*. Frequently, in his letters, Mazarin speaks of himself as a third person, to deceive any one into whose hands the letters might fall. Finally, the curious signs ≇ ★ indicate the affection or love of the Cardinal for the Queen and of the Queen for the Cardinal.

written it gladly. To see the pleasure with which it was received makes me recall another time, which indeed I do recall almost every minute. Though you may doubt it, if I could make you see my heart as well as what I say on this paper, you would be satisfied, or you would be the most ungrateful man in the world; and I do not believe you are that."

The letters of Mazarin are in the same tone. "*Mon Dieu!* How happy should I be and you satisfied," he writes from Brühl, in May 1651, "if you could see my heart, or if I could write what is in it! You would not find it difficult in that case, to agree that never was there a friendship approaching that which I entertain for you. I confess to you that I little imagined that it would go so far as to deprive me of all contentment, when my time is employed in anything else than in thinking of you."[1]

He knew the extent of his empire, did this astute Italian, and he exulted in reminding his royal conquest of it. "If you were nearer the *sea* [Mazarin], I believe that you would be more pleased. I trust that that will be soon."

It has frequently been claimed that the Queen and the Cardinal were secretly married. Such was the tradition preserved at the Palais-Royal, as the letters of the Duchesse d'Orléans, mother of the Regent, prove.[2] The same charge, too, is to be found in many of the pamphlets published during the Fronde, and has been accepted by more than one historian of weight, who argue that a woman of Anne's extravagant piety

---

[1] For the rest of this letter, see p. 25 *infra*.

[2] "The Queen-Mother, widow of Louis XIII, did more than love Cardinal Mazarin; she married him."—"Correspondance complète de Madame, Duchesse d'Orléans," *publiée par* G. Brunet, 1855, II, p. 3.

From an engraving after the painting by Mignard

CARDINAL MAZARIN

would have recoiled with horror from any connection
unsanctioned by Holy Church.

Those who hold this view, of course, start with the
assumption that Mazarin was only in minor Orders, and
therefore would have been free to marry had he been so
disposed. This was certainly the opinion of his contemporaries, and the Abbé de Laffmas, in a rhyming
letter which he addressed to the Cardinal in 1649, says :—

> Vous êtes un grand cardinal,
> Un homme de haute entreprise,
> Vingt fois abbé, homme de l'église,
> Quoique ne soyez *in sacris*. . . .

Aubery ("Histoire de Cardinal Mazarin") and Victor
Cousin (" La Jeunesse de Mazarin) pronounce also for
the negative, as does M. Chéruel (" Histoire de France
pendant la minorité de Louis XIV "). On the other
hand, Amédée Renée, in his " Nièces de Mazarin," and
that indefatigable unraveller of historical mysteries
M. Jules Loiseleur maintain that Mazarin was in full
Orders. The latter writer's arguments are interesting.

" The minutes of the proceedings of the consistory
of 16 December 1641," he writes, " preserved in the
Vatican Archives, at which he (Mazarin) was preconised
cardinal, qualifies him as cardinal of Saint Jean-de-
Latran. No mention is made of his quality of priest,
mention useless, in point of fact, and which would have
been without any object, since his title of canon is spoken
of, which supposes that quality. When an ecclesiastic
is spoken of as canon or bishop, no one thinks of adding
that he is a priest ; that goes without saying.

" Perhaps it may be objected that the kings of France
were honorary canons of various churches, and that
possibly Mazarin may have received the same honour.
To this we reply that the minutes of the proceedings of

the consistory do not speak of Mazarin as an honorary canon, but as an ordinary canon : *canonicus Lateranensis.* Further, Saint Jean-de-Latran is a Roman church, and only persons in Holy Orders were admitted to the canonicates of these kind of basilicas."[1]

These arguments seem sound enough, but M. Loiseleur was apparently unaware at the time when he wrote his book of the existence of a letter of the Cardinal which M. Chéruel cites in his "Histoire de France pendant la minorité de Louis XIV." This letter, addressed to one of his confidants, Elphideo Benedetti, was written when Mazarin was in exile at Brühl in 1651, and had some thought of visiting Rome. "As for the difficulty created by the Bull which deals with those not in Orders, one ought," he writes, "especially to consider the deprivation of the right of voting in the Conclave, and, in regard to that, I should desire to know whether, *in the event of my taking Holy Orders*, I should have the right of voting without any other dispensation being necessary." This passage, in the opinion of M. Chéruel, is a conclusive proof that Mazarin was only a lay cardinal, and most people, we think, will be inclined to agree with him.

M. Loiseleur, however, is on much surer ground when he proceeds to argue that, whether Mazarin was a lay cardinal or a cardinal-priest, he would equally have been unable to contract a marriage without a special dispensation from the Pope, and that such a dispensation had never been granted, except on the condition of the intending Benedict resigning his membership of the Sacred College.

"M. Michelet," says he, "is correct in asserting that there are examples of cardinal-princes whom Rome has

---

[1] "Problèmes historiques."

discardinalized, when some great political necessity obliged them to marry. We do not think that many such examples may be cited, but there is one at least. It is that of Cardinal Jean Casimir, elected King of Poland in 1649, who was relieved of his vows by the Pope and married his brother's widow, Marie de Gonzague. But, before he married, Casimir V laid aside the purple; he did not remain a cardinal. That is, in fact, the question, and we defy any one to cite a single cardinal, lay or not, whom Rome has permitted to marry and still to remain a cardinal. And Mazarin died a cardinal, for, in his last moments, the Nuncio Piccolomini administered the Indulgence *in articulo mortis*, which the Popes are in the habit of according to members of the Sacred College."

M. Loiseleur then goes on to point out that, if the Holy See, in defiance of all ecclesiastical usage, had accorded Mazarin permission to marry and still to retain the external apparel of his former dignity, the dispensation must have been granted either by Urban VIII, who died 28 July 1644, or by Innocent X, who succeeded him and lived till 1655. But it could hardly have been by Urban, he says, for we know, from a report of Mazarin's secret police, that, towards the end of October 1643, three nuns of Val-de-Grâce, intimate friends of the Queen, took upon themselves to send her Majesty a vigorously-worded remonstrance on the subject of her relations with the Cardinal, a remonstrance which would have been entirely purposeless, if, at this period, these relations had been legitimated by marriage. "Nor is that all. Certain notes of the Cardinal's fourth *carnet*, which comprises the end of the year 1643 and the beginning of 1644, and other notes of the fifth *carnet*, which extends down to 28 August of the latter year, show us that about the time of the death of Urban VIII the convents were still inveighing against Mazarin, influenced principally by his scandalous relations with the Queen, a fact which is inexplicable, supposing that a dispensation had been granted by the Pope; for the Queen, who had no secrets from her good friends of Val-de-Grâce, would not have failed to close their mouths by communicating to them the dispensation, if it had existed, and Père Vincent,[1] to whom was attributed the celebration of the marriage, would not have found himself included in the recriminations consigned to the famous *carnets*."

"As for Innocent X," continues M. Loiseleur, "he remained throughout his pontificate the bitter and persistent enemy of Mazarin, and no one in Europe was less likely to go out of his way to do the Cardinal a favour."

This would seem to us to render a marriage between the Cardinal and Anne of Austria extremely improbable, though it is just conceivable, as more than one writer has suggested, that Mazarin may have intimidated Innocent X, by the threat of the annexation of Avignon, into granting the necessary dispensation and also into maintaining silence in regard to it.

[1] Saint-Vincent de Paul.

CHAPTER II

Beginning of the Fronde—The Cardinal sends his nieces to Val-de-
Grâce—His plans for their establishment—Declines the offer of
Cardinal Barberini to marry his nephew to Laure Mancini—Looks
with favour upon the Duc de Candale—Arranges a marriage between
Laure and the Duc de Mercœur—The Prince de Condé opposed
to the match—Intrigues of the Marquis de Jarzé to supplant the
Cardinal in the affections of the Queen—His presumption punished
by Anne of Austria—Mazarin insulted by Condé—Renewal of the
civil war—The Cardinal leaves the kingdom—Exultation of his
enemies—The *Mazarinades*—The cardinal's nieces follows him into
exile—He establishes himself at Brühl—Marriage of the Duc de
Mercœur and Laure Mancini—Mazarin continues to direct affairs in
France—He raises an army and recrosses the frontier—His letter to
the Queen—He joins their Majesties at Poitiers—Return of his nieces
to Paris—Battle of the Faubourg Saint-Antoine and death of Paul
Mancini—Hatred of the Parisians against Mazarin—His second
exile—Tender letter of the Queen to the Cardinal—He is recalled to
France—His triumphant return.

BUT to return to the Mancini.

At the beginning of the year 1649, civil war
broke out—that curious medley of tragedy and bur-
lesque known as the Fronde, and on 5 January the
Court quitted Paris for Saint-Germain, while the
Cardinal's nieces were confided to the care of the nuns
of Val-de-Grâce. August found Court and Cardinal
once more at the Palais-Royal, the Treaty of Ruel
having cleared the air for the time being. But Mazarin,
perceiving that a second storm was brewing, judged it
best to allow his nieces to remain in security.

In the meanwhile, he had begun to busy himself with

plans for their establishment in life ; plans in which, it is hardly necessary to observe, the happiness of the young ladies themselves counted for very little. The eldest of the Mancini sisters, Laure, was now fifteen, and suitors had already begun to present themselves. Cardinal Barberini had made overtures on behalf of his nephew, a Colonna ; but Mazarin demurred to this proposal and suggested in preference one of the younger girls, who was still at Rome in a convent ; for, wrote he, " your proposition would disarrange the plans I have made for establishing all the others in France." This Mancini offered as a *pis-aller* was without doubt Marie, who was one day to become the wife of another Colonna. She was then at most ten years old, which fact, however, did not prevent her politic uncle from drawing up the articles of the marriage-contract.

At the time this letter was written, Mazarin had cast a favourable eye upon the Duc de Candale, the heir of the Épernons, " the first nobleman of the Court in good looks, magnificence, and riches, whom all the men envied, and whose regard all the gallant ladies desired to merit ; if they were not able to make him the trophy of their glory."[1] We may presume that the riches and the renown of his House counted for far more in the Cardinal's eyes than the good looks. But the young gentleman was in no hurry to exchange the rôle of Lothario for that of Benedick, and nothing came of the project ; though the probability of the duke allying

---

[1] Madame de Motteville, "Mémoires." Bussy-Rabutin, in his "Histoire amoureuse des Gaules," has traced the following portrait of this personage : " The Duc de Candale had blue eyes, a well-made nose, irregular features, a large and disagreeable mouth, very beautiful teeth, and golden blond hair in the greatest profusion possible to imagine ; he had an admirable figure, dressed well, and had the air of a man of the first quality."

himself with one of the other sisters was a frequent topic of discussion down to 1668, when a fever, or, if we are to believe Daniel de Cosnac, poison administered by a jealous husband, cut short his career of gallantry and plunged half the ladies of the Court into an ecstasy of grief."[1]

It was perhaps fortunate for Laure Mancini that M. de Candale was so reluctant to enter the holy estate, since a gentleman of so very susceptible a disposition could scarcely have been expected to make a model husband. Soon, however, another and—for the lady at least—a far more desirable *parti* was forthcoming, in the person of the Duc de Mercœur, whose father, the Duc de Vendôme, was the son of Henri IV and the beautiful Gabrielle d'Estrées. Mercœur had none of the ardent blood of his grandparents, or of the ambitious and turbulent disposition of his father and brother, the

[1] His friend Saint-Évremond describes, with all the interest of a public event, the universal grief which his untimely death occasioned among the fair : " The last years of his life, all our ladies cast their eyes on him. The most retiring did not allow themselves to sigh in secret ; the most gallant disputed for him, and desired to possess him as their most glorious conquest. After having divided them in the interests of gallantry, he reunited them in tears by his death. Those whom he had once loved recalled their old sentiments, and imagined that they had still to lose what they had already lost. Several who had been indifferent to him flattered themselves that they would not have been always thus, and, laying the blame on death, which had forestalled their happiness, they wept for this amiable man of whom they might have been the beloved. Finally, there were even some who regretted him through vanity, and one saw unknown ladies insinuate themselves into this commerce of tears, in order to get the credit of being gallant."

More than one disconsolate beauty cut off her hair in despair at the news of his death, among them the Marquise de la Baume, niece of the Maréchal de Villeroi, " who had the most beautiful fair hair in the world." The celebrated Comtesse d'Olonne, one of the latest of Candale's loves, Mlle. de Montpensier tells us, spent the whole night in tears, and on being questioned by her husband as to the cause of her grief, " begged him to forgive her and confessed that she had loved him (Candale) dearly."

Duc de Beaufort, the famous " *Roi des Halles*," but was in all respects an excellent man, amiable, pious, and gentle. Vendôme had grown weary of opposition to the Court, which had brought him nothing but exile and imprisonment, and was ready enough to accept the good things which an alliance with the Cardinal's family would ensure him ; while, on his side, Mazarin hoped to oppose the influence of Vendôme to that of the Prince de Condé and to gain over Beaufort.

The marriage was agreed upon. Vendôme was to receive the admiralty. Mercœur was to have for dowry 600,000 livres and the first vacant government. But Condé had become more troublesome than all the Frondeurs ; he had compelled Mazarin to enter into an agreement not to marry his nieces without obtaining his sanction, and, though he had at first raised no objection to the alliance, as the time for its consummation approached, he became opposed to a step which would make Mazarin less dependent and Vendôme more powerful, and declined to sign the contract. He now accused the Cardinal of having broken faith with him in regard to the government of *Pont-de-l'Arche*, in Normandy, and began to intrigue vigorously against him. Prompted by the prince, one of his protégés the Marquis de Jarzé, "who was by nature brusque, conceited, satirical, and frivolous," dared to raise his eyes to the Queen, in the hope of supplanting the Cardinal in her mature affections. This intrigue became an affair of State, which greatly preoccupied both the Regent and her Minister, and, on the advice of the latter, Anne administered a severe and well-merited rebuff to the presumptuous Jarzé. Madame de Motteville, an eye-witness, has left us the following account of this little comedy :—

"As Jarzé knew, to some extent, by the dismissal of

his friend Madame de Beauvais (a waiting-woman of the Queen, who had lent herself to the designs of Jarzé and had just been exiled on the Cardinal's demand), his position at Court, he thought to execute a clever stroke of policy by appearing to know nothing and to fear nothing. But the hour had come when he was fated to be punished for his presumption. The Queen, having it in her mind to rebuke him, did not fail the moment she saw him to attack him and to say to him, in a contemptuous tone, these very words: 'Really, M. de Jarzé, you are very ridiculous. I am told that you play the lover. A pretty gallant, forsooth! I pity you; they will have to send you to the Petites-Maisons. Though it is true that we need not be astonished at your madness, since it is inherited!'—meaning by that his grandfather, Maréchal de Lavardin, who was passionately in love with the late Queen, Marie de' Medici, and about whom her husband Henri IV used to jest with her.

"Poor Jarzé was overwhelmed by this thunderbolt. He dared not say a word in his justification. He stammered and left the cabinet, full of trouble, pale and undone. In spite of his mortification, he perhaps flattered himself with the reflection that the adventure was a fine one, the crime honourable, and that he had no cause to be ashamed of the accusation. The whole Court was instantly full of the event; the *ruelles* of the ladies rang with the sound of the royal words. The name of Jarzé was heard everywhere in Paris, and the provinces quickly had their share of it."

Jarzé's disgrace and the refusal of the Queen to pardon him put the *comble* upon the discontent of Condé. The hollow truce could not last long, and it was broken on the day when the haughty soldier addressed to the Cardinal a letter bearing on its cover the insulting words, "*All' illustrissimo signor Facchino.*"

The arrest of the princes Condé, Conti, and Longueville, on 18 January 1650, did not arrest the disorder, and, seeing the revolt gaining ground in the provinces, the Parliament of Paris, fulminating decrees against him[1] and Gaston d'Orléans at the head of the Fronde, Mazarin judged it prudent to leave the kingdom. On the night of 6–7 February 1651, he quitted the Palais-Royal, in disguise, followed by the Comte de Broglie and another gentleman, and took the road to Havre. Here he stopped to liberate the imprisoned princes, who had been transferred thither from Marcoussis at the end of the previous November,[2] after which he continued his journey to the frontier, by way of Abbeville and Doullens.

The Frondeurs sang pæans of triumph over the discomfiture and disappearance of their enemy. The pamphlets—those famous *Mazarinades*, which had rained upon the Cardinal since the beginning of the Fronde—redoubled in numbers and bitterness, and whole volumes might be filled with the libels in prose and verse that flowed from the pens of the opposition scribes and rhymesters in the spring of 1651. "The care that the Cardinal bestowed upon his person and his dress, his beautiful white hands, his carefully-trimmed moustache, his lemonades, his *ragoûts*, his pastry, even his bread, all those importations of refined elegance and

---

[1] On 3 November 1750, the Parliament condemned Mazarin to be hanged in effigy in four different places. "*Que ledit Cardinal,*" ran the decree, "*reconnu coupable du crime de traison a été condamné d'être pendu en effigie . . . le 3 November* 1650."

[2] Montglat says: "The Cardinal asked the princes for their friendship, but they, judging truly of the situation, promised him 'all that he wanted of it.'"

Italian voluptuousness; his palace, with its picture-galleries, its statues, and its vast stables—all furnished material for the satirist:

> Adieu, donc, pauvre Mazarin !
> Adieu, mon pauvre Tabarin ;
> Adieu, *l'oncle aux Mazarinettes* ;
> Adieu, père aux marionettes ;
> Adieu, le plus beau des galans ;
> Adieu, buveur des lemonades ;
> Adieu, l'inventeur des pommades ;
> Adieu l'homme aux bonnes senteurs ![1]

Needless to say, the "Mazarinettes" and every member known and unknown of the Minister's family had their share in this deluge of facetiousness and obscenity, for few of the lampoons were of so harmless a character as the specimen we have just cited, and no abuse, no insinuation, no accusation was too gross to heap upon the exiled Cardinal; nor was the reputation of the Queen-Mother respected, as the pieces entitled *Les Soupers des Fleurs de lys* and *Le Custode du lit de la Reine*[2] will testify.

A decree of the Parliament of Paris had expelled the nephew and nieces of the Cardinal from France. The latter quitted the capital almost immediately after their uncle, and joined him at Péronne, whither Maréchal d'Hocquincourt had conducted them. It was well that they did not delay their departure, otherwise they might have been roughly handled. Popular credulity suspected the Cardinal of being concealed in Paris; and a report spread that he was at Val-de-Grâce, disguised as a

---

[1] Amédée Renée, "Les Nièces de Mazarin."

[2] The writer of this libel, one Claude Morlot by name, was condemned to be hanged, but was rescued by the mob, who put the archers and the executioners to flight and pulled down the gibbet.

nun, and that the Queen went there secretly to visit him—

> On disoit que le Mazarin
> Tous les jours chantoit au lutrin
> En habit de religieuse.

It was also believed that the nieces had taken refuge in the city ; crowds collected before the houses in which they were said to be concealed, and ransacked several of them from cellar to attic.

> La canaille rien ne trouva,
> Mais jura de mettre en cent pièces
> Tous ceux qui logeroient les nièces.[1]

It is evident from the fact that Mazarin did not deem it necessary to send the children to their parents in Rome that he was of opinion that his exile would be but a temporary one. He left Péronne, with his nieces and nephew, to establish himself in some town beyond the frontier. At Clermont, in Argonne, he was received by Maréchal de la Ferté, in spite of the decrees of the Parliament, while Fabert, the commandant of Sedan, begged him to take refuge there, although an order wrung from the unfortunate Queen directed her friend to leave the realm. The Cardinal declined Fabert's offer, but left his young relatives in his charge until he had decided upon his place of exile. He finally chose the town of Brühl, within a short distance of Cologne.

One of the most interesting episodes of Mazarin's sojourn at Brühl was the marriage of Laure Mancini. Laure, as we have already mentioned, had been betrothed to the Duc de Mercœur, eldest son of the Duc de Vendôme and brother of "*le Roi des Halles*." But the renewal of the civil war had caused the marriage to be postponed, and the ruin of the Cardinal's fortunes

[1] Loret, "La Muse historique."

encouraged a belief that it would never take place. The amiable and honest Mercœur, however, was faithful to his engagements and to the sentiments with which the beautiful Laure had inspired him, and, ignoring the decrees prohibiting all communication with the exiled Minister, set out for Brühl, where he espoused privately, but in good and due form, his young bride, furnished with the consent of the King, the Queen, and even of Gaston d'Orléans, who subsequently vainly pretended to have revoked it.[1]

Such disinterestedness appeared the height of folly to the selfish courtiers, and, on his return to Paris, the poor duke found himself rallied on all sides, and held up to ridicule and odium by the pamphleteers of the Fronde. Moreover, he had to submit to a trying ordeal, for Condé, furious at the marriage, accused him in the Parliament of having infringed its decrees, by having had relations with the Cardinal and his family, and Mercœur, as a *pair de France*, had to appear before the assembled Chambers to give an explanation of his conduct. He defended himself to the best of his ability, asserting that the marriage had taken place prior to the flight of the Cardinal, and that he had undertaken the journey to Brühl to see not the Minister, but his wife. The Parliament directed that the marriage contract should be laid before it, and the scene terminated by a decree " prohibiting the said Mancini from entering the kingdom or residing therein under pretext of this union."

The Queen had taken great interest in this matter,

[1] The marriage contract was subsequently renewed at the Louvre (29 May, 1654) before the King's notaries, in the presence of their Majesties, the Duc d'Anjou, and other distinguished persons. The Cardinal gave his niece a dowry of 600,000 livres in cash, and the King presented the happy pair with the sum of 100,000 livres.

and was highly indignant at the insulting treatment to
which the Duc de Mercœur was being subjected. " She
charged me," writes de Retz, " to implore *Monsieur*
[Gaston d'Orléans], in her name, to prevent this affair
from being carried any further ; she spoke to him with
tears in her eyes, and showed me plainly that she was
always herself most sensible to what she believed most
affected the Cardinal." [1]

Thus the astute Italian, even in the midst of his
misfortunes, had succeeded in marrying his niece to a
grandson of Henri IV. But his *Carnets* show us that
he had hoped for greater things. He had hoped to
make a "*grand coup*," by marrying the two brothers at
the same time to two of his nieces. " If one could
completely gain over the Duc de Beaufort by an alliance,"
he writes, " I could give the two nieces to the two
brothers, and give the younger [Beaufort] the government of Paris, and treat even for that of Île-de-France.
And, with that, one would make a *grand coup*, for,
possessing the affection of the people in the said town,
he would be in a position to one day render some
considerable service to the King."

From his retreat at Brühl, Mazarin continued to
direct the policy of his party in France. With the
Queen he kept up an active and secret correspondence,
by means of his confidential agent Bartet and other
skilful emissaries. A part of this correspondence still
exists, and shows us Mazarin adroitly combining sage
political counsel with assurances of the most ardent
devotion.

[1] " Mémoires du Cardinal de Retz."

Mazarin to the Queen.

"From Brühl, xi May 1651.

"*Mon Dieu!* How happy should I be and you satisfied, if you could see into my heart, or if I could write to you what is in it! You would not find it difficult, in that case, to agree that never was there a friendship approaching that which I entertain for you. I confess to you that I little imagined that it would go so far as to deprive me of all contentment, when my time is employed in anything else than in thinking of you.

"I wish, also, that I had the power to express my hatred for those indiscreet persons who labour without ceasing to make you forget me and to hinder us from meeting again : in a word, it is proportioned to the friendship which I bear you. They are mistaken, if they hope to see in us the effects of absence ; and if that Spaniard said that the mountains of Guadarrama have great difficulty in dividing two good friends . . .

"If my misfortunes are not speedily remedied, I cannot answer for being wise to the end, for this great prudence ill accords with a passion such as mine.

"Perhaps I am wrong, for which I crave your pardon ; but I believe that, were I in your place, I should have already gone far to find a way for the Friend to see me again. . . . Write to me, I entreat you, and say if I shall see you and when : *for this state of things cannot last,* even should I perish. The greatest enemy that I have in the world, I should love as my own life, and with all my heart, if he could contrive so that I might see Sérafin [the Queen] again. . . ."[1]

And for his sake the Queen, this woman ordinarily so

---

[1] Published by Amédée Renée, "Les Nièces de Mazarin."

indolent, so changeable in her affections, braved every-thing : the outrageous attacks of the rhymesters of the Fronde, the mockery of high and low, the civil war, ready to lose her crown, and her son's crown also, rather than abandon the man who possessed her heart.

On the advice of the Cardinal, the Queen feigned to be reconciled to Condé, the intention being to render him an' object of suspicion to the Frondeurs. In this she succeeded, and that doughty intriguer, indignant at finding that all the promises that had been made to him were not kept, declined to attend the Bed of Justice of 7 September, 1751, at which the young King, being then fourteen, declared himself of age, and retired to his government of Guienne, where he prepared for war, and did not hesitate to ally himself with the Spaniards.

After a year's residence at Brühl, Mazarin resolved to make an attempt to re-enter the kingdom. During the early days of his exile, he appears to have been in considerable financial embarrassment. The greater part of his property, including his palace and its treas-ures, had been confiscated by a decree of the Parliament, and, as he had brought very little money away with him, his family suffered some privations. After a while, however, the Queen contrived to provide him with funds, and by January 1652, he was in possession of sufficient to raise an army of 6000 men, at the head of which he repassed the frontier.

On learning of their enemy's return, the Parliament hastened to set a price on his head. The decree directed that his library and his furniture should be sold, the proceeds to go towards the sum of 150,000 livres offered to the person who should deliver him up alive or dead. This library, formed at such great expense, was sold by auction and dispersed, the King's uncle, Gaston d'Orléans, a rival bibliophile, spitefully insisting that it should be disposed of in detail.[1]

Seeing the moment of his reunion with the Queen approaching, Mazarin redoubled the expressions of tenderness in the letters which he addressed to his middle-aged Dulcinea. Maréchal de Villeroi had insisted on the King and Queen undertaking a journey to Poitiers, and afterwards to Guienne, with the object of placing as great a distance as possible between them and the Cardinal.

"The poor man ought to know," writes Mazarin, "that the friendship which 22 [the Queen] has for 26 [Mazarin] is easily proof against other things than a separation of a hundred leagues more, and that the interposition of a part of the world between these two persons would not be capable of terminating it, whatever one might say. I promise you that until 26 [Mazarin] can be with you, who will tell you more in an hour than I could write in two months, I will communicate with you every three or four days to give you my news. However, I thank you for the suggestion you have made, for there is nothing so obliging, and I see very well that your heart speaks, and that I am greatly deceived if you have not as much friendship for me as 26 has for 22, whom you know well enough has more merit than any one in the world, saving you only

---

[1] Mazarin felt the loss of his books keenly. "I notice," he writes from Pont-sur-Yonne, 11 January 1752, "the precipitation with which they wish to sell my library, and I am informed that his Royal Highness [Gaston d'Orléans] insisted that it should be sold in detail, in order to injure me the sooner. It will be a fine thing to read in history that Cardinal Mazarin, having taken so much care for thirty years to enrich, with the most beautiful and rarest books in the world, a library which he intended to present to the public, the Parliament of Paris decreed that it should be sold, and the money accruing therefrom should be employed to cause the said Cardinal to be assassinated."

of the number, since, without contradiction, there is no one who can contest that quality with you."

Mazarin, at the head of his troops, who wore the green scarf of his House, entered Sedan, where his devoted friend Fabert received him with open arms. He seems to have left his nieces in charge of this loyal soldier until his fate should be decided, after which he resumed his march towards Poitiers, accompanied by his nephew Paul Mancini, a youth of great promise, who was generally popular.

In spite of all the efforts of the Parliament to prevent his return; in spite of the deputation which that body despatched to Poitiers, to demand of the King that he should "keep this foreigner at a distance, not only from his counsels, but also from the whole extent of the lands which owed him obedience, and even from the frontier"; in spite of all obstacles, on 30 January, 1752, Mazarin arrived at Poitiers, riding in triumph in the King's coach, preceded by Louis himself and his little brother, the Duc d'Anjou. The Queen, we may presume, received the Cardinal with at least as much favour as had her son, and the same evening Mazarin supped with their Majesties.

A week later the Duchesse de Mercœur and Olympe Mancini, escorted by their brother Paul, re-entered Paris. A journal of the time announced their arrival as follows :—

"The 3rd of this month of February arrived here, by the Porte Saint-Antoine, the nieces of his Excellency preceded by the Princesse de Carignan,[1] the Princesse

---

[1] Marie de Bourbon (1606–92), daughter of Charles de Bourbon, Comte de Soissons (1566–1612) and Anne de Montafié, and wife of Prince Thomas François de Carignan, son of Charles Emmanuel the Great, of Savoy.

Louise, her daughter, Maréchal de Guébriand, the Marquis d'Ampus, and a number of ladies of condition. They alighted at the Hôtel de Vendôme, where the dowager-duchess, accompanied by several ladies, welcomed them with the greatest marks of affection, which were principally bestowed on the Duchesse de Mercœur, her daughter-in-law. Then, having been conducted to the Louvre, they were favourably received by their Majesties, after which the Queen caused them to be conducted into the apartment which had been prepared for them in that residence. In the evening, they were splendidly entertained by the Princesse de Carignan, who provided for them every possible diversion. . . . Since, they have permitted them to receive after dinner the visits full of honour and affection which the ladies of the Court and town rendered them."[1]

The cordial welcome extended to the sisters by the Princesse de Carignan would appear to suggest that she already regarded with a favourable eye the possibility of an alliance between Olympe Mancini and her son, Prince Eugène de Savoie-Carignan, which actually took place five years later. But the Cardinal, who always made a point of never showing any eagerness for the establishment of his nieces, pretended not to notice it.

Scarcely had Mazarin returned, when the troubles recommenced more violently than ever. Failing in an attempt to get the Cardinal proscribed anew, Condé began a regular war against the Court, and gained some unimportant successes over Maréchal d'Hocquincourt, who commanded the royal army. The object of the prince was apparently to get possession of the person of the young King. But Turenne, recalled by an urgent

[1] Cited by Lucian Perey, " Le Roman du Grand Roi."

message from Louis, quitted the army which was confronting the Spaniards and hastened to Bléneau, where, on 7 April, he saved the rest of the Royalists and Louis himself, who was at Gien, and, in the event of defeat, would in all probability have fallen into his rebellious kinsman's hands. Three weeks later, Turenne and d'Hocquincourt gained a fresh success over Condé at Étampes, where the latter lost over a thousand men. A futile attempt at negotiations on the part of the prince followed, after which he quitted his post at Saint-Cloud and crossed the Seine, with the intention of occupying Charenton. Hard pressed, however, by the royal troops, he was compelled to throw himself into the Faubourg Saint-Antoine, where, on 2 July, a battle was fought, which would undoubtedly have ended in the total destruction of Condé's army, had not *la Grande Mademoiselle* persuaded the citizens to open their gates to the retreating Frondeurs and turned the cannon of the Bastille on the victorious Royalists. " *Voilà un coup de canon qui a tué un mari !* " Mazarin, who had watched the fighting from a place of safety, is reported to have exclaimed, when the first gun was fired, meaning thereby that *Mademoiselle* had destroyed all chance of ever becoming the consort of Louis XIV.

The combat was a sanguinary one, and the Cardinal had the grief to learn that, amongst the Royalist officers most severely wounded, was his nephew Paul Mancini, who, though barely fifteen years of age, had recently been appointed *mestre de camp* of the Régiment de la Marine, and had fought with the greatest gallantry at the head of his men. The young officer was conveyed to Saint-Denis, where the Court had established itself, and the surgeons pronounced his wound a very dangerous one. However, since he had youth and an excel-

lent constitution on his side, they held out some hope of
his recovery, provided that he could be ensured absolute
rest. Unhappily, the Court was obliged to leave Saint-
Denis, where the King was not considered in safety, and
Mazarin, fearing to leave the lad to the tender mercies
of Condé's defeated soldiery or the populace of Paris,
who might have vented upon him their hatred of his
uncle, gave directions that he was to be removed in
a litter. This journey proved fatal to the poor youth,
who died the following day, at Pontoise, a few hours
after receiving the brevet of colonel of the Chevau-
légers of his guard from Louis XIV's own hands.

Mazarin, who did not ordinarily evince much sensibility where members of his family were concerned, was
in despair at the death of his nephew ; he had reckoned
on the favour of the King, who was much attached to
the boy, to ensure him a brilliant future, and had entertained for him a sincere affection. With the idea of
perpetuating his memory, he composed a lengthy epitaph
in which Mancini himself is supposed to recount to
those who pass by his touching history.

The Cardinal's grief was little respected by the Fronde,
whose pamphleteers made it the occasion to pour upon
him a deluge of abominable invectives and cynical
pleasantries. To understand, indeed, the hatred with
which the Minister was regarded, it is necessary to
peruse some of these *Mazarinades*, unprofitable reading
though they be ; for their authors did not hesitate to
declare that Mazarin combined in his own person all the
vices of both modern times and antiquity ; and the
ignorant mob believed them. One scribe went so far
as to publish a pamphlet entitled " Le Pacte de Mazarin
avec le démon," in which he asserted that the Cardinal
" had given his soul and body to the devil, on condition

of becoming the richest and most powerful man in Europe, beloved of fair ladies, and of dying in his bed." This contract was supposed to have been entered into at Rome in the year 1632.

It is singular to reflect that the Minister who was the object of all this scurrilous abuse had, whatever his faults may have been, never wavered in his fidelity to the country of his adoption, while those who vilified him were the mouthpieces of men who intrigued and even fought with the enemies of France.

The inveterate hatred with which the partisans of Condé, the Parliament, and the Parisians generally regarded Mazarin had been rather accentuated than appeased by the Royalist successes in the field, and though the citizens opened negotiations with the King, they firmly declined to return to their allegiance until the Minister was removed. The Queen was naturally violently opposed to such a demand ; but Mazarin himself advised compliance, well knowing that his exile would be but a brief one ; and Anne finally consented, at the same time intimating in unmistakable terms that she was acting under constraint.

The Cardinal left Pontoise on 19 August 1652, having recommended as first minister Prince Thomas de Savoie, while his faithful henchmen Servien and Le Tellier remained at their posts. He proceeded to Bouillon and thence to Cologne, from which city he kept up an active correspondence with the Queen, and continued to direct all her actions. She, on her part, carried out his instructions with the utmost docility, taking upon her own shoulders all the odium which some of them aroused, and did not cease to urge the return of her beloved Minister in the most tender and impassioned terms.

"I know not when I ought to look for your return," she writes, "since new obstacles to hinder it are constantly arising. All that I can say is, that I am very weary, and bear this delay with great impatience, and if 16 [Mazarin] knew all that 15 [the Queen] suffers in this way, I am sure that he would be touched. I suffer so much at this moment that I have not the strength to write for long, nor do I know too well what to say. I have received your letters almost every day, without which I know not what would happen. Continue to write as often, since you afford me some consolation in the state in which I am. . . . At the worst, you have only to throw the blame for the delay on 15 [the Queen], who is a thousand times ≸ [yours] and until her last sigh. The child [the Duc de Mercœur] will tell you everything. Adieu ; I can write no more, and he [Mazarin] knows why. . . ."

At length, all difficulties having been overcome, the Cardinal was recalled. His return was preceded by a considerable service to the State. At his own expense he raised and equipped a body of troops in the neighbourhood of Liège, and joined Turenne, who was laying siege to Bar-le-Duc. In spite of the severity of the winter, the Cardinal displayed so much activity and enthusiasm that those about him found it difficult to believe that he had ever exchanged the sword for the *soutane*. The place surrendered after a brief resistance, and, on 9 February 1653, Mazarin re-entered Paris in a blaze of glory. The King, followed by the greatest nobles of the Court, went to meet the returning Minister as far as Bourget, insisted on his entering his coach, and brought him in triumph to the Louvre, where a magnificent suite of apartments had been prepared for him.

And — singular transformation ! — the same people

D

who, but six short months before, had execrated the very name of the Italian adventurer, now received him with shouts of welcome. "The time of storm was past," says Hénault, "and one respected in him a fortune which so many trials had been powerless to overthrow."

CHAPTER III

Mazarin summons a second detachment of his family to France—Marie Mancini's account of her childhood and of the journey to France— Marriage of the Prince de Conti to Anne-Marie Martinozzi—Their married life—Arrival of Laure Martinozzi, Marie, Hortense, and Philippe Mancini, and their mothers in Paris—Character of Madame Mancini—Her dislike of her daughter Marie—She persuades the Cardinal to send Marie to the Couvent de la Visitation—Hortense joins her sister—Remarkable progress of Marie in her studies—Letters of Marie and Hortense to the Cardinal—Marie leaves the convent and joins the Court at La Fère—A *mariage manqué*—Marie returns to her mother—Marriage of Laure Martinozzi to the Prince of Modena—Marianne and Alphonse Mancini brought to France—A practical joke—Harsh treatment of Marie by her mother—Marie's studies—Illness of Madame Mancini—Beginning of the friendship between Marie and Louis XIV—Death of Madame Mancini—And of the Duchesse de Mercœur.

AFTER the Fronde, Mazarin, with all his enemies out-witted and incomparably the wealthiest subject in Europe, devoted himself to still further strengthening his authority by new and brilliant alliances for his family. On 18 April 1653, he wrote to his father, in Rome, to acquaint him with his intention to bring his niece, Anne-Marie Martinozzi, to France, and to request him to confer with the French Ambassador to the Vatican and "make all the preparations he judged necessary." At the same time, he demanded of his sister, Signora Mancini, her son Philippe, and her eldest remaining daughter Marie. The last named, in a rare little work entitled "La Verité dans son jour, ou les Véritables

Mémoires de M. Manchini, connétable Colonne,"[1] has
left us some interesting details of her childhood, which
help us to understand her character and the original turn
of her mind :

"Rome witnessed my birth, of a family illustrious
enough to make itself esteemed for its own renown, and
which needed not the glory of Cardinal Mazarin to enable it to take a sufficiently high place in the chief city
in the world. At the age of seven, my mother, to whom
I appeared less beautiful than my sister Hortense, to-day
Duchesse de Mazarin, placed me in the Campo Marzio,
convent of the Order of Saint-Benedict, with the idea
of having me brought up in the religious life. At the
end of two years, although my mother had much less
inclination for me than for my sister, she did not fail to
be touched by my feeble health ; and, attributing my in-
disposition to the close confinement in which I was kept
and to the impure air which I breathed in the convent—
which, in fact, was very unhealthy—she took me away
and made me return to her.

"About two years after I had left the convent, my
uncle, the Cardinal, whose fortune had already reached
its height, desired, for the example of the . . .[2] to increase
it still further by allowing others to participate therein ;

[1] This book, published in Spain, but which bears no date, must not
be confused with the better known "Apologie ou les Véritables Mémoires
de Madame Marie Mancini, connétable de Colonna, écrits par elle-même.
A Leide, pour l'auteur, chez Jean von Gelder, à la Tortue, 1678," or
with "Les Mémoires de M. L. P. M. M. (Madame la Princesse Marie
Mancini) Colonne G. Connétable du royaume de Naples. A Cologne,
chez Pierre Marteau, 1676." The latter work is apocryphal, while the
"Apologie" would appear to have been written from the manuscript of
"La Vérité dans son jour," which Marie Mancini had confided to a
person of the name of Brémont. Brémont, without altering the facts,
which are identical in the two works, altogether perverted the style in
his efforts to improve it.
[2] An illegible word.

and this obliged him to summon to him my mother and my aunt Martinozzi, with orders to each of them to bring her eldest daughter. This direction seemed to exclude my sister Hortense, as being the younger ; but her beauty had given her the elder's privilege in the inclination of my mother, who did not, however, fail to explain to me my uncle's wishes, and would no doubt have been pleased if I had declined to obey him, a matter concerning which I had no difficulty in coming to a decision, inasmuch as she bade me choose between going to France or remaining in Rome with my aunt and consecrating myself to God in a cloister. To which, I remember, that I replied that there were convents everywhere, and that when it pleased Heaven to inspire me with pious aspirations, it would be as easy to follow them in Paris as in Rome ; moreover, that I was not yet old enough to decide so important a matter.

" This answer disabused my mother of the error under which she had hitherto lain and made her determine to bring me ; and, to spare herself the resentment which the fact of my being preferred to my sister had occasioned her, she brought us both.

" We accordingly embarked in a Genoese galley, which that republic, which had a very particular regard for the Cardinal, had sent for us. I shall not pause here to describe this moving mansion, since it would be necessary to consume too much time in depicting all its beauties, its spruceness, its richness, and its magnificence ; and it will be enough for me to say that we were treated as queens during our voyage, and that the tables of sovereigns were not served with more pomp and splendour than was ours four times a day.

" We disembarked at length at Marseilles, in May 1653, where my aunt, who was a little too scrupulous,

for a long time declined to receive the corporation of
the town, who begged to be permitted to pay their
respects, being unable to make up her mind to the
form of salutation in vogue in France.[1] This delicacy
was at last overcome, though with great difficulty, and
afforded material for laughter to many people, who were
astonished, and with reason enough, that she made so
much mystery over a formality sanctioned by custom
and justified by so long a voyage.

"From Marseilles we passed to Aix, where we were
received by the governor of the province, who was at
that time the Duc de Mercœur, the first French noble
who had up to then allied himself with the Cardinal,
having espoused Laure Mancini, my eldest sister, whom
he himself had demanded at Cologne, at the time when
his Eminence was obliged to withdraw thither. We
remained eight months in this town of Aix, where the
duke my brother-in-law entertained us in the most
magnificent manner conceivable, and where my sister,
his wife, came to join us two months later, and contributed in every possible way to make the time pass
agreeably."

While the second detachment of the Cardinal's family
was at Aix, where Madame de Mercœur busied herself
with instructing her young sisters and cousin in the
etiquette of the French Court, devoting particular attention to Marie, whose early education, partly owing to
her ill-health and partly owing to the indifference with
which her mother regarded her, had been much
neglected, Mazarin was employed in concluding arrangements for the union of his family with Royalty itself,

---

[1] This consisted in embracing the women and in allowing the men to
kiss the lady's hand.

From an engraving by Frosne

ARMAND DE BOURBON, PRINCE DE CONTI

by an alliance between Anne-Marie Martinozzi and the Prince de Conti, younger brother of Condé.

Armand de Bourbon, Prince de Conti, who was at this time about thirty-four years of age, had been originally destined for the Church, and though he had resisted the imposition of hands ecclesiastical, had received as his appanage many rich abbeys, such as Saint-Denis, Cluny, and Lérens. In person, he was short and slightly deformed, defects which were atoned for by a strikingly handsome face and charming manners. Always under the influence of his celebrated sister, Madame de Longueville, he joined the Fronde, and when Mazarin returned from his second exile, was engaged in defending Bordeaux against the royal troops, in company with the Duc and Duchesse de Longueville and the Princesse de Condé and her son the Duc d'Enghien. When at length the city surrendered, he found himself in a humiliating position. In disgrace at Court, his large fortune almost entirely gone, and crippled with debt, he was one day bewailing his lot and comparing it with that of the Duc de Candale, who had commanded the Royalists besieging Bordeaux, when his secretary, the poet Sarrazin, advised him "to do as M. de Candale was about to do." (A marriage between Candale and one of the Cardinal's nieces was then being talked of). Conti caught at his secretary's suggestion as a drowning man catches at a straw, and, though his almoner, Daniel de Cosnac, afterwards Archbishop of Aix, opposed the project, the counsels of Sarrazin prevailed, and he was despatched to Paris to conduct the negotiation.

The secretary broached the subject to the Minister,[1]

[1] According to one account, it was the Cardinal who, some little time before this, had broached the matter to Sarrazin, and had offered him a considerable bribe to put the idea into his master's head.

who, although overjoyed at the prospect of a union between a member of his family and a Prince of the Blood, was faithful to his character, and succeeded in beating his prospective nephew down several hundred thousand livres in the matter of the dot.

From the "Mémoires" of Cosnac, which contain many curious details about this affair, it would appear that Conti had given Sarrazin *carte blanche* in regard to the choice of his princess, observing that it was a matter of perfect indifference to him which of the young ladies was allotted him, since it was the Cardinal and not a wife that he desired to espouse. Sarrazin, good servant that he was, proved himself worthy of so much confidence, and demanded for his master the most beautiful and the most virtuous of the nieces—Anne-Marie Martinozzi, to wit. Poor Anne-Marie would vastly have preferred accepting the homage of the fascinating Candale, to whom she had practically been promised. But her uncle's wishes were law; and, besides, the duke regarded the matter with the same eye as the prince— it was the Cardinal whom he proposed to espouse ; and, by no means unwilling to prolong his career of gallantry, withdrew his pretensions without hesitation.

It is sad to relate that, while these negotiations were in progress, the Prince de Conti was preparing himself for the duties of matrimony by frequenting public *bals masqués* and other questionable entertainments, and leading generally so dissipated a life that his health remained seriously affected for some time afterwards.

The betrothal took place on 21 February 1654, at the Louvre, and, on the following day, the marriage was celebrated, by the Archbishop of Bourges, in the Queen's Chapel. The bride wore "a dress of brocade, enriched with pearls of very great price, and was conducted to

From an engraving after the painting by Beaubrun

ANNE MARIE MARTINOZZI, PRINCESSE DE CONTI

the chapel by their Majesties, *Monsieur*, the Prince de Conti, Cardinal Mazarin, and several other leaders of the Court."

The Prince de Conti had certainly every reason to consider himself a fortunate man, for not only did his marriage restore to him all the offices and dignities he had lost by his conduct during the Fronde, plus a handsome dowry, the government of Guienne, and a magnificent hotel on the Quai Malaquais, which the Cardinal, in a fit of generosity, subsequently erected for him at his own expense, but it brought him an extremely beautiful wife, who joined to her loveliness " much sweetness of temper, much intelligence, and good sense."[1]

The union proved a happy one, in spite of occasional fits of jealousy on the prince's part, for which his wife, who, though at the time of their marriage " merely an honest pagan," soon became a *dévote* of the most rigorous type, seems to have given him not the shadow of a cause,[2] and in spite, too, of his own occasional lapses from the path of virtue, during one of which he attempted ineffectually to pose as the lover of

[1] Madame de Motteville, "Mémoires." If we are to believe contemporary gossip, Conti would not appear at first to have fully appreciated his good fortune. He was ashamed of his marriage, and vented his ill-humour on Sarrazin, whom he smote on the head with a pair of tongs, inflicting injuries whereof the unfortunate poet died. This tragic incident gave rise to the following quatrain :—

> Deux charmants, deux fameux poëtes,
> Disciples de Marat, Du Cerceau, Sarrazin,
> Ont éternisé les pincettes.
> Le premier par ses verses et l'autre par sa fin.

[2] Once, not long after the marriage, Louis XIV, then seventeen, was so imprudent as to attempt to make love to the princess, who received his advances so very ungraciously, that, the following day, the Cardinal compelled her to apologize to his Majesty. Conti, who was then in Spain, informed of what had occurred, sent orders for his wife to join him immediately. Few husbands, in those days, showed a like discretion.

Madame de Sévigné. These lapses, as was the case with
the celebrated Duc de Joyeuse, were generally followed
by violent fits of penitence and devotion, and at length,
under the twofold influence of his wife and his sister
Madame de Longueville, religion triumphed, and he
became sincerely devout. "The beauty of his penitence," says Madame de Motteville, "surpassed the
ugliness of his faults"; but it would have perhaps
been as well for his reputation with posterity if he
had refrained from publishing his indictment of the
theatre, wherein this erstwhile patron of Molière gravely
informs us that a troupe of actors is "a troupe of
devils," and to amuse oneself at the theatre is to
"delight the demon."

The Princesse de Conti favoured Jansenist doctrines,
and, after her husband's death, which occurred in 1666,
became the protector and patroness of Port Royal. She
was also extremely beneficent; at least two-thirds of the
wealth with which her uncle had endowed her were
dispensed in charity, and an inscription on her tomb in
Saint-André-des-Arts informs us that, during the famine
of 1662, she sold all her jewellery to feed the starving
poor of Berry, Champagne, and Picardy. She died six
years after her husband, leaving two sons, one of whom
married Mlle. de Blois, daughter of Louis XIV and
Louise de la Vallière, and died at the age of twenty-
four; while the other survived to be the highest
ornament of his house.

Some few weeks before the Conti-Martinozzi marriage, the second detachment of the Cardinal's family
had left Aix for Paris. Mazarin did not deem it advisable that his young relatives should proceed directly to
the capital, but instructed them to break their journey

at the Château de Villeroi, near Corbeil, where their uncle visited them, to assure himself that they had benefited sufficiently by the lessons of the Duchesse de Mercœur to pass muster at Court. The result of his examination being satisfactory, he gave orders for them to proceed to Paris, where they arrived at the beginning of February, and were immediately presented to their Majesties, "who received them with marks of extraordinary kindness." The courtiers, of course, followed suit, and overwhelmed the little strangers with attentions; while even the rhymesters of the Fronde, who had so lately been holding Mazarin and all his belongings up to ridicule and odium, now vied with one another in chanting their praises :

> Les Mancini, les Martinosses,
> Illustres matières de noces !

The new arrivals assisted at the marriage of their cousin to the Prince de Conti and the brilliant fêtes which followed it, where the beauty of the little Hortense Mancini seems to have been particularly remarked upon. Three months later (7 June), the King, who had just attained the age of fifteen, was crowned at Rheims, and Philippe Mancini had the honour of being selected as one of the bearers of the Holy Ampulla. It may here be remarked that Mazarin, who had been deeply attached to Paul Mancini, always entertained a strong aversion to Philippe, who had no merit, in his eyes, save that of being of his own blood, and whom he invariably treated with the greatest harshness and severity.

Madame Mancini, or *de* Mancini, as she was now called—for, by the Cardinal's desire, his relatives, since their arrival in Paris, had prefixed the French territorial prefix to their names—was allotted to a suite of apartments in the Louvre, where Marie and Hortense lived with her. She appears to have been a singularly unpleasant kind of woman, ill-tempered, bigoted, and superstitious. (She believed with equal fervour in the power of saints and of astrologers.) What affection she had to bestow was concentrated on three of her daughters—Madame de Mercœur, Olympe, and the little Hortense. Marie she could not endure, and, as we have seen, had only brought her to France with extreme reluctance. She now advised her brother to send the girl to a convent, hoping that, once there, she would remain there. The Cardinal was far from sharing his sister's feelings with regard to his niece ; but, inasmuch as Marie, at this time a thin, sallow-complexioned, and ungainly child, did not strike him as likely to create a favourable impression at Court, he decided to do as Madame Mancini suggested, and the girl was accordingly sent to the Couvent de la Visitation, in the Faubourg Saint-Jacques, " to see," as his Eminence expressed it, " if she would not put on a little flesh."

Here, two months later, she was joined by her little sister Hortense, " who was too much of a child to remain at Court, to which her beauty had introduced her, and where every one was so pleased to see her, even up to *Monsieur*,[1] who, child though he was, could not live without her. His Eminence added that she was a little too obstinate, to which, he said, the liberty she had been allowed to enjoy in the great world had too much contributed." [2]

The abbess of the Couvent de la Visitation was Mère Elisabeth de Lamoignon, sister of the First President of

---

[1] The Duc d'Anjou, afterwards Duc d'Orléans, the King's brother.

[2] " La Vérité dans son jour, ou les Véritables Mémoires de M. Mancini, connétable Colonne."

the Parliament of Paris, "who was charged to instruct us and to teach us the language and all that she considered necessary for girls of our age and rank."[1]   Madame de Lamoignon quickly perceived that in Marie she had no ordinary pupil. The young girl was singularly gifted, and learned with extraordinary rapidity. The most difficult subjects did not seem to present any difficulties to her, and so marvellous was her memory that she was able to retain whole pages from tragedies and poems. Moreover, she was an indefatigable student, the reason being that, young though she was, she was well aware that, if she wished to occupy a place at Court, the object of all her desires, her only chance was to atone by the graces of the mind for her lack of physical attractions.

The abbess did not fail to render an account of the astonishing progress made by her pupil to the Cardinal, who expressed himself much gratified ; but he had conceived a great affection for Hortense, who remained the favourite among his nieces to the end of his life, and it was she who addressed to her uncle requests which Marie would never have dared to make. Thus, two months after entering the convent, we find her writing to the Cardinal the following letter :—

Hortense de Marcini to Cardinal Mazarin.

"1 July 1654, Couvent de la Visitation,
"Faubourg Saint-Jacques.

"MONSEIGNEUR,—I have been too long in this place without giving myself the honour of writing to your Eminence. I had intended to wait until I was more proficient in writing, but I am impatient to know if the little Hortense is still honoured by your remembrance. She is striving hard to learn how to serve God and

[1] *Ibid.*

to make herself very wise, in order to merit this favour. If your Excellency would be willing to favour me with one of his visits, as he promised me, that would be the summit of my happiness. If I cannot have this honour, at least I beg your Eminence very humbly to remember to give instructions to M. Colbert touching that which he promised me every month for my diversion and for giving alms to the poor ; and also your Eminence will not forget that the time since I have been at home, which is nearly a month, ought to be reckoned, and my sister Marie nearly three. I should be grieved, loving her as I do, were she to have no share in your liberalities. She begs to be honoured by your remembrance, since, like myself, she has no other desire than to render ourselves worthy of the quality of

"Your very humble and obedient niece and servant, who loves you with all her heart,

"HORTENSE DE MANCINI."

The Cardinal, through the Bishop of Coutances, lost no time in making a satisfactory response to this appeal, and both sisters write to thank him. Here are their letters, that of Marie being a singularly graceful and charming one for a girl only thirteen years of age :—

Marie de Mancini to Cardinal Mazarin.

"This 9 July, Couvent de la Visitation,
"Faubourg Saint-Jacques.

"MONSEIGNEUR,—I lack words to express the sentiments of respect and gratitude that I have for the kindness and care your Eminence has for us. Monseigneur de Coutances has just given us fresh proofs of it, since he has assured us that we have always a share in the honour of your remembrance. He has brought us thirty pistoles [three hundred francs] and some fans, on behalf of your Eminence ; and what has transported us with admiration, is to find that, in the midst of your important occupations, you condescend so far as to think of matters so nearly concerning our persons. It is for me a powerful incentive to study to perfect myself, and to be one day so happy as to give you cause not to disown me.

" I am, etc."

Hortense de Mancini to Cardinal Mazarin.

" Sainte-Marie de la Visitation.

" MONSEIGNEUR,—I am transported to find that you have done your little Hortense the honour to think of her. Monseigneur de Coutances will be able to express to you my joy, and especially when he gave me the presents on your behalf. I believed that it was true what he told me, that you always love me a little. It is that which makes me pray to God with all my heart for your Eminence, that you may have the kindness to continue that favour. That God may preserve you in health, the while I shall strive to do everything possible not to be unworthy of the quality of your . . . . etc. . . . ."[1]

Among her accomplishments, Marie now numbered drawing, and, desirous of doing everything possible to establish herself in the good graces of her all-powerful uncle, she conceived the idea of sending him for his fête-day a portrait of Hortense, which she had recently finished.

[1] Published by Lucien Perey, " Le Roman du Grand Roi."

Marie Mancini to Cardinal Mazarin.

"18 August 1655.

"MONSEIGNEUR,—Since in ten days' time it will be the festival of the saint whose name your Eminence bears, I cannot allcw it to pass without offering to your Eminence this little portrait of my fashioning. I know that you love very much her whom it represents, and I shall esteem myself happy if, when you look at it, you do me the honour to remember me, and to believe that we shall not fail to offer earnestly, on that day, our prayers to our Lord for your preservation, having nothing so much at heart as to prove to you my desire to live and die in the respect and obedience which I owe to you, etc."[1]

Marie had been an inmate of the Couvent de la Visitation some eighteen months, when, one day in October 1655, she received a letter from the Cardinal informing her that she was to leave it and join the Court, which was then at La Fère, in Picardy. She travelled thither in charge of Madame de Venel, a lady entirely devoted to Mazarin's interests, who became a little later *gouvernante* to his three younger nieces, heartily glad, we may suppose, to exchange the dull monotony of the convent for the gaiety and bustle of Court life, and was received very graciously by her uncle.

In his letter, Mazarin had said nothing about the motive which had prompted him to send for his niece, which was a matrimonial one. He had, as a matter of fact, arranged, or believed that he had arranged, a marriage between Marie and Armand de la Porte, only son of the Maréchal de la Meilleraye.

[1] Published by Lucien Perey, "Le Roman du Grand Roi."

In the eyes of the old aristocracy of France, the La Portes were little better than parvenus. The marshal himself, though a relative by marriage of Richelieu, was the grandson of an advocate, while, if Saint-Simon is to be believed, the founder of the family was only a humble doorkeeper, whence came the name of La Porte. Saint-Simon, however, as is well known, had a remarkably fertile imagination, particularly where persons whom he disliked were concerned. On the other hand, the marshal, by methods into which it were perhaps indiscreet to inquire too closely, had succeeded in amassing an enormous fortune, and had obtained permission to hand over to his son his lucrative post of Grand Master of the Artillery, as well as his governments. Altogether, thought his Eminence, poor, plain Marie might consider herself an exceedingly fortunate girl.

But the Cardinal and the marshal, in making their calculations, had forgotten one unimportant detail, namely, to assure themselves of the consent of the prospective bridegroom. The latter had seen Marie and Hortense at the time of their first appearance at Court, and, while he had scarcely noticed the former, had fallen desperately in love with the latter, notwithstanding the fact that she was then barely ten years old. He now flatly declared that he would wed Hortense or no one ; that from the first moment he had seen her, he had loved her with such devotion that, if he were not permitted to marry her, he would retire to pass the rest of his life in a convent. And one day, the object of his adoration tells us, he confided to the Duchesse d'Aiguillon that so overmastering was the passion which consumed him that " provided he could marry Hortense, he cared not if he died three months later." These words, the writer adds, were duly reported to the Cardinal, who, indignant at the Grand Master's refusal of his elder niece's hand, exclaimed contemptuously, "I would rather give Hortense to a lackey than allow him to marry her."[1] However, as we shall see, he subsequently came to view the matter in a different light.

In the winter, the Court returned to Paris. Marie was not a little afraid that after this *mariage manqué* she would be sent back to the convent. But her uncle, not a little impressed by the girl's intelligence, had resolved to definitely emancipate her and she, therefore, returned to her mother at the Louvre. Shortly afterwards, Hortense also quitted the Visitation, and was taken charge of by her eldest sister, Madame de Mercœur, who allowed her a good deal of liberty, of which the young lady did not fail to take the fullest advantage. Olympe, as the eldest unmarried sister, had already a separate suite of apartments of her own.

Mazarin could afford to regard the failure of his first attempt to establish Marie Mancini in life with comparative equanimity, since, in the previous summer, he had succeeded in arranging a brilliant alliance for another of his nieces, Laure Martinozzi, younger sister of the Princesse de Conti, who was then sixteen, a little the junior of her cousin Olympe Mancini. The memoirs of the time have left us no details in regard to the appearance of Laure Martinozzi, who was only a bird of passage, though, as an anonymous rhymester, whom Amédée Renée cites in his "Nièces de Mazarin," qualifies her as a "Roman beauty," it is probable that she did not want for attractions. However, whether she was beautiful or not, she resembled her elder sister in other respects, inasmuch as she was

[1] "Mémoires de la Duchesse de Mazarin."

pious, intelligent, and amiable; and when Alfonso d'Este, only son and heir of the reigning Duke of Modena, demanded her hand in marriage, there can be no doubt that he—or rather his agents, since he married her by proxy without ever having seen her—exercised a wise discretion in preferring her to Olympe, who was deeply mortified at being passed over. Personal considerations, however, probably counted for very little in this alliance. Modena needed the support of France against Spain, which was then pressing with all her weight upon the petty sovereigns of Italy, and Duke Francesco I, as capable a statesman as he was a soldier, perceived that an alliance with the family of the virtual ruler of France would assure him what he desired.

The marriage was celebrated at Compiègne, in June 1655, Prince Eugène de Savoie, afterwards the husband of Olympe Mancini and the father of the celebrated commander, acting as proxy for the Prince of Modena in the gorgeous ceremonial, which was precisely the same in all respects as if the bride had been a daughter of France.

A few days later, the young princess set out for Italy, accompanied by her mother Madame Martinozzi, the Duc and Duchesse de Noailles, and a numerous suite. Madame Martinozzi remained for some time at Modena with her daughter, and then returned to her house in Rome, where she passed the rest of her life.

From the marriage of Laure Martinozzi and Alfonso d'Este, two children were born: a son, who succeeded his father, in 1662, as Duke Francesco II, and a daughter, Marie Beatrice, who married James, Duke of York, after the death of his first wife, Anne Hyde, and became Queen of England and mother of the old Pretender, so that, but for the Revolution, the blood of

Mazarin might have continued to flow in our sovereigns' veins.

During the minority of her son, the Duchess of Modena acted as regent, and governed her little State with both wisdom and firmness (" *virile donna*," one of her biographers calls her), in politics remaining faithful to France and Louis XIV. Afterwards she joined her mother in Rome, where she continued to reside until her death.

The Duc and Duchesse de Noailles had been entrusted by Mazarin with another mission, besides that of escorting the Princess of Modena to her future home. They were charged to bring from Rome the little Marianne Mancini, the youngest of the five sisters, who had remained behind in that city, under the care of one of her aunts, when her mother set out for France, and, with her, her little brother Alphonse. On their homeward journey, they stopped at Modena, where, as cousins of the new princess, they were received with great ceremony, and an address presented to them by the municipal authorities, to which Marianne replied with much aplomb in a jargon of her own, a mixture of Italian and French. Although only six years old, the little girl was extraordinarily precocious, and on her arrival in France, quickly became a great favourite with the Cardinal and the Queen and the pet of the Court, which her gaiety and amusing repartees greatly diverted. His Eminence, when in a good humour, was in the habit of playing on the child singular tricks. Here is one which her sister Hortense relates in her " Mémoires," and which, though somewhat *gai*, is too characteristic of the morals of the time to be omitted :

" Another thing which afforded us much diversion at

this time was a jest which the Cardinal played upon the future Duchesse de Bouillon, the little Marianne, who was then six years old ; she was very gay, very lively, and used to make repartees far in advance of her age. The Queen used to divert herself greatly with them, as did also the Cardinal, who permitted himself the greatest liberties with her, and delighted to tease her more than any one. The Court was then at La Fère. One day, in the Queen's apartments, Mazarin amused himself by rallying Marianne on some gallantry that he pretended that she had, and ended by reproaching her with being with child. The resentment which she showed diverted every one so much that it was agreed to continue to rally her about it. . . . This went on so long as was thought necessary to make her believe the thing probable ; yet she refused to believe anything, and always defended herself with a great deal of heat, until, one fine morning, she found between her sheets a little child. You cannot imagine the astonishment and grief she was in at this sight. . . . The Queen came to console her, and wanted to be godmother, and all the Court came to congratulate the *accouchée*. They pressed her hard to tell them the name of the father, and she replied, with an air of mystery : 'It can be no one but the King or the Comte de Guiche, because they are the only men who have ever kissed me.'"[1]

Such were the pleasantries of the time, and the manner in which the characters of young girls were formed !

Little Marianne, like Marie, lived with her mother, but, whereas Madame Mancini treated the child with the utmost indulgence, for the elder sister she had nothing but harshness and severity. "My mother," writes Marie, "had become so bad-tempered that she

[1] "Mémoires de la Duchesse de Mazarin."

was unbearable ; and, as I was the least loved and the only one exposed to her ill-humour—my sister Olympe being in a separate apartment, and my sister Hortense being with Madame de Mercœur, under the care of Madame de Venel, who brought her up with much kindness and tenderness—I confess that I passed a very unpleasant time, and that nothing equalled my grief. To increase my misery, I had, for my only retreat, the worst of lodgings, and for my only companion an old *femme de chambre* called Rose, who had brought us up, and considered myself, besides, as being on the eve of entering a convent."[1]

The habitual harshness of her mother, indeed, made so great an impression upon the sensitive girl, that long after Madame Mancini's death had freed her from her thraldom, and she had become one of the divinities of the Court, she somehow found it difficult to realise that she was not still under her iron rule.

"Education," she writes, "is the richest gift that fathers can bestow on their children after that of giving them birth ; but it is of great importance that it should be accompanied by kindness : too great severity serving only to despoil them of affection ; love and fear being almost always incompatible. This was my own experience ; for even after my mother had been dead two years, my imagination, obsessed by the fear which had remained to me, represented her still living in my thoughts, and, even when waking, it seemed to me that I saw her, and that thought alone occasioned me incredible pain."[1]

Poor Marie's troubles had, however, one beneficial result. The pleasures of the Court, in which her sisters freely indulged, being interdicted to her by her mother,

----

[1] "La Vérité sur son jour."

and being left to her own resources almost the entire day, she sought to while away the long, lonely hours by reading, and, thanks to the splendid library wherewith the Cardinal was gradually replacing the collection dispersed in 1652, she had no lack of books. She read with avidity all the most celebrated French and Italian authors, and, with her wonderful memory, what she read was seldom forgotten. Poetry, and in particular Ariosto, was her favourite study, but she did not neglect more serious subjects, such as history, politics, and philosophy. And thus it came about that this little Cinderella, neglected and misunderstood, was, at an age when most young girls of to-day are still in the schoolroom, one of the most cultured women of her time, who, when at last she took her place in the great world, did not fear to converse with men like Lionne and Servien, La Rochefoucauld, and Saint-Évremond.

In the latter part of the year 1656, Madame Mancini fell ill. Her malady, the nature of which we are not told, if not exactly induced, was certainly aggravated by superstition. She was, as we have mentioned, a devout believer in astrology, of which science her late husband, Lorenzo Mancini, would appear to have been a singularly successful exponent. His predictions, according to his widow, proved almost invariably correct. He had predicted the death of their son Paul, killed in the combat of the Faubourg Saint-Antoine, and also his own death, on the very day on which it had occurred ; and, among those which remained to be fulfilled, he had predicted that she herself would die in her forty-second year, which she had but partly completed.

During her illness, which was not at first considered serious, the King did her the honour to visit her every evening, and it is to these visits that may be traced the

beginning of the friendship between his Majesty and
Marie Mancini which was to cause so much perturba-
tion in high places three years later.

Madame Mancini, Marie tells us, had strictly forbidden her daughter to enter her room when any
visitors happened to be present.   But, in order to reach
the elder lady's apartment, the King had to pass through
a room adjoining that of Marie, who very frequently
contrived to enter it unobserved about the time at
which her sovereign might be expected to arrive.
Louis, on his part, never failed to stop to talk to the
girl, whose lonely life he could not help pitying ; "and
these few minutes of conversation sufficed to make my
sad and mournful days pass more quickly, and I
returned to my solitude less afflicted than before."[1]

Towards the end of the year so dreaded by Madame
Mancini, her illness took a turn for the better, and she
began to entertain hopes of her ultimate recovery.
However, about the middle of December, she had a relapse, and on the nineteenth of the same month she died,
the victim, apparently, partly of her own superstitious
fears and partly of the ignorance of the surgeons who
had attended her, and, as a last resource, had administered to the sick woman a powerful emetic.

The approach of death did not effect any change in
her feelings towards the daughter whom she had always
treated with so much harshness and injustice, and
almost her last act was to implore the Cardinal to send
Marie to a convent, " because she appeared to her of a
bad disposition, and because her husband, a famous
astrologer, had predicted that she would be the cause of
much evil."[2]

Madame Mancini was buried in royal state, and a

[1] " La Vérité sur son jour."   [2] Madame de Motteville, " Mémoires."

solemn service, celebrated in the name of the general
assembly of the clergy of France, was held at the
Church of the Augustins for the repose of her soul, at
which the Bishop of Montauban preached and availed
himself of the opportunity to deliver a fulsome eulogy
of Mazarin and his family. Her death, however,
caused no interruption in the gaieties of the Court, and
the same ladies who in the morning had assisted at the
funeral service, her niece the Princesse de Conti among
them, figured in the evening at the performance of the
ballet of "l'Amour malade," in the great hall of the
Louvre, at which the young King, who represented the
languishing god, " danced," says the *Gazette de France*,
" with so much grace and majesty that one may say that
never had one seen so much sweetness and charm as
in the person of this great prince."

The Duchesse de Mercœur was on the eve of giving
birth to her third child when Madame Mancini died.
Although deeply affected by her mother's death, nothing
occurred during her confinement to occasion her friends
any uneasiness ; but, a few days later, "half her body became suddenly paralysed and she lost the power of speech."
The Cardinal was sent for in hot haste and hurried to
his niece's bedside, but, being reassured by the doctors
in attendance, returned to the Louvre, where the King
was again dancing in the ballet of " l'Amour malade." As
he was leaving, word was brought him that Madame de
Mercœur was much worse. Throwing himself into the
first coach he could find, he drove at full speed to the
Hôtel de Vendôme ; but, on reaching the sick-room, he
learned that the duchess was dying, and, being unable to
speak, she could only smile at him. " As she did not
suffer," says Madame de Motteville, "and was still con-

scious, death caused in her none of those terrible changes which it makes in others. A beautiful vermilion, which the fever gave her, had enhanced her natural beauty. I heard those who saw her in this state declare that she appeared to them the most beautiful woman possible to imagine, and her beauty increased their regret. The Cardinal was so affected that he could not refrain from giving expression to his grief, and the sobs he uttered appeared to proceed from a lively emotion." [1]

The valuable, but little-known, "Mémoires" of Daniel de Cosnac, who was present at Madame de Mercœur's death, contain some interesting details about the last hours of this good and amiable woman, who, firm in her faith and conscious of a blameless life, had a smile and a flash of gaiety, even in the very presence of the King of Terrors.

"Ten days passed without her experiencing any inconvenience. I spent part of these ten days in her chamber, and found her more cheerful than she had been since her mother's death. I rallied her on her delicate state and because she kept her bed while she looked and felt so well, when she told me that she could not rid her mind of a thought which she had had during her confinement : it was that she would never leave her bed again. I laughed at this apprehension, and Madame de Venel, her *dame d'honneur*, being in her room, she began to speak of her death again, laughing the while. Among other things, she said that when she died, she would not be able to refrain from laughing at the grimace Madame de Venel would make. I found her so well and in such good spirits that I said to her, 'Madame, to-morrow you must dress, and we will dine by your fireside. . . .'" At noon on the morrow, I came to the Hôtel de Vendôme. As I was mounting the steps, I

[1] Madame de Motteville, "Mémoires."

From a contemporary print

LAURE MANCINI, DUCHESSE DE MERCŒUR

was told that Madame was very ill. All that she had said the previous day returned to my mind. Having inquired of her how she did, she answered with difficulty, and, with her right arm, she proceeded to raise her left, and, showing it to me, told me that she could feel neither the hand nor the arm. The doctors maintained that her life was in no danger. . . . But she was overtaken by such drowsiness that they began to fear that her brain was affected. They ordered her to be cupped, which was done in so cruel a manner that the poor princess cried out in a way that pierced one's heart. She looked at me, as if to implore me to stop them tormenting her thus. This lasted all day. In the evening, the doctors began to change their tone. The Cardinal came himself to administer the Sacraments. She appeared so beautiful in this sad state that one could not realise that she must so soon die. At the foot of the bed she perceived Madame de Venel, who was weeping. The princess noticed her grimaces ; she turned her eyes in my direction, and when they encountered mine, she glanced towards Madame de Venel and began to smile, recollecting without doubt what she had said to me the previous day."

The Duc de Mercœur, who had been devotedly attached to his wife, was prostrated with grief. He retired into a convent of the Capuchins, where he remained for some time. Although still young, he did not think of remarrying, but became a priest, and died a cardinal and legate of the Holy See in France.

By his marriage with Laure Mancini, the duke had three sons, of whom the eldest was the famous soldier, Louis Joseph, Duc de Vendôme, and the second, Philippe, Grand Prior of the Order of Malta, celebrated for his wit and debauchery.

CHAPTER IV

Marriage of Olympe Mancini to Prince Eugène de Savoie, Comte de Soissons—Friendship between Olympe and Louis XIV—His Majesty's visit to the Hôtel de Soissons—Early *galanteries* of Louis XIV—Olympe and *la Grande Mademoiselle*—Marie Mancini takes her place at Court—Her appearance—Growing attachment between her and the King—Beneficial results of her influence over Louis—Fatal accident to Alphonse Mancini—Mazarin's grief at his nephew's death—His dislike of his surviving nephew, Philippe Mancini—The Comtesse de Soissons and Louis XIV—Incident at the Maréchale de l'Hôpital's ball—The Court follows the army—Louis XIV's visits to Turenne's headquarters at Mardyck—Surrender of Dunkerque—Dangerous illness of the King—Alarm in Paris—Colbert's letter to Mazarin—The King recovers—Passionate grief of Marie Mancini—Indifference of the Comtesse de Soissons—The Court at Fontainebleau—Louis XIV's attentions to Marie.

MADAME DE MERCŒUR died on 9 February 1657, and, ten days later, the second of the Mancini sisters, Olympe, was married to Prince Eugène de Savoie, Comte de Soissons, son of Prince Thomas de Carignan-Savoie. The date of the marriage had been fixed some time before the death of Madame de Mercœur, and the Cardinal, who always feared the unexpected, did not wish it to be postponed. It was a brilliant match for Olympe. Of the House of Savoy by his father, grandson of Charles V by his grandmother, and of the blood royal of France by his mother, Marie de Bourbon, daughter of Charles de Bourbon, Comte de Soissons, it would have been difficult to find a husband of greater consideration or of higher birth. Moreover, Mazarin had caused the title of Comte de Soissons to be revived in favour of his new nephew,[1] and Olympe thus became the wife of a Prince of the Blood, and was called, to distinguish her, *Madame la Comtesse.*

The marriage contract was signed on 19 February 1657, in the King's apartments, in the presence of their Majesties, *Monsieur*, the Cardinal, the Princesses de Conti and de Carignan, and others.

"The following day," says the *Gazette de France*, "this distinguished company repaired to the Queen's apartments, the Comte de Soissons escorting his betrothed, who was dressed in a gown of silver cloth, with a bouquet of pearls on her head, valued at more than 50,000 livres, and so many jewels that their splendour, joined to the natural *éclat* of her beauty, caused her to be admired by every one. Immediately afterwards, the nuptials were celebrated in the Queen's chapel. Then the illustrious pair, after dining with the Princesse de Carignan in the apartments of Mlle. de Mancini, ascended to those of his Eminence, where they were entertained to a magnificent supper, at which the King and *Monsieur* did the company the honour of joining them, although preparations had only been made for members of the family."

The two following days were devoted by the bride to receiving the visits of the Court. "On the 20th, the Queen, who, on this occasion, acted, so to speak, the part of mother to the Comtesse de Soissons, accompanied her to Notre-Dame to hear Mass, and then returned with her to the Louvre, whither came her mother-in-law, the Princesse de Carignan, to conduct her to the

---

[1] The last Comte de Soissons was Louis de Bourbon, brother of the Princesse de Carignan. He was killed at the battle of La Marfée, in 1641, and, as he left no legitimate issue, the title had become extinct.

Hôtel de Soissons, and testified to her, by her joy and the rich presents which she made her, how great is the satisfaction with which she regards this marriage."

Olympe was also well satisfied with the arrangement, notwithstanding that she had, at one time, hoped for a higher destiny—for nothing less than a throne ; not a ducal one, such as her cousin Laure Martinozzi shared, but the first throne in Europe.

Desirous of confining the royal favour as far as possible to himself and his family, Mazarin had from the first encouraged the intimacy between the young King and his elder nieces, which had begun from the time of the arrival of the latter in France. It was Olympe to whom Louis attached himself. Brought up, so to speak, with the King, who was the same age as herself, she had taken more share than her sisters or cousin in his boyish amusements, and the preference he had always shown for her increased as he grew older. Olympe's quickness and tact were remarkable even in her childish days. Even then she never forgot that her playfellow was a King, whose favour was to be won, a possible lover whose homage was to be secured, and shaped her course accordingly, ever ready to enter into the pursuits of the young sovereign, to divine his tastes, to anticipate his wishes.

Although never beautiful, the girl improved vastly in appearance as the years went by. At the age of eighteen, Madame de Motteville, who had drawn so unflattering a portrait of her on her arrival in France, thus describes her : " Her eyes were full of fire, her complexion had become beautiful, her face less thin, her cheeks took dimples which gave her a fresh charm, she had fine arms and beautiful hands." And the chronicler adds : " She certainly seemed charming in the eyes

of the King, and sufficiently pretty to indifferent spectators."

The attachment of the King for Mlle. Olympe soon
became an affair of importance, which greatly occupied
both Court and town. People began to ask themselves
whether the Cardinal, who did not find even Princes of
the Blood too highly placed for his nieces, and who had
lately married one to the heir-apparent of a reigning
duke, would set any bounds to his ambition. Mazarin,
as we shall presently show, had very different matrimonial views for his young master ; but he certainly
seems to have looked with a far from unfavourable eye
upon Louis's penchant for Olympe, which enabled him
to keep the King under his care, and ambitious and
possibly hostile beauties at a distance ; and his star
shone with such brilliancy just then that Olympe became the divinity of the Court, and every one hastened
to burn incense at her feet.

Anne of Austria, on her side, regarded her son's
attention to the young lady with complacency, though
Madame de Motteville tells us that she could not endure to hear any one speak of the affair as one that
might perchance become legitimate. " The greatness of
her soul had a perfect horror of such abasement."
Another queen, the eccentric Christina of Sweden, who
passed through France in 1656, was of a different
opinion, and declared that " it would be very wrong
not to let two young people so admirably suited to one
another marry as soon as possible."

As we have seen, nothing came of this affair, for
Louis showed no inclination to abase himself, and
Olympe soon came to the conclusion that her best
chance of obtaining the power and influence she coveted
lay in some less illustrious union. Her mortification

was intense at seeing her cousins, Anne-Marie and
Laure Martinozzi, preferred by the Prince de Conti
and Alfonso d'Este, nor was it lessened when the
Marquis de la Meilleraye, to whom the Cardinal offered
her, as he had previously her sister Marie, gravely
assured his Eminence that he wished to marry "*pour
faire son salut*," and that, as he felt an inconceivable
aversion to Olympe, marriage with her would be "*juste-
ment le grand chemin de la damnation.*"

Compensation, however, for these disappointments
was forthcoming in her union with the Comte de
Soissons, which raised her to the rank of a Princess
of the Blood, and provided her with an indulgent
husband, who adored his wife when he was at home,
and whose frequent absences with the army gave her
ample opportunity for enjoying the society of her
admirers.

Louis XIV did not testify the least annoyance at the
announcement of the marriage, and his cheerful looks at
the ceremony caused the Queen to remark to Madame
de Motteville, who had endeavoured to disquiet her on
the matter : "Did I not tell you that there was nothing
to fear from this *liaison*."

In spite, however, of the perfect indifference shown
by the King at the moment of the marriage, he continued to visit the lady with the greatest regularity ;
indeed, scarcely a day went by on which his Majesty's
coach did not stop at the gate of the Hôtel de Soissons;
and Olympe, basking in the rays of the royal favour,
rapidly took her place as the brilliant, intriguing great
lady that Nature intended her to be.

It may, perhaps, be asked of what character were
the relations between the King and countess. We
are inclined to think that the young sovereign was

hardly so indiscreet with the matron as he had been with the maid, as, from the confidences of contemporary writers, it would appear that the age of innocence had passed for him.

When Louis was but sixteen, his attention was attracted by a certain Mlle. de la Motte d'Argencourt, "who had neither dazzling beauty nor extraordinary intelligence, but whose whole person was agreeable." His predilection for her society became so very marked that the Queen and Mazarin grew uneasy, and the former, one evening when Louis had conversed with the young lady rather longer than she deemed prudent, rebuked him sharply and openly. The monarch received the maternal reprimand "with respect and gentleness"; but it would not appear to have had much effect, for, shortly afterwards, we hear of him speaking to Mlle. de la Motte "as a man in love, who was no longer virtuous," and assuring her that, if she would only return his affection, he would defy both the Queen and the Cardinal. The lady, however, from motives either of virtue or policy, declined to entertain his proposals, and the Queen having pointed out to her son that "he was wandering from the path of innocence," the King was moved to tears, confessed himself in his oratory, and then departed for Vincennes, in the hope that a change of scene might assist him in subjugating his passion. After a few days' absence, he returned, fully determined never to speak to Mlle. de la Motte again; but, "not being yet wholly strengthened," so far departed from his resolution as to dance with her at a ball, with the result that he was on the point of succumbing once more, when the Queen and the Cardinal put an end to the affair by packing the damsel off to a convent at Chaillot, where, Madame de Motte-

F

ville assures us, "she led a life that was very tranquil and very happy."[1]

The Queen's vigilance was, however, powerless to save the young sovereign from the wiles of the intriguing *femme de chambre*, Madame de Beauvais, the same lady who had lent herself to the schemes of the presumptuous Jarzé, and had received a term of exile for her pains. Madame de Beauvais, called by her royal mistress "*Cateau la borgnesse,*" was very far from being beautiful, while her youth was only a memory; but she was "a woman of experience," who possessed "*l'humeur galante au dernier point*"; and she had the distinction of opening that famous list which contains the names of La Vallière and Montespan.

After this singular debut, the monarch addressed the same homage to "*une petite jardinière,*" by whom he had a daughter, who was brought up without scandal and married secretly to a gentleman of some position. Then we hear of a *galanterie* with the beautiful Duchesse de Châtillon, beloved of the great Condé; of an unsuccessful attack upon that impregnable fortress of virtue, the Princesse de Conti; and of an equally abortive attempt to woo a marvellous young beauty, Élisabeth de Tarneau by name, "who had the prudence to refuse him so much as an interview." From all of which it will be gathered that the French ecclesiastic who gravely assured the Pope that Louis at twenty was "as chaste as he had been on the day of his baptism," must have been either a most unblushing prevaricator of the truth or singularly ill-informed in regard to the doings of the Court.

To judge by the Comtesse de Soissons's subsequent history, she was not the kind of woman to be over-

[1] "Mémoires de Madame de Motteville."

fastidious as to the means she employed to retain in her chains this illustrious captive. It is true that other chains often drew him away; but Olympe knew how to make the most of her good fortune. It was much that the King remained constant, at least in his visits, and left her all the prestige of favour.

On the strength of this favour, the young lady seems to have given herself intolerable airs, and to have treated even members of the Royal Family with the coolest insolence. *La Grande Mademoiselle*,[1] reconciled with the Court in the early summer of 1657, installed herself at Saint-Cloud, prior to rejoining their Majesties, who were then in Flanders. Although she had been so long absent from the Court, *Mademoiselle* was well informed of all that went on there, and was, in consequence, very curious to see the lady to whom the King was reported to be paying so much attention. Olympe, being then enceinte, had been compelled, to her intense disgust, to remain in Paris, and was in a very bad humour when her mother-in-law, the Princesse de Carignan, brought her to visit the princess, who has left us the following account of their interview :—

"'I bring you my daughter-in-law,' said Madame de Carignan to me, ' she is enceinte; she came in a litter.' I went to receive her; Madame de Carignan paid me many compliments. As for her daughter-in-law, she said nothing. It was warm, and there were a great many people about me; and I said to Mlle. de Guise and to Madame d'Épernon : 'Pray take the Comtesse de Soissons into my cabinet, lest she should be incommoded here, and I will join her in a moment'; which they did. Madame de Carignan remained with the rest of the com-

[1] Anne Marie Louise d'Orléans, Duchesse de Montpensier, eldest daughter of Gaston d'Orléans (*Monsieur*), younger brother of Louis XIII.

pany. The Comtesse de Soissons was for a long time silent, when all of a sudden she asked me : ' Why do you not wear your ruffles like other people ? ' I told her that they inconvenienced me. To which she answered : ' If you think that it makes your arms look more beautiful, you are mistaken.' She then added : ' My mother-in-law is very tiresome ; she is so afraid that I shall hurt myself that she follows me everywhere.' I paid her a thousand compliments on the obligations under which the Cardinal had placed me ; said that I loved all who belonged to him ; that her marriage had given me the greatest joy, and that I hoped to see her often and to be friends with her. To all of which she answered me not a word. I did not find her so pretty as I had been told, and, when I looked at her, I could not understand how the King had ever fallen in love with her. I praised her very much in every way ; she received it all with an indifference and in a silence which astonished every one."

The mortification of the Comtesse de Soissons at being prevented from following the Court to Flanders, which resulted in her showing such a peculiarly unpleasing side of her character to *Mademoiselle*, was due to the fact that she was just then occupied in doing her utmost to combat Louis XIV's penchant for her sister Marie, and feared that, during her enforced absence from the field, it could hardly fail to make material progress.

Soon after Olympe's marriage, the Cardinal had permitted Marie to take the place at Court of which her mother's dislike had so unjustly deprived her. " The death of my mother and the marriage of my sister Olympe," she writes, " having rendered me more independent, and, enjoying all the privileges belonging to the right of the eldest, of which I was in possession, I

passed a life of sufficient tranquillity and began to taste
its sweets. Contentment of mind always contributes to
the favourable development of the body, and the condition in which I found myself at that time was a
sufficiently convincing proof of it for me. I was not
recognisable, and I am able to say that prosperity had
been of as much advantage to my mind as to my body,
and had greatly augmented its vivacity and gaiety."[1]

In point of fact, Marie's appearance, like that of
Olympe, had already improved to a really remarkable
degree. Her features, though too irregular for beauty,
were good; she had large and brilliant black eyes,
splendid teeth, and a delightful smile; while the extreme mobility of her countenance endowed her with a
singular charm. Her complexion was of the purest
olive; her hair jet black and abundant; her figure supple
and well made, and she had very pretty hands and feet.
In a word, she had become a dangerously attractive
young woman, who, without ever approaching the perfect loveliness of her sister Hortense, was perhaps more
capable of inspiring a true passion. Louis XIV is the
proof of it. His liking for the girl, which had begun
during his visits to her dying mother, increased rapidly
now that her participation in the gaieties of the Court
threw them constantly together, and, during a visit to
Fontainebleau which the Court paid in the autumn of
1657, it became apparent to all that this liking was
gradually developing into a much warmer feeling.

The young monarch, as we have related, had already
made several excursions into the realms of gallantry;
but, though he had loved, he had never been beloved,
perhaps because, as one writer suggests, he was still very
timid with women: a callow youth, who blushed and

---

[1] "La Vérité sur son jour."

paled when a pretty girl held his hand, and who mingled
with unlawful pleasures floods of remorseful tears. The
thought that he had at last excited a *grande passion*, one
of those turbulent emotions which he felt to be equally
the due of his handsome face and fine figure and of his
exalted position, could not be otherwise than soothing
to his vanity. He began to pay increased attention to
Marie Mancini, and the more he saw of her, the more
she pleased him. He spoke to her " *avec application*,"
says Madame de Motteville, and was carried away like
a straw before the hurricane.

And there can be no doubt that Marie loved him—
loved, that is to say, the man apart from the king. The
" Mémoires " of her sister Hortense, who, it goes without saying, was her confidante, leaves us in no uncertainty on this point.

" As she (Marie)," she writes, " had a serious attachment for the King, she would have been very glad to
see me affected by a similar weakness. But my extreme
youth did not permit me to attach myself to anything,
and all that I could do to oblige her was to show some
particular complaisance towards those of the young
people we saw who diverted me most in the childish
games which then occupied my attention. The presence
of the King, who seldom stirred from our lodging,
often interrupted us. Although he lived among us
with a marvellous kindness, he had always something
so serious and so solid, not to say majestic, in all his
ways, that he could not help inspiring us with respect,
even contrary to his intention. My sister alone was
undisturbed, and you can easily understand that his
assiduity had charms for her, who was the cause of it,
because it had none for others. As the things which
passion does make us seem ridiculous to those who have

never known what that passion is, my sister's exposed her very frequently to our raillery."[1]

Soon the King's predilection for Mlle. Marie's society became the all-absorbing topic of conversation, and rumours of it reached Queen Christina of Sweden, who one day remarked, in her blunt way, to Louis: "If I were in your place, I should marry a person whom I loved." As for Marie, if she had not been already aware of the growing attachment of the young monarch, the attention of the courtiers, and particularly of the ladies, towards her would soon have revealed it.

Mazarin, in its early stages, seems to have viewed the very marked inclination of the King for his niece with complacency, probably regarding the affair as a mere boy and girl attachment, and even lent himself to it, so far as to provide the young lady with a number of ravishing toilettes, which enabled her to more than hold her own in the Court festivities. The Queen, on her part, placed no obstacle in the way of her son's attentions, preferring to see him engaged in what she imagined to be a harmless flirtation than imperilling his salvation by wearing the chains of the Duchesse de Châtillon or some other notorious beauty.

The young girl's influence over her royal admirer increased daily. Olympe had shared his pleasures, accommodated herself to his tastes; Marie sought and succeeded in inspiring him with a desire to share hers. Although skilled in all bodily exercises—horsemanship, dancing, and the use of arms—Louis XIV, at the age of twenty, was profoundly ignorant. His mind was one which required stimulating, and no one had as yet taken that trouble. The germs of those qualities which made a great monarch of a man of mediocre intel-

[1] "Mémoires de la Duchesse de Mazarin."

lect were there, but these germs had had neither light nor air to expand. "Marie Mancini became his friend, and it was like an irruption of the sun into an enclosed and gloomy spot. He learnt and understood more in six months than he had since he came into the world.

"She opened to him the world of heroes—heroes of love, heroes of constancy and self-sacrifice, heroes of glory. She revealed to him the sentiments great or subtle, passionate or noble, which made life precious. She reproached him with his ignorance, and constituted herself his preceptress, teaching him Italian, filling his hands with poems, romances, and tragedies, reading to him herself verse and prose, in an amorous voice, with intonations which soothed or intoxicated him. She accustomed him to serious conversations with men of age and merit, excited him to emulation, and aided him to acquire nobility and correctness of expression. To her is due also the little taste for the arts that he possessed.

"He owed her more than all that. She made him ashamed of being without ambition, without dreams either worthy or unworthy, without desires more lofty than the choice of a costume or a *pas de ballet*—made him, in a word, remember that he was King, and gave him the idea of being a great king. He never forgot the lesson."[1]

Louis, who had loved the girl at first because she loved him and intended that he should reciprocate her passion, ended by loving her spontaneously, from a nobler motive, because he recognised in her a superior mind, contact with which opened to his own unknown horizons.

[1] Arvède Barine, "Princesses et grandes dames : Marie Mancini."

From an engraving after the drawing by Wallerant Vaillant

LOUIS XIV

The close of the year 1657, was marked by an unto-
ward event, which occasioned Mazarin profound sorrow.
His youngest nephew, Alphonse Mancini, who had
arrived in France at the same time as his little sister
Marianne, had been sent, like his brothers Paul and
Philippe before him, to the Jesuit College at Clermont,
from which glowing accounts as to his progress in his
studies reached the gratified Cardinal. During the
Christmas festivities, he was playing with the other
scholars, when, tired of their ordinary games, some one
suggested that they should toss one another in a blanket.
All went well until it came to Alphonse's turn to
undergo that not over-pleasant experience, when the
little Abbé d'Harcourt, who was very weak, allowed the
corner of the blanket he held to slip from his hand, with
the result that Alphonse fell to the floor and fractured
his skull. Four surgeons were quickly on the spot, but
all their skill was unavailing, and the unhappy lad died
on 16 January 1658. "He had nearly completed his
studies," says *Mademoiselle*, "and showed remarkable
intelligence. He was *un esprit vif*, and the Cardinal, I
have heard people say, had entertained such great hopes
for him that he was about to remove him from college,
and intended to keep him near his person and accustom
him to affairs, to have him to sleep in his own chamber,
speak of everything before him, and show him all the
despatches that he received and wrote." Mazarin was
in despair at Alphonse's death, which he appears to have
felt even more keenly than that of his brother Paul.
On receiving the news he left for Vincennes, where he
shut himself up for ten days and refused to see any one.

By the irony of fate, Philippe Mancini, the only
nephew who now remained to the Cardinal, was precisely
the one whom Mazarin could not endure, and for whom

he always evinced the greatest aversion. However, if Philippe, who was an amiable young man, though some-what frivolous, had not succeeded in gaining his uncle's favour, he had won the affection of the King, who, in January 1657, appointed him captain of his company of Musketeers, Charles de Baatz de Castelmore, Comte d'Artagnan, the hero of Dumas's immortal romance, being nominated lieutenant of the same company, in order that his military knowledge might supplement that of his superior officer.

The winter of 1657–8 was a particularly brilliant one at the Court, balls, fêtes, and ballets following one another in rapid succession. The taste which the King had early evinced for the last of these entertainments showed no sign of diminishing, and he figured in nearly all of them, together with Marie Mancini. At the same time, his Majesty continued to visit the Hôtel de Soissons and to pay considerable attention to its mistress ; probably, he feared to incur that lady's resent-ment by a too abrupt desertion, foreseeing that she might prove a dangerous enemy.

The countess, on her side, though perfectly well aware that her younger sister had already supplanted her in the royal affections, pretended to ignore it, and in public lost no opportunity of flaunting her intimacy with his Majesty. *Mademoiselle* writes :—

" Madame la Maréchale de l'Hôpital gave a ball, to which we went in masks and dressed in gold and silver stuffs and caps and plumes ; the men wore silk stockings and coats covered with embroidery. When we entered, we wore our masks, which, however, we immediately removed. . . . We repaired to a room magnificently decor-ated for refreshments, but, as there was only one cover and one armchair, the King said to me, ' Sit down there, my cousin ; it is your place.' I cried out at that, as if he spoke in jest ; he rejoined, 'Who will take it ?' The Comtesse de Soissons smiled and said : ' I will sit there.' In fact, she proceeded to take it, although *Monsieur*, the King's brother, said, ' Do not go there.' This familiarity with the King surprised me, for it was not so before I left the Court. All seated themselves at table ; the King was the last to sit down, saying, as he did so, 'Since there is no other seat but this, I must needs take it." He helped himself to no dish that he did not offer to others, and begged us to eat with him. For myself, who had been brought up in the greatest respect for etiquette, all this astonished me very much, and it was long before I could accustom myself to it.

"On my preparing to leave, the King said to the Comtesse de Soissons, ' Let us take my cousin home.' She said that she was quite willing. We set off at full speed, and so quickly that the King's Guards, who were on horseback, had great difficulty in keeping up with us. The streets of Paris were so unsafe at night at this period, that the King said gaily, seeing his Guards so far behind the coach, ' How delighted I should be if robbers would attack us !' His Majesty's coach was left far behind, so that until it came up, we walked on the terrace in the court of the Luxembourg, the 3rd of February, at three o'clock in the morning, as if it were the month of July."

In the course of that winter, Louis XIV had a passing fancy for a certain Mlle. de la Motte-Houdan-court, whom several writers confound with the Mlle. de la Motte d'Argencourt already mentioned. ' Nothing was talked of but this new friendship of the King," says *Mademoiselle;* "and all the men were glad, hoping that it would make him more gay." The Queen and the Cardinal, however, nipped the affair in the bud. " The King was closeted for three hours with her Majesty and his Eminence, and at the break up of the conference took no more notice of La Motte."

At the end of April 1658, the King and Queen quitted Paris and proceeded to Amiens; and Turenne having resolved to lay siege to Dunkerque, the Court established itself at Calais, from which town Louis paid frequent visits to Mardyck, which Turenne had made his headquarters.

On these visits, the King was only accompanied by a small escort, and did not bring with him any of the comforts and luxuries with which he usually travelled; but shared Turenne's quarters, though that general was very indifferently lodged, and his soldier's fare. Under ordinary circumstances, this rough life might have had no ill effects upon his Majesty; but summer arrived with almost tropical heat, water was difficult to procure, while the decomposing bodies of those who had fallen in the campaign of the previous year and lay but half buried in the sand, tainted the air and rendered the camp a perfect plague-spot.

On 23 June, Turenne having defeated the relieving army under Condé and Don Juan of Austria, in the Battle of the Dunes, Dunkerque capitulated; but the rejoicings over this success did not last long, as a week later Louis XIV fell dangerously ill of a malignant fever, the result of the hardships he had voluntarily undergone during his visits to the army, and of breathing for entire days the pestilential air of Mardyck.

For a fortnight, the young King was in great danger, and the doctors in attendance could only hold out very slight hopes of his recovery. Paris was in consternation, and the Holy Sacrament was exposed in all the churches; while the *protégés* of Mazarin were in the utmost alarm, fearing that Louis's death might involve their patron's downfall.

"We are in the gravest anxiety here in regard to the illness of the King," writes Colbert to the Cardinal. "M. de Langlade, who will bring this note to your Eminence, will be able to tell you the bad news that reached us yesterday evening. God grant that it may not be true! But, in God's name, Monseigneur, let your Eminence give orders to some one to despatch a courier daily to this town, as I am of the opinion of all your Eminence's servants, that it is of very great importance that we should be advised every moment of what is happening in so delicate and grave a matter. If the news be good, we shall take steps to make it public; if it be bad, we shall use it as appears to us most advantageous for the service of the King and of your Eminence."[1]

This letter was written on 7 July. The news of the following day was very grave: the doctors had practically abandoned hope, and the Viaticum had been administered; and the houses of Colbert and other important persons who were believed to be in receipt of private information were besieged by excited crowds.

As a forlorn hope, a doctor from Abbeville, Du Saussois by name, who enjoyed a great local reputation, was called in, and, after a long consultation with Vallot, first physician to the King, it was decided to try the effect of an emetic wine, a remedy then but little known. The experiment was attended with complete success; in a few days the royal patient was declared out of danger,

[1] Letter cited by Lucien Perey, " Le Roman du Grand Roi."

and on 22 July was so far recovered as to allow of his being removed to Compiègne by easy stages.

One can well imagine the varied feelings which animated the Court during that fortnight of anxious suspense, while the King's life and all that depended upon it trembled in the balance : the anguish of the Queen ; the feverish anxiety of Mazarin, divided between grief for the master to whom he was tenderly attached and fears for his own position in the event of the illness having a fatal termination ; the ill-concealed joy of the personal friends of *Monsieur;* the painful uncertainty of those who knew not whether to weep for the declining or to pay court to the rising sun. To few indeed, we fear, save the devoted mother, did the thought of the premature death of the young prince occasion a genuine and disinterested grief ; but, among these last, no one was so much remarked as Marie Mancini, who, unable to conceal or to moderate her feelings, gave way to a despair which was the talk of the whole Court. "Marie," writes Madame de la Fayette, " had testified an affection so violent, and had so little concealed it, that when he grew better every one spoke to him of the grief of Mlle. de Mancini, and perhaps in the sequel she spoke of it to him herself. In short, she gave proof of so much passion, and broke through so completely the restraints which the Queen-Mother and the Cardinal imposed upon her, that one may say that she constrained the King to love her."[1]

In striking contrast to the passionate grief of Marie, her sister Madame de Soissons evinced the most profound indifference during the King's illness. "She did not show the regret that one would have expected of her," says *Mademoiselle,* "in view of the friendship

[1] "Histoire de Madame Henriette d'Angleterre."

that the King had shown for her. The Queen said to her one day, 'Every time I see you, I desire to weep; you make me think of my grief.' She made no reply whatever, but turned and inquired of those who were with her, 'What did the Queen say?'"

In the early autumn, the Court removed from Compiègne to Fontainebleau, where, as is so often the case with persons who have recently passed through a dangerous illness, Louis XIV gave himself up with whole-hearted zest to every kind of pleasure, and gaiety reigned supreme. There were balls and fêtes, performances by the French and Italian players, excursions by water, and picnics in the forest. On one occasion, *Monsieur* gave a "collation," at the hermitage of Franchard, whither the whole Court proceeded on horseback and in gala dress. The King, who was in high spirits, took into his head to ascend the rocks which surrounded the hermitage—"the most inconvenient possible to imagine," says *Mademoiselle*, "and where you would have supposed only goats could ever have been before." He was accompanied in this perilous adventure by Marie Mancini, while the Marquis d'Alluye lent his assistance to Marie's friend, Mlle. du Fouilloux. On reaching the summit, Louis, in a spirit of mischief, sent orders to the rest of the party, who had remained in the garden of the hermitage, to follow him, preceded by a band of violin players, which *Monsieur* had provided for the entertainment of his guests. We were obliged to obey," continues *Mademoiselle*, "though it was not without difficulty; and we no sooner resolved to venture than we found ourselves obliged to return. I am surprised that no one was hurt, for we ran the greatest risk of having our arms and legs broken, and even of fracturing our skulls. I think that the prayers of the good hermit must have preserved us. After supper, we returned *en calèche*, accompanied by a number of men bearing torches, and, on our arrival, went to the play."

During the visit to Fontainebleau, the intimacy between Louis XIV and Marie Mancini made rapid progress: and, if Marie had had to wait longer than her sisters for her share of the good things of life, she was now abundantly compensated. Neither the Queen nor the Cardinal placed any obstacle in the way of her enjoyment of the society of her royal admirer, although the jealous Comtesse de Soissons complained bitterly to her uncle of Louis's predilection for her younger sister. But Mazarin still believed, or more probably feigned to believe, that the affair was of no consequence, and made no attempt to interfere. From Marie's "Mémoires," however, it is evident that his Majesty's passion was now approaching a high temperature, and that the fact was patent not only to herself, but to the whole Court.

"The King's kindness was so great, that we lived on terms of familiarity with both him and *Monsieur*, and, since this familiarity permitted me to say what I thought with a certain degree of freedom, perhaps I said it with some agreeableness. I continued still to do the same during a visit that the Court paid to Fontainebleau (for we followed it everywhere), and, on my return from this visit, I perceived that I did not displease the King, as I had already sufficient knowledge to understand that eloquent silence which often persuades more than all the fine speeches in the world. Perhaps, also, the penchant and the inclination that I had for his Majesty, in whom I recognised more merit than in any one in his realm, rendered me more intelligent in this matter than I had been on another occasion.

"However, the testimony of my eyes was not enough to cause me to believe a matter of this consequence ; but the courtiers, who are as so many eyes which watch over the actions of kings, perceiving also, as well as myself, his Majesty's inclination, speedily confirmed me in the opinion that I had formed by their extraordinary respect and deference. And the attentions of the King, the magnificent presents which I received, his care, his *empressements*, and the kindness that he showed for me in all things, soon ended by persuading me altogether."[1]

On the return of the Court to Paris, it was remarked that the King did not resume his accustomed visits to the Hôtel de Soissons ; while, on the other hand, not an evening passed on which he did not engage the younger sister in conversation, his manner on these occasions partaking far more of that of the lover than of the gracious sovereign. An event of the highest importance, however, now arrived to interrupt what that young lady calls her "ravishing prosperity."

---

[1] "La Vérité dans son jour."

G

CHAPTER V

Mazarin's project of marrying Louis XIV to the Infanta Maria Theresa
—Negotiations between France and Savoy in regard to the King's
marriage with the Princess Margherita—The Cardinal arranges a
meeting between the two Courts at Lyons—His object—Departure
of their Majesties and the Court for Lyons—"The King always
near Mlle. de Mancini"—He ignores the Comtesse de Soissons—
Incident at Dijon—Arrival at Lyons—Meeting between Louis XIV
and the Princess Margherita—*Empressement* of the King—Arrival of
a secret envoy from Spain with an offer of peace and the Infanta's
hand — Conversation between Louis XIV and Marie Mancini —
Sudden change in the King's attitude towards the Princess Margherita
—The Duke of Savoy and Hortense Mancini—Rupture of the
marriage negotiations with Savoy—The Princess Margherita and her
mother leave Lyons—Marie Mancini makes a great resolve—Intimacy
between her and Louis XIV at Lyons—A watchful *gouvernante*—
The Court returns to Paris.

FOR more than fifteen years, and through many strange
vicissitudes, Mazarin had steadily pursued the project of marrying Louis to the Infanta Maria Theresa of
Spain. His object for desiring this union was twofold.
In the first place, a closer connexion between France and
Spain would leave the Emperor isolated in Europe and
render him practically impotent. In the second, it was
more than possible that it might, sooner or later, be
the means of giving the crown of Spain to the House
of Bourbon, for, as his letters to the French plenipotentiaries at the Congress of Westphalia indicate, the astute
Cardinal had resolved to so frame the marriage-contract
that there would be little difficulty in contesting the

validity of any renunciation of her rights on the part
of the Infanta.[1]

Since 1648, when the Peace of Westphalia was concluded with the Emperor, more than one attempt had
been made to conclude peace on the basis of another
Franco-Spanish marriage.   But, as Philip IV had no
male issue, and the Infanta would, in consequence,
have carried with her to France the right of succession
to the crown of Spain, the Court of Madrid had
hitherto received the Cardinal's proposals with marked
coldness.

Of late, however, the situation had been materially
modified.   In 1657, the Queen of Spain had given
birth to a son, an event which placed two lives between the Infanta and the throne, and very sensibly
diminished that princess's matrimonial value ; while
France had gained great advantage in the field, and it
was becoming increasingly difficult for Spain, with troops
disheartened by defeat and an impoverished Treasury,
to continue the struggle.

Indirect negotiations were accordingly opened, but as
the Court of Madrid showed its customary vacillation,
Mazarin resolved on a very adroit manœuvre, with the
object of forcing it to come to a decision.

For some time past both France and Spain had been
making great efforts to secure the alliance of Savoy, a
State which had been originally on the side of France,
but had now for many years maintained a strict neutra-
lity.   Savoy was then governed by Christine de France,
second daughter of Henry IV, and widow of Victor
Amadeus I, who, on the death of her husband in 1637,

---

[1] Mr. J. B. Perkins, " France under Richelieu and Mazarin."

had been declared Regent and guardian of her son, Charles Emmanuel II, and her three daughters.[1]

The Duchess, a shrewd and sagacious woman, a worthy daughter of Henry IV, at first declined to commit herself to either side. When pressed by Mazarin, however, she finally replied that she would take the part of France, on condition of the marriage of Louis XIV to her second daughter Margherita. The Cardinal did not see his way to satisfy her in this matter, having more exalted views for his young master ; but after the Battle of the Dunes, with Flanders half conquered and the Milanese greatly weakened by the capture of Valenza and Mortara, he was naturally reluctant to pause in his triumphant career, and, since he was unable to push his conquests in Italy without a passage for French troops through Piedmont and the assistance of Savoy, he determined, in the event of a definite refusal from Madrid of the Infanta's hand, and the consequent prolongation of the war, to agree to the Duchess's terms. He, therefore, accepted the project of marriage, but under the reservation that no definite decision should be arrived at until Louis XIV had had an opportunity of seeing the Princess Margherita ; and he requested the Duchess to bring her daughter to Lyons, the place which he had selected for the interview. Christine readily accepted this proposition, and the end of November 1658 was fixed for the meeting of the two Courts.

No secrecy whatever was made of the proposed meeting, Mazarin hoping that so soon as the news reached Madrid, Philip IV would hasten to intervene with an offer of his daughter's hand, when, of course, he intended

---

[1] Charles Emmanuel II had been declared of age in June 1648, but his mother continued to keep the authority in her hands down to the time of her death, 27 December 1663.

to break off immediately all negotiations with Savoy. It was a masterly move, and, as we shall see, was attended with complete success.

When this journey to Lyons was first mooted, Louis XIV had decided to proceed thither accompanied only by the Cardinal and his gentlemen-in-ordinary, leaving the Queen and the rest of the Court in Paris. Subsequently, however, he begged his mother to accompany him, declaring that he did not like to part from her for even a brief period, and that her assistance was essential to enable him to arrive at a decision on a matter of such importance. The Queen consented willingly enough, and determined to take with her *Mademoiselle*, all her maids-of-honour, and the Cardinal's nieces, who always formed part of her entourage.

In the opinion of Marie Mancini's latest biographer, Lucien Perey, it was that young lady who had induced the King to make this alteration in his plans, knowing that, in the event of the Queen going to Lyons, she would accompany her, and would thus be in a position to bring all her influence to bear upon Louis to prevent him deciding in favour of the Princess Margherita.

It is very probable that a similar idea had occurred to Mazarin. The Cardinal could no longer pretend to be ignorant of Louis's attachment to his niece, but as yet he had not judged it necessary to interfere. Underrating the independence and obstinacy of the girl's character, he hoped to find in her a useful instrument, who, if occasion arose, would endeavour to influence the King's mind in the direction which he himself thought desirable. It would certainly be extremely vexatious if, when Philip IV, as he confidently expected him to do, should offer his daughter's hand and peace along with it, Louis should have fallen in love with the Princess Margherita and insist upon marrying her. In that eventuality, he might count upon Marie to save the situation.

On 26 October, the King and Queen, after hearing Mass at Notre-Dame, set out for Lyons, accompanied by a numerous and brilliant suite. During the first day's journey, his Majesty remained in his coach with his mother, *Mademoiselle*, and the Princess Palatine,[1] the *surintendante* of the Queen's household. But on the morrow, as the weather was fine, he suggested to *Mademoiselle* that it would be more pleasant on horseback. " Mlle. de Mancini, some of the Queen's ladies, and myself did as he proposed. The King was always near Mlle. de Mancini, with whom he conversed in a most gallant manner."[2]

The journey resembled an official progress. Some leagues from every town of importance the royal cortège was met by the gentry of the neighbourhood dressed in their bravest attire, who escorted it as far as the gates, where the magistrates and citizens waited to receive their young sovereign, whom few of them had ever seen, and who, after running so many risks during the Fronde, had but lately had so narrow an escape from death. Everywhere the utmost enthusiasm prevailed ; on all sides nothing was heard but praises of the young monarch ; his handsome face, his fine figure, the skill with which he managed his high-spirited horse, the grace with which he acknowledged the salutations of his loyal subjects—all delighted the crowds who flocked to do him homage.

[1] Anne de Gonzague, second daughter of Charles de Gonzague, Duc de Nevers, and wife of Prince Edward of Bavaria, "Count Palatine," fourth son of Frederick V, Elector Palatine. She must not be confused with her niece, Charlotte Elizabeth, the second wife of *Monsieur*.

[2] "Mémoires de Mademoiselle de Montpensier."

At Dijon, where, on his arrival, the King was met by all the *noblesse* of Burgundy, with the Duc d'Épernon, the governor of the province, at their head—the Court remained for a fortnight. The States of Burgundy were at that time sitting, and Mazarin hoped that the presence of their sovereign would serve as a spur to their loyalty, and induce them to vote larger subsidies than was their custom.

The King was in the highest spirits. He danced every evening, and all the principal people in the province, and even in the town, *Mademoiselle* tells us, came to watch him. Every evening, too, he ordered a grand collation in lieu of supper, thanks to which arrangement he did not sup with the Queen, but remained "four or five hours talking with Mlle. de Mancini." On the other hand, the poor Comtesse de Soissons was entirely ignored by her former admirer, and in a manner so pointed as to suggest that she had contrived to displease seriously his Majesty, presumably by complaining to the Cardinal about his intimacy with her sister.

"During the journey," writes *Mademoiselle*, "the King did not address a word to the Comtesse de Soissons, and at Dijon it was the same. One day, he did something which was remarked by all, although a mere bagatelle. During a collation, the Queen sent to him to ask for some rissoles, and I made the same request. He sent some to the Queen, with whom the Comtesse de Soissons was supping, but finding them insufficient, she sent to ask for more. The King then sent word that he had enough for her and for me, but that there were not enough left for himself and his company. Every one believed that this was intended to apply to the Comtesse de Soissons."

Before the Court quitted Dijon, the fine weather with which it had been favoured since leaving Paris had broken up ; notwithstanding which, Louis XIV still continued to perform the greater part of each day's journey on horseback. The cold and rain had driven *Mademoiselle* and most of the fair equestrians to the shelter of the coaches ; but Marie Mancini braved the elements and remained his Majesty's inseparable companion as far as Lyons, which was reached on Monday, 28 November.

Next morning, the Queen received warning that Madame Royale—as the Duchess of Savoy was called in France—and her daughter would reach Lyons on the following Friday, 2 December. Their Majesties, the Cardinal, *Monsieur*, and *Mademoiselle* went forward to meet their guests. *Mademoiselle* rode in the royal coach, an honour which was also accorded to Maréchal de Villeroi, the governor of the Lyonnais. Grooms followed leading the gentlemen's horses.

"We found all the road filled with splendid equipages," writes *Mademoiselle*. "Madame Royale and M. de Savoie, her son,[1] had a great number of mules, with muleteers and magnificent housings, some of black velvet, others of crimson, with their arms embroidered on them in gold and silver. The mules of all persons of rank had their bells. We met the *litière du corps* of Madame Royale, preceded by twelve pages dressed in black bordered with black velvet, followed by her guards with an officer at their head. These wore black casaques braided with gold and silver. There was

---

[1] Charles Emmanuel II, Duke of Savoy. He married Jeanne Baptiste de Nemours, and died in 1675, leaving a son, Victor Amadeus, born 1666, who married Anne-Marie d'Orléans, daughter of *Monsieur* by his first marriage with Henrietta of England, and was father of Marie Adélaïde of Savoy, Duchesse de Bourgogne.

another litter belonging to Madame Royale, and several others. We met a number of coaches, each drawn by six horses, followed by footmen in livery, all being evidence of a great Court. When they heard that Madame Royale was near, they came to inform the King, who immediately mounted his horse and went to meet her. The Queen said: 'I confess I am impatient to know what the King will think of the Princess Margherita.' Yet she showed neither desire for nor dislike to the marriage, but observed: 'If I could have the Infanta, I should be overwhelmed with joy. Nevertheless, I cannot but be content with what pleases the King. At the same time, I think that he would prefer the Princess of England.'"[1]

Presently Louis came galloping back, threw himself from his horse, and approached the Queen's coach. "*Eh bien!* my son?" exclaimed Anne of Austria. The King replied, "She is much smaller than Madame la Maréchale de Villeroi; her shape is the most graceful conceivable. Her complexion——" He paused for a moment, and then added, "Olive-coloured; and it becomes her well. She has beautiful eyes; she pleases me, and I find her to my liking."

Immediately afterwards the Duchess of Savoy appeared; the coaches stopped, and the two princesses descended to greet one another. After an exchange of compliments, which appears to have revealed Madame Royale in the light of a confirmed flatterer, that lady and her two daughters entered the Queen's coach. The moment they were seated the King began to talk to the Princess Margherita "as if he had known her all his life," to the great astonishment of *Mademoiselle*,

[1] Henrietta-Anne, daughter of Charles I and Henrietta-Maria.

for the King was naturally cold towards strangers, and " very little inclined to be sociable."

When Lyons was reached, the King conducted the Duchess of Savoy to the apartments which had been prepared for her reception in the archbishop's palace, while the Queen retired to her cabinet, where she was immediately joined by the Cardinal, who said : " I have some news to tell your Majesty which she does not expect, and which will surprise her to the last degree." " Is it that the King, my brother, sends to me to offer the Infanta ? " eagerly inquired the Queen, " for that is what I least expect." " Yes, Madame, it is that," rejoined the triumphant Minister.

The Cardinal's stratagem had indeed been crowned with complete success, for almost at the same moment as the Duchess of Savoy and her daughters had entered Lyons by one gate, Pimentel, a special envoy from Philip IV, had entered by another, bearing an offer of peace and the Infanta.[1]

Marie Mancini had not formed part of the suite which had accompanied their Majesties to meet the visitors from Savoy, but had remained at Lyons. So soon, however, as the royal party returned, she hastened to inquire of *Mademoiselle* what sort of impression the young princess had made upon the King. To which that lady—not, we may be sure, without a spice of malice—replied : " It seemed to me that she pleased him greatly."

---

[1] Pimentel, travelling in the strictest incognito, since he was unprovided with a passport and ran the risk of being made prisoner, if his identity were discovered, had arrived at Mâcon on 19 November, from which town he wrote to the Cardinal to acquaint him with the important mission with which he was charged. Mazarin, however, kept his arrival a profound secret, and his dramatic appearance on the very day of the entry of the Princess Margherita had been carefully arranged by the Minister.

Marie said nothing ; but the same evening she had a long and very animated conversation with his Majesty. What passed on this occasion is a matter for conjecture, as etiquette obliged those present to remain at a distance. *Mademoiselle*, however, pretends that the young lady was heard to say, in a sarcastic tone, to her companion : " Are you not ashamed, Sire, at their wishing to give you so ugly a wife ? "

However that may be, by the following morning the King's attitude towards the Princess Margherita had completely changed. He called upon her at an early hour, in order, so it was said, that he might have a view of her figure *en déshabillé*, since it was rumoured that she was humpbacked, but was as cold as he had been assiduous in his attentions on the day of her arrival ; conduct, which greatly disconcerted the Duchess of Savoy, though the princess herself did not appear to notice anything. In the evening, at the Queen's, it was worse still. " The King never ceased talking to Mlle. de Mancini before the Princess Margherita, to whom he did not address a single word." From which it would appear that, whatever Marie may have taught her royal admirer, good manners had certainly not been included in the curriculum.[1]

The following day, the Princess Margherita's brother,

---

[1] It is very improbable that, as several writers have suggested, the sudden change in Louis XIV's attitude towards the Princess Margherita was due to some hint he had received from Mazarin rather than to the influence of the jealous Marie, since Montglat, a well-informed and trustworthy chronicler, tells us that the Cardinal was at first inclined to regard Pimentel's mission with considerable suspicion : " He feared that it was merely a ruse of the Spaniards to cause the Court of Savoy to leave Lyons discontented and offended, to the end that, on its return to Piedmont, it might enter into a treaty with them and abandon France, in order to avenge the insult which it had received, and that afterwards they would refuse to give the Infanta to the King."

the Duke of Savoy, a handsome and amiable young man, arrived at Lyons. He, like his sister, had come with matrimonial intentions, having some thought of offering his hand to *Mademoiselle*, and, in default of her, to one of the Cardinal's nieces. Notwithstanding her immense fortune, the Amazonian princess did not please him, and he speedily transferred his attentions to the beautiful Hortense Mancini, to whom it was an open secret the Cardinal intended to bequeath the bulk of his wealth. Mazarin would have been willing enough to conclude so brilliant an alliance for his favourite niece ; but the Duke was not content with handsome settlements and the prospect of great wealth. He demanded that Pignerol, which belonged at this period to France, should be ceded to him, a proposition which the Minister declined even to consider.

Some days passed without any discussion taking place between the two Courts in regard to the object which had brought them together, during which Louis XIV showed the same coldness to the Princess Margherita and the same *empressement* towards Marie Mancini. In the meanwhile, Pimentel remained at Lyons, strictly preserving his incognito and seeing no one, except Mazarin. The Duke of Savoy, although unaware of the arrival of the Spanish envoy, became convinced that the Cardinal was merely using his sister as a pawn in his political game, and his dissatisfaction being increased by the failure of his own matrimonial negotiations and a trivial dispute with *Monsieur* over a question of precedence,[1] took his departure in anger, exclaiming, if

[1] " He (the Duke of Savoy) behaved to the King with great respect ; but as, since the Regency, the Duke of Savoy, his father, had obtained the favour of his Ambassadors being received as those of crowned heads, this advantage, which he held only under the kindness of the King and the facility of the Minister, caused him to have the audacity to refuse to

we are to believe *Mademoiselle* : " Adieu, France, and for ever. I quit thee without regret."

The Duchess of Savoy, less clear-sighted than her son, and, besides, much more eager for the match, refused to abandon hope ; and the Cardinal, consummate diplomatist though he was, found the situation distinctly embarrassing, since he was unwilling to break off definitely all negotiations with Savoy until he had satisfied himself that no serious hitch was likely to arise in those which he had to conduct with Spain. Finally, however, the Duchess learned of the arrival of Pimentel, and, in a great state of agitation, sought out the Cardinal and peremptorily demanded a positive answer. Mazarin, perceiving it useless to dissemble further, then informed her of the proposals which had been received from Philip IV, adding that it was the imperative duty of his young master to take this the only means of giving peace to Europe and terminating a war which had already lasted for more than twenty years, and the prolongation of which could serve no useful purpose.

Madame Royale became " pale as death," and " considered whether she should swoon away," but, by a great effort, recovered her composure, and replied, with dignity, that she fully comprehended the exigencies of the political situation, and the advantages which France would derive from the marriage of Louis XIV with the Infanta, but that she demanded at least some guarantees for the Princess Margherita, in the event of anything arising to prevent the King from espousing Maria Theresa.

visit *Monsieur*, because he did not give him his right hand. The difference was in reality so great between them, that the late Duke, his father, never covered his head in Madame Royale's presence, and in all things, notwithstanding his position as husband, he showed her the greatest respect."—" Mémoires de Madame de Motteville."

But if the Duchess succeeded in restraining her feelings in the presence of the Cardinal, she gave full vent to her chagrin and indignation before *Mademoiselle*, who, calling upon her later in the day, found her "greatly changed," and saw that she had been weeping bitterly. Evening, however, came, and, with it, the Cardinal, bringing a paper signed by the King's own hand, "wherein he undertook to espouse the Princess of Savoy, if within a year from that date his marriage with the Infanta had not been concluded."[1] To this document Mazarin, "who was somewhat conscience-stricken," added a handsome present: a pair of fine diamond earrings, a number of other trinkets, and a quantity of perfumes and fans; at sight of which, the disconsolate Duchess straightway dried her tears and hurried off to show her earrings to the Queen. "She talked of nothing else, and every one admired the happy change from tears in the morning to gaiety in the evening." As for the Princess Margherita, the innocent victim of all these intrigues, no change was observable in her. "She always preserved an admirable tranquillity, and acted in the matter as if it had concerned another."[2]

The Duchess of Savoy and her daughters took their departure a few days later, their Majesties accompanying them a little way on their homeward journey. "Madame Royale wept; her eldest daughter a little. As for the Princess Margherita, she only shed a few tears, which appeared to be rather those of anger than of tenderness."[3]

On returning to Lyons, the Queen declared herself much relieved at having got rid of "all those people," and made sport of the Duchess for having wept, observ-

[1] "Mémoires de Montglat."
[2] "Mémoires de Mademoiselle de Montpensier." [3] *Ibid.*

ing that she was "the most consummate actress she had ever seen." She said nothing against the Princess Margherita, "for she admired her conduct and the firmness and strength of mind with which she had borne all that had happened." This poor princess, after losing the most splendid crown in the world, was reduced to marrying a petty Italian prince, the Duke of Parma. She died in 1663, the same year as her mother, the Duchess Christine.

A few days after the departure of the Princesses of Savoy, news arrived that the Queen of Spain had given birth to another son, and Philip IV wrote a very affectionate letter to his sister to announce this happy event, which confirmed her hopes for peace and the marriage of Louis with the Infanta.

The Court remained at Lyons until the end of the following January. Marie Mancini was ill for some days, during which the King visited her constantly. We may surmise that her illness was not wholly unconnected with the events which were passing around her. She had abandoned herself unreservedly to her passion for the King, to the intoxication of a reciprocated attachment, doubly sweet to one whose life up to that time had been so sad and lonely, without troubling herself to reflect what must be the ultimate issue of a sentiment of this nature between two persons of such very different stations. She had, in fact, thought only of the present and closed her eyes to the future. The arrival of the Princess Margherita, and the favourable impression which she was reported to have made upon the King, had abruptly opened them, and aroused her to a full comprehension of the danger which threatened her. Her passionate and violent nature awoke, and, with it, the pride and ambition which were the dominant traits in her character. The thought of being supplanted, even nominally, in the heart of the man she loved by another woman was intolerable to her ; the thought of being deposed from the place which she had come to look upon as rightfully hers was even more bitter. Overestimating the extent of her influence over Louis, she flattered herself that, even if circumstances had not come to her aid, she would still have experienced little difficulty in weaning the King from any desire he might have had to wed the Princess Margherita ; and, though she could not disguise from herself that in the Infanta, or rather in the great interests which the Infanta represented, she had a far more formidable foe to contend with, she was in no way dismayed. Nor did she intend to rest content with a defensive attitude ; she herself was resolved to enter the lists as a candidate for this dazzling prize. Too proud and too shrewd to become the mistress of the King, she foresaw that the young sovereign's passion could ere long be goaded to the point of marriage ; and, that resolution once taken, she firmly believed that neither the opposition of the Queen and the Cardinal, nor the duty he owed his realm, would be able to turn him from his purpose.

On her recovery from her illness, Marie, "charmed with the King's fidelity and the power she had over him, resumed her usual post, which was always near him, talking with him and following him wherever it was possible, and the satisfaction she felt in believing herself beloved made her love still more him whom she already loved too much." [1]

---

[1] "Mémoires de Madame de Motteville." Madame de Motteville had not accompanied the Court to Lyons, but she was kept well informed of all that was passing there by her friends' letters.

Louis XIV certainly gave the young lady ample excuse for her conduct. He scarcely quitted her side. Every morning, he called upon her ; every evening, he invited her to share his collation ; then accompanied her to the Queen's, and when her Majesty had retired for the night, escorted her home. "At first he followed her coach, next he acted as coachman, and finally he took a seat inside." He was lodged, as were Marie and her sisters, in the Place Bellecour ; and on moonlight nights the two young people often promenaded in the Place until a very late hour. If his Majesty went to the play, he invariably took Marie with him and installed her by his side at one end of the tribune reserved for him ; the other being usually occupied by *Monsieur* and *Mademoiselle*.

All these attentions naturally made a great stir ; nothing else was talked of, either by the Court or the public, but the King's passion for the Cardinal's niece. His Eminence, though frequently confined to his house by the gout, was, of course, perfectly well aware of all that was happening. Still, he made no attempt to interfere. So far the King's attachment had served a useful purpose in preserving Louis from the wiles of ambitious beauties, who might have endeavoured to undermine his own influence, and, in particular, in detaching him from all thought of marriage with the Princess of Savoy ; and as yet he could not bring himself to believe that his young master could be so regardless of his own dignity, and so indifferent to the interests of his kingdom, as to desire to carry the affair to its legitimate conclusion.

That he might be tempted to carry it to its illegitimate one was in the Cardinal's opinion far more probable ; the moonlight promenades in the Place

H

Bellecour had occasioned him no little uneasiness; and he accordingly enjoined upon Madame de Venel, the *gouvernante* of Marie and her sisters, to keep the strictest watch over her charges. The young ladies slept upon the ground-floor, and the windows of their chamber, which opened on to the Place, were so low as to afford an easy means of access to any one who desired to enter. The *gouvernante* promised implicit obedience, and kept her word, the result being an amusing incident.

"Madame de Venel," writes Hortense, "was so accustomed to her profession of guardian (or rather of spy), even at night, that she rose in her sleep to see what we were doing. One night, as my sister Marie lay asleep, with her mouth open, Madame de Venel, coming, all asleep as she was, to grope in the dark, happened to thrust her finger into her mouth so far, that my sister, starting out of her sleep, made her teeth meet in the lady's finger. Picture to yourselves the amazement that they were both in, when they were thoroughly awake, to find themselves in this position. My sister was extremely angry at this inquisition. Next day, the story was related to the King, and all the Court laughed over it." [1]

The Court left Lyons at the end of January 1659. The weather was bitterly cold, notwithstanding which Louis XIV announced his intention of making the greater part of the journey on horseback. *Mademoiselle* and most of the elder ladies preferred the warmth and shelter of their coaches, but several of the younger readily agreed to accompany his Majesty and his suite, this mode of travel providing excellent opportunities for flirtation. Among these, it is hardly necessary to observe, was Marie Mancini, who, attired in a velvet

[1] "Mémoires de la Duchesse de Mazarin."

justaucorps trimmed with fur and a black velvet cap decorated with a plume, presented, we are assured, a particularly charming appearance, and had the honour of her sovereign's escort nearly the whole of the way, the rest of the equestrians being careful to keep at a respectful distance, so as not to embarrass the lovers. As the Cardinal and the jealous Comtesse de Soissons were making the return journey, as far as Nevers, by water, and Madame de Venel remained in her coach with Hortense, who was very susceptible to cold, there was no one to interfere with her enjoyment of the King's society, and she was in the highest spirits, while Louis shared her good humour. "The King," writes *Mademoiselle*, "was in a much better humour since he had fallen in love with Mlle. de Mancini; he was gay, and talked to every one."

CHAPTER VI

Marie Mancini's confidences—Alarm of Anne of Austria and Mazarin
at the King's passion for Marie—Louis XIV plays a practical joke
on Madame de Venel—Visit of Don Juan of Austria to Paris—His
jester and Marie Mancini—The "debauch of Roissy"—Philippe
Mancini disgraced and imprisoned by the Cardinal—Pimentel in Paris
—Astonishment of the Spanish envoy at the King's attentions to
Marie—Increasing alarm of the Cardinal and the Queen—Louis XIV
demands the Cardinal's permission to marry his niece—Question of
Mazarin's conduct in this matter considered—Painful scene between
the King and Anne of Austria—The Cardinal determines to exile
Marie—Despair of the King and firmness of Mazarin—Interview
between Louis XIV and Marie—The pearls of Henrietta Maria—
The King's grief—Departure of Marie and her sisters for La
Rochelle.

THE Court was very gay that winter. "On our
return to Paris," writes Marie Mancini, "our
only care was to amuse ourselves; there was not a
day, or, to speak more correctly, not a minute, which
was not devoted to pleasure; and I may say that never
had time been spent as we spent it. His Majesty,
wishing to ensure the continuance of our amusements,
commanded all who formed our circle to amuse us in
turn. There was nothing but a succession of entertainments and balls; and although these frequently took
place in country spots, there was, nevertheless, nothing
more magnificent; to be convinced of which, it will be
enough to know that these entertainments were given
by persons of the first quality, and that love, which is
full of resource and inspires everything into which it

enters, arranged them with care. For, in a word, there was not a cavalier who did not take part in them. The Grand Master[1] put forth every effort to please my sister Hortense, the Marquis de Richelieu took the same care for Mlle. de la Motte-Argencourt,[2] the Marquis d'Alluye for Mlle. du Fouilloux, whom he subsequently married, in whom his Majesty and myself had the utmost confidence, and several others who had similar engagements, and of whom space forbids me to speak here. The gallant adventures which accompanied our entertainments and our promenades would demand a whole volume ; so I shall pass over them in silence, and content myself with recounting one, which will show with what delicacy the King loved, and that he lost no opportunity of giving me proof of it. It was, if my memory does not deceive me, at Bois-le-Vicomte, as I was walking very quickly under a row of trees, his Majesty wished to give me his hand, and mine, happening to strike, although rather lightly, against the pommel of his sword, he drew it sharply from its scabbard and threw it far away. I know not how to describe the manner in which he performed this action; there are no words to express it."

Since his return from Lyons, indeed, the King's passion for Marie had increased in a positively alarming manner, and they were scarcely ever apart. "The King never came into the Queen's presence without Mlle. Mancini," says Madame de Motteville. "She followed him everywhere and whispered in his ear, in the presence of even the Queen herself, undeterred by the respect

[1] The Grand Master of the Artillery, Armand de la Porte, Marquis de la Meilleraye, afterwards Duc de Mazarin.

[2] Apparently, she means Mlle. de la Motte-Houdancourt. Mlle. de la Motte-Argencourt had been sent to a convent (see p. 65 *supra.*)

and decorum which she owed her. . . . The King's attachment to the Cardinal's niece gave the Queen pain. She
feared a result that would be unworthy of the King ;
and she desired that the Infanta, bringing him a pure
heart that was wholly his, might not find his heart
already occupied by an affection in every way unworthy
of him, through the boldness which she knew existed in
the girl's disposition. At this moment, these intentions
seemed to be in keeping with what he owed himself ;
but a passion, however feeble, when fed and sustained
by another stronger and more violent, might change
them ; and this was what the Queen feared.

Mazarin, too, who, as we have seen, had not opposed
the King's inclination so long as he believed it might
serve his own ends, was becoming seriously alarmed ;
for, even supposing that Louis had no serious intentions, such conduct was in the highest degree indiscreet
on the part of a sovereign who proposed to contract an
alliance with the proudest house in Europe, and might,
if rumours of it were to reach Madrid, prove a formidable hindrance to the progress of the negotiations with
Spain. Both he and the Queen, accordingly, resolved
to put an end to the affair as speedily as possible, and,
in the meanwhile, took Madame de Venel into their confidence, and bade her keep the strictest watch over the
movements of Mlle. Marie.

Madame de Venel promised obedience, and set about
her congenial task with such good-will as to draw upon
her the dislike of the King. "One day, when the King
was distributing sweetmeats to the ladies of the Court,
in boxes gallantly ornamented with different coloured
ribbons, Madame de Venel received hers and opened it.
But what was her terror to see emerge a dozen mice, a
kind of animal of which, it was known, she entertained

the greatest horror! Her first impulse urged her to precipitately quit the company; but, immediately calling to mind the promise which she had given the Queen never to let Mlle. de Mancini out of her sight, she retraced her steps and re-entered the apartment. The King, who had just seated himself on a sofa with Mlle. de Mancini, and was already felicitating himself on the success of his enterprise, astonished at seeing Madame de Venel return so soon, said to her : 'What! Have you recovered from your alarm already, Madame?' 'No, Sire,' replied she, 'it is because I have not recovered from my alarm that, in order to regain my courage, I thought it necessary to keep close to the son of Mars.' And, with that, she seated herself on the sofa between them."[1]

In the meantime, the negotiations with Spain were progressing steadily. Pimentel had arrived in Paris soon after the return of the Court from Lyons, and numerous interviews had taken place between him and Mazarin, in which the principal bases of the treaty had already been agreed upon. The advent of Pimentel had greatly perturbed Marie Mancini, who was still more alarmed when, in March 1659, Spain made a further step in advance, and Don Juan of Austria, natural son of Philip IV and the actress Calderona, came to visit the Queen on his way from Flanders to Madrid. Don Juan came incognito, notwithstanding which the Queen addressed him as " My nephew," and he was lodged at the Louvre. He gave himself very haughty airs, even in the presence of the King, and scarcely deigned to notice *Monsieur* and *Mademoiselle*, to their intense mortification.

[1] Manuscript "Mémoire sur Madame de Venel," published by Lucien Perey, " Le Roman du Grand Roi."

According to the custom of the time, the Prince had with him a jester, a girl called Capitor, the fame of whose wit had preceded her. She arrived in Paris shortly after her master, dressed as a man, with closely-cropped hair, a hat, and a sword. "She was ugly and cross-eyed," says *Mademoiselle*, "but had an infinitude of wit, and was a very pretty fool. The King took so great a fancy to her that she never quitted the Louvre. The Queen and *Monsieur* were greatly diverted by her, and I myself also."

But, alas! Señorita Capitor was continually talking of and praising the Infanta, a habit which did not at all tend to commend her to Marie Mancini, who conceived the greatest dislike to her, spoke of her as "the fool," and jeered at her. Capitor retaliated and let fall some biting jests at the young lady's expense, which duly reached the latter's ears, and so enraged her that she complained to the King, who gave orders that the girl should be sent away. The Queen, *Monsieur*, and *Mademoiselle*, and nearly all the ladies of the Court, made her presents, and many begged her to mention them to the Infanta. The King derided these last, and "the Queen perceived that Mlle. de Mancini allowed no opportunity to slip of ruining in the mind of Louis XIV all those who, whether near or far, belonged to the Infanta." [1]

Shortly after the departure of Don Juan, an incident occurred which, for a moment, diverted attention from Marie Mancini to her brother Philippe, and "obliged the Court to praise the Cardinal not only in his presence, but in all places."

A party of gay young noblemen, amongst whom was Philippe Mancini, the Marquis de Manicamp, the

[1] "Mémoires de Mlle. de Montpensier."

Comte de Guiche, and Bussy-Rabutin, were invited by
the Comte de Vivonne, First Gentleman of the Chamber,
to spend Holy Week with him at his country-house at
Roissy; and, by a singular coincidence, the King's
Almoner, the Abbé Le Camus, was also one of the
guests. People were not slow in recounting the most
unheard-of things in regard to the doings of this
pleasure-party, so out of place during the Holy Days.
"They were accused of having chosen the time with
sacrilegious intent, the least of which was the eating of
meat on Good Friday; they were even accused of
having committed certain impieties, unworthy not
only of Christians, but of men of sense."[1] It was said
that they had eaten a sucking-pig, after causing it to be
baptized by the Abbé Le Camus; nor was it long
before the sucking-pig became a man, whom they had
killed and partially devoured. As a matter of fact, they
had done nothing worse than play some harmless practical joke on a notary who happened to be passing that
way, and who was so little offended that he subsequently joined them at supper. Their real offence,
however, lay in having composed a song in which
various prominent members of the Court were somewhat roughly handled. Very imprudently, a copy of
this song was circulated, and eventually found its way
into the hands of the Queen, and from hers to the
Cardinal's, who, "to show that he did not intend to
protect the crime, determined to punish all the accomplices in the person of his nephew, whom he dismissed
from the Court and his presence," and imprisoned in
the citadel of Brissac.

This action on the part of the Cardinal was the more
unjust since, according to Bussy-Rabutin, who, as we

[1] "Mémoires de Madame de Motteville."

have mentioned, was one of the party, the luckless Mancini, seeing the turn events were taking at Roissy, had quitted the company soon after his arrival and shut himself up in his room, and on the morning of Good Friday had returned to Paris. But Mazarin, who heartily disliked his nephew, was delighted at the opportunity of proving that he did not favour his family. Moreover, the intimacy existing between the young man and the King did not at all commend itself to his Eminence, who suspected that, if occasion arose, Philippe might be employed as an intermediary between Louis XIV and Marie ; and the pretext for getting rid of him seemed too good to be lost.

The negotiations with Spain continued to advance. Pimentel was again in Paris, occupying a suite of apartments at the Palais-Mazarin, and he and the Cardinal were constantly closeted together.[1] It was an open secret that everything hinged upon the marriage between Louis XIV and the Infanta, for the concessions demanded by France were such as, in ordinary circumstances, Philip IV would most certainly refuse, but might accord without loss of dignity to his son-in-law.

For some time, Pimentel kept within the walls of the Palais-Mazarin, and did not show himself in public, a precaution which is somewhat difficult to account for, in view of the fact that all Paris was aware of his visit and its object. At length, however, the preliminary negotiations having been concluded, he accepted an invitation to attend a magnificent fête given by the Minister Lionne at his château at Berny. The King and Queen, the Cardinal, Marie Mancini, and nearly the

---

[1] As the Palais-Mazarin was not yet finished, the Cardinal still occupied his apartments at the Louvre.

whole of the Court were present, and the entertainment was worthy of the illustrious guests. There was a concert, a play, and a splendid supper, followed by a display of fireworks on the canal, and the festivities terminated with a ball. His Majesty complimented his host warmly on the entertainment he had provided, declared that he had never visited a country-house which he had admired more, nor enjoyed himself so much in a single day. The latter statement was probably true enough, seeing that, undeterred by the presence of Pimentel, he did not quit Mlle. Mancini's side for a moment, to the intense astonishment of the Spanish envoy, who, although he had heard rumours of the King's infatuation, had not yet had an opportunity of seeing the lovers together. So scandalized was he at such conduct on the part of a monarch who aspired to the hand of his master's daughter, that on the morrow he could not refrain from unbosoming himself to Mazarin.

The Cardinal was now thoroughly alarmed. The remonstrances which he had addressed to his niece, and the hints he had from time to time thrown out in the presence of his young sovereign, had fallen on barren ground ; and it appeared to him that the King had deliberately chosen the fête at Berny to flaunt his passion in the face of the whole world.

The Queen, on her side, was no less disquieted ; she could no longer conceal from herself the extraordinary influence which this young girl exercised over her impressionable son. Very submissive hitherto to his mother's wishes, Louis seemed now to trouble himself very little about them, and, in certain circumstances, did not fear even to brave them openly. A recent incident had shown her this but too plainly.

During the Carnival, a very gorgeous ballet had been performed at the Court, in which Marie Mancini had particularly distinguished herself, and, as the reigning favourite, had of course been rewarded with loud applause. To please her, the King announced that the ballet would be danced again during Lent. This decision was extremely repugnant to the Queen, who remonstrated with her son in the strongest terms, finally declaring that, if he kept to his intention, she would not only refuse to be present, but would go to spend Lent at Val-de-Grâce. "*Eh bien!* You can go," retorted the King brusquely. Then Marie, delighted to find that she had only to express a wish for it to be obeyed, herself begged the King to do as her Majesty desired, a request with which Louis at once complied.

It had been decided that the final negotiations with Spain should take place at Saint-Jean-de-Luz, where Mazarin and Don Louis de Haro, the Spanish Prime Minister, were to confer together and draw up the terms of the definitive treaty; and the Cardinal pointed out that it was imperative that the King and Queen should follow him to Bayonne, in order to be at hand in the event of any serious difficulty arising. Anne of Austria, therefore, implored her son to give her his solemn assurance that he would raise no opposition to the projected marriage with the Infanta; to which Louis replied, coldly and evasively, that he had no intention of opposing it, but that there was time enough to consider it, as the conditions of the treaty had not yet been decided on by either side.

The King did not fail to render an account of what had passed between his mother and himself to Marie, vowing that nothing should induce him to consent to the match, and that he would wed no one but her;

while the girl, on her side, left no means untried to confirm him in this resolution, and to prejudice his mind against the Cardinal and the Queen. "The opposition of the Cardinal," says Madame de la Fayette, whose recital is confirmed by all contemporary "Mémoires" and by numerous unpublished documents, "only served to embitter her against him and to cause her to render him all kinds of ill turns. She did not do the Queen any less injury in the mind of the King, both by condemning her conduct during the Regency, and by informing him of all that malice had invented against her. Finally, she succeeded in making herself so absolutely mistress of his mind, that, during the time that the preliminary negotiations in regard to the peace and the marriage were in progress, he demanded of the Cardinal permission to espouse her." [1]

Some historians maintain that Mazarin was for a moment allured by the prospect of seeing his niece Queen of France, and that, had it not been for the strenuous opposition of Anne of Austria, he would have allowed Louis XIV to have his way. This contention appears to rest principally on a supposed conversation between the Cardinal and the Queen, which is related by Madame de Motteville in her "Mémoires." "The aversion which the Queen entertained for Mlle. de Mancini," she says, "was greatly increased by a speech which her uncle made to her. He was the slave of ambition and capable of ingratitude, and had an innate desire to prefer his own interests to those of every one else. His niece, intoxicated by her passion and persuaded of the power of her own charms, had the presumption to imagine that the King loved her enough to do all things for her; and accordingly

[1] "Histoire de Madame Henriette d'Angleterre."

she let her uncle know that on the terms on which she stood with the King, it was not impossible that she might become Queen, provided he would contribute his influence to further her ambition. The Cardinal could not refuse himself so fine an adventure, and he one day spoke of it to the Queen, laughing at the folly of his niece, but in a manner so ambiguous and embarrassed that he allowed her to see clearly enough what he had in his mind to cause her to reply in these words: 'I do not believe, Monsieur le Cardinal, that the King could be capable of such baseness; but, if it were possible that he should think of it, I warn you that all France will revolt against you and him, and that I will put myself at the head of the rebels and induce my second son [Philippe, Duc d'Anjou] to join them.'"

M. Chantelauze pronounces without hesitation for the authenticity of this conversation. He pretends that Madame de Motteville's evidence is "above suspicion," that it is "irrefutable," because "no one had more knowledge of the private affairs of the Queen."[1] On the other hand, the best-informed biographers of both Mazarin and Marie Mancini, such as M. Chéruel, M. Amédée Renée, M. Charles Livet, Lucien Perey, and Mr. J. B. Perkins, are unanimous in discrediting it. They point out that, in the first place, the writer, who was a bitter enemy of Mazarin, does not venture to assert that she had her information from the Queen's own lips. In the second, that the Cardinal was at this time, as Madame de Motteville herself admits, a few pages further on in her "Mémoires," absolute master of the Queen's mind,[2] and it is, therefore, in the highest

[1] "Louis XIV et Marie Mancini."
[2] "The Cardinal exercised so absolute an empire over the Queen's mind that she did not dare to do anything without his advice, and that he did not allow her to dispose of a simple benefice."

From an engraving after the painting by Sir Peter Lely

MARIE MANCINI

degree improbable that she would have addressed him
in such terms. And, finally, that the surer record of
Mazarin's letters, and his conduct throughout the affair,
show that he had always resolutely opposed a step which
would not only have been fraught with disaster to
France, but would have been fatal to his own interests.
" Mazarin," says Mr. Perkins, " had nothing to gain by
it and much to lose. He would become the uncle of a
queen, instead of the successor of Richelieu. To have
his niece the Queen of France might, under some circumstances, have gratified his vanity, but the negotiations for the Spanish alliance had been practically
arranged when the passion of Louis XIV reached its
height. The Cardinal would have sacrificed the treaty
which he believed would help to ensure him permanent
fame ; he would have incurred the enmity of the nation
for the continuance of the war ; the enmity of the
Queen for interfering with her favourite scheme, and
the enmity of Louis so soon as his passion had abated,
and he realised that the greatest prince in the world had
made a misalliance. Had Marie been able to control
the King's policy, it would not have advanced the
interests of Mazarin. He already possessed to the
fullest extent the affection and confidence of Louis XIV,
and he had little hold on his niece, who was impatient,
ungovernable, and wasted very little love on her
uncle." [1]

The Queen, learning from the Cardinal of the unheard of step which her son had just taken, summoned him to her cabinet, when she employed every
argument she could think of to divert him from his
purpose, appealing in turn to his sense of duty, his

[1] " France under Richelieu and Mazarin."

honour, and his delicacy. All was in vain. "The young King was no longer his own master; he belonged to those black eyes which looked into his own from his *lever* to his *coucher*, at table, in the drive, at play, and in the dance, in every nook and corner of the Louvre; to those burning eyes which accompanied the murmurs and cries of a tragic and passionate voice."[1] His reply to his mother's entreaties was to fly into a violent passion, and vow that no one save Mlle. Mancini should share his throne. He left the Queen plunged in the depths of despair, already perhaps seeing in imagination her idolised son the byword of Europe, the Cardinal's schemes ruined, France and Spain once more at one another's throats, and she herself, like her mother-in-law Marie de' Medici, condemned to wander in exile and die miserably in a foreign land.

Meanwhile, Mazarin had had an interview with his niece, with equally fruitless results. The girl obstinately declined to renounce her love and her ambition, nor could he obtain from her the smallest concession. As he was on the point of starting for the Pyrenees to meet the Spanish plenipotentiaries, and recognised the imprudence of leaving Marie behind him to labour for an end totally opposed to his own, he at once resolved to remove her out of the reach of the infatuated King, and accordingly informed the young lady that it was his intention to send her and her sisters, Hortense and Marianne, in charge of Madame de Venel, to La Rochelle.

Marie does not appear to have been greatly distressed at this announcement, since she could not bring herself to believe that the King would permit the Cardinal to carry out his resolve; while, when Mazarin requested

[1] Arvède Barine, "Princesses et grandes dames: Marie Mancini."

the Queen to break the news to her son, Anne declined
and implored him not to separate the lovers, as she
feared that, in his first indignation at learning of the
forthcoming exile of his mistress, Louis might create
some scandal which would put an end to the negotiations for his marriage with the Infanta.

Mazarin, however, was adamant, and, as the Queen
refused to act as his ambassador, he ordered his niece to
acquaint Louis XIV with his decision. The announcement threw the young monarch into the last excess of
grief and indignation. He vowed that no power on
earth should separate him from his beloved; he
threatened to publicly disgrace the Cardinal, and for
three whole days he did not address so much as a word
to his mother. Finding the Minister inflexible, he
suddenly changed his tone, threw himself at the feet of
the Queen and the Cardinal, and besought them on his
knees to grant the dearest wish of his heart. "I will
marry Mlle. de Mancini," said he; "I will break with
the Infanta; I will do anything rather than see her
suffer for love of me."

The Cardinal replied, that "having been chosen by
the late King, his father, and since by the Queen, to
assist them with his counsels, and having hitherto
served them with inviolable fidelity, he was resolved not
to abuse the confidence reposed in him by suffering him
to commit an act so contrary to his reputation; that he
was master of his niece, and would stab her to the heart
rather than elevate her by so great an act of treason."[1]

Such was the King's grief, that Anne of Austria, in
spite of the horror with which such a misalliance inspired
her, could not refrain from begging the Cardinal not to
insist on the exile of his niece. But Mazarin, remem-

[1] "Mémoires de Madame de Motteville."

I

bering the vast interests at stake, was not to be diverted
from his purpose, and all that Louis could obtain from
him was a formal promise to grant him an interview
with Marie during the forthcoming journey of the
Court to Bayonne.

On leaving the Queen and the Cardinal, Louis
hastened to Marie Mancini's apartments, which were
situated above his own, to acquaint her with the result
of the interview. He did not conceal from her that he
despaired of shaking her uncle's resolution, but sought
to comfort her by the assurance that nothing should
induce him to wed the Infanta or to abandon the hope
of overcoming the opposition of his mother and
Mazarin.

Marie was but partially consoled by these promises.
"Why," she asked, "if your Majesty is so determined,
does he permit this order of exile to be executed?
Does he not see that, if I am once sent away, the
Cardinal can easily send me further, perhaps even to
Italy, according to his good pleasure, and separate us
for ever?"

The King endeavoured to reassure her, pointing out
that the promise which Mazarin had given him that
they should meet during the journey of the Court to
the South was a proof that he had no such intention.
To these assurances he added the most tender protestations, nor did he leave her until he had succeeded, as
he imagined, in somewhat allaying her fears.

Left to herself, the unhappy Marie gave full vent to
the despair which she had with difficulty restrained
during the visit of the King; the blind confidence
which she had hitherto reposed in him was beginning
to waver. "This would be," she writes, "the place
to speak of the intentions which his Majesty is said to

have had in my favour, did not modesty forbid me, and, for the same reason, I shall not enlarge upon the obvious displeasure which the prince felt at witnessing my departure. But I cannot keep silence in regard to the grief which this separation occasioned me ; nothing in my life affected me so sensibly ; all that one is able to suffer appeared to me as nothing in comparison with this absence ; there was not a moment when I did not desire death as the only remedy for my woes. Briefly, I was in a condition which neither what I have just said nor the strongest expressions could possibly explain."

During the few days' grace which Mazarin had allowed his niece, the King did not quit her side, seeking by every means in his power to prove to her that she alone occupied his thoughts ; and, undeterred by the remonstrances of the Queen and the Cardinal, lost no opportunity of proclaiming the passion and grief which the coming separation occasioned him. A chance of testifying to the lady and the whole Court that he was very far from abandoning the hope of seeing her one day Queen of France happened to present itself at this moment, and the infatuated youth hastened to take advantage of it.

Henrietta Maria, the widowed Queen of Charles I, then residing at Saint-Germain, desired to sell a magnificent string of pearls, in order to add to her meagre budget (the unfortunate princess subsisted entirely on Louis XIV's bounty, and had been compelled to part little by little with nearly all her jewels). Marie Mancini had greatly admired these pearls on the rare occasions on which the Queen had worn them at Court, and no sooner did Louis learn that they were for sale, than he gave orders for them to be purchased, to present to his inamorata. Marie tells us that she at first refused to accept them, sorrowfully pointing out that henceforth she would have no opportunity of wearing them. "But his Majesty insisted in a manner so pressing, and accompanied his request with words so full of promise," that eventually she allowed herself to be persuaded.

For the money required for the purchase of these pearls—78,000 livres—Louis, who never possessed a sol of his own, had to apply to Mazarin, who, we may presume, gave orders for its payment with a very bad grace, though somewhat consoled by the reflection that the jewels would remain in his family. He was still less pleased when his Majesty demanded a further sum of one thousand pistoles, without informing him of the object for which it was required. The Cardinal suspected, and with good reason, that the money was intended for the payment of certain secret agents, in the event of his placing any obstacles in the way of the King corresponding with his niece. However, he was unable to refuse the money.

Three days before the departure of Marie and her sisters for La Rochelle, Mazarin left for Vincennes, perhaps to be out of the way when the final leave-takings should take place ; and the King took advantage of his absence to seek an interview with his mother, who, he flattered himself, might prove more amenable to reason, with the Cardinal no longer at hand to support her. In this, however, he was mistaken.

"The evening preceding the day of Mlle. de Mancini's departure," says Madame de Motteville, "the King came to the Queen in a state of profound depression. She drew him aside and spoke to him for a long time ; but, as the sensibility of the heart which loves demands solitude, the Queen herself took a light which stood on her table, and, passing from her chamber into her bath-room, requested the King to follow her. After they had been about an hour together, the King came out with swollen eyes, and the Queen followed him, so touched by the state in which she was obliged to place him, that it was easy to see that the King's suffering cost her much. At that moment, she did me the honour to say to me, in a low tone : 'I pity the King ; he is both loving and reasonable ; but I have just told him that I am certain that he will one day thank me for the pain I have caused him ; and, from what I see in him, I do not doubt it.'"

During this interview, Louis had used every persuasion to gain his mother over to his side, but without success. He had, however, obtained a renewal of the promise to permit him to see Marie again during the journey to the South ; while, before leaving for Vincennes, the Cardinal, perceiving the state of exasperation into which the coming separation from his mistress had thrown his young sovereign, and judging it to be the wisest course to humour him so far as possible, had consented to a regular correspondence being established between the lovers.

From the Queen's apartments, Louis passed to those of Marie, to mingle his tears with hers, and to renew the vows which he had already made so many times. Hortense Mancini was the only witness of this interview, which lasted until a late hour, when the King returned to his own apartments, "mournful, silent, and without speaking to any one."

The following morning, 22 June 1659, he again repaired to Marie's apartments, and did not leave her till the hour fixed for her departure, when he conducted her to her coach, "allowing his grief to be perceived by every one." It was then that Marie Mancini addressed to her royal lover those well-known words so full of tenderness and of reproach : "*Sire, vous êtes roi, vous pleurez, et je pars !*"

The King leant towards her and murmured some words in her ear which were inaudible to those standing by. Whatever they were, they do not appear to have afforded the poor girl much consolation, for she threw herself back in the coach, and, sobbing bitterly, murmured to Hortense : "Ah! I am abandoned!"

The coach drove away, and Louis XIV, having taken a hurried leave of his mother, entered his own and set off for Chantilly, where he remained for some days, "in order to recover his equanimity."

CHAPTER VII

Departure of Mazarin for the Pyrenees—Illness of Marie Mancini—
Angry scene between Louis XIV and Anne of Austria—The King
writes every day to Marie—Uneasiness of the Cardinal—His letter
to the King from Poitiers—Arrival of Marie and her sisters at La
Rochelle—Marie promises to submit to her uncle's orders—But has
no such intention—Letter of Mazarin to Louis XIV from Montlieu
—Violent scene between the King and the Queen-Mother—Letter of
the Cardinal to Louis XIV from Libourne—Anxiety of Mazarin—
His outspoken letter to the King from Cadillac—Evasive reply of his
Majesty—Eloquent letter of Mazarin from Saint-Jean-de-Luz—His
anxiety to prevent a meeting between the King and Marie during the
journey of the Court to the South—His letter to the Queen—Madame
de Venel ordered by Anne of Austria to bring the Cardinal's nieces to
Saint-Jean-d'Angely.

ON 26 July, the King and Queen visited Mazarin at
Vincennes, for a final conference before his departure for the Pyrenees, at the conclusion of which the
Cardinal started for Notre-Dame-de-Cléry, where he
intended to rejoin his nieces and accompany them part
of the way to La Rochelle.

On his arrival, he found Marie in a high fever, the
result of the violent emotion which she had lately
undergone, and, for some days, the poor girl's condition
was such as to cause her relatives no little uneasiness.
The King, who had returned to his solitude at Chantilly,
was in ignorance of the illness of his mistress, and was,
in consequence, greatly surprised at receiving no reply
to the long and tender letters which he daily despatched
to her. At length, however, the Comte de Vivonne,

who, it had been arranged, was to act as intermediary in
the event of Marie not being able to address herself
directly to the King, received warning of the young
lady's plight from one of her waiting-women, and communicated the news to his Majesty. Louis at once
started for Fontainebleau, where the Court then was,
and despatched one of his Musketeers to Notre-Dame-
de-Cléry, charged with a letter for Mazarin, commanding
him to treat his niece with every possible consideration
and kindness, and to inform him immediately of her
state of health, and a second for Marie, the contents of
which we can well imagine. All the Court knew of the
departure of the Musketeer, and the Queen, whom his
Majesty had greeted on his arrival with icy coldness,
ventured to inquire of her son what news he had of
Mlle. Mancini. Upon which the King " flew into a
violent passion, crying out in a voice so loud that he
could be heard by those in the adjoining apartment, that
it was useless to ask news about those whom one
intended to kill."

To his Majesty's letter, the Cardinal replied that his
niece " had had a little fever, through want of sleep,
but that she was now in good health and covered with
confusion at the honour which you have done her."
" I love her as I should," he continues, " and I shall
give her proof of it as I ought, in response to the
affection which she shows for me, and her resignation
to what I desire of her, which will always be very greatly
to her advantage." To the Queen, Mazarin wrote with
a good deal more candour : " Marie is more afflicted than
I can express, but she shows herself entirely resigned to
my wishes, and that she will never have any others."

Other messengers, bearing letters from the lovelorn
prince—" all very long and very tender," the lady tells

us—continued to follow the Cardinal and his nieces on their journey southwards. At Chambord, a Musketeer overtook them with *five* letters for Marie, and another for Mazarin. An hour later, came yet another epistle, accompanied by a " speaking portrait " of his Majesty for Mlle. Mancini, who was at no pains to conceal from her uncle the joy which the gift occasioned her. In short, the letters rained upon them day and night in a perfect deluge, to the intense annoyance of the Cardinal, who, in authorizing a correspondence between the King and his niece, had not bargained for anything of this nature, and began to fear that, in separating the lovers, he had only added fuel to the flame.

Not only did the Cardinal find the letters too numerous, but the method chosen by the King of communicating with his beloved, by means of special couriers, was very far from commending itself to him. In the first place, he was advised that it had become the universal topic of conversation at the Court, which meant that it must sooner or later reach Madrid. In the second, the system deprived him of all chance of surveillance, and prevented him from obtaining, through the good offices of his faithful ally, Madame de Venel, any knowledge of the contents of the bulky epistles he saw arriving. He, accordingly, begged his Majesty to abstain from direct communication with his niece, and to send his letters by the ordinary Court couriers, under cover to Colbert, to be forwarded by him to his relative Colbert de Terron, Governor of La Rochelle, who, like the future Comptroller-General, was believed to be devoted to his Eminence's interests.

On reaching Poitiers, Mazarin parted from his nieces, the latter continuing their journey to La Rochelle, while the Cardinal took the road to Bayonne. Before quitting Poitiers, however, Mazarin wrote to the King as follows :—

Mazarin to Louis XIV

". . . The confidante [the Queen] has written to inform me of the state in which she found you, and I am in despair, for it is absolutely necessary that you remedy it, if you do not wish to be unhappy, and to make all your faithful servants die of grief. The means which you employ are by no means calculated to cure you, and, unless you resolve in earnest to alter your conduct, your malady will grow worse and worse. I conjure you by your glory, by your honour, by your duty towards God, by the welfare of your kingdom, and by everything which is able to affect you, to labour strenuously to master yourself, and not to make the journey to Bayonne unwillingly; for, briefly, you will be guilty before God and before men if you go not thither with the purpose with which you ought to go, by reason, by honour, and by interest. I trust that the person you wot of (Marie Mancini) will contribute materially to that end, since I have spoken to her in the terms which were necessary to dispose her so to do."[1]

This urgent letter did not produce the smallest effect upon the King. He sent, as Mazarin had requested, letters by the ordinary couriers ; but this did not prevent him from despatching to Marie other messengers, bearing epistles not less voluminous than those entrusted to the couriers of the Court, and, "instead of making

[1] This and the other letters of Mazarin to Louis XIV, Anne of Austria, and Madame de Venel which appear in this volume are in the Archives of the Ministère des Affaires Étrangères and the Bibliothèque Nationale, and have been published, wholly or in part, in several works, notably by M. Chantelauze, in his "Louis XIV et Marie Mancini."

use of the remedies which might be able to moderate his passion, omitted nothing which might serve to augment it,"[1] so that the poor Queen wrote to the Cardinal that she was in the last stage of anxiety as to the ultimate issue of the affair. As for Marie, the daily arrival of the welcome epistles from Fontainebleau had naturally revived the hopes that her uncle's determined action had temporarily crushed. " There are scarcely any misfortunes," she writes in her " Mémoires," " which do not flatter themselves by some hope to mitigate their grief. I did not refuse this remedy to mine, when I saw that his Majesty thought of nothing but despatching couriers to me charged with five letters of several pages ; and, taking into consideration the fact that the peace was not yet concluded, and that there were great obstacles to overcome, I dared sometimes to promise myself that it would not be concluded."

It is hardly necessary to observe that Marie's letters were not less numerous and voluminous than those of the King, and, inspired as they were by genuine devotion, contributed to keep alive a passion of which the roots were too deep to be easily eradicated. It is unfortunate, indeed, that not even one of these letters has been preserved, for they must have been well worth reading.

The faithful Madame de Venel did not fail to acquaint the Cardinal with the continuance of the correspondence. " Matters," she writes, " seem to me a little worse than they seemed to you, and it would perhaps be not without advantage to the service of your Eminence, if it were possible to examine the contents of the first packet despatched from La Rochelle." With characteristic discretion, the lady begs her employer not to make

---

[1] Mazarin to the Queen, July 1659.

any reply to this portion of her letter, and to burn it so
soon as read.

At the same time, Mazarin was receiving very disquieting reports from Fontainebleau in regard to the
health of the King, whom his chief physician, Vallot,
declared to be " suffering from fever and insomnia, and
to be growing sensibly thinner." On the other hand,
the Cardinal's *âme damnée*, Bartet, reported that Louis
appeared to be less incensed against his mother, and that
" it was hoped that the deplorable effects produced on
his Majesty's mind as regards the Queen tended to
diminish."

The Cardinal's nieces and their *gouvernante* arrived at
La Rochelle on 11 July, and were received as though
they had been Princesses of the Blood ; cannon fired
salutes, the municipal authorities waited upon them to
pay their respects, and at night the town was illumin-
ated. A day or two after their arrival, Marie wrote
to her uncle a letter, in which she did not attempt to
conceal her weakness, but promised submission to his
wishes. "I have seen, by what you have written and
by what Madame de Venel has received, your orders
to me to subordinate my feelings to yours ; that will
not be an easy matter. I recognise always more fully
my weakness, notwithstanding which, I have no other
desire than to do all my life all what you may command
me, and what I shall see is likely to please you. It will
not be accomplished without great difficulty, for the
thought causes me furious suffering."

This letter was quickly followed by another, in which
she promises to cease writing to " the person he wots
of (the King), if such were his desire," and concludes
by declaring that she is " resolved to obey him and to
keep all her life the quality of his humble servant."

These assurances appear to have been intended to throw the Cardinal off his guard. The King had not failed to recommend his inamorata to take measures to secure the good-will of all those about her who might prove of service to her, " even engaging her to promise them in his name whatsoever she might judge necessary to gain them over to their cause"; and, while the young lady was assuring her uncle of her desire to obey him in all things, she was busily employed in executing his Majesty's instructions. Thus a secret struggle was going on between the Cardinal and Marie; the one endeavouring to make himself acquainted with the contents of the lovers' correspondence, the other striving to evade the vigilance of the Argus-eyed spies placed around her by her uncle.

Under date 12 July, we find the chief of these, Madame de Venel, informing the Cardinal that she "has experienced great difficulty in having Mademoiselle's letter enclosed as his Eminence had instructed her." "She argues the matter warmly," the *gouvernante* continues, "and says that she cannot conceive why, when the letters can be sent direct, I cause them to be despatched by a circuitous route. However, she gave it to me, and I sent it to M. Colbert."

But, if Marie consented to entrust some of her letters to the King to the care of the Cardinal's agents, his Eminence was not long in ascertaining that these were very far from being the only ones she despatched to Fontainebleau, and that nothing else was talked of at the Court but the arrival and departure of the messengers of love. In great alarm, he wrote to the King, urging him in the strongest terms to put an end to the correspondence.

Mazarin to the King.

"Montlieu, 12 July 1659.

"You will find enclosed a packet which has been addressed to me at a place near La Rochelle, and you will permit me to tell you, with the respect and submission that I owe you, that, although I have always carried my complacency for what you have desired to the last extreme, when I perceived it possible to do so without prejudice to your service and glory, nevertheless, my reputation is at stake, and also that of a person whom you honour with your kindness [Marie Mancini], and who will assuredly receive an irreparable injury, if you have not the goodness to break off the correspondence which you carry on with her with so much publicity. I conjure you to do so, and, although, being as you are the most just and the most reasonable of all men, I ought not to doubt that, from this motive alone, you will accord me this favour, I desire, notwithstanding, to receive it as the greatest recompense you are able to give me for the small services that I have had the happiness to render you ; and I venture also to say that you owe it, too, to yourself at the present juncture, when you are on the eve of undertaking a journey for an object which is not in accord with the aforesaid correspondence, which does you more injury than if the person in question were at the Court, and you were frequenting her society, as you did in Paris.

"If you were aware of how people speak of it in the aforesaid place, and if you knew what was said about it at Fontainebleau and among the persons who accompany me, you would not be annoyed at my supplications, and you would not wait for them to give orders concerning it.

"I have also a number of advices which have reached me from Flanders, Germany, and other places, which speak of all this with a freedom which has astonished me. And, as I desire your credit more than anything which can concern myself, I am not able to refrain from acquainting you with all these particulars, in order that, being free to reflect upon them, you may be free to do that which I beg of you very humbly. I ask your pardon, if I press you in a matter which will not perhaps be at first to your liking, and to believe that I would willingly consent to give my life to have the happiness of never proposing to you anything but agreeable things which were consistent with decorum and your private reputation, which I assuredly desire more than life.

"I beg you to confer with the confidante [the Queen] concerning this matter, and to believe me the most devoted of your servants."

Louis XIV had hitherto received the Cardinal's letters without testifying any resentment. But it was otherwise with those which Mazarin addressed to the Queen, and which the latter had the imprudence to read to him. In one of these, the Cardinal indulged in some very plain speaking about his niece, whom he accused of openly boasting of the favour of the King, and added that she was altogether unworthy of the young sovereign's affection. On hearing this, Louis quite lost his temper, and upbraided his mother in the most violent manner, accusing her of having embittered the Cardinal's mind against his niece, and vowing that he would never forgive her, since, previous to Marie's departure for La Rochelle, she had promised the contrary. Then he wrote to Mazarin in terms more measured, but very firm, informing him that he himself was the best judge of what persons were worthy of his affection, and stood in need of no lesson from him, although he was willing to believe that the Minister had spoken entirely in his (the King's) interest.

To this letter, which caused him much uneasiness, the Cardinal replied at once and sought to excuse himself.

Mazarin to the King.

"Libourne, 14 July 1659.

"Magalotti has delivered to me your letter of the first of this month, and I have been surprised at what you write me concerning the person [Marie] about whom I have written to the confidante [the Queen]; for I well understand that you know her, and that you are incapable of bestowing your affection easily on persons undeserving of it. Moreover, I not only thought that possible, but I believed that they boasted about it, which is certainly the case ; and it was essential to your reputation that this report should not be circulated, and that every one should be deceived. Nevertheless, I am greatly beholden to you for the way in which you write to me regarding this matter, assuring you that I am touched as I ought to be by all the kindness that it pleases you to bestow on me.

"The confidante [the Queen] informs me, by her letter of the 1st, that she has not had reason to be satisfied with you on a certain occasion, and recalls what she wrote to me the preceding day. I have not yet received that letter, and I am suffering the greatest anxiety conceivable, not knowing what it contains, and being in despair at the slight which the confidante thinks she has received, although I cannot imagine that the matter is of importance. For, if such were the case, even though I might die on the way, I should take post to repair to the place where you are. But I do not understand how that can be, since you have not done me the honour to write to me about it. I shall pass an anxious time until I receive an explanation.

"I send you a note, wherein I am instructing Colbert to pay to Blouin[1] one thousand pistoles, or eleven thousand livres. He will find this sum, and larger sums, should you require them; and you must know once for all that, since I have nothing which is not yours, you may dispose of what belongs to me up to the last sol; and you cannot do anything which could afford me greater pleasure."

The Queen's delayed letter reached Mazarin, at Cadillac, on 16 July. It recounted the violent scene which her Majesty had had with Louis XIV, and threw the Cardinal into the last stage of anxiety. He replied immediately as follows :—

Mazarin to the Queen.

"Cadillac, 16 July 1659.

"I have received, by the ordinary courier, your letter of the 9th, concerning which I wrote to you. I suffer much uneasiness, but its contents have given me still more, and to such a degree that I thought of setting out to return; and I believe that I should have done so, had it not been for the scandal and the consequences that a resolution of such importance would have produced at the present juncture.

"I fear to lose my reason, for I can neither eat nor sleep, and I am overwhelmed by grief and anxiety at a time when I am greatly in need of tranquillity."

---

[1] First valet-de-chambre to the King.

K

The poor Cardinal did not exaggerate the condition into which the Queen's news had thrown him. His anxiety, indeed, brought on a violent attack of gout, complicated by gravel, which necessitated his remaining at Cadillac for some days longer, and the consequent postponement of the Conferences with the Spanish pleni-potentiaries, which were to have opened on 20 July.

On the same day on which he wrote to the Queen, Mazarin also despatched a long and urgent letter to Louis XIV, which he entrusted to one of his own guards, with orders to travel at the utmost speed and to bring back the King's reply without the delay of a moment. Never did subject, never did Minister, ad-dress to his sovereign language more eloquent, more outspoken, or more courageous.

Mazarin to the King.

"Cadillac, 16 July 1659.

" . . . . Even if you had not commanded me so precisely as you have done to speak to you with all freedom, where your service was concerned, I should not fail to do so at this juncture, although I knew that it would be distasteful to you, and that I should run the risk of losing your good graces.

"I have seen what the confidante [the Queen] has written me touching your displeasure and the way in which you have expressed it to her. But, since I know that her affection for you is proof against everything, and that your natural goodness, as well as your duty, gives you much uneasiness, so soon as you are aware of having displeased her, and that you return at once to testify to her the utmost tenderness, that will not occasion me much distress. But I confess to you that I

am extremely grieved to learn, from the advices which
are received from all quarters, of the manner in which
people speak of you, at a time when you have done me
the honour to announce to me that you were resolved to
devote yourself with extraordinary application to affairs,
and to set earnestly to work to become in all things the
greatest king in the world.

"Letters from Paris, Flanders, and elsewhere advise me that you are no longer recognisable since my
departure, and that not because of me, but on account of
some one who belongs to me [Marie Mancini]; that you
have entered into engagements which will prevent you
giving peace to all Christendom and rendering your
State and your subjects happy by your marriage, and
that if, to avoid so great a calamity, you pass on to
make it, the person you espouse will be most miserable,
and that through no fault of her own.

"It is said (and that is confirmed by letters from the
Court to persons in my suite) . . . . that you are always
shut up to write to the person you love, and that you
waste more time in that way than you did in conversing
with her when she was at Court. It is further said that
I approve of this and connive at it, in order to satisfy
my ambition and hinder the peace.

"It is said that you are at variance with the Queen,
and even those who write in the mildest terms say that
you avoid her as much as possible.

"I find, moreover, that the consent I gave, at your
earnest request, to an occasional interchange of news
between yourself and this person has ended in a continual commerce of long letters; that, in fact, you write
to her every day and receive a reply. And when couriers are wanting, the first who sets out is charged with
as many letters as days have elapsed since you were able

to despatch them, which cannot be without scandal, and I may say without some injury, to this person's reputation and mine.

" What is worse, is that I have recognised, by the answers which this person has made me when I have sincerely wished to advise her for her good, and by the advices that I have had from La Rochelle, that every day you omit nothing to entangle her more and more, assuring her that your intentions are to do things for her which ought not to be, and which no man of your station could wish to do, and which, in short, are, for several reasons, impossible.

" . . . God has established kings (after matters which concern religion, for the maintenance whereof they ought to use every possible means) to watch over the welfare, security, and repose of their subjects, and not to sacrifice that welfare and repose to their private passions ; and when there have appeared persons so unhappy as to oblige, by their conduct, the divine Providence to abandon them, histories are full of the revolutions and miseries they have drawn upon their persons and States.

" And, therefore, I solemnly warn you not to hesitate any longer, for though, in a certain sense, you are the master to do as you please, yet must you give account of your actions to God for the saving of your soul, and to the world for the saving of your credit and reputation. . . . If your subjects and State were so unhappy that you did not take the resolution which you ought, nothing in the world could prevent them from falling into greater evils than they have yet suffered, and all Christendom with them. And I can assure you, from certain knowledge, that the Prince de Condé and many others are watching closely to see what will

come of this matter, hoping, if things fall out in accordance with their wishes, to derive great advantage from
the plausible pretext which you will give them, on
account of which the said prince will have no doubt
about securing the support of all the Parliaments, the
great personages, and the nobility of the realm, nay, all
your subjects generally ; and, moreover, will not fail to
loudly proclaim that I have been the counsellor and the
solicitor of all that you have done.

"I am also obliged to tell you, with the same frankness, that, if you do not alter without any delay your
conduct, and do not master the passion which at present
dominates you, so that every one sees that not only
will the projected marriage be accomplished, but that
you do it willingly, and in the hope that it will prove
happy, as well as the person you will espouse, it is impossible that the aversion you entertain towards it, and
the ill-treatment the Infanta is likely to receive, will not
be known in Spain, since, on the eve of your marriage,
you do nothing to prevent it being seen, in a thousand
ways, that all your thoughts and affections are elsewhere. In which event, I hold it certain that they
will take at Madrid the same resolutions which we
ourselves should take in a like case to this. That is
why I implore you to consider what blessing you can
expect from God and men if, for this cause, we are compelled to recommence the most sanguinary war which
has ever been seen, with as much prejudice as we have
reaped advantages in the past, and as God has favoured
your cause and the pious intentions which you and the
Queen have always had.

"I point all this out to you the more plainly, because
Pimentel, during the journey, observed to me, on two or
three occasions, that you were too much in love to wish

to marry so soon, and that people had written to him
the same thing from Flanders, in terms which occasioned
him much uneasiness.

"I conclude all this discourse by declaring to you
that, if I find not, by the answer which I implore you
to make me with all speed, that there is room for
hope that you are taking, without reservation, the path
that is necessary for your own welfare, for your honour,
and for the preservation of your kingdom, I have no
other course open to me, in order to give you this last
mark of my fidelity and of my zeal for your service,
than to sacrifice myself, and, after giving into your
hands all the benefits with which it has pleased the late
King, yourself, and the Queen to overwhelm me, to
embark, with my family, to go and pass the remainder
of my days in some corner of Italy, and to pray to God
that this remedy which I shall have applied to your
malady may bring about the cure which I desire above
all things in the world, being able to say, without
exaggeration and without using the terms of submission
and respect I owe you, that there is no affection com-
parable to that which I have for you, and that it
would be impossible for me to prevent myself dying of
grief, should I see you do anything which may blacken
your reputation and expose your person and your State.

"I believe you know me well enough to credit that
what I write comes from the depths of my heart, and
that nothing can prevent me from turning back and
carrying out the resolution of which I have just spoken
to you, if I see not, by the answer that you will make
me and by your future conduct, that you have mastered
the passion to which you are at present enslaved. . . ."

While awaiting the King's answer, the unhappy

Cardinal received several alarming letters from Madame de Venel, in one of which she informed him that a special courier had just arrived from his Majesty, with a letter for Mlle. Mancini, after perusing which the young lady had informed her waiting-women that the King was coming to visit her on his way to Bayonne.

Louis XIV's reply to the letter from Cadillac, together with two other letters, written respectively on the 16th and 20th inst., reached Mazarin at Saint-Jean-de-Luz, and occasioned him more uneasiness than ever. The young monarch skilfully avoided giving a categorical answer to the Minister's demand—that is to say, to break off his relations with Marie ; but he expressed his willingness to follow in all things the counsels of the Queen. The Queen, it would appear, alarmed by the change in her son's health and his unhappiness, no longer supported Mazarin as loyally as heretofore, and Louis had good hopes of ultimately bending her to his will.

Here is the reply which the Cardinal made to the King's letters.

Mazarin to the King.

"Saint-Jean-de-Luz, 27 July 1659.

"My pain giving me a short respite, I take up my pen to inform you that I am in receipt of your letters of the 16th, 20th, and 22nd of this month, among which is the reply that you have had the goodness to make me to the despatch which I wrote you from Cadillac. You do me the great honour to tell me that you are persuaded that I desire nothing but your credit and the welfare of your State, and that, in consequence, you are more than ever resolved to follow my counsels ; but, at the same time, you do the contrary. I begged you to write no

more to La Rochelle, and you replied that that would be
too hard for you, and that the confidante [the Queen]
had approved your reasons ; so that I must conclude
that I have influence over your mind, and that you have
the goodness to follow my counsel, provided it happens
to accord with your own wishes.

"You only speak now about following those of the
confidante, because, in some fashion, they are in accord
with your own ; and, without entering into any further
explanation in regard to my letter from Cadillac, you
assure me beyond measure of your benevolence and of
your desire to defer to my counsels, but without telling
me anything definite of your wishes concerning the
matters on which I have to negotiate with Don Luis
[de Haro].   You conclude by saying that you will not
fail to follow the counsels of the confidante, and that
you have no doubt that this will meet with my approval ;
that is called, in good French, evading the question and
giving change.   You are the master of your conduct,
but you cannot compel me to approve of it, when I
know for certain that it is prejudicial to your honour, to
the welfare of your State, and to the repose of your
subjects.   Finally, as I could not commit a greater crime
in regard to you than to disguise from you matters of
importance to your service, I declare to you that I can
know neither repose nor contentment, if I do not see,
by the results, that you are obtaining the mastery over
yourself, for otherwise all is lost, and the only remedy
which remains for me to employ is *to withdraw and to
take away with me* the cause of the evils which we are
on the eve of seeing arrive.

"I have the ambition which an honest man ought to
have, and perhaps, in certain things, I go too far. I love
my niece dearly, but, without exaggeration, I love you

still more ; and I am more interested in your credit and
the preservation of your State than in anything in the
world. Wherefore, I can only repeat what I did myself
the honour to write to you from Cadillac, and, although,
just at present, it is not agreeable to you, I am sure that
you will one day love me well for it, and that you will
have the kindness to confess that I have never rendered
you a more important service than this one. The confidante loves you with the utmost tenderness, and it is
impossible for her, as it is impossible for me, not to
treat you with consideration. Although she is aware
that your wishes are often not in accordance with
reason, she does not interfere, because she is not proof
against the sight of your suffering. For myself, I
believe that I have for you the same affection as the
confidante ; but this affection renders me only the more
firm and resolute to oppose what is absolutely contrary
to your reputation and service ; for, were I to do otherwise, I should be helping you to ruin yourself.

"You take the trouble to tell me that you are ready
to believe what I write concerning the things that are
said about you and the correspondence you are carrying
on with La Rochelle, but that neither you nor the confidante have heard any one speak about it. That no one
should speak to you of it does not surprise me ; and, as
for the confidante, she cannot know what I know ; but
assuredly she is acquainted with many things which she
does not tell you, from fear of displeasing you.

"I greatly wish that M. de Turenne had had the
courage to inform you of what is being said concerning
this affair of yours, when you would have known that
I state nothing on my own authority. To conclude, I
answer you that all Europe argues about this passion of
yours, and that every one speaks of it with a freedom

which is very prejudicial to us. At Madrid, even, the affair has created a scandal, for they have not failed to write from Flanders and Paris, with intent to break off the negotiations for the projected alliance and prevent the execution of the peace. When I shall have the honour to see you, I will show you papers which will make you understand more about this matter than I have written to you. And, unless you remedy it without any delay, the affair will grow more serious every day, and will become incurable.

"I ought further to complain of the great care you take to send to La Rochelle what I write to you. Consider, I beg of you, if that be courteous towards me or advantageous for you, and if that be the way to contribute towards the cure of the person to whom you write. . . ."

This eloquent and persuasive letter produced no more effect upon Louis XIV than those which had preceded it. Madame de Venel reported from La Rochelle that special couriers continued to arrive from Fontainebleau, bringing not only letters from the King to his beloved, but also the letters which the Cardinal had written to his young master, in consequence of which, Marie was so exasperated against her uncle, that she refused even to write to him to felicitate him on his restoration to health.

Soon a new subject of alarm presented itself to the anxious Minister. The Court was making preparations for its departure for Bayonne, and, as will be remembered, the King had obtained the formal permission of the Cardinal and the Queen to allow him to see Marie Mancini again on his way to the South. Mazarin was fully resolved to do everything possible to induce Louis

XIV to renounce this project; but, in view of the King's determination and the weakness of Anne of Austria, he was at a loss how to proceed. He foresaw that this interview would not only have the effect of fanning the flame of a passion which absence had been powerless to extinguish, but might create a scandal at the very opening of the Conferences. It was indeed, he thought, more than possible that the infatuated young King was actually counting upon it to bring about a rupture with Spain. The anxiety which this thought occasioned him aggravated his disease and brought on a serious relapse, so that for several days he was obliged to cease all correspondence. On his recovery, he wrote to the Queen, imploring her to prevent the meeting he had so much cause to dread at all costs.

Mazarin to the Queen.

"Saint-Jean-de-Luz, 29 July 1659.

" I have been extremely mortified at not having been in a fit state to write to you for some days, since that is for me one of the greatest consolations that I can have, and particularly in the agitation of mind in which I am. I have read your four letters several times, and I cannot thank you enough for the continuation of your kindness, but for which I should pass a worse and a more unhappy life, seeing that I am separated from you and from the confidant [the King], and the latter does not do the things that I should wish, in order to oblige every one to regard him as the wisest of all kings, who prefers the grandeur and glory of his State to every other consideration and pleasure. I see plainly, by your letters and by those of the confidant, that your affection for him has not allowed you to continue firm; but assuredly he will do himself some injury; and, for myself, I do not change my opinion, and I confirm to the confidant, in a letter which I am writing him, the same things which I wrote to him from Cadillac. You will see the letter, and it is impossible for you not to approve of my reasons, if the compassion which you feel towards him, when you see him suffering, does not prevent you from so doing.

"I complain to the confidant that he has written to La Rochelle all that I have written to him. I am assured of it, and he has treated me very ill in behaving in this way.

"Marianne writes to me to complain of Hortense, and with reason, for she is always closeted with Marie, whose confidante she is, and both of them drive away Marianne, so that she can never remain with them.[1] I observe that Hortense is taking the same road as the other, and that she has less deference for Madame de Venel than her sister has. You may judge how much annoyance this occasions me; but I promise you that, in one fashion or another, I shall put the matter right, whatever may happen. It is a great misfortune when one has reason to be dissatisfied with one's family.

---

[1] Marianne had written to her uncle: "I make use of another hand besides my own to let your Eminence know the miseries which my sisters inflict upon me, and, if he does not believe me, he can ascertain, through Madame de Venel, that I adhere strictly to the truth. For five or six days, they have not allowed me to enter their room, but have driven me out with the greatest fury imaginable. Marie is unwilling to suffer any one, save Hortense, near her. I beg your Eminence to find some remedy for this. I know not what to do, and Madame de Venel herself is very angry with them. I have nothing else to tell you this evening."

The explanation of this state of affairs is that the worthy Madame de Venel had persuaded Marianne to spy upon her sisters; to inform her whenever she saw Marie writing a letter, and even to listen at the key-hole to the conversations between her and Hortense, and that the little girl had been detected.

" Madame de Venel does all that she can, but they have little regard for her. I trust that the confidant [the King] will have the kindness to accord me the favour of not going to see them ; for assuredly that would be badly received, and the scandal would be a public one. But, should I be so unfortunate as to fail to obtain so reasonable a request, and your good offices be powerless to effect anything against the strength of his passion, I implore you, *a mas no podo*, to make my nieces come with Madame de Venel to Angoulême, and to write her a letter in which you will order her to bring them to the same place, because you wish to see them as you pass through ; and after they have remained there a night, you will arrange for them to return. I beg you, in that case, to send a gentleman to carry your letter to Madame de Venel and accompany them ; but, in God's name, do everything possible to avert this blow, which, in whatever way it comes, cannot fail to have a very disastrous effect. . . ."

The Queen either could not or would not attempt to prevent the dreaded interview ; but she wrote to Madame de Venel, directing her to bring her charges to Saint-Jean-d'Angely. The bearer of the letter, M. du Fouilloux, brother of Marie's friend and a great favourite of the King, brought also a long letter from his Majesty to Mlle. Mancini. His arrival and the news he brought caused that young lady the greatest joy, and threw poor Madame de Venel into the utmost consternation, for, having received no orders on the subject from the Cardinal, she knew not what to do. She at once despatched a courier to his Eminence, to inform him of what had occurred and the impossibility, under the circumstances, of refusing to obey the commands of the Queen.

Madame de Venel to Mazarin.

"10 August 1659.

"MONSEIGNEUR,—The letter which I am sending to your Eminence will serve as my excuse. I am, with very sensible displeasure, compelled to set out without having had a word of advice from your Eminence regarding what I ought to do. . . . For the love of God, let your Eminence have the goodness to advise me what I should do, since I would prefer to die rather than have the unhappiness to displease your Eminence. M. du Fouilloux, who has brought the Queen's letter, has instructions to attend Mesdemoiselles to Saint-Jean. I shall not fail to send word to your Eminence of what happens there.

"I am, etc.

"P.S.—Mesdemoiselles will sleep to-morrow (Monday) at Surgères, and Tuesday at Saint-Jean, where the Court will arrive on Wednesday."

CHAPTER VIII

Interview between Louis XIV and Marie Mancini at Saint-Jean-
d'Angély—The King more enamoured than ever—Letter of Marie
to her uncle—Angry letter of Mazarin to Madame de Venel—Alarm
of Marie, who seeks to pacify the Cardinal—Marianne's verses—
Continuation of the correspondence between the King and Marie—
Remarkable letter of Mazarin to Louis XIV—Curt response of his
Majesty—The King accuses Anne of Austria of embittering the
Cardinal against his niece—Letters of Mazarin to the Queen-Mother
and the King—Despair of Louis XIV at finding that all obstacles to
his marriage with the Infanta have been surmounted—Marie Mancini
breaks off all correspondence with the King—Letter in which she
informs her uncle of her resolution—Joy of the Cardinal—His letters
to Madame de Venel and his niece.

THE Cardinal's nieces left La Rochelle on 11 August and reached Saint-Jean-d'Angely the following day, where they awaited the Court, which did not
arrive until the morning of the 13th. In his letter,
the King had informed Marie that he intended to precede the Queen and reach the town an hour before
her. Such, however, was his impatience to behold once
more the object of his adoration, that he arrived fully
two hours earlier than he was expected. "He alighted
immediately at our lodging," writes Hortense, "and,
after the first salutations had been exchanged, he passed
into the reception-room, where he conversed alone with
Marie until the moment when they came to warn him
of the arrival of the Queen. He then entered our
coach and escorted us to the Queen, who received us
with all the graciousness imaginable. Marianne was

so touched that she remained like one petrified, being unable to utter a word. Finally, she began weeping, which was very unlike her."[1]

The Princesse de Conti and the Comtesse de Soissons were with the Queen when the girls arrived. The latter had never forgiven her younger sister for having supplanted her in the King's affections, and, with characteristic spitefulness, now endeavoured to do the lovers an ill turn, by inviting Marie to sup with her and vowing that she would take no refusal. But Marie was equal to the occasion, and replied that she would come with pleasure, if the King did not intend to do her the honour of visiting her. When the Queen sat down to the card-table—Anne of Austria divided her time between cards and devotional exercises—Louis XIV escorted the young ladies to their lodging, and remained with them until he was summoned to join his mother at supper. He returned immediately afterwards, and stayed until two o'clock in the morning. Hortense was present during a part of the time, and assures us that "nothing could equal the passion which the King showed and the tenderness with which he asked of Marie her pardon for all that she had suffered for his sake." He promised to do everything possible to obtain the Queen's consent for them to rejoin the Court at Bordeaux, and would have remained until an even later hour, had not Marie, fearing the malicious interpretations which the Comtesse de Soissons might put upon so long an interview, begged him to leave her.

The following morning, Marie and her sisters repaired again to the Queen's lodging, where the King was awaiting them. They accompanied her Majesty

[1] "Mémoires de la Duchesse de Mazarin."

to Mass, at the conclusion of which the Queen took leave of them and continued her journey. Before she left, Marie, on Louis XIV's advice, begged her permission to rejoin the Court. Anne of Austria did not like to refuse openly ; but took refuge behind the Cardinal, and replied that she would give it her willingly, providing his Eminence were agreeable. Marie knew well enough what his Eminence's answer was likely to be ; nevertheless, as the King had set his heart on her following the Court, she did not despair of being ultimately successful.

Louis XIV remained at Saint-Jean-d'Angely for some hours after his mother's departure, the whole of which time was passed in earnest conversation with Marie, when it was agreed that the girl should use every endeavour to conciliate her uncle, since an apparent submission to his wishes seemed to be the only possible means of terminating her exile. Finally, " after some tears had been shed on both sides," the King succeeded in tearing himself away, and continued his journey to Bordeaux ; while Marie and her sisters returned to La Rochelle, M. du Fouilloux, by his Majesty's orders, again escorting them.

The interview had revived all the girl's hopes. She had found the King more devoted than ever and more than ever resolved to brave both his mother and the Cardinal. He was perfectly aware of the difficulties which were certain to arise during the forthcoming negotiations, notably in regard to the Prince de Condé, whose demand to be restored to all his honours and dignities would certainly be supported by the King of Spain, and strenuously opposed by Mazarin. It was quite possible that this matter alone might prove an insurmountable obstacle to the conclusion of peace, in

L

which eventuality the chief objection to his marriage with Marie Mancini would be removed.

A few days after her return to La Rochelle, Marie addressed to the Cardinal the following letter :—

Marie Mancini to the Cardinal.

"La Rochelle, 22 August 1659.

"MONSEIGNEUR,—I have seen the letter which your Eminence has done Madame de Venel the honour to write to her,[1] and I should suffer the greatest grief possible to conceive, if you were able to doubt my affection and respect. I know too well the obligation which I am under to you not to render all my life an absolute submission to your orders. I should be in despair were your Eminence to doubt it. I have no good opinion of myself, and, even if I had, I should always submit to your orders. I feel that my welfare is in your hands, and I am tranquil, well knowing that you will have the goodness to assure it. If I have done anything to displease your Eminence, let me know of it, for I submit blindly to your wishes.

"Your Eminence is aware of the journey which we have just undertaken by the Queen's command. You will admit that I required to be extremely submissive to return to La Rochelle without allowing the mortification I experienced to be observed, and you have seen that, in this affair, I have had sufficient control over myself. Be persuaded that I am not oblivious of the obligation under which I am to you, and that I would lose my life rather than fail to prove to you the submission which makes me, with respect, etc."[2]

---

[1] Presumably, a letter written from Saint-Jean-de-Luz on 14 August, in which Mazarin had expressed in very strong terms his anger at the folly and obstinacy of his niece.

[2] Published by Lucien Perey, "Le Roman du Grand Roi."

The tone of this letter is obviously the result of the advice given by the King to his inamorata at Saint-Jean-d'Angely. It did not, however, produce the effect upon the Cardinal which the writer expected. Informed by Madame de Venel of all that had taken place during the meeting between the lovers, Mazarin could hardly doubt that his Majesty's passion for his niece was as lively as ever, and he had, moreover, received from the Comtesse de Soissons a highly-coloured account of the manner in which Marie had treated her on that occasion, to which the countess joined some very unpleasant innuendoes respecting the *tête-à-têtes* which her sister had had with the King. He did not, in consequence, condescend to acknowledge Marie's letter ; but wrote a very angry one to Madame de Venel, and concluded by expressing his opinion that his niece was "going the right way to make herself the most unhappy woman of her age." This letter was duly shown by the *gouvernante* to her charge, with whom it provided food for very serious reflection. The imprudent girl had at first troubled very little about displeasing the Cardinal, believing that the King's love would be able to protect her against any extreme measures on her uncle's part. However, her continued exile and the veiled threats which his Eminence's letters contained had begun to alarm her. She was too intelligent not to perceive that Mazarin was resolved to promote at all costs the true interests of France and his master, and that, unless, as the King had himself advised her, she could contrive to conciliate him by a pretence of submission to his wishes, she was not unlikely to find herself shut up in a convent for the remainder of her days ; not, of course, in France, where Louis XIV could have interfered to prevent it, but in Italy. She therefore wrote to the Cardinal a very long and very humble letter, defending herself against the charge of discourtesy to Madame de Soissons, to whom she promised to write very often and to testify "all kinds of affection," from which his Eminence would be able to judge how entirely submissive she was to his orders.

This time Mazarin allowed himself to be persuaded, and wrote to the Comtesse de Soissons recommending her to behave " with more prudence and moderation " in regard to her sister. He feared that otherwise she might incur the displeasure of the King, even more than she had already contrived to do, which would not at all have suited the Cardinal's plans.

In the midst of his grave political occupations and of the ceaseless anxiety which the continuance of Louis XIV's passion for his niece occasioned him, Mazarin did not neglect the most trifling matters. Thus, learning from Madame de Venel that Marianne was somewhat unwell, he wrote to Vallot, the King's first physician, begging him to prescribe for her by letter, which the doctor did, and sent the Cardinal reassuring reports as to the health of his favourite. The future patroness of La Fontaine—and Pradon—had even thus early shown her taste for *belles lettres*, and was in the habit of addressing to her uncle rhyming epistles modelled, apparently, on Loret's " Muse historique," which, to judge from the following specimen, written after her visit to Saint-Jean-d'Angely, must have afforded his Eminence much amusement.

Marianne to the Cardinal.

" 18 August 1659.

" J'ai eu la plus grande joie
De voir la reine et le roi.
Mais le plaisir a été bien court
De ne voir qu'un instant la Cour.

Vous nous laissez longtemps
Languir à La Rochelle,
Nous autres pauvres pucelles.
Vous ne songez non plus à nous,
Que si nous étions des loups-garous.
Il me semble que vous ne devriez pas
Oublier des nièces qui ont tant d'appas.
Qui vous aiment si fort
Qu'elles aimeraient mieux la mort,
Qu'être longtemps en absence
De votre noble Éminence.
Pour moi qui suis votre chère nièce
Je me mettrai en mille pièces
Pour obéir toujours aveuglément
Et vous donner contentement.
La reine nous a donné
Quatre montres en vérité
Que sont les plus belles
Qui soient dans La Rochelle ;
Ma sœur Hortense a eu
La plus belle montre de tout.
Je voudrais bien coucher avec vous
Et que fussiez mon époux,
Monsieur, je vous supplie,
Traitez-moi sans cérémonie,
Car ce serait plutôt moi
Qui vous devrait faire la loi.
Ou madame de Venel ment
Ou vous ne lui écrivez pas souvent,
Elle se trouve fort en peine
Quand elle a nouvelle de la reine
Qui l'oblige de partir ;
Craignant fort le démentir
Elle pleure et se tourmente,
Rendez-la donc plus contente
Et moi je vous dis adieu
Parce que je vais prier Dieu."[1]

[1] Published by Lucien Perey, " Le Roman du Grand Roi."

The Cardinal's belief in Marie's assurances of submission did not last long.   Madame de Venel reported, under date 27 August, that the young lady had received two bulky epistles from the King almost at the same time, to which she had replied at equal length. To add to his uneasiness, Louis XIV wrote to him to plead the cause of his beloved, assuring the Cardinal that Marie's feelings towards his Eminence were very different from what he seemed to imagine, and begging him to show himself more indulgent and less of a scold. The poor Cardinal, who was suffering from "a furious attack of gout," appears to have quite lost his temper. He wrote to Madame de Venel, telling her to inform his niece that she might spare herself the trouble of writing to him any more, "since he knew very well what was in her mind and the value he ought to place in her professions of affection for him."   And he addressed to the King a long and eloquent letter, in which he drew a most unflattering portrait of Marie, and conjured him, in the strongest possible terms, to master this passion, which threatened to prove so disastrous to the interests of France and his own reputation.

Mazarin to the King.

"28 August, from Saint-Jean-de-Luz.

"I beg you to be persuaded, once and for all, that I know not how to render you a greater or more important service than to speak to you with the freedom which you have had the kindness to permit me to do where your service is concerned, and particularly on matters of consideration and importance, with which assuredly you have no servant capable of dealing with the zeal that I shall employ.

" I shall begin by telling you, in reference to your letter of 13 August, which treats of the kindly feeling which the person who is in question has for myself, and of the other things which it has pleased you to write to her advantage, that I am not surprised at the manner in which you speak, since it is your passion for her which prevents you, as is commonly the case with persons in a like state to yourself, from understanding her true character ; and I answer that, were it not for this passion, you would be of the same opinion as myself that this person has no affection for me, but, on the contrary, regards me with much aversion, because I do not flatter her follies ; that she has unbounded ambition, a capricious and passionate disposition, contempt for every one, no control over her actions, and a predilection for committing all kinds of extravagant things ; that she is more unreasonable than ever since she had the honour of seeing you at Saint-Jean-d'Angely ; and, instead of receiving your letters twice a week, she now receives them every day. In short, you will perceive, as I do, that she has a thousand faults and not a single good quality to render her worthy of your kindness. In your letter, you affirm your belief that my opinion of her is the result of the bad offices which people render her. Is it possible that you are under the impression that I, who am so discerning and skilful in affairs of importance, am in entire ignorance of those which concern my family ? Can I entertain any doubt as to the intentions of this person in regard to myself ? when I see that she never fails to do in all things the contrary to what I order her ; that she turns the counsels I give her regarding her conduct into ridicule ; that the presumptuous acts she commits in the sight of all the world are prejudicial both to her own honour and my own ; that she wishes to make herself mistress and change all the orders that I give in my house; and that, to conclude, despising all the care that I have employed, with so much affection, earnestness, and address, to place her in the right way and make her prudent, she persists in her follies, and intends to become the laughing-stock of the world?

"If the bad behaviour of this person were injuring only herself and me, I might disguise my feelings. But, since the evil is augmenting daily, and this connection is doing irreparable harm to the reputation and tranquillity of my master, it is impossible for me to tolerate it; and I shall be compelled, in the end, to take resolutions whereby every one will be convinced that, where your service is in question, I am prepared to make every sacrifice.

"And if I am so unhappy as to find that the passion which you cherish for this creature prevents you from realising the importance of the affair, nothing remains for me save to carry out the resolution with which I acquainted you in my letter from Cadillac;[1] for, to be brief, there is no power which can deprive me of the absolute authority which God and the laws have given me over my family. And you will one day be the first to pay tribute to the service which I shall have rendered you, which will assuredly be the greatest of all, since, by my resolution, I shall have placed you in the way to be happy, and, along with that, to be the most glorious and the most accomplished king on earth.

"I return to the person under discussion, who believes herself more assured than ever of being able to dispose absolutely of your affection, since the new promise you made her at Saint-Jean-d'Angely, and, if you

---

[1] His resolve, if all other means of bringing the King to reason failed, of resigning his post of chief Minister and carrying off Marie and her sisters to Italy. See p. 134 *supra.*

are obliged to marry, I know that her intention is to render the princess you wed unhappy all her life, which cannot happen without rendering you the same, nor without exposing you to a thousand grievous inconveniences ; for you cannot expect the blessing of Heaven if you, on your part, do nothing to deserve it.

" Since that last visit [the interview at Saint-Jean-d'Angely], which I always knew would be fatal, and which, for that reason, I strove to prevent, you have recommenced writing to her every day, not letters, but whole volumes, giving her an account of even the most trifling happenings, and reposing in her the utmost confidence, to the exclusion of every one else ; in such a way that your whole time is occupied in reading her letters and in writing your own. And what is incomprehensible, is that you employ every imaginable expedient to excite your passion, while you are on the eve of your marriage. Thus, you are labouring to render yourself the most unhappy of all men, since there is no condition more insupportable than a marriage which is contrary to one's inclination.

" But tell me, I entreat you, what is this girl's intention, when once you are married ? Has she forgotten her duty so far as to believe that, if I were so dishonourable a man, or, to speak more plainly, so infamous as to approve of it, she will be able to assume a position which will dishonour her ?[1] Perhaps she imagines that she can act thus without any one murmuring, since she has gained every one's heart. But she is greatly deceived, since her conduct has aroused so much feeling against her amongst all who are acquainted with her, that I should find it hard to name one who has any esteem or goodwill for her, save Hortense, who is a child whom she

---

[1] That is to say, become the King's mistress.

has won over by flattery and by giving her money and other things ; having found, so I conceive, some treasure, since she refused to accept the money which I ordered Madame de Venel to give her to any amount she desired, when she went to La Rochelle.[1]

"The greatest good fortune which can happen to this person, is for me to set matters in order without delay, and if I cannot render her prudent, which I believe to be impossible, at least to prevent her follies being any longer patent to the world, since, otherwise, she will run the risk of being ruined.

"You will hear all this with astonishment, because the affection which you bear her leaves you no room to discern clearly what concerns her. But for myself, who am not preoccupied, and who, whatever the cost may be, desire to serve you at this juncture, which is the most important of your life, even if it should cost me my own, I see the truth as it is, for otherwise I should be committing a kind of treason. For the rest, let things happen as they will, since I am prepared to die, provided it be in the execution of my duty and in serving you, as I am obliged to do, particularly in this matter, with which no one except myself can know how to deal.

". . . I do not doubt that she [Marie Mancini] is aware of all that I have the honour to write to you; but, very far from fearing that, I desire it passionately ; and would to God that I believed her capable of giving sound counsel concerning the affairs about which you take the trouble to inform her, for I should willingly ask to be relieved of this anxiety ! But I confess to you

---

[1] This is a palpable hit at the King, who had been supplying Marie with money wherewith to secure the good-will of those about her and facilitate the correspondence between the lovers.

that at my age, and in the midst of all the occupations
by which I am overwhelmed, and in which it seems to
me to be sufficient happiness to serve you with credit
and with advantage to your State, it is intolerable for
me to find myself disturbed on account of a person
who, for all kinds of reasons, ought to tear herself in
pieces in order to relieve me. And what distresses me
to the last degree, is that, instead of sparing me this
sorrow, you contribute thereto, by giving this wretched
girl courage and resolution to act as she is doing.

"I was altogether relieved in my mind by what you
took the trouble to write to me, and by the manner in
which you had begun to conduct yourself after my
despatch from Cadillac ; and I believed that you had no
other thought than to prepare the way to be happy
in your marriage, which could only be by putting an
end to the passion which had rendered itself mistress
of your mind. But I have seen, with sensible grief,
that since this fatal visit [the interview at Saint-Jean-
d'Angely], which I would have prevented at the cost
of my blood, everything is in a worse condition than
before. And it is unnecessary for you to explain the
matter differently, for I cannot doubt it, and I may say
that I know all as well as you. Consider after that,
I beg of you, what must be my condition, and if the
world contains a more unhappy man than myself, who,
after having always applied himself zealously to augment
your reputation and to procure, by all the most difficult
means, the triumph of your arms, has the grief to
behold a person related to him on the point of over-
turning everything and of compassing your ruin, if you
continue to give a free rein to the passion which you
have for her.

"Can I, without injury to the fidelity which I owe

you, and without betraying my obligations, abstain from warning you that you are taking a road altogether contrary to decorum and to the happiness to which you ought to aspire, since, on the eve of your marriage, you are abandoning yourself more than ever to your passion ? For whatever power you may have over yourself, and whatever progress you may have made, on the advice of her whom you love, in the art of dissimulation, you cannot conceal your aversion for this marriage, although it be the most advantageous and the most glorious that you can possibly contract. You lay yourself open to receive proofs of the wrath of God, if you proceed to marry a princess whom you do not love, with the intention of living on bad terms with her, as the other person [Marie] threatens to do with her whom you wed.

"I find myself greatly embarrassed . . . about concluding the final negotiations in regard to your marriage ; since it seems to me I am promising what cannot be performed, and that I am contributing to the establishment of a state of things which will render miserable an innocent girl who is deserving of your affection [the Infanta].

"It is time for you to come to a decision and to declare your intentions without any concealment ; since it is a thousand times better to break off all negotiations and continue the war, without troubling ourselves about the misery of Christendom and the injury which your State and your subjects will thereby receive, than to conclude this marriage, if it will produce only your unhappiness and that of your kingdom.

"All this is what the passion, the fidelity, and the zeal that I have for your service constrains me to represent to you with the freedom that I ought, as an old servant who desires only your credit, and who has more interest and obligation than any one else, not only in telling you the truth, but, further, in sacrificing his life for so good a master as yourself. Finally, I protest to you that nothing can prevent me dying of grief, if I see a person who is so dear to me as you occasion more unhappiness and disaster than I have rendered you service since the first day I began to serve you."

Never had Mazarin found himself in a more difficult or more embarrassing position. "This affair," wrote he subsequently to Colbert, "is perhaps the most delicate in which I have ever been engaged, and which has occasioned me the greatest uneasiness." He passed the three or four days before he received the King's answer in a state of the most painful anxiety, though he had the art to conceal his apprehensions and to persevere in the boldness of his language. "I flatter myself that I rendered you a very important service twenty-four hours since," he writes to the King, the day following that on which he had addressed to him his memorable letter, "having written to you with the freedom and candour which a faithful servant who has more interest than any one else in your reputation and happiness ought to employ. I await your reply with great impatience, since by it I must regulate my conduct and form the resolution which I shall deem capable of delivering you from the passion whereby you are at present possessed."

Louis XIV's answer, which reached him on 3 September, was very different from what he had expected, and filled him with consternation. The young monarch, madly in love as he was, had resented Mazarin's strictures upon the character and conduct of his niece as so many insults to himself, and, though the contents of the document are not known, there can be no doubt, from the letters which the Cardinal immediately addressed to the King and Queen, that it must have contained a stinging rebuke.[1] A letter from the latter reached him by the same courier who brought his Majesty's reply, and related that, on the arrival of Mazarin's letter, there had been a painful scene between mother and son, in which Louis had again accused the Queen of embittering the Cardinal against his niece, and had declared his resolution of listening to no more advice from either of them.

To Anne of Austria, Mazarin replied :—

Mazarin to the Queen.

" 3 September, Saint-Jean-de-Luz.

" I am in despair at seeing, from all that you have the goodness to write to me, the grief which you are experiencing.   Would to God that I were able to afford you relief in shedding all my blood, for I would do so with the greatest joy imaginable !   The answer of the confidant [the King] is conceived in terms which show me plainly enough that he has no more affection for me or consideration for his own interests.   Consequently, I have no alternative, save to execute his orders to abridge the time of the marriage, and after having signed the contract and the articles of peace, which will be glorious and advantageous for his person and his State, to take the resolution which will be the best calculated to deliver him from my importunities and the best for his service ; praying God with all my heart to bless my intentions."

[1] According to Choisy, Louis XIV wrote that Mazarin might do as he pleased, and that if he abandoned the conduct of his affairs, many others would willingly take charge of them.

From an engraving after the painting by Mignard

ANNE OF AUSTRIA, QUEEN OF FRANCE

"Here," remarks Marie Mancini's biographer, Lucien Perey, "the Cardinal observes more tact than in his letter to the King. He was well aware that the Queen, so weak when confronted by her son, could only hope to hold her own against him on rare occasions; and he, therefore, makes use of the most powerful incentive to rouse her to action, namely, the threat of his own departure. We have seen how much Anne of Austria had suffered during the Cardinal's exile at Cologne. From that time, the links which united them had been given a new strength, and he well knew the effect which the fear of a fresh separation would produce on her mind. Nothing, then, could have been more adroit than the phrase which we have just read."[1]

The tone of Mazarin's letter to the King is very different from that of 28 August. Then the Minister was imperious and determined; now he is all humility and submission, though the conclusion is not without a touch of dignity.

Mazarin to the King.

"Saint-Jean-de-Luz, 3 September.

"SIRE,—Immediately on receipt of your letter, I take up the pen to give myself the honour of telling you that, although your answer is rather terse, I recognise sufficiently your intentions and the situation of your mind as regards myself. Your kindness has never permitted you up to now either to write or to speak to me as you have on this occasion. It does not, however, cause me surprise, for, since the journey to Lyons, I have always doubted very much whether, if I were not sacrificed to the person in question, I should not be to some other.

[1] "Le Roman du Grand Roi."

"Had you taken the trouble to examine my letter, you would have found therein ample grounds for expressing to me your gratitude for what I wrote to you, actuated by a pure and disinterested motive for your service, reputation, and honour; and you would not treat me extravagantly as you do, in telling me that I have a bad opinion of you and that I believe you to be a liar. I should not deserve to live, if I had such thoughts about my master. But I tell you the truth without failing in the respect I owe you, when I maintain that the passion you have for the person whom you love [Marie Mancini] prevents you from seeing her faults, and that I know that she has no affection for me, notwithstanding what you have taken the trouble to write to me to the contrary. For, without doing you any wrong, I think that I know better what she is and the manner in which she has conducted herself towards me. If you are angered with me, as you say at the commencement of your letter, you have only to order me to the place to which you desire me to repair to feel the effects of your indignation, and I shall not fail to obey you. Be sure, at least, that, without making the slightest protest, I shall publicly announce that you are in the right and that I am culpable.

"You have, however, too much sense of justice to wish to deprive me of honour in payment for my services; and it is quite sufficient, it appears to me, to deprive me of life and all that I possess in the world, without depriving me of the liberty that laws divine and human give me to dispose of my family.

"I implore you very humbly to pardon me, if I have importuned you over much, assuring you that I shall do so no more in the future. Finally, to abridge the time

of your marriage, I shall sign the articles relating to it
and those of the peace, according to your orders, which
done, I shall go to end my days in the place to which
you may be pleased to order me, satisfied with having
had the happiness to serve for thirty years the King,
your father, and yourself, without your army or your
affairs having suffered any loss of reputation. I
demand only this favour, that you will be persuaded
that, whatever may be my fate, I shall be to the last
moment of my life the most faithful and the most
devoted creature that you have."

Up to this moment, Louis XIV seems to have really
believed that some obstacle would intervene to prevent
the conclusion of peace and his marriage with the
Infanta ; the wish being in all probability father to the
thought. But the Cardinal's letter, humble and submissive though it was, spoke of the treaty as a thing
already assured, and showed him that the Minister
anticipated no difficulties other than those of his
Majesty's own creating. His eyes were opened, and
he saw that it was no longer possible for him to draw
back, unless he desired to take upon himself the entire
responsibility for the continuance of a sanguinary and
useless war, and the universal opprobrium which such
an action must involve. His grief was terrible, and in
the next letter he wrote to Marie Mancini he was unable
to conceal from her his apprehensions.

The receipt of the King's letter threw the poor girl
into the direst distress. She recognised at once how
futile had been the hope, to which she had clung so
tenaciously, that the young monarch's devotion to her
would be proof against the pressure of the immense
interests arrayed against them. A letter from Mazarin's

M

creature Ondedei, Bishop of Fréjus, confirmed her fears, and, finally, she learned, through Colbert, that Maréchal de Gramont had received orders to proceed to Madrid, to make a formal demand for the Infanta's hand, on behalf of his master. Her pride, stronger than her love and her grief, asserted itself, and urged her at least to secure to herself the credit of being the first to break the ties which her lover seemed powerless to preserve. She immediately resolved to cease all communication with the King, and forthwith wrote to the Cardinal to inform him of her determination and her willingness to submit to his orders.

Marie Mancini to the Cardinal.

"La Rochelle, 3 September 1659.

"MONSEIGNEUR,—I believe that presently your Eminence will have reason to be satisfied with me, owing to the course which I intend to adopt. I have begged the King to consent that I should write to him no more, and to do the same also for me.

"Your Eminence has only to cause him to show you the letter which I have written to him, and he will see that I am not deceiving him. To conclude, I entreat your Eminence very humbly to believe that I have no other thought than to conform in all things to all his intentions and to follow implicitly all his commands.

". . . I shall esteem myself very happy, if once you can be fully persuaded of my submission and gratitude. I am, as I should be, Monseigneur, your Eminence's very humble . . .

"MARIE DE MANCINI."[1]

[1] Published by Lucien Perey, "Le Roman du Grand Roi."

This letter was accompanied by one from Madame de Venel, confirming the good news. "From the moment when the King gave her [Marie] to understand that there was no obstacle in the way of his marriage," wrote the *gouvernante*, "her conduct has undergone a complete change; her countenance is altogether different; she is gay, amuses herself, and behaves as Seneca would have done on a like occasion; she has made so many moral reflections that all the philosophers combined could not have known so much as she does. I assure you, Monseigneur, that the sight of her present conduct occasions me all the joy imaginable."

We can well imagine the relief of the anxious Cardinal on receiving these letters, as unexpected as they were welcome. He had opened his niece's with serious misgivings; but, after perusing the first few lines, his joy was such that he summoned the Bishop of Fréjus to listen to its contents. Then he sat down and wrote to Madame de Venel a letter expressive of his delight at finding that his niece had at last proved amenable to reason, and referring to that young lady in terms strangely different from those which he had employed in his celebrated letter to the King.

Mazarin to Madame de Venel.

"Saint-Jean-de-Luz, 8 September.

"I confess to you that I have not for a long time experienced a pleasure so great as that which I have received in reading the letter which my niece has written me, and the news that you give of her present state of mind, after she had become aware that the King's marriage was absolutely decided upon. I never doubted her intelligence, but I mistrusted her judgment, and particularly in a matter wherein a strong passion, accompanied by so many circumstances to render it furious, left no room for reason to act.

"I reply to you again that it affords me the greatest conceivable joy to have such a niece, seeing that, of her own accord, she has taken so generous a resolution, and one so much in conformity with her own honour and my satisfaction. I am acquainting the King with what she has written to me and what she has done. I am assured that his Majesty will esteem her the more for it, and, if France knew of the manner in which she has conducted herself in this matter, it would desire for her every kind of happiness and give her a thousand blessings. But I am in a sufficient position to make her feel the results of my affection and of the inclination that I have always had for her, which has only been interrupted, because it appeared that she had none for me and attached no importance to my counsels, although they had no other end than her own happiness and peace of mind.

"I beg you to express to her, on my behalf, that I love her with all my heart; that I am about to give serious consideration to the question of marrying her and making her happy, and that she will be so to the last degree, if she applies herself earnestly to profit by the affection which I have for her and the esteem I feel for her, on account of the action which she has just done; for I declare to you, without exaggeration, that it would be difficult to expect the like in a person of forty years who had lived all her life among the philosophers.

"And, since she is pleased to indulge in moral reflections, you must tell her from me that she ought to read the books which have been well spoken of in that connection, particularly Seneca, wherein she will find matter to console her and to confirm her joyfully in the resolution she has just taken.

" I am persuaded that she loves too much her honour, advantage, and reputation to make the least change in that ; and you must tell her from me that I should be in despair if such were to happen, and that she would lose the merit of the finest action that she could possibly do all her life.

" I do not send a long answer, because this letter will serve for her.   I desire her to take every opportunity of writing to me, and to express to me freely all her senti- ments ; for I shall be enchanted to contribute, by my replies, to place her in a position to be loved and esteemed by all, and to procure, in all kinds of ways, her contentment.

" It is necessary for her to take walks and indulge in every kind of amusement which may contribute to keep her mind in the state of tranquillity I desire for her ; and, if money for her diversions be required, you have only to apply for it to the Sieur de Terron,[1] who will refuse nothing which you may ask of him."

And, the same day, the Cardinal addressed to his niece the following letter :—

Mazarin to Marie Mancini.

" Saint-Jean-de-Luz, 8 September.

" You could not give me a greater joy than by writing to acquaint me with the resolution at which you have just arrived.   I pray God with all my heart that it may please Him to assist you, so that you may carry it out, as you ought to do, for all kinds of reasons, being able to tell you, without flattering you, that you could do nothing in your whole life which would give you more honour and glory than what you will derive

---

[1] Colbert de Terron, Governor of La Rochelle.

from the action which you have just done. I am writing
at length to Madame de Venel. That is why I shall
not say anything further here, since I could only repeat
to you the same things. I beg you only to be assured
of my regard and affection, and that I shall not delay in
giving you proofs of it on all occasions."

CHAPTER IX

The King declines to accept Marie Mancini's decision and continues to
write to her—She refuses to reply to his letters—Letter of Mazarin
to the King—Reports of Madame de Venel—The Cardinal's nieces
remove from La Rochelle to Brouage—Letter of Marie to her uncle
—The King persists in writing to Marie, who, however, continues
inflexible—Letters of Mazarin to his nieces—Rhyming response of
Marianne—The Cardinal sends his confidential agent Bartet to
Bordeaux to keep watch upon the actions of the King—His reports—
The Comtesse de Soissons, at Mazarin's request, endeavours to regain
her former influence over Louis XIV—The King sends Marie a
present of a little dog—Treachery of Colbert de Terron, Governor
of La Rochelle, to the Cardinal—Marie begs her uncle to find a
husband for her—And expresses a preference for Prince Charles of
Lorraine—The Constable Colonna demands her hand—Reports of
Bartet in regard to the King and the Comtesse de Soissons—The
countess, by the Queen's order, writes to her sister—Despair of
Marie—Mazarin sends the Bishop of Fréjus to Brouage to propose
to his niece the Colonna marriage—She refuses—Letters of the
Cardinal and the King to Marie—Return of the Mlles. Mancini to
Paris—Severe orders of the Cardinal as to the manner in which they
are to conduct themselves—Letters of the King to Marie—A touch-
ing incident—Amusing letter of Marianne Mancini to the Cardinal—
Prince Charles of Lorraine.

IN the meanwhile, Louis XIV, at Bordeaux, had
received Marie's letter, in which the girl announced
to him her intention of writing to him no more, and
begged him to cease all communication with her. The
letter appears to have occasioned his Majesty as much
astonishment as pain, although, aware as he was of the
proud and passionate character of his mistress, he ought
certainly to have foreseen something of this nature.
However, he could not bring himself to believe that she

would persist in such a resolution, and immediately wrote her an expostulatory letter four pages in length.

"The ordinary courier of this evening," writes Madame de Venel to the Cardinal, "brought a letter of four pages for Mlle. de Mancini. After receiving it, she told me that she desired to reply for the last time ; that she had forgotten in her previous letter to beg the King to burn her letters, and wished to do so. She repeated that it would be for the last time. I answered her : 'But what is your pleasure that I should write to his Eminence, after the letter which you made me write him by the last courier, and which you read ?' She responded angrily : 'Tell him that I am writing to him [the King].'"

The King, though deeply wounded by Marie's persistence, still refused to believe that she would continue to resist his importunities, and wrote her letter after letter ; but the girl's pride sustained her, and after the brief note begging him to burn the letters he had received from her, not even the most passionate entreaties could wring so much as a line from her. Overwhelmed with grief, Louis had, nevertheless, courage enough to endeavour to conceal his sufferings from those about him, and, to find some distraction from his melancholy reflections, turned his attention to the negotiations which were in progress on the frontier. It was then, perhaps, that he began to comprehend something of the great service which the Cardinal had rendered him in combating with so much resolution a passion which, if it had been allowed to take its course, would have been fraught with such disastrous consequences both to himself and his kingdom. Any way, he appears to have regretted the angry and imperious tone of the letter which had caused Mazarin such consternation, and now wrote to the Minister in the most affectionate terms, begging him to forget the rebuke which he had then administered to him and to continue to write to him with the utmost freedom. To which the delighted Cardinal hastened to reply.

Mazarin to the King.

"Saint-Jean-de-Luz, 14 September 1659.

"If I received with joy the terms wherein it pleased you to write to me on the last occasion, you will readily believe that your letter of the 11th, which I have just received, has rendered me the most contented man in the world, in seeing to what degree it pleases you to honour me with the assurances of your friendship. And, although you render me justice when you tell me that you recognise clearly that I have no other end in all that I have written to you, save your credit, your tranquillity, and the welfare of your service, I am, notwithstanding, under infinite obligations to you for the same ; and, whatever resolution I had taken to the contrary, I shall execute with pleasure the order which you give me, always to write to you freely all my opinions in matters which concern your service.

"I have not dared to inform you how satisfied I am with the person you wot of [Marie Mancini], for I feared that perhaps it might not be agreeable to you, for which reason I addressed myself to the confidante [the Queen], well knowing that she would tell you everything.

"I entreat you now to profit by the grace that God has bestowed on you in giving you so excellent an example to follow, and you will see that, if you take a generous resolution to endeavour to obtain the mastery over yourself, you will have peace of mind and will give it also to the said person, and you will place yourself also in a position to find happiness in your marriage, for I assure you the Infanta will give you reason to be so.

"To conclude, I know not how to tell you how much I love the person whom I did not believe capable of an action such as she has just done, and I esteem her the more, inasmuch as it was the only remedy capable of placing you in a position to conquer your passion."

During this unexpected crisis, Madame de Venel sent daily bulletins to the Cardinal, who had strictly enjoined upon her to give him immediate warning should she note the slightest sign of wavering on the part of his niece.

"Mademoiselle," writes the *gouvernante*, under date 10 September, "has received her letter [from the King] as usual, but she will make no reply to it. She did me the honour to tell me this evening that she will never write any more. . . . She will go to Brouage next week, to amuse herself for some days."

And again, on 15 September :

"Mademoiselle starts to-morrow for Brouage. Mademoiselle's state of mind is better than your Eminence could possibly desire, and very assuredly I believe it entirely at ease. Saturday last, she did not write, nor did any one write a line on her behalf. She amuses herself very well ; she is just now playing at blindman's buff with M. de Lionne. If she finds Brouage more to her liking, she will remain there ; if not, she will return here to await what your Eminence will have the goodness to do for her. Assuredly, the letter which your Eminence wrote her has entirely confirmed her in her generous resolution."

And then, on the morrow, from Brouage :

" Mesdemoiselles arrived yesterday in this town in good health ; the garrison gave them the best reception they could ; cannon fired salutes, and the intendant entertained them magnificently. Mademoiselle fortifies herself every day in her generous resolution ; she has never been so gay ; she plays for high stakes, and won thirty pistoles off the intendant."

In a further letter, dated the 20th, the Cardinal was informed that " Mademoiselle de Mancini had received no letter by that day's courier," and that " Mademoiselle's mind appeared very tranquil."

On her arrival at Brouage, Marie herself hastened to write a reassuring letter to her uncle.

Marie Mancini to the Cardinal.

"Brouage, 15 September.

" MONSEIGNEUR, — I cannot omit to thank your Eminence for all the kindness and affection which you express for me. For my part, at present, I do everything possible to find distraction. I arrived yesterday at Brouage, where we were accorded the most courteous reception possible to imagine. Since your Eminence has the kindness to wish that I render him an account of all that I do, I will tell him that I amuse myself the most part of the time at play, and have won thirty pistoles. Play treats me in the most unkind manner imaginable ; we do not play for high stakes—indeed, we could not play for smaller ones—but I persist in losing. The rest of the time I amuse myself by reading, particularly Seneca, wherein I remark a thousand beautiful things, which I find in addition to those of which you have told me.

" . . . I cannot say anything more to your Eminence, save that he will see by the manner in which I shall conduct myself that I have no other desire than to do my duty and to please him, and thereby to merit all the kindness which he has shown for me. I promise your Eminence that henceforth I will write very often to *Madame la Comtesse*,[1] and that I will testify to her all kinds of affection, with the greatest joy imaginable, since by that you will judge of my submission to your orders. . . . "

In her "Mémoires," Marie informs us that she had resolved to go to Brouage, a dull little coast town, hemmed in by salt marches, because the solitude of the place accorded better with her state of mind than the gaiety and bustle of the thriving port of La Rochelle. Her latest biographer, Lucien Perey, however, ascribes to her a different motive :

" She had not forgotten her uncle's threat to remove her by force out of the King's reach ; the King had not concealed it from her ; and, in the alternations of despair and of fleeting hope to which she was a prey, the poor child still believed, for a moment, in the possibility of the Spanish marriage being broken off ; in which event, it would have been easier for her to escape from that place in a little boat belonging to the fishermen, of whom there were a great number at Brouage, than from the port of La Rochelle, full of large vessels, to all the officers of which she was known. We have every reason to believe that this advice had been given her by the King, before the interruption of their correspondence."[2]

Louis XIV continued to write every day to his

---

[1] Her sister Olympe, Comtesse de Soissons.
[2] " Le Roman du Grand Roi."

inamorata, who, however, remained inflexible in her resolution not to reply, and sent her uncle renewed assurances of her entire submission to his wishes.

Marie Mancini to the Cardinal.

"October 1659.

". . . I received to-day a little letter from the King. It contained but two lines, wherein he expresses to me the joy that he experiences in observing that your Eminence is so satisfied with me. I confess to you that I have had no small difficulty in preventing myself from writing to him, and what gives me strength to do it is my duty and my desire to satisfy your Eminence. I wish thereby to make you understand that I am the most devoted of nieces."

Mazarin replied, praising her firmness, which, he declared, was such as no longer to permit him to fear any change, and assuring her that he would lose no opportunity of giving her proofs of his affection, and that she would find in him "not only a good uncle, but a father who loved her with all his heart." He advises her to seek distraction, to go and spend a few days in the pretty Isle of Oléron, recommends her to hunt and to fish and to entertain her friends, and informs her that he has directed Madame de Venel to supply her with all the money she may require.

The Cardinal also wrote to his other nieces. He begs Hortense to take no heed to what Marianne says in disparagement of her writing and her style, as he is quite satisfied with both, but to continue to write to him. He praises Marianne's verses, which afford him great pleasure, advises her, when she is at a loss for a rhyme, to seek her sisters' assistance, and concludes by assuring her that no one loves her as he does.

Marianne was much flattered by his Eminence's letter, and lost no time in sending him further proofs of her proficiency in verse-making.

Marianne to the Cardinal.

" Ier October 1659.

" Dès que j'ai reçu votre lettre
Elle m'a donné une si grande joie
Qui si l'on m'eût fait roi !
Je suis si aise que mes vers
Vous divertissent quoiqu'ils soient de travers !
Mais ils sont fort beaux pour une personne de mon âge,
Qui n'est pas volage.
Vous avez écrit à ma sœur Hortense
Qu'elle écrive tous les ordinaires
Et je crois que ses vers
Ne seront pas de bon air
Quand ils seraient du meilleur air, je pense
Que les miens les effaceront
Car ils ont plus d'esprit et de raison.
Vous me dites de prier mes sœurs d'achever mes rimes,
Mais j'ai l'esprit trop magnanime.
Ma sœur Hortense m'a prié je ne sais combien
De finir sa lettre qui ne vaut rien ;
Elle m'a fort étourdie
Et lisant toutes ses folies,
Et moi je vous dis sagement :
Je veux que vous soyez mon amant
Et je vous aimerai tendrement
Jusques au jour du jugement." [1]

In spite of the reassuring letters which he received from Marie, confirmed as they were by the daily reports of Madame de Venel, Mazarin was still far from satisfied that the affair which had caused him such terrible anxiety was definitely at an end. The persistence with which Louis XIV continued to write to the

[1] Published by Lucien Perey, " Le Roman du Grand Roi."

girl, notwithstanding her obstinate refusal to reply to his letters, seemed to indicate that his Majesty's passion had been very far from extinguished by the unexpected turn events had taken, and caused the Cardinal much uneasiness. He felt the necessity of having a confidential agent near the person of the King, who could be trusted to discharge there a similar function to that which Madame de Venel exercised so efficiently at Brouage ; and, accordingly, despatched his confidant Bartet to Bordeaux, ostensibly on a mission to the Queen, but in reality to keep watch over his Majesty and furnish his patron with a full and particular account of all his actions.

Bartet's reports did not tend to allay the Cardinal's apprehensions. He wrote that the King seemed greatly depressed ; that he was always very reticent on the subject of the Infanta, and did not appear to take the faintest interest in what Bartet, who had lately been in Spain, had ventured to tell him about that princess. Moreover, he appeared to have no heart for the gaieties of the Court, and had declined to be present at a ball given by *Monsieur*. On the other hand, when a company of strolling-players, which had recently visited La Rochelle, gave a performance at Bordeaux, his Majesty had attended it, and had questioned the actors as to whether the Mesdemoiselles Mancini had patronised their entertainment. Bartet added that, during the evening, the King seemed very sad and did not speak a word to any one.

The Cardinal, on his agent's advice, now resolved to enlist the good offices of the Comtesse de Soissons, and begged her to leave no means untried to recover the influence over the King of which her younger sister had deprived her. The ambitious and jealous Olympe consented readily enough, and made "every imaginable advance" to his Majesty, who, touched apparently by her anxiety to please him, received her back into some degree at least of her former favour. But alas! the Cardinal's satisfaction at this news was very short-lived, for almost directly afterwards he heard that the King had sent to Brouage a present of a little dog, one of the offspring of his beloved lapdog Friponne, with a collar round its neck, on which was inscribed, "À Marie de Mancini." Nor was his vexation lessened by his learning from Bartet that the departure of the little dog was known to all the Court, and that the Queen was "greatly disturbed."

This news was followed by intelligence of a far more alarming character. The letters of the King to Marie had, as we have mentioned, been addressed under cover to Colbert de Terron, the Governor of La Rochelle, who had handed them to Madame de Venel, to be passed on to her charge. There can be little doubt that, on more than one occasion, Terron and the *gouvernante*, acting on Mazarin's instructions, had made themselves acquainted with the contents of these interesting epistles, by a method which had effectually baffled detection. Now, however, the Cardinal learned, to his amazement, that the governor, whom he had hitherto believed to be entirely devoted to his interests, had been playing him false; that the letters from the King which he had handed to Madame de Venel were not the only ones from his Majesty which had reached La Rochelle; that, by the King's orders, the faithless Terron had held long and frequent conversations with Mlle. Marie, seeking by every possible argument to shake the girl's resolution to hold no further communication with her royal lover, and encouraging her to

hope that, since it had been found impossible to cele-
brate Louis XIV's marriage with the Infanta before the
following spring, it might not after all take place.

It is amusing to note that his Eminence's informant
was none other than Louis XIV's own confidential valet-
de-chambre, Blouin, "whom the Cardinal had purchased
body and soul."

Mazarin was, of course, furious with Terron,[1] who,
however, entrenched himself behind the express orders
of the King; and the Cardinal was, in consequence, compelled to overlook his delinquency and derive what
consolation he could from an assurance that he was
deeply penitent and would offend no more, but would
deal with future epistles from his Majesty "as his
Eminence might be pleased to order him."

This discovery troubled Mazarin beyond measure,
for it showed him that Louis's passion was still as
lively as ever, and he had serious doubts whether his
niece would continue to resist the entreaties of her
lover. He, accordingly, determined to take without
delay a step which would put an end to the affair altogether, at least so far as marriage was concerned.

In the early days of her rupture with the King, while
suffering all the anguish of wounded pride, Marie had
begged her uncle to find a husband for her as speedily
as possible, to save her from the humiliations to which
she felt that she would be subjected, should Louis XIV's
marriage with the Infanta find her still unwed. At the

---

[1] The devoted Colbert was greatly enraged at his relative's treachery,
which, he wrote to the Cardinal, was a reflection on the whole Colbert
family, and made him feel unworthy to subscribe himself his Eminence's
very faithful servant. So incensed was he that he even talked of proceeding to La Rochelle to mete out punishment to his faithless kinsman
with his own hands; and the Cardinal had to send him orders to forego
his intended vengeance.

N

same time, she had expressed a strong disinclination to become the wife of a foreign prince, above all of an Italian or a Spaniard, and had intimated her preference for Prince Charles of Lorraine, nephew and heir of the reigning Duke, the eccentric Charles IV, of whose good qualities she had heard much while at Court. The Cardinal was more than a little doubtful as to the wisdom of his niece's choice, deeming that the greater the distance he could contrive to place between her and Paris, the better it would be for the peace of mind of all parties concerned. But, since it appeared to him to be advisable to humour her at this juncture, he now wrote to inform her that he was sending the Bishop of Fréjus to Brouage, with proposals of marriage on behalf of the Prince of Lorraine. As a matter of fact, he had had no dealings whatever with the prince in question, and was at that moment in constant communication with Don Pedro Colonna, whom he saw almost every day during the Conferences, with the view of marrying his wayward niece to the latter's nephew, Lorenzo Onofrio Colonna, Principe di Palliano, Grand Constable of the kingdom of Naples, one of the greatest noblemen of Italy and Spain. Don Pedro wrote to his nephew, at Rome, strongly urging the advantages of a union with the family of the wealthy and all-powerful Minister ; and the Constable accepted the proposition with alacrity, notwithstanding that he was perfectly aware of Marie's love-affair, which, indeed, was by this time the talk of all Europe.

Louis XIV's marriage with the Infanta having been definitely postponed until the spring, it had been decided that the Court should spend the winter in Provence, and accordingly, on 7 October, it left Bordeaux and proceeded by easy stages to Toulouse, where it arrived a week later. The Cardinal, of course, remained at Saint-Jean-de-Luz, to discuss with the Spanish plenipotentiaries the last clauses of the Treaty of the Pyrenees, which was finally signed on 7 November; but his confidant Bartet accompanied the Court and did not fail to notify his Eminence of all that happened during the journey.

"The King," he writes, "has found means to play cards all the way from Bordeaux. On the second day, he quitted the Queen's coach and entered that occupied by the Comtesse de Soissons and Madame d'Uzès. They contrived a table, on which they played high enough to lose three or four hundred pistoles. Up to this time, the loss is not the ladies'; it is the King who loses."

And again:

"The King has resumed his relations with the countess; he has recommenced to talk and laugh with her, so that matters are progressing as well as one could desire. They dined every day in the coach without leaving it. The Comte de Soissons has also resumed with the King his former manner of paying court to him. The servants and those about them are certain that things are going from good to better."

And then, in a third report:

"The King lives on such good terms with M. and Madame de Soissons that nothing could possibly be better. His Majesty entertained them, three days since, with a ball and a play, and afterwards they partook of *médianoche*[1] together, having passed more than three hours in conversation, perhaps of things past rather than of those of the future."

---

[1] *Médianoche* was a meat supper eaten at midnight on fast-days. It was a custom which had been introduced into France from Spain. There was considerable diversity of opinion among the devout as to its lawfulness.

Bartet adds that he has exhorted the countess to make even greater efforts to attach the King to her than those which she had employed "previous to the storm raised by her sister"; that he has had occasion to reproach her with a lack of warmth in her manner towards his Majesty, which has caused him (Bartet) "inconceivable anxiety," and that though he hopes for the best, the fact that he has once witnessed his Majesty escape from the lady's hands "into those less merciful," makes him a trifle dubious as to the ultimate issue.   He concludes by urging that the countess should be appointed *dame d'honneur* to the future Queen.

From all of which it will be gathered that Mazarin, who, in his memorable despatch to the King, had expressed such righteous horror at the possibility of Marie Mancini "assuming a position which would dishonour her" and imperilling the wedded happiness of the Infanta, had not the smallest objection in the world to seeing her elder sister playing the same rôle, if thereby his own ends might be served.

In Bartet's reports to the Cardinal, Anne of Austria appears in a far from favourable light. "The Queen," he writes, "does not know herself for joy at the renewal of the King's relations with the Comtesse de Soissons. I believe that she will be still more pleased if the news flies to Brouage, where it will doubtless soon arrive."

It would appear that the Queen's horror of the misalliance which her son had contemplated was such that she was ready to welcome every means whereby he might be weaned from so disastrous a step, and even the taking of a mistress on the eve of his marriage was regarded by her with complacency, since it seemed to afford a kind of guarantee against any revival of his passion for Marie Mancini.   For that unfortunate girl,

Anne had conceived the most violent aversion, and
Bartet's belief that the news of the *rapprochement* between the King and the countess would soon reach
Brouage proved well founded, for the Queen, with a re-
finement of cruelty, directed Madame de Soissons to
inform her sister of the fact, a command which that lady
joyfully obeyed.

Poor Marie was in despair on learning that the first
result of her generous renunciation had been to pave
the way for the triumph of her detested sister, and
wrote forthwith to the Cardinal.

Marie Mancini to the Cardinal.

" Although I wrote two days ago to your Eminence,
I cannot prevent myself from troubling you again, to
tell you of all the grief I am suffering, and you can form
some idea as to whether I have reason. The Comtesse
de Soissons has written to me and informed me that the
King has done her the honour to converse with her as
he did formerly, and that she believes that I have
already heard this news, since the King had told her
that he had already written to me himself. These are
the very words of the countess's letter.

" Your Eminence can see by that, that, even in this
century of ours, there are Job's comforters. But, since,
by obeying you, I have afforded her reason for offering
me these condolences, I ask of you two things : one, to
prevent them making mock of me, and the other, to
remove me out of reach of their railleries, by marrying
me speedily, which I very humbly implore you to do."

This letter caused Mazarin profound uneasiness. If
Marie, goaded to fury by the taunts of the Comtesse de
Soissons, were to break her resolution so far as to com-

plain to the King, and the latter were to discover that the countess's letter had been written by order of the Queen, the result would be exceedingly unpleasant; and it might very well happen that his task would have to be begun all over again. He, therefore, determined to raise a new barrier between the lovers by acceding to his niece's request to find a husband for her without delay.

At the beginning of November, Ondedei, Bishop of Fréjus, arrived at Brouage. He was the bearer of the most affectionate messages from Mazarin, who assured his niece that her happiness was his chief consideration, and that he was desirous of doing everything in his power to further her wishes in regard to Prince Charles of Lorraine. At the same time, he was instructed to tell her that this project presented great difficulties, and that her uncle had found a far more suitable husband for her in the person of the Constable Colonna, already mentioned, whom he was most anxious that she should accept. The bishop hastened to add that, of course, the Cardinal left her perfectly free to decide the matter for herself, nothing being further from his intention than to force her into a marriage contrary to her inclinations. Marie refused even to consider the matter; and, though Ondedei remained some days at Brouage, and had several lengthy conversations with the girl, with the object of impressing upon her the advantages of the Colonna marriage, he was unable to alter her decision. On his departure, he carried away with him the following letter for the Cardinal :—

Marie Mancini to the Cardinal.

"November 1659, Brouage.

"MONSEIGNEUR,—I have several things to tell your Eminence regarding the proposal which M. de Fréjus has made to me on your behalf. . . . M. de Fréjus will be able to explain my feelings to your Eminence better than I can express them ; but, above all, I beg you to be persuaded that I leave absolutely to him [Mazarin] what relates to myself, and am prepared to do everything he may wish. Nevertheless, I am obliged to tell you that I could not be happy at Rome, and that I might even render the person who married me unhappy, for it would be impossible for me to accustom myself to the way of living in that country. Let not your Eminence imagine that I have other reasons for remaining in France. If an alliance with the Prince of Lorraine cannot be arranged, as I am aware that it presents many obstacles, let your Eminence choose whoever he may approve of, gentleman or prince, provided that it be soon. That is all I ask of him, since I am beginning to grow very weary of this place.

" Monseigneur de Fréjus will be able to inform you better of the state in which he finds me, and, if you were to see me sometimes, I should arouse your compassion."[1]

The Conferences with Spain terminated on 12 November, and, the following day, Mazarin started for Toulouse to rejoin the Court, where he arrived on the 22nd. The Bishop of Fréjus arrived a few days later and informed the Cardinal of the result of his mission to Brouage, laying stress on the state of exasperation into which the King's relations with the Comtesse de Soissons had thrown Marie. He counselled the Cardinal to endeavour to pacify her without delay, if he desired to avoid some awkward scandal.

On the other hand, Mazarin had discovered, on his

[1] Published by Lucien Perey, " Le Roman du Grand Roi."

arrival at Toulouse, that the intimacy between the King
and the Comtesse de Soissons was more apparent than
real ; so much so indeed that he began to fear that his
Majesty was dissimulating. He, therefore, spoke to
him of Marie in very affectionate and sympathetic terms,
adding that it would, perhaps, be as well for Louis to
assure her himself of his remembrance and regard.
Then he wrote to his niece a soothing letter, informing
her that "the person for whom she had the utmost
esteem [the King]" had charged him to assure her that
nothing was capable of making him change, whatever
people might say or write to the contrary, on the ground
of appearances which had no foundation. He also
promised not to press the Colonna marriage, "although,"
he adds, "I know that the Constable Colonna, head of
a family so illustrious, so accomplished and so handsome
a prince, with a rent-roll of two hundred thousand
crowns, is assuredly one of the most brilliant matches
possible to find, and Cardinal Colonna, his uncle, has
written to me several times, soliciting the marriage with
great eagerness, since he prefers it to all others."

As it had been decided that the Court should remain
in the South until after Louis XIV's marriage with
the Infanta, Mazarin judged it safe to put an end to
Marie's exile, and, accordingly, gave directions for his
nieces to return to Paris, whither they set out at the
end of December. Scarcely had they started, however, when the poor Cardinal had a terrible fright,
for the King, growing weary of the monotony of the
provinces, suddenly announced his intention of passing
the rest of the winter in Paris. Mazarin was in the
utmost consternation, for, if his Majesty were to carry
out his resolution, he did not doubt that all his
work would be undone in a very short time. Happily

for his peace of mind, troubles arose at Aix and Marseilles, and provided him with a specious pretext for persuading the King to remain in Provence.

During their journey to Paris, Hortense and Marianne both fell ill, and, in consequence, the little party did not reach the capital until the end of January, where their arrival was announced by the rhyming chronicler Loret in the following verses :—

> ". . . Les illustres Mancines
> Du Louvre à présent citadines,
>
> . . . .
>
> Jeudi, dans la maison du Roi,
> Arrivèrent en bel arroi.
> Les trois pucelles triomphantes
> Qui valent vraiment les Infantes,
> Mademoiselle Mancini
> Dont le mérite est infini :
> A savoir l'illustre Marie,
> Qui, sans aucune flatterie,
> Fait voir un cœur placé des mieux,
> Et digne du destin des dieux."[1]

The Cardinal had given orders for his nieces to take up their quarters at the Palais-Mazarin ; but, for some reason, at the last moment, these were countermanded, and poor Marie had, in consequence, to return to her old apartments at the Louvre, where every object served to remind her of the lover who had spent so many hours there with her. To add to the bitterness of her regrets, the portraits of the Infanta seemed to be everywhere, and the few ladies whose visits her uncle had authorized her to receive could talk of nothing else but the approaching marriage.

The ratification of the Treaty of the Pyrenees

---

[1] "La Muse Historique," 1 February 1660.

(23 January 1660) was celebrated everywhere by public rejoicings, and Marie was compelled, by the Cardinal's orders, to assist at the *Te Deum* at Notre-Dame, while, the same evening, she attended a grand display of fireworks at the hotel of Maréchal de l'Hôpital, Governor of Paris. " I could not prevent myself from reflecting," she writes in her Memoirs, "how dearly I had paid for this peace over which all showed so much joy, and no one thought that, but for the sacrifice I had made, the King would perhaps have refused to allow his marriage to be accomplished." However, in the midst of these trying circumstances, the girl showed much strength of character, her natural pride coming to her aid and enabling her to disguise the bitterness of her feelings.

If Marie had hoped to find some liberty in Paris, she had counted without her uncle. The Cardinal's orders did not permit his nieces to see more than a very limited number of people, and their vigilant *gouvernante* took care that they should not be infringed. His Eminence was anxious, above all things, that the young ladies' conduct should provide no material for gossip, and he regulated most minutely everything which concerned them.

" They must conduct themselves with discretion in Paris," he writes to Madame de Venel, " for many people will keep a close watch on the behaviour of my nieces. I am perfectly willing for them to amuse themselves, but in such a way that no one can find anything to babble about. As for their visiting, they must go, on their arrival, to see the Queen of England,[1] and pay her a visit once a month. They must also visit from time to time Madame de Carignan and Madame

---

[1] Henrietta Maria, widow of Charles I.

de Vendôme, and be careful to caress my great-nephews; and Madame d'Angoulême the younger, who is the friend of our family and very virtuous, Madame de Villeroi, and Madame de Créqui. And I do not wish that my nieces should go to the play, unless in the company of one of the last-mentioned ladies.

" I do not doubt that my nieces will be very satisfied with the manner in which Madame Colbert will treat them, for, besides the affection which she has for my family, they may derive much profit from her conversation. I shall be very pleased to learn that the said lady is often with my nieces, when they will act as they should, if they pay her great attention, with which I shall be very pleased."

Poor Marie's dejection continued, and the prospect of being compelled to assist at the fêtes in honour of the approaching marriage, preparations for which were being made on all sides, did not tend to promote a more cheerful frame of mind. At the beginning of March, she received a letter from her uncle, enclosing one from the King, to which the Cardinal directed her to reply. His Majesty's letter was couched in coldly conventional terms, and the girl did not doubt that it was the outcome of a plot hatched between the Queen, the Cardinal, and the Comtesse de Soissons to show her that Louis's love for her was dead. To Mazarin she replied :—

Marie Mancini to the Cardinal.

" March 1660.

" Monseigneur,—I am in receipt of the letter which your Eminence has done me the honour to write to me, and I do not intend to fail to obey your orders in despatching an answer to the letter which you have sent me. I assure you that it is conceived in the terms which you would desire. What troubles me, are the reports which are going about, and which cause me to doubt greatly whether I possess the honour of his [the King's] friendship.

". . . I look forward with great impatience to the month of May, when I hope to have the honour of seeing you, and expressing to you my gratitude for all your kindness."

Some days later, Marie received another letter from Louis XIV, enclosed, like the first, in one from her uncle ; and this time she replied to it without sending the letter to the Cardinal. But the King's letter caused her nothing but pain, since all that she heard confirmed her in the belief that he was paying the most assiduous court to the Comtesse de Soissons, while, at the same time, expressing some impatience at the delays to which his marriage was being subjected. Her only desire now was to awaken, in her turn, Louis's jealousy and marry before him.

All the ladies of Paris were now busily engaged in selecting the toilettes which they intended to wear at the festivities which would follow the return of Louis XIV and his bride to their capital. While awaiting the Cardinal's orders respecting those which he desired for his nieces on this auspicious occasion—for Mazarin, as we have said, regulated everything which concerned them—Madame de Venel caused all the costly gowns which the girls had left in Paris on their departure for La Rochelle to be laid out for their inspection. One day, on entering her room, Marie found a particularly dazzling confection spread out upon her bed, and, on catching sight of it, burst into a passion of tears.

Neither Madame de Venel nor Hortense, who were both present at the time, understood the cause of her grief; but when the *gouvernante* had retired, Hortense endeavoured to calm her sister and inquired why she was weeping so bitterly. "The last time that I wore that gown," replied Marie, "he [the King] said to me : 'That toilette becomes you ravishingly, *my Queen !*'" And, the next day, she informed Madame de Venel that nothing could induce her ever to wear the gown in question again.

The young girls grew very weary of the monotonous and secluded life which their uncle's orders compelled them to lead, and complained bitterly to Madame de Venel, who, in her turn, lamented in her letters to Mazarin the ill-humour of her charges. She was also much exercised in her mind at Marianne's constant demands for money. "Mlle. Marianne, if she were a preacher, would never preach, save to beg for money," she writes. "Besides what she has had from your Eminence since we arrived here, I have often given her a pistole, and sometimes two." The money, it would appear, was lost at the card-table.

The Cardinal was very angry with Marianne ; but a letter which he received from that young lady, or rather the postscript thereof, completely disarmed him.

Marianne to the Cardinal.

"Paris, the 13th of the month of April 1660.

"MONSEIGNEUR,—It is a long while since I have done myself the honour of writing to your Eminence ; but that was from fear of troubling you, for you have so many affairs to attend to that I believed you would not do me the honour to read my letters. I shall experience

the greatest conceivable joy when the marriage is concluded, for I hope soon to have the honour of seeing
the Queen and your Eminence, whom I await with
great impatience. I beg of you to often recall to mind
Marianne de Mancini.

"P.S.—Monseigneur,—As Madame de Venel refuses
to give me any money without your Eminence's orders,
I entreat you to tell her to do so, since I am greatly in
need of it. I am dying of fear lest my pockets may
be lined with the skin of the devil, for the cross always
escapes from them.[1] I believe that those of my sisters
are not more blessed than mine, as they are scarcely
richer than myself. I offer for you in all my letters the
same prayer as in this one, which is that I may always
retain your affection, etc.

His Eminence, we are assured, laughed till the tears
ran down his cheeks over the idea of pockets lined
with the devil's skin ; the Queen was equally amused,
and the request of the audacious Marianne was promptly
granted.

One of the few diversions which Mazarin permitted his
nieces was that of taking an occasional constitutional in
the garden of the Tuileries, always, it is needless to say,
escorted by Madame de Venel. The Cardinal had also
given instructions that they were to go very simply
dressed and masked, as he did not wish them to excite
attention. At first, Marie had taken but little pleasure
in these promenades, and had often excused herself, on
one plea or another, from accompanying her sisters ;
but, on a sudden, she began to evince quite an affection
for the Tuileries and was often the first to propose a
walk there. The Argus-eyed Madame de Venel quickly

---

[1] The pistole bore on its reverse side the cross of Savoy.

perceived that this change had coincided with the appearance in the gardens of a handsome young man of distinguished appearance, who seemed to regard Mlle. Marie with rather more attention than was perhaps quite consistent with good breeding, without, however, venturing to address her.   Nor was it long before she made the further discovery that the gentleman in question was none other than that very Prince Charles of Lorraine to whom Marie had so earnestly begged her uncle to marry her in preference to the Constable Colonna.

Thereupon, the *gouvernante*, to the intense disgust of her charges, was forthwith seized with a diplomatic illness, which made it impossible for her to leave her room, and, in consequence, for the young ladies to visit the Tuileries for some days.   Madame de Venel, of course, employed the interval in writing to Mazarin, to acquaint him with this new development and to ask for instructions.   The same courier carried to the Cardinal a letter from Marie, bitterly complaining of the conduct of Madame de Venel, who would not permit her to go out, and whose ill-humour, she declared, " occasioned her more suffering than his Eminence could possibly imagine."   The writer concluded by asserting that "her only hope of escaping these mortifications, and of ending the torment to which she was at present subjected, lay in his Eminence's return."

To Madame de Venel's astonishment, the Cardinal seemed inclined to ignore the attentions of Prince Charles of Lorraine, and that prince, in default of obtaining permission from the *gouvernante* to visit her charges, continued to follow them so assiduously in their walks and drives that soon all Paris was talking of it.

CHAPTER X

Journey of Philip IV and the Infanta to the frontier—Indifference of
Louis XIV to the preparations for his marriage—Letters of the King
to the Infanta—Her reply—The marriage by procuration—Portrait
of Maria Theresa—The King's present to his bride—Interview
between the King of Spain and Anne of Austria at the Île des
Faisans—Interview between the two kings—Marriage of Louis XIV
and Maria Theresa at Saint-Jean-de-Luz—Marie Mancini and Prince
Charles of Lorraine—Letter of Marie to the Cardinal after the
marriage of the King—Louis XIV makes a pilgrimage of love to
La Rochelle and Brouage—Charles IV, Duke of Lorraine, becomes
the rival of his nephew for the hand of Marie Mancini—Intrigue of
Mazarin to excite the King's jealousy against Prince Charles of
Lorraine and Marie—Visit of the Cardinal's nieces to Fontainebleau
—Icy reception of Marie by the King—Her grief and mortifica-
tion—Mazarin objects to his niece's marriage with Prince Charles, and
urges her to accept the Constable Colonna—She again refuses.

AT the conclusion of the Conferences at the beginning
of November 1659, Mazarin had pushed on the
arrangements for the royal marriage with all possible
expedition. Owing, however, to the feeble health of
Philip IV, which rendered a journey to the frontier so
late in the year out of the question, it had been found
necessary to postpone the happy event till the following
April. Further delay occurred, owing to the leisurely
manner in which the Spaniards made their preparations;
and it was the end of March before the King of Spain
and his daughter left Madrid.

So soon as Louis XIV was informed that his bride-
elect had set out upon her journey, he quitted Avignon,

where the Court then was, and approached the frontier
to receive her. But Philip IV, who deemed it indispen-
sable to his own and his daughter's dignity to travel
with a retinue which extended for six leagues and
required four thousand sumpter-horses and mules to
transport their baggage,[1] moved with unconscionable
slowness, halting at various towns to allow his loyal
subjects to entertain him with bull-fights, masquerades,
and other amusements, so that it was not until 3 June
that Fontarabia was reached, some six weeks later than
had been originally intended.[2]

Louis XIV evinced a most profound indifference to
the preparations which were being made for his wedding,
save so far as regarded the horses, equipages, and
liveries. In those which concerned the Infanta, he
seemed to take not the faintest interest. However,
since it was necessary to express to his *fiancée* the joy he
was supposed to feel at her approach, he obtained permission to write to her, and despatched the following
letter. It will be observed that he addresses the princess
as if she were already Queen.

---

[1] "The wedding-garments of the bride-elect, twenty-three complete
attires, were contained in twelve trunks lined and covered with crimson
velvet, the hinges, the locks, and the keys being of silver; twenty other
trunks covered with russia leather contained the linen. There were
also six trunks lined with crimson satin, their hinges, bars, and locks
being gold enamelled. Two of them contained presents for the Duc
d'Anjou (*Monsieur*), and the others presents to be distributed among the
ladies of the French Court. No less than fifty sumpter-horses were
required to carry the articles for the Infanta's toilette, and twenty-five
more for exquisite hangings and tapestry. In addition to all this, there
were special robes and liveries for the entry into Paris, a sedan-chair
adorned with silver, worked like Flanders lace, and for charity and other
gifts the Infanta had 50,000 pistoles."—Bingham's "Marriages of the
Bourbons."

[2] According to a letter in the Thurloe State Papers, which is cited by
Bingham, the wedding had been originally fixed for 20 April, and the
Court had intended to be in Paris again by the end of May.

Louis XIV to the Infanta.

"Auch, 25 April 1660.

"I take advantage, with the greatest conceivable pleasure, of the permission which has been given me to write to your Majesty, and to assure her myself of all the passion I feel for Her. I envy the happiness which this gentleman [the bearer of the letter] will have in beholding her sooner than myself, and although I have commanded him to represent clearly to your Majesty to what degree I shall esteem myself happy when I can explain to her my feelings by word of mouth, I very much doubt whether he will succeed in acquitting himself as I should wish. In short, my impatience is greater than I can possibly express, and, without the consolation that I have in seeing that we are drawing nearer to each other, nothing could prevent me from coming to her in person. In the meantime, my favourite conversation is to speak of the perfections of your Majesty and to listen to the accounts which I hear of them from all parts. I am entirely your Majesty's.

"L."

From her childhood, Maria Theresa, notwithstanding the fact that France and Spain were at war, had always regarded Louis XIV as her future husband,[1] and the portraits which she had seen of him, and the glowing terms in which the Maréchal de Gramont had depicted his young master, when he came to Madrid to demand her hand, had contributed to arouse in her a feeling which was hardly distinguishable from love. Knowing nothing of the Mancini affair, she believed that the

---

[1] According to Madame de Motteville, her mother had told the princess that to be happy she must either be Queen of France or a nun.

above letter expressed his Majesty's true sentiments towards her, and was duly enchanted with it.

Soon after the Court arrived at Saint-Jean-de-Luz, where the marriage was to be celebrated, we find Louis again writing to his bride-elect.

Louis XIV to the Infanta.

"Saint-Jean-de-Luz.

"Seeing your Majesty approach and my happiness with her, I cannot contain my joy, and, although it is impossible to express what I feel, I do not hesitate to send to your Majesty the Comte de Noailles, Captain of my Guards, in whom I have every confidence, to tell you that my delight is beyond all expression. I am enchanted to think that I am on the eve of being able to assure you of this in person. I desire it with a passion which has no equal, and which, in a word, corresponds to the merit of your Majesty. "L."

To this letter the princess hastened to reply, though in more measured terms.

The Infanta to Louis XIV.

"Fontarabia, the 3rd of June 1660.

"SEIGNEUR,—I have received the letter which your Majesty has sent me by the Comte de Noailles, accompanied by the demonstrations of attachment and joy which our nearer approach occasions your Majesty, and which this nobleman has assured me he has remarked in you. I have received this assurance with all the deference due to the gallantry of your Majesty and demanded by the good fortune of having obtained so great a favour. I shall endeavour always to deserve it, by conforming to the wishes which your Majesty

imposes on me, desiring that God will grant you every
felicity such as I desire.   "MARIA THERESA."

On 3 June 1660, the day on which the Spanish
Court reached Fontarabia, the marriage by procuration
was celebrated. The ceremony was performed by the
Bishop of Pampeluna, Don Luis de Haro acting as
proxy for the King of France, with the Bishop of
Fréjus as best man. The bride wore a kind of close-
fitting white cap, which entirely concealed her hair, and a
white satin gown embroidered with gold and precious
stones, which, says Madame de Motteville, a witness
of the ceremony, "made her resemble those Spanish
Madonnas whose figures are invisible beneath the
profusion and stiffness of their robes woven with gold
and silver, and whose heads are buried in enormous
ruffs." The chronicler, however, adds that her beauty
triumphed over her unsightly dress, "an infallible proof
of its greatness," and proceeds to give us a detailed
description of the princess's charms, from which it
would appear that Maria Theresa must have been a very
ordinary-looking young woman indeed, with fine blue
eyes and an abundance of fair hair, but with a diminutive
figure, heavy features, a dull white complexion, and bad
teeth.

From other sources we learn that, though of a
virtuous and kindly disposition, she entirely lacked the
faculty of pleasing, and was *gauche*, timid, ignorant, and
bigoted to the last degree. In short, a greater contrast
in every way to poor Marie Mancini it would have been
impossible to conceive.

On the following day (Friday, 4 June), Louis XIV
sent his wedding-present to his bride, accompanied by
the following letter :—

Louis XIV to the Queen.

"Saint-Jean-de-Luz, 4 June 1660.

" To receive at the same time a letter from your Majesty and the news of the celebration of our marriage, and to be on the eve of enjoying the happiness of seeing you, are assuredly subjects of indescribable joy to me. My cousin, the Duc de Créqui, First Gentleman of my Chamber, whom I send expressly to your Majesty, will communicate to you the sentiments of my heart, in which she will observe always more and more an extreme impatience to be able to tell her of them myself. He will present her also with some trifles from me."

These trifles consisted of a large casket, of which *la Grande Mademoiselle* has left us a description. It was of sandal-wood inlaid with gold, and contained everything that one could possibly imagine in the shape of jewels in gold and diamonds, such as watches, gloves, mirrors, patch-boxes ; little scent-bottles of all kinds ; cases in which to put scissors and tooth-picks ; miniatures to place in a bed ; crosses, chaplets, rings, bracelets ; a smaller casket, in which were pearls, diamond earrings, and a box for the crown jewels. " In short," says *Mademoiselle,* " one could not easily conceive that a present so magnificent and gallant had ever been seen before." [1]

The same day there was a private meeting between Philip IV and Anne of Austria, who had not seen one another for forty-five years, on the Île des Faisans, where the Conferences had been held.[2] The Queen hastened

[1] "Mémoires de Mlle. de Montpensier."

[2] The Île des Faisans was a little island in the Bidassoa, but a few hundred feet long ; the northern half belonged to France, the southern to Spain.

forward with open arms to embrace her brother, who, however, received her in the most ceremonious manner and merely pressed her hands, though he appeared to be no less moved than Anne. A little later, Louis XIV arrived on horseback, accompanied by some of his gentlemen. He came incognito, and did not enter the room where their Majesties and his bride were conversing, but remained at the door, and, " thrusting his head between the shoulders of Don Luis de Haro and the Cardinal, for a good quarter of an hour regarded the Infanta, who, at a sign from Don Luis de Haro, cast her eyes on the King of France and turned pale." As Louis XIV was there incognito, the Spanish King did not salute him and pretended to take him for some private French gentleman. But he remarked, with a smile, to his sister : " *Tengo lingo hierno !* " ("I have a handsome son-in-law.") When the Infanta embarked on the Bidassoa to return to Fontarabia with her father, Louis accompanied the barge, riding along the bank, hat in hand, followed by a number of French and Spanish nobles.

Two days later (6 June), the two kings met officially, for the purpose of swearing to observe the Treaty of the Pyrenees. They entered the conference chamber, followed by the grandees of their respective realms, and, after hearing the Treaty read, knelt down at a small table opposite one another, with a copy of the Gospels between them, Louis being on French territory, Philip on Spanish,[1] and took the oath to respect it. On rising from their knees, they embraced, and, crucifix

---

[1] With a punctilious regard for diplomatic etiquette, the building erected for the Conferences had been placed exactly in the centre of the island, and, while the northern part of the principal apartment was French territory, the southern was Spanish ground.

in hand, promised eternal friendship. Then Mazarin went to the window and waved his hand, whereupon some cannon stationed by the French on the northern bank of the river fired three discharges, which were answered by those of the Spaniards on the opposite shore.

On the morrow, the whole of the two Courts met at the Île des Faisans, when Philip IV, after an affecting leave-taking with his daughter, formally handed her over to her husband, and took his departure for Madrid with the same pomp as he had come, while the French Court returned to Saint-Jean-de-Luz, where on 9 June the second marriage ceremony took place.

Between the house occupied by Anne of Austria, where the Infanta had passed the last two days, and the church of Saint-Jean a gallery had been erected, a little higher than the street, and along this the royal party made their way. All were on foot. First came the Prince de Conti, accompanied by two gentlemen, bearing blue wands covered with fleurs-de-lys ; Mazarin, in full canonicals, followed ; after the Cardinal walked the King, who was dressed in cloth of gold covered with black lace, and wore no jewels ; and behind his Majesty came the bride, conducted by *Monsieur*, while her *chevalier d'honneur*, M. de Bournonville, walked on her left hand. "She wore a petticoat of violet velvet covered with little fleurs-de-lys, a royal mantle of the same colour also covered with little fleurs-de-lys, the facings being of white cloth edged with black ermine. The royal mantle extended, without exaggeration, ten ells ; Mlle. de Valois held one corner, Mlle. d'Alençon the other,[1] and the middle, which, as I have said, was

[1] Mlles. de Valois and d'Alençon were the younger daughters of Gaston d'Orléans.

ten ells in length, was carried by the Princesse de
Carignan. All the princesses wore veils, which stretched
about four ells, on their heads ; they were of black
crépon, and their ends were held by three gentlemen.
The Queen-Mother followed ; her trailing veil was
carried by the Comtesse de Flers. *Mademoiselle* came
next, and M. de Mancini held her veil." Throughout
the procession to the church and the marriage ceremony,
which was performed by the Bishop of Bayonne, the
young Queen wore a gold crown, so heavy that her
dame d'atours (Mistress of the Robes), the Duchesse de
Navailles, stood behind her holding it, lest its weight
should prove too much for her. At the conclusion of
the ceremony, medals of gold and silver bearing the
portraits of the King and Queen were distributed
amongst the people.

From the naïve confidences of Madame de Motteville, it would appear that, for the rest of that memorable day, Louis XIV showed himself as much charmed
with his bride as if the match had been one of inclination, instead of policy ; while, during the days which
followed, " the Queen testified towards the King the
most lively affection, and took pleasure in revealing her
passion to the eyes of all."

While Louis XIV was spending his honeymoon at
Saint-Jean-de-Luz, Marie Mancini, in Paris, had become the object of the most marked attentions on
the part of Prince Charles of Lorraine. Madame de
Choisy, mother of the famous abbé of that name, and
a lady who, according to Mlle. de Montpensier, was
" very much given to match-making," had suggested
the match to the prince, and, having taken counsel with
a certain Abbé Buti, a very adroit Italian, whom Marie

From an engraving by Nanteuil

PRINCE CHARLES (AFTERWARDS CHARLES V) OF LORRAINE

employed occasionally in her service, the latter, "notwith-standing the watchfulness of Madame de Venel, found means to acquaint her with the intentions of Prince Charles."[1]

Marie received these overtures very favourably; indeed, as her latest biographer very justly remarks, she would have been less than a woman had she be-haved otherwise. At the moment when the return of Louis XIV and his bride was about to expose her to the sneers or compassion of the Court, a handsome young prince, heir to a great name and a great fortune, had become a suitor for her hand. Nor was this her only motive. "Mademoiselle," wrote Madame de Venel to the Cardinal, "desires to cause uneasiness to him who has occasioned her so much." One thought, in fact, possessed her mind : to be married before the arrival of the King ; to show her faithless lover that another had been ready and anxious to possess the treasure which he had esteemed so lightly.[2]

An interview was arranged with the prince, and was quickly followed by others. Marie was delighted with the handsome face, the charming manners, and the in-telligence of her suitor ; all that she had heard of him was abundantly confirmed, and she felicitated herself on her acumen in having informed the Cardinal of her preference for him, even before she had made his acquaintance. But to affirm, as do M. Chantelauze and Arvède Barine, that she fell passionately in love, shows, we think, an inability to appreciate her character, and is, moreover, disproved by the sequel.

The prince, on his side, seems to have become as completely fascinated as the King had been, though

1 " Mémoires du Marquis de Beauvau."
2 Lucien Perey, " Le Roman du Grand Roi."

how much of this was due to the lady's personal charms and how much to the renown with which the passion of Louis XIV had invested her is, of course, difficult to say.   Any way, he neglected no opportunity of testifying his devotion, and Madame de Venel's post was, in consequence, very far from a sinecure.   The *gouvernante*, needless to remark, kept the Cardinal informed of all that was happening ; but Mazarin sent no precise orders and appeared inclined to allow matters to take their course.

It is probable that an alliance with the House of Lorraine would have been very favourably regarded by the Cardinal, had it not been for the fear that, in leaving Marie at the French Court, the King's passion might reawaken, in which case he could not doubt that the girl would use all her influence over Louis's mind to revenge herself upon the Minister who had thwarted her passion and her ambition.   He determined, therefore, to adopt a waiting policy, and to come to no definite decision on the matter until the King returned with his bride to Paris, when he would be better able to judge whether his niece might remain at the Court without danger.

A few days after the royal marriage, that young lady wrote to her uncle.

Marie Mancini to the Cardinal.

"Paris, 20 June 1660.

"MONSEIGNEUR,—I have experienced the greatest conceivable joy on learning that all is concluded, and that, in consequence, it will not be long before I have the happiness of seeing you.   You can well understand that I have so many reasons to cause me to desire your return that it will be necessary for me to acquaint you with them in detail, after I have the pleasure of seeing you. I am well persuaded that after having established so gloriously the interests of France, you will think of those of the person in the world who is with the utmost sincerity yours," etc. etc.

In spite of this letter, it must not be supposed that the marriage of Louis XIV had not occasioned the girl the keenest anguish. But, as we have already observed, pride with her was always stronger than love, and she was now feverishly impatient to obtain the Cardinal's consent to her marriage with Charles of Lorraine and have the affair publicly announced before the return of the Court to Paris.

If Mazarin had for a moment flattered himself that the much-desired union with the Infanta had extinguished the King's passion for Marie Mancini, and that, therefore, it would be safe to allow the latter to remain at the French Court, he was speedily undeceived. Their Majesties quitted Saint-Jean-de-Luz about the middle of June, and travelled towards Paris by easy stages, receiving in every town through which they passed the most enthusiastic demonstrations of loyalty and delight. On reaching Bordeaux, Louis XIV suddenly announced his intention of leaving the two queens to continue their journey to Saint-Jean-d'Angely and going to pay a visit of three days to La Rochelle and Brouage. He desired, he said, to travel incognito, accompanied only by two or three of his gentlemen.

The consternation of the Cardinal may be imagined. At the moment when he believed, or at least hoped, that the King was wholly occupied with his young bride,

and had no thought to spare for Marie, this fatal
passion was so little extinguished that his Majesty
proposed to break his journey, in order to make a
pilgrimage of love to those sacred spots which had
witnessed the sufferings of his mistress! And if such
were now the feelings which possessed him, what would
they be when he returned to Paris and found himself
once more in the presence of his enchantress, and
began to institute the inevitable comparisons between
her grace, vivacity, and intelligence, and the *gaucherie*,
timidity, and ignorance of the Queen!

Anne of Austria was equally alarmed, but Louis had
given his orders in a tone which did not admit of any
opposition; and the sole concession which Mazarin
was able to obtain from him, in order to minimize the
scandal which this romantic escapade could not fail to
arouse at Court, was permission to accompany the
King as far as La Rochelle, on the plea that, as he
was governor of the country of Aunis, it would appear
strange if he did not do the honours to his sovereign.

Leaving the Cardinal at La Rochelle, to continue his
journey to Paris, Louis proceeded to Brouage, accompanied only by three young noblemen, of whom one
was Philippe Mancini, but lately released from his imprisonment at Brissac, which had been greatly prolonged
by a foolish attempt to escape.

The King stayed two days at Brouage, during which
he made no effort to conceal the melancholy which
oppressed him; and Philippe wrote to Marie that his
Majesty "wept much, as he walked by the sea in the
evening; that he remained there until very late at
night, and sighed deeply." He added that the King
had expressed a wish to occupy the same room in the
château which had been allotted to her.

The immediate result of this escapade was that the Cardinal sent imperative orders to Colbert to cause his nieces to remove at once from the Louvre to the Palais-Mazarin, "since he did not deem it expedient that they should be lodged at the Louvre when the King and Queen arrived in Paris."

Those young ladies looked forward to the arrival of the Court with very different feelings. Hortense and Marianne, the latter of whom had at Easter made her first communion, without, however, becoming any the more serious, to judge by the nonsense verses which she continued to address to her uncle, could talk of nothing but the coming festivities. Marie, on the other hand, anticipated the coming of the King with an ever-increasing dread, and could scarcely bear to visit the Louvre, "for fear that her countenance might betray her."[1]

To add to her anxieties, the Cardinal, though prodigal in promises, had as yet taken no steps in regard to the proposals of Prince Charles of Lorraine, who continued to pay her the most assiduous court. Since the romantic pilgrimage of the King to Brouage, the doubt which Mazarin had always entertained as to the wisdom of allowing his niece to remain at the French Court had given way to certainty, and he was now firmly resolved that the Constable Colonna, and no one else, should be her husband. In the meanwhile, the position of affairs in Paris had become much complicated, owing to the attitude of Prince Charles's uncle, the Duke of Lorraine, which provided the Cardinal with an excellent pretext for delay.

This eccentric personage, who, according to the expression of Voltaire, passed his life in losing his States

[1] Letter of Madame de Venel to Mazarin, 7 July 1660.

and in levying troops in order to reconquer them, had shown himself on his accession to the ducal crown of Lorraine the implacable enemy of Louis XIII. He had given an asylum to Gaston d'Orléans, after that prince's conspiracy against Richelieu, and had induced him to marry his sister Marguerite, to the intense disgust of the King of France. Later, he allied himself with the Emperor Ferdinand II, and went about, at the head of a body of mercenaries, burning, pillaging, and committing all manner of atrocities. However, he did not remain faithful to his allies, who revenged themselves by luring him to Brussels, where he was arrested and conducted to Spain. A five years' imprisonment in the Castle of Toledo was terminated by the Treaty of the Pyrenees, which restored to him Lorraine, but gave the Duchy of Bar and the Clermontois to France; and it was his anxiety to recover his lost dominions which led him to interfere in the affairs of his nephew and Marie Mancini. But let us listen to his biographer, the Marquis de Beauvau :—

"We know the ill-will of Charles IV towards Prince Charles of Lorraine. Far from favouring his project (i.e. the marriage with Marie Mancini), he opposed it openly, loudly expressed his indignation against those who supported it, and went so far as to indulge in threats. Such a scandal could not fail to wound the feelings of the Cardinal. But the Duke sought to persuade him that he was only opposed to the marriage of his nephew, *because he desired to espouse Mlle. de Mancini himself,* and despatched the Duc de Guise to him to make a formal demand for her hand.

"At the same time, in order to break off his nephew's commerce and his project of marriage, he proceeded to pay frequent visits to Marie de Mancini, and to employ every kind of cajolery and persuasion to induce her to believe that he proposed to marry her himself.

"And, the better to win over Madame de Venel to his cause, he threw one day into her lap a jewel which she had refused to accept from his hand. On which, it happened that the lady, having dropped it into the knee-piece of her boot, it fell to the ground, and was discovered by a lackey, who profited thereby, since neither the Duke nor Madame de Venel cared to lay claim to it."[1]

Far from being discouraged by this rebuff, the Duke sent an ambassador to Madame de Venel, to inform her that the Cardinal had practically accorded him his niece's hand, and had promised him the restoration of his confiscated States, by way of a dowry—a statement which must have considerably astonished his Eminence, when it reached his ears; that the only obstacle he feared was the aversion of the lady, which, however, he hoped to be able to overcome with the aid of the *gouvernante*, to whom he promised mountains and marvels, if she would consent to assist him.

That discreet lady replied that she was much flattered by these proofs of his Highness's confidence, though deeply offended by the offers which accompanied them; but that she could, of course, do nothing in the matter, since Mlle. de Mancini was far too well-brought-up a young lady to regard any suitor, save with her uncle's eyes. And forthwith sent an account of the whole affair to the Cardinal.

Charles IV was quite correct in his belief that Marie regarded him with aversion, for not only was he interfering with her plans in regard to his nephew, but he was himself, apart from his rank, very far from the

[1] "Mémoires du Marquis de Beauvau."

kind of suitor to appeal to a young girl of her temperament and education. He was fifty-six years of age, "with eyes like those of a cat," coarse in his tastes, coarse in his manner, and still coarser in his conversation ; while his matrimonial vagaries and innumerable amours were the talk of Europe. He had married, *en premières noces*, Nicole, eldest daughter of Henri *le Bon*, Duke of Lorraine, and it was through her that he had secured the ducal crown. Soon afterwards, however, he declared this union annulled, and married the beautiful and witty Beatrix de Cusane, Princesse de Cantecroix. It was only after the consummation of this new marriage that Charles appealed to the Vatican to confirm the nullity of the first ; upon which the Princess Nicole solicited on her side the nullity of the second. The Pope decided in favour of Nicole, and excommunicated the Duke, who, however, ignored the Bull, and continued to live with the Princesse de Cantecroix, who followed him in all his travels and was surnamed his "*femme de campagne.*" Nicole died in 1657, but the Duke refused to ratify his marriage with Beatrix, and it was not until the latter lay on her deathbed that he consented to marry her by proxy.[1]

In spite of the discouraging reception accorded his ridiculous pretensions by Mlle. Mancini, Charles IV continued to press his suit. "The Duke of Lorraine," writes Marie, "perceiving the intention of his nephew, and fearing that the marriage would not bring his

[1] This prince, some years later, became deeply enamoured of the daughter of an apothecary, Marianne Pajot by name, who is described as a marvellous beauty, and the contract for a morganatic marriage was already drawn up, when Louis XIV, at the instance of the Duke's sister, the Duchesse d'Orléans, put an end to the romance, by causing the fair Marianne to be carried off and shut up in a monastery. Finally, at the age of sixty-two, the amorous Duke espoused Louise d'Aspremont, a maiden of thirteen summers, by whom, however, he had no children.

Eminence over to his [the Duke's] interests, and that, as the true successor of this prince, he might receive from the Cardinal advantages to the prejudice of the Duke, decided to forbid him absolutely to pay court to me, and took his place, without reflecting that, at his age, he was unable to fill it worthily, and that his persistence in following me to the Cours de la Reine and the Tuileries could not meet with the same success as the attentions of his nephew."[1]

Mazarin, who was of course kept informed of all these proceedings by Madame de Venel, must have smiled grimly, since he was fully determined in his own mind that neither uncle nor nephew should wed the girl. But though he gave no direct encouragement to either of the princes, he still allowed Marie to believe that he looked with favour upon the suit of the younger, foreseeing that Prince Charles's passion for his niece might ere long be turned to good account.

Firmly resolved though he was to remove Marie for ever out of the King's path, by marrying her to the Constable Colonna, the Cardinal was fain to admit that the execution of his project offered serious difficulties. Marie, as we have seen, had rejected the proposed alliance in the strongest possible terms, and to attempt to force her into it would be worse than futile, as Louis XIV would most certainly interfere. A surer means, however, presented itself to the Minister's mind. The young King was intensely proud; Marie was the same. Let Mazarin but once succeed in awakening Louis's anger and jealousy, by inducing him to believe that Marie had already found consolation for her blighted hopes in the love of Prince Charles of Lorraine, and all would be easy. The King would treat

[1] "La Vérité dans son jour."

P

her with coldness and disdain in the presence of the whole Court. The girl, unaware of the cause, and bitterly humiliated at such conduct on the part of the sovereign by whom, but a few months before, her slightest wish had been so eagerly anticipated, would ask nothing better than to place half Europe between the Court of France and herself. Then her uncle would represent to her the objections to her marriage with Prince Charles of Lorraine and the advantages of the Colonna alliance; and there could be little doubt what her decision would be.

The plan was no sooner conceived than executed. The Comtesse de Soissons, who had come to Paris to give birth to a son, received her orders, and, on rejoining the Court, lost no time in recounting to the King the minutest details regarding her sister and Prince Charles of Lorraine : their walks in the Tuileries, their drives on the Cours de la Reine, the devotion of the prince, the pronounced encouragement which his advances had met with from the lady, and so forth ; and we may be very sure that the tale lost nothing in the telling. Anne of Austria, on her side, ably seconded the countess's efforts, and neglected nothing whereby the gossip of the capital concerning the lovers might reach her son's ears. The pride of the monarch revolted ; however, he took steps to verify what was told him, but every one he questioned confirmed it, for appearances were in its favour. At length, on 13 July, the Court arrived at Fontainebleau, where it was to remain until the preparations for the solemn entry of the King and Queen into their capital were completed. Louis XIV's first care on meeting the Cardinal was to inquire if it were true that his niece was to wed Prince Charles of Lorraine. Mazarin replied that the

alliance was one which he greatly desired, and showed
the King the letters he had received from Marie and
Madame de Venel. Louis read them. " *Cela est bien !* "
he observed coldly, as he handed them back, while a
dark flush of anger mounted to his brow. He could
no longer doubt that he was replaced! He, the King
of France! " Few men allow themselves to be replaced; Louis XIV never allowed it, not through
vanity, but through monarchical faith. To reign alone
on the throne; to reign alone in the hearts of those
whom he honoured with his affection; the one appeared
to him as much a matter of divine right as the other."[1]
Was the greatest sovereign in the world to be exposed
to the misadventures of vulgar lovers? The very
thought was intolerable!

Mazarin heard the words, marked the angry flush
on his sovereign's brow, and, assured of the success of
his scheme, returned to Paris, and ordered his nieces
to proceed at once to Fontainebleau and salute their
Majesties.

Marie, as we may suppose, obeyed with the utmost
reluctance. "I felt," she tells us, "that, in entering the
presence of the King, I was about to reopen a wound
which was not completely healed, and of which absence
would have been better calculated to cure me." However, there was no gainsaying the Cardinal's commands,
and, on 22 July, she set out with her sisters for Fontainebleau, all three arrayed in superb toilettes, which their
uncle had ordered for the occasion and the preparation
of which had delayed their visit until this date.

On their arrival, the girls were ushered into the
presence of the King and Anne of Austria; the young
Queen was not present, having postponed all formal

[1] Arvède Barine, " Princesses et grandes dames : Marie Mancini."

receptions until after her entry into Paris. Marie, as the eldest, was the first to advance to salute the Queen-Mother, in so painful a state of agitation that she scarcely dared to raise her eyes from the ground. On presenting herself before the King, however, she raised them involuntarily, and met those of Louis fixed upon her with a look so cold and contemptuous that she felt as if turned to stone. So overcome was she indeed, that she had scarcely strength to make the three curtseys prescribed by etiquette before retiring.[1]

But she was not to escape so easily. Just as she reached the door, the Queen-Mother, who had not failed to observe the icy reception which the King had accorded her, called her back, and, desirous of prolonging the punishment of the girl whose misplaced ambition had occasioned the Cardinal and herself such torments of anxiety, began to felicitate her upon her approaching marriage. By an heroic effort, the unhappy Marie succeeded in mastering her emotion, and answered that she was as yet in ignorance of her uncle's plans in regard to her future. The Queen would have questioned her further, but Mazarin, who was present and feared that Anne was going too fast and might disclose their plot to its victim, created a diversion by beginning to jest with Marianne, and the subject was allowed to drop. At length, the girls withdrew, and Marie, hastening to the apartment which had been allotted them, gave way to a passion of grief, which the sympathetic Hortense essayed vainly to calm. "I could not have imagined," she writes, "that his Majesty would have received me with such coldness and indifference, and

[1] The first immediately after saluting the Queen, the second in the middle of the room, and the last at the door. All the curtseys had to be performed while walking backwards, the lady kicking away her train as best she might.

I must acknowledge that the astonishment and mortification I experienced made me wish every moment to return to Paris."[1]

However, she was compelled to remain at Fontainebleau for some time longer, and to strive, as best she might, to conceal the grief and mortification which consumed her beneath a smiling countenance. This was no easy task, nor was it rendered any the easier by the conduct of the Comtesse de Soissons, who took a malicious pleasure in rallying the poor girl on her low spirits whenever the King happened to be within hearing. "You find the time pass slowly when you are away from Paris," she observed to her one day; "nor am I surprised, since you have left your gallant there." To which Marie, who entertained no doubt that her amiable sister was endeavouring to embitter the King's mind against her, coldly replied: "That is possible, Madame"; a remark which appears to have still further alienated his Majesty.

Louis XIV, indeed, felt the deepest resentment against her whom he had not yet succeeded in forgetting. He thought bitterly that at the very moment that he was making his romantic pilgrimage to Brouage, this woman whom he had so dearly loved was giving to another the heart which he had imagined to be his for ever. "In his first indignation he did not pause to reflect," remarks the lady's sympathetic biographer, Lucien Perey, "that his marriage had reduced Marie to despair. He did not make allowance for the height from which she had fallen, for the suffering and the irritation which she experienced on seeing these same courtiers, who, a year before, had treated her with the deference due to a queen, to-day rally her pitilessly or affect a compassion more humiliating still."[2]

[1] "La Vérité dans sans jour." [2] "Le Roman du Grand Roi."

The testimony of a trustworthy eye-witness shows us that, notwithstanding all her efforts, the luckless girl was quite unable to disguise her feelings :

"She was beside herself with fury and despair ; she found that she had lost, at the same time, a very amiable lover and the most splendid crown in the world. A temperament less passionate than hers would have safe-guarded her from giving way to her feelings under such circumstances. As it was, she abandoned herself to rage and anger." [1]

One day, she sought out her uncle and demanded if he were acquainted with the reason of Louis's treatment of her. The Cardinal, chuckling over the success which was attending his Machiavellian scheme, assured her that the King's attitude was but assumed, in order to deceive the young Queen and the public ; that his regard for her was still as warm as ever, and that, once she was married, all would be changed. He added that, since all eyes were fixed upon her and the King, and every word which passed between them was faithfully reported to Maria Theresa, he must beg her to give him a solemn promise that she would not attempt to demand any explanation of his Majesty.

Marie was very far from being satisfied with the Cardinal's assurances. But the promise was given and faithfully observed, though it must have been a cruelly hard task, for Louis now began to push his resentment so far as to vaunt in her presence the perfections of the Queen. "It is the fault of our sex," she says in her "Mémoires," "to be unable to endure to hear others praised, even though they may deserve it. But, if the praise be bestowed by one whom we love on a person

---

[1] Madame de la Fayette, "Histoire de Madame Henriette d'Angle-terre."

who robs us of his affection, nothing is more painful, nothing more cruel. The King often made me experience this. . . . And the orders that my uncle had given me never to demand an explanation of this matter prevented me from condemning him unheard. However, the emotions of my heart carried me away and obliged me to reveal my feelings two or three times to his Majesty, who received my complaints so ill that I resolved to say nothing further to him about it."

Then she goes on to tell us that, " finding that her disease required a remedy," she proceeded to put into practice " a part of what Ovid advises in order to conquer love," which, however, seems to have been no more efficacious than the precepts of Seneca which she had studied at Brouage ; that she removed from her sight every object that was capable of keeping her passion alive, and, " seeking a specious pretext to banish it from her heart, begged her sister Hortense to tell her all the evil she could of the King." [1]

Notwithstanding the bitter mortification which the conduct of Louis XIV was occasioning her, Marie was still desirous of marrying Prince Charles of Lorraine, for whom, if she had no love, she had certainly conceived a very warm friendship and esteem. But the moment she ventured to broach the subject to the

---

[1] Hortense, in her " Mémoires," confirms this : " On the return from the frontier, we were sent for to Fontainebleau, where the Court was. The King treated my sister somewhat coldly, and this change began to make her resolve to marry into Italy. She would often pray me to tell her as many ill things of the King as I could. But, apart from the fact that it was rather difficult to speak ill of such a prince as he, who lived among us with a charming sweetness and familiarity, my age, which was then only twelve, did not permit me to quite understand what was required of me, and all that I could do to help her, stricken with grief and loving her tenderly, was to weep for her misfortunes with her, until she might bear me company in weeping for mine."

Cardinal, his Eminence raised every conceivable objection. The prince, he pointed out, was only the heir-presumptive of his uncle, who, being always ready to marry all kinds of women, would be sure to take unto himself another wife ere long, and very probably have a son, in which event the alliance would be quite unworthy of the niece of Cardinal Mazarin! How much better would it be for her to accept the proposals of the Constable Colonna, one of the greatest noblemen of Italy, who, from all accounts, was, personally, quite as desirable a husband as Prince Charles, and whose future, moreover, was not dependent on the caprices of any relative!

Marie flew into a violent passion, declared that nothing should induce her to wed the Constable, and accused her uncle of wishing to break the promises he had made her a score of times not to send her away from France or force her into any marriage contrary to her inclination. The Cardinal shrugged his shoulders, declared that his beloved niece was under an entire misapprehension, that he had not the slightest intention of forcing any alliance upon her; but that he felt it to be his duty to represent to her the inconveniences and advantages of those which happened to present themselves at that moment. Then he left her, with an assurance that there was no need for haste, and that she could take as long as she pleased to consider the matter.

Mazarin, having sown the seed, could afford to wait for the harvest, which, he felt sure, could not be long delayed, since the moment was now approaching when the unhappy Marie would be called upon to face an even more trying ordeal than that which she had had to encounter at Fontainebleau.

CHAPTER XI

Marie Mancini witnesses the entry of the Queen into Paris—Description of this pageant—Despair of Marie—She consents to marry the Constable Colonna—Visit of the Marchese d'Angelelli to Paris—Fête at the Palais-Mazarin—Illness of the Cardinal—His treatment of Anne of Austria—His last counsels to Louis XIV—His anxiety to see Marie wedded to the Constable—Hortense and her suitors—Marriage of Hortense to the Marquis de la Meilleraye—Death of Mazarin— "God be thanked; he has gone!"—His fortune—His will—Explanation between Marie and Louis XIV—The King implores Marie to break with the Constable Colonna—She refuses—Her marriage by procuration—Her departure for Italy—A disastrous journey—The Archbishop of Amasia—Meeting between Marie and the Constable at Milan—Letter of Louis XIV to Madame de Venel—Dangerous illness of Marie at Loretto—Her arrival in Rome—Letter of Louis XIV to the Constable Colonna.

ON 26 August, the King and Queen made their famous entry into Paris by way of the Porte Saint-Antoine, and Marie Mancini, by her uncle's orders, was compelled to accompany his Eminence— who was too unwell to take part in the procession—and her sisters to the hotel of Madame de Beauvais, first *femme de chambre* to Anne of Austria, who had invited the Queen-Mother, the widowed Queen of England and her daughter, the ill-fated Henrietta, the Princesse Palatine, the Duchesses de Noailles and de Chevreuse, and other ladies of the Court, to witness the spectacle. At one of the upper windows sat Madame Scarron, the future Madame de Maintenon, who, though very much esteemed in fashionable society for her wit and beauty, was not yet a member of the Court. "Madame de Beauvais, the King's first adventure ; Marie de Mancini, his first love, and Madame Scarron, who was to be his last, met together to witness the entry of Maria Theresa. Do they not make a piquant picture ?"[1]

The pageant was worthy of the occasion. In the Faubourg Saint-Antoine, a superb throne had been erected, supported by four columns and crowned with a dome. Twenty steps led up to the pavilion, which was open on three sides. It was hung with rich tapestries, and, seated under a daïs, the King and Queen received the homage of their faithful subjects. All the corporate bodies, lay and clerical, presented their duty and swore allegiance to their sovereign.[2]

This ceremony concluded, the cortège started for the Louvre. The King, wishing to leave all the honours of the entry to the Queen, did not ride with her in the triumphal car, but rode some distance in front, preceded by a glittering procession of troops, noblemen and gentlemen, and the retainers of various great personages.

Nothing in this procession attracted more attention than Mazarin's Household, which, in the enforced absence of his Eminence, was marshalled under the direction of his intendant Colbert. "It was headed by seventy-two baggage-mules : the first twenty-four with trappings simple enough ; the next twenty-four with trappings finer, richer, and more splendid than the handsomest tapestries that you ever saw, and silver bits and bells ; in short, a magnificent sight, which evoked general admiration. Afterwards twenty-four pages went by, followed by all the gentlemen and

---

[1] Lucien Perey, "Le Roman du Grand Roi."
[2] Bingham's "Marriages of the Bourbons."

officers of his household, a very large number. Next
came twelve carriages, each drawn by six horses, and then
his Guards. His Household took an hour to pass by.
Afterwards came that of *Monsieur*. I forgot, in speaking of the Cardinal's, to mention twenty-four horses
splendidly caparisoned, and themselves so beautiful that
I could not take my eyes off them. *Monsieur's* Household appeared after this very mean. Then came the
King's, truly royal, for nothing in the world could have
been more splendid. You know better than myself of
what it is composed, but you cannot imagine the beauty
of the horses on which the pages of the royal stables
rode ; they came prancing along, and were handled most
dexterously. Then came the Musketeers, distinguished
by their different plumes ; the first brigade wore white ;
the second, yellow, black, and white ; the third, blue
and white ; and the fourth, green and white. After
this, came pages-in-waiting, with flame-coloured sur-
touts covered all over with gold. Then M. de Navailles,
at the head of the light cavalry—all this magnificent ;
next Vardes,[1] at the head of the Hundred Swiss ; he
wore a uniform of green and gold, which became him
very well.

"Then . . . No, I think the gentlemen of quality
followed the light cavalry ; there were a great many of
them—all so magnificent that it would be difficult to
select any one in particular. . . . The Comte de Guiche[2]
rode all alone, covered with embroidery and precious

---

[1] Francois René du Bec-Crespin, Marquis de Vardes, son of Henri IV's
mistress, the Comtesse de Moret, by her second marriage with the Marquis
de Vardes. He was a consummate courtier, and likewise a consummate
scoundrel. See p. 245 *et seq. infra.*

[2] Armand de Gramont, younger son of Antoine II, Duc de Gramont,
and nephew of Philibert de Gramont, the hero of Count Hamilton's
"Mémoires."

stones, which sparkled delightfully in the sun. He was surrounded by servants in rich liveries, and followed by some officers of the Guards."[1]

The Maréchaux de France preceded the King, before whom they bore a brocaded canopy. "The King was attired in a suit of silver brocade covered with pearls and adorned with a marvellous number of carnation-coloured and silver ribbons, with a superb plume of carnation-coloured and white feathers clasped by a cluster of diamonds; his belt and sword were of the richest workmanship. He was mounted on a splendid Spanish horse, a dark bay, with its trappings of silver brocade and its harness sewn with precious stones.

"The Queen's pages-in-waiting, in superb liveries, followed. Then came the *calèche* of her Majesty, which might be more fittingly described as a triumphal car. It was covered, inside and out, with gold-wire embroidery, an entirely new invention, on a silver ground, the outside, both front and back, adorned with festoons in relief, all embroidered with gold and silver wire. The canopy likewise was embroidered, both inside and out, with the same kind of embroidery, and was supported by two columns encircled with jasmine and olive blossoms, symbolical of Love and Peace. All that part of the *calèche* which is usually made of iron was of silver-gilt, and even the wheels were gilded.

"This marvellous car was drawn by six pearl-coloured Danish horses, whose manes and tails reached to the ground, caparisoned and covered with trappings of the same embroidery, and all of them of such rare beauty that no painter could possibly hope to do them justice,

[1] Letter of Madame de Maintenon to Madame de Villarceaux, 27 August 1660, "Correspondance Générale de Madame de Maintenon," i. 71.

From an engraving after the painting by Beaubrun

MARIA THERESA OF AUSTRIA, QUEEN OF FRANCE

and all that one can say is that they were *chefs-d'œuvre*
of Nature, made expressly to take part in this pageant.

"The princess [the Queen] was attired in a robe on
which gold, pearls, and precious stones made up a
brilliant and imposing combination, while her coiffure
was resplendent with the Crown jewels, which, however, lent far less *éclat* to her appearance than her own
charms."[1]

"One can easily picture," remarks Lucien Perey,
"what Marie suffered during that day, and the bitter
thoughts that the triumph of the Queen aroused in her
mind. How many times had she dreamed, intoxicated
by the promises and the passion of the King, of thus
entering the Louvre, Queen and triumphant! And, to
crown her punishment, she was forced to assist at the
spectacle of that joyous and enthusiastic crowd, and to
listen to the acclamations which greeted the woman who
had replaced her. Yet, if she had been alone, and had
been able to give way to her grief! But she had to
submit to this torture before Anne of Austria, before
her uncle, to whom she was indebted for it, and before
the ladies of the Court, some of whom betrayed their
sympathy by glances of compassion."[2]

Resolved at all costs to disguise her feelings, the
unhappy girl, summoning to her aid all her strength of
character, succeeded in enduring to the end this terrible
ordeal, without betraying by word or look the anguish
which consumed her. No sooner, however, had she
regained the Palais-Mazarin and her own room, than
her strength gave way and she fainted. Madame de
Venel, who had doubtless anticipated some such *dénoue-
ment*, was quickly at hand with restoratives; but scarcely

[1] *Gazette de France*, 3 September 1660.
[2] "Le Roman du Grand Roi."

had her charge recovered consciousness and perceived
the *gouvernante*, than she entreated her to leave her,
" since she could not endure the sight of her."

Madame de Venel, not altogether displeased, we may
presume, with such a tribute to the efficiency with
which she had discharged the duties of her post, hurried
off to acquaint the Cardinal with his niece's condition.
Mazarin, however, knew when to let well alone ; and,
perceiving that any interference from him at this juncture was more likely to delay than to hasten the end
which he had in view, left the girl to her grief. His
policy was justified, for, the following morning, Marie
requested an interview with her uncle, informed him
that she was willing to accept the Constable Colonna as
her husband, and begged that he would at once announce
her approaching marriage to the Court.

Transported with joy at the success of his scheme,
Mazarin hastened to write to the Marchese d'Angelelli,
a friend and confidant of the Constable, who had been
the intermediary between him and the Cardinal, to
inform him of his niece's decision. The marquis, who
was at Brussels, at once set out for Paris, where, quickly
perceiving the true cause of Marie's resolution, he
neglected nothing to diminish the aversion which she
had for the match, painting the Constable in the most
advantageous colours, and expatiating on the delights
of Rome and the splendid position which would be hers
as the wife of so great a personage.

He might have spared himself the trouble ; the girl
had not the smallest intention of changing her mind,
since, in the interval, she had been subjected to a fresh
ordeal. A fortnight after the entry of the King and
Queen into Paris, the Cardinal had given a grand fête
to their Majesties at the Palais-Mazarin, one of the

features of which had been a supper served with a magnificence which had never been seen before. And at this supper Marie, who, as the eldest of his Eminence's unmarried nieces, was called upon to do the honours to the queens, had had the unspeakable humiliation, as it seemed to her, of waiting upon her triumphant rival with her own hands. That evening put the *comble* upon her punishment. Henceforth, she had but one desire : to shake the dust of Paris off her feet as speedily as possible.

Ever since his return from the Pyrenees, Mazarin's health, which had been infirm for some time past, had been steadily failing. His constitution was naturally good, but there can be no doubt that the enormous amount of work which he voluntarily imposed upon himself had gone far to impair it, and the three months he had spent on the marshy banks of the Bidassoa, in the midst of incessant labours and anxieties of all kinds, had hastened the progress of his malady. Early in 1661, his condition grew rapidly worse, and his physicians felt it their duty to warn him that his end was near.

Anne of Austria was in despair; while the King, who entertained a genuine affection for the Minister who had stood to him in place of a father, and who, whatever his faults may have been, had never spared himself in his sovereign's service, was scarcely less affected. Both their Majesties established themselves at Vincennes, where the Cardinal lay ill, and it was rarely that a day passed on which the Queen-Mother did not come to sit by the dying man's bedside and lavish upon him the most tender care. But Mazarin showed no gratitude ; for eighteen years he had been acting a

part, and now, in the very presence of death, he probably felt that it was time to have done with it. "He
treated her as if she were a chambermaid," says Montglat ; "and when they came to tell him that she was
mounting the stairs to his room, he frowned, and
said before his valets : 'Ah ! that woman will be the
death of me ; she worries me so. Will she never
leave me in peace ?"[1]

His conduct towards Louis XIV was very different,
and proves that the almost extravagant professions of
loyalty and devotion which his letters to his sovereign
contain must have been dictated by genuine feeling.
He now gave him at great length his last counsels,
urging him strongly to take upon himself the chief
direction of affairs, to limit the Parliament of Paris to
its judicial functions, and to reduce taxation, so far as
the necessary expenses of the Government would permit. He also advised him to avail himself of Colbert's
services in the finances, and to keep a careful control over
the operations of Fouquet. And all his directions, save
those relating to the two persons just mentioned, were
carefully committed to writing by order of the King.[2]

Two private matters greatly exercised the Cardinal's
mind during his last hours : one was the future of
Marie, the other that of her sister Hortense.

Mazarin was feverishly anxious to get the former safely
wedded to the Constable Colonna, for until that was accomplished, he was in constant dread lest some chance
might reveal to Louis the true state of the girl's feelings
towards him, and bring about a revival of his passion.
However, many vexatious delays occurred, and the Cardinal did not live to see his wish gratified.

[1] "Mémoires de Montglat."
[2] Mr. J. B. Perkins's "France under Richelieu and Mazarin."

Hortense's establishment in life occasioned him scarcely less anxiety. When it is remembered that the young girl was gifted with quite extraordinary beauty, and that it had long been an open secret that her uncle intended to bequeath her the bulk of his vast wealth, it is not surprising that her suitors should have been well-nigh as numerous as those of Penelope. The Cardinal, however, was hard to please, and the majority of them were very quickly sent about their business. Among those, however, whose pretensions received more consideration at his hands, excluding Charles Emmanuel of Savoy, of whom mention has been made elsewhere, were two future sovereigns, Pedro II of Portugal and Charles II of England.

Why Mazarin refused the overtures of Pedro, then Regent of his future kingdom, does not appear to be known ; but it is not improbable that, since Portugal was at war with Spain, he feared that the marriage of his niece to its ruler might be resented by the latter country, and interfere with the progress of the negotiations for peace.

However that may be, political considerations were certainly responsible for his rejection of Charles II's suit. During the Conferences at the Île des Faisans, Charles journeyed thither in the hope of inducing France and Spain to assist him in an attempt to recover his kingdom, and, with the idea of binding Mazarin to his cause and, at the same time, of replenishing his empty purse, asked for Hortense's hand. But the Cardinal was resolved not to break with the existing Government in England, so long as there was a possibility of renewed war with Spain ; and, besides, in common with nearly all Continental statesmen, considered Charles's chance of recovering the throne which

Q

his father had forfeited a very remote one, even with foreign aid. And so he gracefully declined the honour by insisting that, " so long as a cousin of his Majesty's (i.e. Mlle. de Montpensier) remained unmarried, he must not think of a simple demoiselle."[1]

Could Mazarin have foreseen that, in a few months from that date, without a single European sovereign stirring a finger to help him, the King would come to his own again, his answer would, no doubt, have been a very different one ; and, indeed, scarcely was Charles seated on the throne than the Cardinal, judging him to be still in need of money, sent Bartet to London to offer him Hortense and five million livres with her. Henrietta Maria, who had just concluded the marriage of her daughter with *Monsieur*, showed herself very favourable to the Cardinal's project, and urged her son to accept the lady and the dowry. But Charles's position was growing stronger daily ; the signs of hostility which had at first manifested themselves in the Parliament and the army had almost entirely disappeared ; while his counsellors were, of course, as strongly opposed to the match as had been Mazarin to an alliance between his own sovereign and Marie Mancini. And so, to the intense mortification of the Cardinal, the King, not, we may suppose, without a biting jest or two

[1] Mr. Osmund Airy, " Charles II." Mlle. de Montpensier, in her "Mémoires," says that the day after the Cardinal arrived at Saint-Jean-de-Luz, having signed the peace, he came to pay her a visit, and said : " The King of England has proposed to marry my niece Hortense. I replied that he did me too much honour, but, so long as there were first cousins of the King to marry" (meaning Mlle. de Montpensier), " I must decline." Mademoiselle adds that she thanked him, and strongly urged him to give Hortense to the King. . . . " I learned that on the death of Cromwell, the Queen of England (Henrietta Maria) had made the same proposal to the Cardinal, who had rejected it. The last time it was M. de Turenne who made it. He took a great interest in that which concerned the King of England."

about the irony of Fate, declined what he had once solicited so humbly.

When Mazarin found that his days were numbered, he resolved to have done with kings and princes, and to give Hortense and her wealth to some French nobleman who would assume and perpetuate his name. He thought of Turenne; but Turenne had an illustrious name, which he was disinclined to abandon, and fifty years, which the young Hortense was even more disinclined to accept. Then there was some talk of the Prince de Courtenay, a descendant of the youngest son of Louis *le Gros*, who could boast of the longest pedigree and the shortest purse of any nobleman in France. But, notwithstanding his illustrious lineage, the Cardinal soon decided that a young man "who had literally nothing but his cloak and his sword" was no fit match for the richest heiress in Europe. Finally, he determined to consult the Bishop of Fréjus, who had been for many years the confidant of his secret missions and family difficulties, and, indeed, very much to him what Père Joseph had been to his great predecessor.

Now, the Marquis de la Meilleraye, Grand Master of the Artillery, whose suit the Cardinal had so contemptuously rejected four years before, had stoutly declined to abandon hope, and had continued to pay Hortense the most assiduous court. During the exile of the three sisters at La Rochelle and Brouage, he had despatched couriers to the object of his adoration with almost as much regularity as had the King to Marie, thereby occasioning poor Madame de Venel much embarrassment; and, knowing the confidence that Mazarin reposed in the counsels of the Bishop of Fréjus and the venal character of that prelate, he had engaged him to plead his cause with the Cardinal, promising him a reward of fifty thousand écus, in the event of his efforts being crowned with success.

At first his Eminence would listen to nothing in La Meilleraye's favour—had he not declared that he would rather give Hortense to a lackey?—but now, on his death-bed, he relented, and, on 28 February 1661, the marriage-contract of Hortense de Mancini and Armand Charles de la Porte, Marquis de la Meilleraye, Grand Master of the Artillery, was signed by their Majesties, at Vincennes, in the Cardinal's sick-room.[1] Then, at his Eminence's request, the King created La Meilleraye a duke, by the title of Duc de Mazarin.[2]

"So soon as the marriage was concluded," writes Hortense, "he [the Grand Master] sent me a great cabinet, wherein, among other rich gifts, there were ten thousand pistoles in gold. I gave a great part of them to my brother and sisters, to console them for my opulence, which they could not see without envy, however much they endeavoured to conceal it. I never put them to the trouble of asking me, for the key always remained in the same place in which it was when they brought it, and they took all they wanted. One day, for want of some better amusement, we threw more than three hundred louis out of the window of the Palais-

---

[1] But the Bishop of Fréjus never got his fifty thousand écus. Hortense writes: "The bishop, won over previously by the Duc de Mazarin, upon promise of fifty thousand écus, neglected nothing to deserve them. But he never received them, for he returned the bond, which was given him, intimating that he would prefer the bishopric of Evreux if he could obtain it. But the King, having disposed of it to another, notwithstanding M. de Mazarin importuning him for the space of two months, M. de Fréjus claimed the fifty thousand écus, which, however, M. de Mazarin was no longer willing to pay."

[2] Mr. J. B. Perkins, in his "France under Richelieu and Mazarin," states that the Cardinal *bequeathed* this title to La Meilleraye; but this is incorrect. The Cardinal was never Duc de Mazarin. He was, however, Duc de Nivernois et Donziois, which duchy went to Philippe Mancini.

Mazarin, to have the pleasure of seeing a crowd of servants which was in the court scramble and fight for them. This prodigality, reaching the Cardinal's ears, caused him so much displeasure that it is believed to have hastened his end."[1]

Mazarin, in fact, died ten days after Hortense's marriage, on Wednesday, 10 March 1661, "meeting death with a good countenance," according to the expression of Madame de Motteville. On the previous Sunday, feeling his end approaching, he sent for M. Joly, at that time curé of Saint-Nicolas-des-Champs and afterwards Bishop of Agen, to whom he confessed, remarking : " I am not satisfied ; I much desire to feel a greater grief for my sins. I am a great criminal, and I have no hope, save in the mercy of God." The following day he received Extreme Unction, " *avec de grands témoignages de piété.*"

On the Tuesday, he requested that Mass should be said in his room, adding that he had perhaps never heard Mass once in his life in the spirit in which the Church intended him to hear it. M. Joly then asked him whether it were not his wish to make some public amends for the bad examples he had given and the scandals he had been guilty of during his life ; to which he replied, "Most willingly," and "taking a holy candle in his hand, with bare head and according to the formula of *amende honorable* and public reparation, he asked pardon of God for all his sins, and begged those whom he had offended to pardon him." Soon afterwards, he was seized with a violent spasm of pain, and was heard to mutter : "Courage ! It is necessary to suffer." About two hours after midnight, M. Joly made him kiss the crucifix, and without any other out-

---

[1] "Mémoires de la Duchesse de Mazarin."

ward sign, save a slight opening of the mouth, he expired.

Marie, Hortense, and Philippe Mancini were in an adjoining room when Bernouin, the Cardinal's *valet de chambre*, came to inform them that his master was no more. "My brother and sister," writes Hortense, "looked at one another, and, for all regret, observed : 'God be thanked; he has gone!' And, to tell the truth, I was scarcely more grieved. It is a remarkable thing that a man of that merit, after having laboured all his life to elevate and enrich his family, should have received from it, after his death, nothing but marks of aversion. But, if you knew with what severity he treated us in all things, you would be less surprised at it. Never had man manners so courteous in public and so harsh in his own house. All our tastes and inclinations were contrary to his, and to that must be added the incredible subjection in which we were kept."[1]

The Cardinal on his death-bed offered to leave his fortune to the King, but this offer, as he no doubt expected it would be, was declined. The amount of that fortune has been variously estimated. Saint-Simon places it as high as 60,000,000 livres, a sum which in purchasing power would represent between ten and twelve million pounds sterling to-day; but the majority of contemporary writers, including the Duchesse de Mazarin, who, as her uncle's residuary legatee, may be presumed to have known something about the matter, estimate it at little more than half that amount, and even this figure is probably somewhat exaggerated. "The most authentic figures as to his fortune," says Mr. Perkins,

[1] "Mémoires de la Duchesse de Mazarin."

" are in a statement prepared by Colbert, in 1658. They show that at that time it was somewhat less than 8,000,000 livres. His income, including his pensions and livings, was about 800,000 livres. This estimate did not include his art collections, his jewels, or the offices and governments which he held, and which passed to his heirs. His fortune also was largely increased after 1658, but it was probably overestimated. Whatever it was, it was an enormous one to have accumulated in the public service, and is a stain upon Mazarin's memory. He might have urged, in mitigation of his offence, that he lived in an age of almost universal public corruption, while it was not his greed, but his opportunities, which exceeded that of most of his contemporaries."[1]

The Cardinal ratified the provisions he had already made for the erection and endowment of the Collège des Quatre Nations, for scholars for Roussillon, Artois, Alsace, and Piedmont, left donations to various charities and legacies to several of his friends ; but the bulk of his wealth was bequeathed to his family. Philippe Mancini had the duchy and peerage of Nivernois and Donziois,[2] which the Cardinal had purchased from the Duke of Mantua, in 1659, half of the Palais-Mazarin, the paintings and statuary in which represented a considerable fortune, the Palazzo Mazarini at the foot of the Quirinal, in Rome, and 600,000 livres in cash. By his uncle's request, he quartered the arms of the Cardinal with his own, and added the name of Mazarini to his patronymic.

The Comtesse de Soissons received only 350,000 livres ; but, in 1660, her uncle had purchased for her,

[1] " France under Richelieu and Mazarin."
[2] Philippe Mancini took the title of Duc de Nevers.

for 250,000 livres, the much-coveted post of Superintendent of the Queen's Household.

Marianne Mancini received 600,000 livres.

Marie, in spite of all the Cardinal's fine promises,
was very badly treated in comparison with her sisters,
since she received nothing but a dowry of 100,000 livres
a year, which Mazarin had promised her on her marriage with the Constable Colonna,[1] 15,000 livres for the
expenses of her journey to Italy, and jewellery to the
value of another forty thousand.

The most favoured of all the Mancini was, of course,
Hortense, who, with her husband, inherited the residue
of her uncle's fortune, including the finer portion of
the Palais-Mazarin and its contents.[2]

Mazarin had died without seeing the marriage for
which he was so feverishly anxious celebrated, and the
fear that it would encounter some obstacle followed
him to the grave. Nor were his apprehensions ground-
less. A few days after the Cardinal's death, Marie,
believing herself released from the solemn promise
which she had given her uncle not to demand of the
King any explanation of the change in his manner
towards her, was unable to resist the temptation of
acquainting his Majesty with all that she had suffered

---

[1] "The said Cardinal," runs the will, "desires that she [Marie] shall
be content with the dowry that he has promised her on her marriage with
the Constable Colonna, which is the most illustrious and advantageous
alliance which could be desired in Italy."

[2] The old Hôtel Tubeuf, the galleries erected by Mansart, and the
dependencies adjoining the Rue des Petits-Champs. This part continued
to bear the name of the Palais-Mazarin. Philippe Mancini had the
buildings newly erected, situated on the Rue de Richelieu and the Cour
de l'Horloge, with part of the former hotel of Duret de Chevry. The
principal entrance of his hotel, which was given the name of the Hôtel
de Nevers, was in the Rue de Richelieu, and is now that of the Bibliothèque Nationale.—Amédée Renée, "Les Nièces de Mazarin."

since his return to Paris : the bitter mortification of finding that the sacrifice she had made for his sake had earned her, instead of his esteem and gratitude, nothing but coldness and disdain, the torture she had endured on the day of his entry into Paris, which was renewed every time she saw the Queen, and so forth.

The result may easily be imagined. As he listened to the girl's burning words, Louis perceived that all that he had been told about her infatuation for Prince Charles of Lorraine was false, and that, in his blind jealousy, he had allowed himself to be made the dupe of a clever conspiracy. All his passion revived, and, casting himself at her feet, he swore that he adored her still, and entreated her to break with the Constable Colonna, promising to take upon himself the whole responsibility for the rupture. But Marie, though deeply moved, was inflexible. What position, she asked, was he able to offer her ? Could it be possible that he imagined that she, whom he had promised to make his wife and Queen of France, would ever stoop to become his mistress ? If the Constable Colonna, she declared, now that her uncle was dead, refused to accept her as his wife, it was her intention to enter a convent.

The King, however, whose passion her resistance only served to inflame, refused to abandon hope. He recommenced to visit her every evening, as had been his custom before her exile to La Rochelle, paid her the most delicate attentions, and strove by every means in his power to induce her to remain in France. Prince Charles of Lorraine, on his side, taking heart of grace from the fact that the Constable Colonna had not yet signed the marriage-contract which had been sent to Rome for his approval, and was commonly credited with a desire to break off the match now that Marie's fortune had proved to be far below what every one had expected, continued to press his suit, and lost no opportunity of testifying his devotion. "The young Prince Charles of Lorraine," writes Hortense, "loved my sister passionately, pressed her to marry him, and continued this pursuit, even after the Cardinal's death. The Queen-Mother, who by no means wished her to remain in France, charged Madame de Venel to break off the intrigue at any cost; but all her efforts would have been useless, had they not been seconded *by certain reasons unknown to any one.* And, although the King had the kindness to offer her [Marie] the choice of any one else in France for a husband, if M. de Lorraine did not please her, and showed himself sensibly displeased at her resolution to leave France, her evil star drew her into Italy."[1]

These reasons, "unknown to any one," must have been perfectly well known to Hortense, who, however, writing only some fifteen years after the events we are relating, was naturally reluctant to publish them to the world. Marie was no Gabrielle d'Estrées or Jacqueline de Beuil to contract a marriage for the convenience of a king; other women might ardently covet the post of royal favourite, and find in the power and influence attached to it abundant compensation for their dishonour; but to her, who had once believed that so very different a destiny awaited her, the position would be intolerable. And she refused absolutely to break with the Constable Colonna.

At the beginning of May, news arrived that the Constable had signed the marriage articles at Rome, and that a courier was on his way with them to Paris. Louis

[1] "Mémoires de la Duchesse de Mazarin."

XIV made no attempt to conceal the chagrin which Marie's coming departure occasioned him, and meeting her an evening or two later in the Queen-Mother's apartments, said : "Destiny, which is above kings, has disposed of us contrary to our inclinations, Madame ; but it will not prevent me from seeking to give you proofs of my esteem and attachment in whatever country of the world you may be." And then, turning to Madame de Venel, who was standing by, he added : "And you, Madame, I beg you to be my surety, and to accompany the Constabless as far as Milan, where the Constable should come to receive her, and to write me a full account of the incidents of the journey."

A few days later, a courier arrived with the expected articles, and the marriage was celebrated in the King's chapel at the Louvre, by the Archbishop of Amasia, afterwards Patriarch of Jerusalem, uncle of the Constable Colonna, for whom the Marchese d'Angelelli stood proxy.[1] The ceremony concluded, Marie was treated as a foreign princess, addressed by their Majesties as "my cousin," and accorded the *tabouret*[2] in the presence of the Queen.

The preparations for departure were soon completed, and, accompanied by the Archbishop of Amasia, the Marchese d'Angelelli, and Madame de Venel, and

---

[1] She had been affianced the previous evening in the King's cabinet, an honour commonly reserved for Princes and Princesses of the Blood.

[2] The *tabouret* was a stool, on which Princes and Princesses of the Blood, foreign princes and princesses, cardinals, dukes and duchesses—in fact, all persons whom it was customary for their Majesties to address as "cousin," had the privilege of seating themselves in the presence of the Queen. Occasionally, as a special favour, it was accorded to other persons. Thus Madame de Montespan, although only a marchioness—she could not be created a duchess, as were Louise de la Vallière and Mlle. de Fontanges, because that step would have involved the elevation of her husband—was given the *tabouret* by Louis XIV, in 1679.

escorted by a hundred mounted guards, under the command of M. de Monceau, one of the gentlemen of the late Cardinal's Household, she set out for Italy. As on the occasion of her departure for La Rochelle, two years before, Louis XIV conducted her to her coach and gravely kissed her hand. He was evidently deeply moved, but no word escaped him. Marie was less self-controlled, and burst into tears as the coach drove away.

They were never to meet again.

The journey to Milan was a most trying and calamitous one, and must have seemed to Marie, who, like nearly all her family, was intensely superstitious, the worst possible augury for the future. A few days after leaving Paris, a fever broke out among the servants, of which more than one of them died. The weather, while crossing the Simplon Pass, was terrible ; the road was in an indescribable condition, and several men of the escort and their horses fell over a precipice and were dashed to pieces. Nor did their disasters end when the mountains had been traversed, for the first evening after their arrival in Italy, the balcony of the house in which Marie was lodged gave way, precipitating a number of the party, who had gathered there to admire the view, to the ground. The unfortunate owner of the house was killed, while several others received more or less serious injuries. "One saw only broken heads, arms, and legs ; one heard only the cries of the injured. It was a frightful spectacle and calculated to move the hardest heart."

To add to the grief and terror which these calamities must have occasioned her, poor Marie was so unlucky as to offend the Archbishop of Amasia, a most unpleasant personage, who appears to have been half mad when sober and altogether so when drunk;[1] and the estimable prelate revenged himself by commiserating his niece on the unhappy fate which, he declared, awaited her with the Constable, whom he depicted as a libertine of the most abandoned kind and a ferocious tyrant, who would keep her a close prisoner in his palace, and, on the slightest suspicion, would not scruple to beat or even to poison her. Nor did he neglect to relate to her, embellished with a thousand gruesome details, the terrible legend of a Princess Colonna, who was immured by her husband in the dungeon of an old castle, where she remained until every one believed her dead, and would assuredly never have seen the light of day again, had not her moans attracted the attention of a passer-by, who informed her relatives of her plight.

The unfortunate Marie was so overcome by the archbishop's discourse, that she announced her intention of immediately petitioning the Pope to annul her marriage, and it required all the efforts of the Marchese d'Angelelli and the Constable's brother, the amiable Abbate Colonna, afterwards Prince of Sonnino, who joined them a day or two after they entered Italy, to reassure her.[2]

A few miles from Milan, the party was met by the Constable Colonna and one of his friends, the Marqués

---

[1] He was the youngest brother of the Constable's father, Filippo Colonna, and was born in 1602. In his youth, he bore the title of Duca di Marsi. Having killed a young nobleman in a duel, he was compelled to leave Rome, and took service with the Spaniards in Flanders. In 1638, stimulated perhaps by remorse for his crime, he returned to Rome and took Orders. He did not, however, deem it necessary to lay aside the manners and morals of the worst type of mercenary soldier with his sword and uniform.

[2] Letter of the Abbé Benedetti to Lionne, Archives des Affaires Étrangères, published by Lucien Perey, "Une Princesse romaine au xvii⁰ siècle : Marie Mancini Colonna."

Spinola de los Balbases,[1] who, at Colonna's request, advanced first to greet Marie, representing himself to be her husband. As the marquis was middle-aged and of far from prepossessing appearance, while she had been led to believe that, to the eye at least, the Constable was all that could be desired, the poor girl was bitterly disappointed, "received his compliments with a coldness equal to her surprise," and, turning to one of her waiting-women, remarked in French, that, "if this were the husband intended for her, she would decline to have him, and that he might seek a wife elsewhere."

The waiting-woman, however, who happened to have seen a portrait of Colonna, recognised him instantly, and pointed him out to her mistress, who was immensely relieved at finding that she had been mistaken.

The Constable, having welcomed his bride, conducted her to a little pleasure-house in the vicinity, where a sumptuous repast had been prepared, after partaking of which, they proceeded to Milan, at whose gates they were received by the Governor, the Duca di Gaetano, and the principal citizens.

Milanese society was, of course, eager to make the acquaintance of the lady who had had the King of France at her feet, and, during the few days which Marie and her husband spent in the city, "the ladies of the first quality vied with one another in giving magnificent entertainments in her honour." "But," continues Marie, "the fatigues of the journey, the grief at finding myself separated from my relatives, and, above all, alas! my sorrow at having left France, rendered me in the worst humour conceivable, which occasioned consider-

---

[1] He was an Italian, although he bore a Spanish title, and a grandson of Ambrogio Spinola, the celebrated general of the Thirty Years War. The marquis, a year or two later, married a sister of Lorenzo Colonna.

From an engraving after the drawing by Giacomo Bichi

LORENZO ONOFRIO COLONNA, PRINCIPE DI PALLIANO,
GRAND CONSTABLE OF THE KINGDOM OF NAPLES

able uneasiness to the Constable, who did everything possible to afford me diversion."[1]

Colonna, on the other hand, seems to have been charmed with his bride, the more so, since he found that certain fears which he had entertained in regard to the nature of her relations with Louis XIV had been without justification. "The Constable," writes Hortense, "who had at first believed that the love of kings could not be innocent, was so delighted to find the contrary in the person of my sister, that he made no account of not being the first who had gained her heart. He lost the bad opinion which, like all Italians, he possessed of the liberty accorded to ladies in France, and decided to allow her the same liberty at Rome, since he found she used it so discreetly."[2]

As Colonna was anxious to reach Rome before the heat of the summer reached its height, he and his young wife only remained ten days in Milan, and then set out on their journey southward, while Madame de Venel and the escort returned to Paris. Immediately on her arrival in Milan, the *gouvernante* had written as Louis XIV had enjoined upon her, giving him a full account of the incidents of the journey; but she appears to have said nothing about the health of the Constabless, who was very far from well. To this letter, the King replied in terms which show the tender interest which he still felt for Marie.

Louis XIV to Madame de Venel.

"Fontainebleau, 20 June 1661.

"MADAME DE VENEL,—I have been very pleased to hear, from your letter from Milan, of the happy suc-

[1] "La Vérité dans son jour."
[2] "Mémoires de la Duchesse de Mazarin."

cess of your journey and the termination of your adventures.

"After having guarded a treasure with the utmost vigilance, there was nothing more honourable than to hand it over in perfect safety to the person to whom it belongs, as you have done, thereby proving still further that you are deserving of the custody of more important ones,[1] which I have resolved to entrust to you the moment I am able."[2]

The Constable and Marie journeyed by easy stages to Loretto, where the latter became so ill that it was impossible for her to proceed further. A violent attack of brain-fever declared itself, and for many days the unhappy girl lay between life and death. Her husband, in despair, sent out messengers to scour the town and all the country round for doctors, and at one time nearly a dozen medical gentlemen were gathered round the sick-bed. All agreed that the illness was a dangerous one, but no one seemed able to propose any remedy which his colleagues felt themselves justified in trying. To make matters worse, the Archbishop of Amasia persecuted the luckless invalid with zealous exhortations, "never entering her room without informing her that no hope of saving her life remained, and that she must prepare for death." At length, two celebrated physicians arrived from Rome, followed closely by Marie's uncle, Cardinal Mancini. The Roman doctors soon got rid of the incompetent throng which beset the house ; the Cardinal, a kindly and practical man, turned

---

[1] As a reward for her services, Mazarin and Anne of Austria had some time before persuaded the King to promise Madame de Venel the post of *sous-gouvernante* to his daughters, should any be born to him.
[2] " Œuvres de Louis XIV."

the archbishop as courteously as he could out of the sick-room, and the Constabless began to mend.[1] At length, she was pronounced fit to continue her journey, and, towards the end of July, arrived in Rome.

During her illness, Louis XIV, who had learned from the Duchesse de Mazarin of her sister's condition, showed himself much concerned, and wrote to Loretto, requesting that a courier should be despatched every day to inform him how she fared. On reaching their destination, the Constable Colonna lost no time in acquainting the King with their safe arrival and of his wife's convalescence, to which his Majesty replied in the following letter, wherein it is not difficult to detect an undercurrent of bitterness.

Louis XIV to the Constable Colonna.

"Fontainebleau, 6 August 1661.

"My Cousin,—After the fatigues of a long journey and a dangerous illness, it is not a small thing that my cousin, your wife, should have at last arrived in Rome in a state of convalescence. I have been very pleased to learn this good news, from the letter which you have written me, trusting that the repose and satisfaction of being with you will soon restore her to perfect health, a consummation which I desire with all my heart. I have remarked also with great pleasure the

---

[1] But one of the doctors to whom she owed her life nearly lost his. Benedetti writes : " Supping one day with the doctors who had been summoned from Rome, the Archbishop of Amasia hastened to furnish them with an occasion to practise their art upon themselves. One of the doctors having dared to contradict him about the cause of Madame's illness, he threw a knife full at his chest, which was intended to kill him, and inflicted so grievous a wound that he was for some days in danger of death. The following morning, the archbishop went complacently to make his excuses, remarking that he had been somewhat heated with wine."

R

sentiments which she has preserved towards myself, and that they are shared by you. Be assured that mine will ever be for you and her such as you will desire them to be, and that I shall joyfully embrace every occasion of proving it to you by my actions."[1]

[1] " Œuvres de Louis XIV."

CHAPTER XII

Failure of Maria Theresa to gain the affection of Louis XIV—The King resumes his relations with the Comtesse de Soissons—But leaves her for Louise de la Vallière—The Marquis de Vardes—He becomes the countess's lover—And intrigues with her and the Comte de Guiche against La Vallière—The Spanish letter—Madame de Soissons and Vardes attempt to supplant La Vallière by Mlle. de la Motte-Houdancourt—Discovery of the authors of the Spanish letter plot—Madame de Soissons exiled, but soon recalled to Court—Marriage of Marianne Mancini to the Duc de Bouillon—Her patronage of men of letters—Her friendship with La Fontaine—She urges him to compose his fables—And his tales—Her intrigue to secure the failure of Racine's " Phèdre."

"DESTINY, which is above kings, has disposed of us contrary to our inclinations," Louis XIV had said on the eve of Marie Mancini's marriage. If such were the case with the girl whom he had so passionately loved, it was even more so with himself. It would, indeed, have been difficult to find a woman more un-suited in every way, save that of birth, to be the consort of the young King of France than the Infanta Maria Theresa. To retain the affections of Louis XIV, a woman required more than beauty : she needed to possess, and to possess in a very marked degree, the faculty of pleasing. This was, in great part, the secret of the influence of Marie Mancini, of the twelve years' empire of Madame de Montespan, of the long ascendency of Madame de Maintenon. The lack of it accounts for the fall of La Vallière from favour, notwithstanding all the claims she had upon the consideration of her royal lover, the brief reign of Mlle. de Fontanges, and the failure of many another empty-headed beauty to make more than the most transient impression upon his Majesty's heart. And it was in this, far more than in physical attractions, that poor Maria Theresa was found wanting.

Her ignorance was profound; she had come, for instance, to France unable even to read, much less to converse, in French, and appears to have experienced the greatest difficulty in obtaining even a superficial knowledge of the language. Reared in the most cramping conditions of Spanish etiquette, her every word and action were governed by the most punctilious regard for ceremonial; while her timidity was such that she was ill at ease in the company of any but her immediate attendants and the Queen-Mother, and positively trembled in the presence of the King, whom, however, she loved with an almost pathetic devotion. Under these circumstances, it is scarcely a matter for surprise that Louis, unable to derive any pleasure from her society, should have sought companionship and amusement elsewhere. Nor had he far to seek.

"The King," writes La Fare, "was on the most intimate terms with the Comtesse de Soissons, whom he visited every day." The intriguing Olympe had received, as the reward of her assistance in the Cardinal's little plot to keep Louis XIV and her sister apart, the post of Superintendent of the Queen's Household, in virtue of which she had become the greatest lady of the Court. But her ambition was far from satisfied : she dreamed of an empire such as no woman had exercised in France since the days of Diane de Poitiers, and was resolved to leave no means untried to attain her goal.

That, however, she was never to reach, nor even to approach. A flirtation with the charming Henrietta of England, who, at the end of March 1661, had become the wife of *Monsieur*, an affair which greatly exercised the minds of the Queen-Mother and Maria Theresa, though it would appear to have been innocent enough, was followed by the rise to favour of the gentle La Vallière; and if his Majesty continued his visits to the Hôtel de Soissons, it was but too evident that it was the high play which went on there rather than the *beaux yeux* of its mistress which was the attraction.

But, though the King remained insensible to the blandishments of the countess, he was not insensible to the mortification which that lady was powerless to conceal at the cessation of those tender passages between them, from which she had hoped so much. Perhaps, he believed that, as with La Vallière, it was the man, and not the king, whom Madame de Soissons loved ; perhaps, he feared that the countess, ever a dangerous person to affront, might vent her displeasure on his inoffensive Louise. Any way, he determined to provide her without loss of time with a new gallant, and, accordingly, ordered his friend and confidant, the Marquis de Vardes, to lay siege to her heart.

A terrible fellow was this Marquis de Vardes. Handsome, brave, audacious, and wholly devoid of scruple, the anecdotes about him are innumerable. There was not a woman so virtuous or so highly placed to whose love he did not presume to aspire ; not a man, however great his skill with the rapier, whom he would not "call out" on the slightest provocation. He fought with the Duc de Saint-Simon, father of the author of the famous "Mèmoires," and the Comte du Lude ; he overcame the resistance of the beautiful Duchesse de Roquelaure, whose virtue had until then withstood all assaults upon it,[1] and even dared to raise his eyes to the Princesse de Conti—she who had publicly rebuffed the advances of Louis XIV himself—and met with no worse fate than a gentle reproof; and there are, indeed, some chroniclers who affect to believe that his efforts in that quarter might eventually have been crowned with success, had it not been for the vigilance of her jealous husband. When we mention that to his skill in fencing and love-making he joined a biting wit and a talent for backstairs intrigue which it would have been difficult to rival, it will be admitted that M. de Vardes was a force to be reckoned with at the Court of *le Grand Monarque*.

M. de Vardes hastened to obey his sovereign's command; he would have obeyed with equal promptitude, though, perhaps, with less willingness, if Madame de Soissons had been a withered dowager of three-score, instead of a handsome young woman of twenty-five, for he prided himself on being a consummate courtier, which meant that there was no action too dishonourable for him to commit in order to gain his Majesty's favour. Olympe, on her side, received his professions of devotion very graciously. Was not her new *soupirant* "the best-made and most amiable man in France"?[2] She was calculating and ambitious, but she was an Italian and naturally ardent. Soon her liking for the marquis had developed into a veritable passion, which was patent to

---

[1] During one of his visits to the duchess, the duke, who was exceedingly jealous, returned home unexpectedly, and, to avoid compromising the lady, M. de Vardes was compelled to take refuge in a cellar, where he remained for two days. On emerging from his retreat, faint with hunger and thirst, and with a fine coat completely ruined, he decided that the game was not worth the inconveniences attached to it, and poor Madame de Roquelaure saw him no more. After an unsuccessful attempt to console herself with *Monsieur*, she died, so the chroniclers say, of a broken heart.

[2] "Mémoires de Daniel de Cosnac."

every one, save her husband, who was the most un-suspicious, or, perhaps, the most complacent, of men. None of the countess's admirers need fear that they would be required to take shelter in the cellars of the Hôtel de Soissons.

But, though Olympe had found some consolation for her wounded vanity in the attentions of Vardes, she was none the less resolved to separate the King and La Vallière. She, therefore, took counsel with her lover and the Comte de Guiche, son of the Maréchal de Gramont, a vain and foolish young man,[1] who had a grudge against La Vallière for having once rejected his addresses, and decided to raise a scandal before which, they judged, the sensitive girl must inevitably succumb.

The plan of the conspirators was to send an anony-mous letter, containing a full, true, and particular account of the manner in which his Majesty spent a great part of his leisure, to the Queen, who, thanks to the exertions of Anne of Austria, was still under the delu-sion that there was " nothing but mere friendship " between her husband and La Vallière. This letter was composed by Madame de Soissons and Vardes, and trans-lated into Spanish by Guiche, who was well acquainted with that language, as Maria Theresa was still so ignorant of French that she might have failed to under-stand it, if the vernacular had been employed. It was then enclosed in an envelope addressed in the hand-writing of the Queen of Spain—which Madame de Soissons had stolen from her royal mistress's apart-ments—in order to make sure of its reaching its destination unopened.

Fortunately for poor Maria Theresa's peace of mind,

[1] But in war, according to Madame de Sévigné, " a hero of romance."

the letter fell into the hands of Donna Molina, a Spanish lady in the Queen's service, who, fearing that it might contain some bad news concerning the King of Spain, who was seriously ill, took upon herself the responsibility of opening it, and promptly carried it to Louis XIV.

The King, having read the letter, "blushed, and appeared surprised at the adventure." He resolved that whoever had had the presumption to meddle with his private affairs should have abundant cause to rue their temerity; but, as the person whom he employed to investigate the matter was none other than Vardes himself, it is hardly surprising that the culprits escaped detection.

Undeterred by the failure of their plot, a few months later, Madame de Soissons and Vardes brought forward a rival to La Vallière, in the person of Mlle. de la Motte-Houdancourt, one of the Queen's *filles d'honneur*, " who, though no sparkling beauty, had drawn away lovers from the celebrated Menneville(one of Fouquet's mistresses).'" She very nearly succeeded in drawing away La Vallière's as well, for she contrived to persuade the King that, although hitherto of unblemished virtue, she was violently in love with him, and wrote him the most eloquent letters, which had been composed for her by Vardes and the countess. Moreover, Louis's passion was stimulated by the rivalry of the Chevalier de Gramont, the hero of Count Hamilton's " Mémoires," who, it appears, had never given the damsel a thought until he found that she was honoured by his sovereign's attentions, when he forthwith concluded that she must be worthy of his. He soon had reason to regret his folly in believing that

---

¹ Hamilton's " Mémoires de Gramont." The King had paid this damsel considerable attention during the winter of 1657–8, but his growing passion for Marie Mancini had prevented the affair going very far. See p. 75 *supra*.

love renders all things equal, for Mlle. de la Motte, who had no use for such small fry as the chevalier when there was a king ready to fall at her feet, complained of his importunities to her royal admirer, and, one fine day, M. de Gramont received a peremptory order to retire from Court.

Meanwhile, poor La Vallière, whom kind friends had, of course, taken care to inform of what was in progress, was plunged in the depths of despair. But Louis, piqued by the resistance of La Motte, who continued to simulate virtue with considerable skill, paid no heed to her reproaches, and pressed his suit with such ardour that the Duchesse de Navailles, the Queen's *dame d'honneur*, who was responsible for the good conduct of La Motte and her colleagues, deemed it expedient to place iron gratings before the windows of her charges' apartments, in order to guard against accidents. This precautionary measure greatly incensed his Majesty, who stigmatized the duchess as "an extravagant reformer of the human race"; and Vardes, quick to perceive his opportunity, now informed the King that he had discovered that the writer of the anonymous letter to Maria Theresa was Madame de Navailles herself; upon which, Louis, without apparently troubling to examine the supposed proofs, promptly banished the poor lady and her husband from Court.

At length, Mlle. de la Motte, acting on instructions from the Comtesse de Soissons, professed herself ready to surrender. She made, however, one stipulation : the instant dismissal of La Vallière. Louis protested, but the lady was inexorable, and it is quite probable that she would have carried her point, had not Anne of Austria, who, though she had no love for La Vallière, had still less for the intriguing maid-of-honour, intercepted a letter written by one of Madame de Soissons's friends to La Motte, and containing overwhelming proof that the girl was a mere tool in the hands of others, and laid it before her son. Highly indignant at the manner in which he had been tricked, the King at once broke off all relations with La Motte, who was shortly afterwards dismissed from the Queen's service, for having received one of her admirers, the Marquis de Richelieu, in her apartments, in defiance of her Majesty's orders.

After this second failure, Madame de Soissons had recourse to other and far more serious methods of warfare against La Vallière—methods which were one day to lead to her disgrace and expulsion from France ; but of this we shall speak later on.

In the meanwhile, it is satisfactory to know that, in 1665, the real authors of the Spanish letter plot were discovered, and the poor Duc and Duchesse de Navailles exculpated, recalled to Court, and reinstated in the royal favour. Had not the conspirators fallen out among themselves, however, it is highly improbable that the truth would ever have come to light. The facts were as follows.

The Comte de Guiche was in love with Henrietta of Orléans (*Madame*), who certainly seems to have given him every encouragement to hope for the best, or worst, though, as in the opinion of La Fare—a writer by no means inclined to credit any lady with virtue who had not given ample proof of possessing it—the princess was " virtuous, though a trifle coquettish," it is improbable that the affair ever went beyond the bounds of a violent flirtation.[1] The Marquis de Vardes also aspired

[1] For further details in regard to the relations between *Madame* and the Comte de Guiche, see Madame de la Fayette's " Histoire de Madame Henriette d'Angleterre," and Julia Cartwright's (Mrs. Henry Ady) " Madame."

to add *Madame* to the list of his conquests, intrigued
against Guiche, whose confidant he was, and succeeded in
getting him sent to Lorraine. So cleverly did he manage
the affair that Guiche left Paris without having the least
suspicion that he owed his separation from his inamorata
to the machinations of the marquis, to whom he arranged
to entrust his correspondence with the princess. In virtue
of his position as intermediary, Vardes enjoyed constant
access to *Madame*, and, having won her confidence, proceeded to make love to her on his own account. At first,
Madame appeared far from displeased at his attentions,
and drove the Comtesse de Soissons frantic with jealousy ;
but her heart still belonged to the absent Guiche, and
she declined to transfer it to the marquis. Angered by
the rejection of his suit, Vardes refused to deliver up
certain very tender letters which the lovers had confided
to his care, and also informed the King of the contents
of a letter of another kind, which *Madame* had entrusted
to him for transmission to her brother, Charles II, in
England. Not content with this treachery, he next
proceeded to let fall some highly injudicious remarks
concerning the princess, and one day observed to the
Chevalier de Lorraine, who was paying court to one of
Henrietta's *filles d'honneur*, that it was a pity that he
wasted his time on the maid, when the mistress was such
an easy conquest. This speech was duly reported to
Madame, who complained to the King, with the result
that one evening M. de Vardes supped in Bastille.

On learning of the misfortune which had befallen her
lover, the Comtesse de Soissons was beside herself with
grief and indignation. Her wrath against *Madame*,
who, she declared, had twice robbed her of him, "first
by love and now by hatred," knew no bounds. Straight
to the King she went, thinking only of revenge, and

determined to repay the probable ruin of her lover by that of Guiche, against whom she proceeded to launch all manner of accusations. He had committed we know not what crime against the State ; he had attempted to betray Dunkerque to the English ; he had written the Spanish letter to the Queen. *Madame*, to whom Guiche had, some time before, confided the truth about that too celebrated epistle, arrived upon the scene almost at the same moment, and denounced Vardes and the countess. Between the two furious women his Majesty must have spent a very unpleasant quarter of an hour, but, by way of compensation, he ended by learning everything.

In the result, Vardes was removed from the Bastille to the citadel of Montpellier, and subsequently banished to his government of Aigues-Mortes, in Provence, where he remained until 1683 ; Guiche was sent on foreign service ; while Madame de Soissons and her husband—who, poor man! was entirely innocent of any complicity in the affair—were ordered to retire to Champagne, of which province the count was governor.

Their exile was not, however, of long duration, and, at the end of a few months, Olympe returned to Paris and resumed her functions as Superintendent of the Queen's Household and her life of pleasure and intrigue. The King, however, seldom visited the Hôtel de Soissons, and treated the countess somewhat coldly, if always with courtesy. To console herself for the loss of Vardes, Olympe took a disciple of his, the Marquis de Villeroi, called by the ladies "*le Charmant*," into favour, and ad-mitted him to her hotel on the same footing as that which that Titan of intrigue and gallantry had formerly occupied. If we are to believe the *chansons* of the time, M. de Villeroi had **more than one** coadjutor in his office of *amant-en-titre;* but that does not seem to be the opinion of the best-informed contemporary writers, and historians like Walckenaer, who accuse the countess of leading a life of depravity, probably do her an injustice. She was far too haughty and fastidious ever to stoop to vulgar amours. Let us, however, leave Olympe for a time to speak of the fortunes of her sisters.

A few days before Mazarin's death, a visitor presented himself at the door of the Cardinal's sick-room, and requested a private interview with his Eminence. It was the famous Maréchal Turenne, to whom Mazarin had once desired to wed Hortense, and he had come to ask for the hand of another of Mazarin's nieces, the thirteen-year-old Marianne, not for himself, but for his nephew, Maurice Godefroy de la Tour d'Auvergne, Duc de Bouillon. Turenne had made the same request some time before, and the Cardinal had promised to consider the matter. Thinking, however, that Marianne was too young to marry, or, perhaps, that he might be able to find for her a more brilliant match, he had as yet returned no definite answer, and the result had been some coolness between him and the marshal. Now, however, that the Cardinal lay on his death-bed, Turenne resolved to be reconciled to his old friend, and, at the same time, to endeavour to gain his consent to the union of their families. It was some days, however, before he was able to obtain the private interview upon which he insisted, and when at length he was successful, the Cardinal seemed disinclined to discuss the question of the marriage, though he was delighted at the visit of the man whose sword had restored his fallen fortunes during the Fronde, declared that he would die his servant and friend, and, drawing a magnificent ring from one of his wasted fingers, begged the marshal to wear it in remembrance of him.

Turenne returned to Paris without even broaching the matter which had brought him to Vincennes, and, following the example of the Marquis de la Meilleraye, had recourse to the good offices of the Bishop of Fréjus. Whether he employed the same means of gaining over Ondedei to his interests as the Grand Master had found so efficacious, is uncertain; but, any way, the bishop agreed to undertake the commission. This time, however, he failed. Mazarin, who was too near death to trouble about a marriage which, unlike that of Marie, was of no particular urgency, answered that Marianne, with her fortune, would never want for a husband, and refused to discuss the subject further. Nevertheless, Ondedei once more proved himself a valuable ally, for, after the Cardinal's death, he succeeded in persuading Anne of Austria, with whom he had great influence—had he not been the confidant of all Mazarin's private affairs?—of the suitability of the match; and on 22 April 1662, the marriage of Marianne and the Duc de Bouillon was celebrated in the presence of the King and Queen, and was followed by brilliant fêtes.

The Duc de Bouillon, a soldier like his celebrated uncle, and, like him, entirely devoted to his profession, proved a kind and indulgent husband, but he had no tastes in common with his wife. When his presence was not required in the field, hunting occupied the greater part of his time; while the duchess, as may be anticipated from her fondness for verse-making, affected intellectual pursuits, and seemed never so happy as when surrounded by a throng of men and women of letters: Segrais, Benserade, Madame Deshoulières, Ménage, and others.

From a contemporary print

MARIANNE MANCINI, DUCHESSE DE BOUILLON

Early in the year 1665, the Duc de Bouillon set out for Hungary, to take service, under Montecuculi, against the Turks, and being indisposed to leave his young wife, who had lately given birth to a son, unprotected amid the dangers of the Court, sent her to Château-Thierry, one of his country-seats, to await his return.

Here it was that Marianne became intimate with the poet La Fontaine, who was to owe so much to her sympathy and encouragement, and, in return, to immortalize her in his verses.

La Fontaine had then just returned to his native town from a three years' residence at Limoges, whither he had accompanied his relative Jannart, the friend of Fouquet and his substitute in the office of *procureur-général* to the Parliament of Paris. He was sadly in need of a new protector to replace his first Mæcenas, languishing in his cell at Pignerol, and he was fortunate enough to find one in the Duchesse de Bouillon. It is probable that the poet had already met the duchess at Fouquet's hotel in Paris before her marriage, but now he was to be afforded an opportunity of seeing her more frequently, and of appreciating her intelligence and kindness. He appreciated her beauty also, for Marianne, though she could not boast the classic features of the lovely Hortense, was in her way hardly less charming, with a dazzling complexion, eyes which sparkled with merriment, a winning smile, and a profusion of soft brown hair. Her figure, though somewhat diminutive, was perfectly formed, and she had beautiful hands and feet, while an infinite grace characterised all her movements.

La Fontaine soon conceived for her a warm and de-

voted admiration, which he expressed both in prose and
verse—

> Vous excellez en mille choses.
> Vous portez en tous lieux la joie et les plaisirs :
> Allez en des climats inconnus aux Zéphirs,
> Les champs se vêtiront de roses.

It is thus that he speaks of her twenty-five years later,
when she went to join her sister Hortense in England,
and his tone remained always the same, "familiarly
respectful and affectionately admiring."

"Nothing authorises the supposition," remarks the
poet's biographer, M. Georges Lafenestre, "that between
the little *grande dame* and the humble, middle-aged
bourgeois there had been any other relations than those
of a very lively sympathy, the result of a common taste
for the same intellectual pleasures, of the same horror
of *ennui*, and of the same indulgence for the raptures of
passion and the frailties of gallantry. La Fontaine has
honestly revealed to us his sentiments, and we have no
reason to suspect his frankness :

> Peut-on s'ennuyer en des lieux
> Honorés par les pas, éclairés par les yeux
>   D'une aimable et vive princesse,
> A pied blanc et mignon, à brune et longue tresse ?
> Nez troussé, c'est un charme, encor selon mon sens ?
> C'en est même un des plus puissants.
> Pour moi le temps d'aimer est passé, je l'avoue ;
>   Je mérite qu'on me loue
>   De ce libre et sincère aveu,
> Dont pourtant le public se souciera très peu.
> Que j'aime ou n'aime pas, c'est pour lui même chose ;
>   Mais s'il arrive que mon cœur
> Retourne à l'avenir dans sa première erreur,
> Nez aquilins et longs n'en seront pas la cause.[1]

---

[1] M. Georges Lafenestre's "La Fontaine." The last line of these
verses was for Madame La Fontaine, whose nose resembled that of her
husband.

However that may be, La Fontaine became one of the familiar friends of the Bouillon household, both in Paris and at Château-Thierry, and this intimacy was indeed a fortunate occurrence for his genius. Although he was forty-four years of age at the time when he made, or renewed, acquaintance with Madame de Bouillon, his reputation was not yet made ; he had only published a little volume, containing "Joconde, la Matrone d'Ephèse" and other poems, and had printed a few fables. He found with this great lady of sixteen summers the spur which his idleness needed and a keen appreciation of his real powers. It was she who marked out the road along which he was to travel, and urged him resolutely to compose his fables, and her lively imagination furnished him with more than one subject.[1] Stimulated by his patroness, La Fontaine's tardy genius at last bore fruit, and so hard did he work under her supervision that he published two years later the first six books of his fables. "But," says the lady's biographer, M. Amédée Renée, "all must be confessed ; it was not only fables which the Duchesse de Bouillon urged the poet to compose. De Retz pretends that Mazarin had pleased Richelieu and his colleagues by 'libertine tales of Italy.' These tales, in fact, had obtained a great popularity, whatever it was that had opened the door to them, and the courtiers learned Italian to read Boccaccio and Poggio, as one learns it to-day to sing a cavatina. The Duchesse de Bouillon took pleasure in the tales which La Fontaine extracted from "The Decameron"; it is a taste that we have no longer, but her time explains and excuses it. Women more severe

---

[1] It was Madame de Bouillon, and not, as some writers have stated, Madame de Sablière, who surnamed La Fontaine "*le Fablier*," which summed up in a single word his vocation.

s

than Marianne amused themselves in similar fashion ; Madame de Sévigné and her rigorous daughter[1] did not object to speak of it in their letters. La Fontaine, charged to amuse his merry châtelaine, enlarged, accordingly, his collection of tales as well as fables. It was not, of course, at the period when she was sixteen years old that Madame de Bouillon showed so pronounced a taste for this light literature ; she did not encourage this badinage until later, and it was to make a diversion to his fables.

When the Duc de Bouillon returned from Hungary and carried off his wife to Paris, La Fontaine followed his patroness, who presented him to her sisters, Mesdames de Soissons and de Mazarin, her brother, the Duc de Nevers, who also cultivated the Muses, and her brother-in-law the Duc d'Albret, afterwards Cardinal de Bouillon, and obtained for him the place of gentleman of the chamber to *Madame*.

With the advent of La Fontaine, came more distinguished members of the Republic of Letters to the Hôtel de Bouillon than those who had formerly been seen there, among them Molière and the old Corneille. For Corneille the duchess seems to have cherished almost as profound an admiration as Madame de Sévigné, and it was this admiration, coupled with her friendship for Madame Deshoulières, whose verses Racine had, perhaps unduly, depreciated, which probably led, in 1677, to her ill-advised attempt to sustain against the author of " Andromaque " and " Iphigénie," a young

[1] The Comtesse de Grignan. But was Madame de Grignan quite so "rigorous" as M. Renée seems to suppose ? There was some talk of an affair which she had with the Duc de Vivonne, Madame de Montespan's brother, at Marseilles ; and the unusual bitterness with which her mother speaks of that nobleman would appear to indicate that it was not wholly without foundation.

and conceited poet named Pradon, author of a couple of indifferent tragedies.

Racine was then at work on his immortal "Phèdre," and the duchess persuaded her *protégé* to compose a play upon the same subject, to be produced at the Théâtre Guénégaud simultaneously with the appearance of Racine's work at the Hôtel de Bourgogne. Such rivalry was, of course, legitimate enough ; five years before, Paris had witnessed a similar duel between Racine and Corneille over the subject of Titus and Berenice, though, on this occasion, both plays had been written at the suggestion of *Madame*, and the secret had been so carefully kept that, until their works were actually in rehearsal, the two poets were altogether unaware that they were competing against one another.

But the same, unfortunately, cannot be said of the methods of Madame de Bouillon to ensure the success of Pradon's play and the failure of Racine's. All went well at the Hôtel de Bourgogne the first evening, the management having taken the precaution to exclude all whom they suspected of being unfavourably disposed towards the author, and the play was accorded a reception which could not fail to satisfy the most exacting dramatist. The following evening, however, matters were very different ; to the chagrin of Racine and the astonishment of the company, every box on the first tier was empty ! The same thing occurred on the following evening and the next after that ; while, to increase the mystery and the poet's mortification, the boxes at the Théâtre Guénégaud were reported as crowded with applauding spectators. The explanation was that the Duchesse de Bouillon had adopted the ingenious device of engaging in advance all the best seats at both houses, filling those at the Théâtre Guénégaud with her friends and leaving the others empty.

The feelings of Racine may be imagined, for that not inconsiderable section of the public which judges of the merits of a play solely by results was beginning to assert that his tragedy was a failure and Pradon's a brilliant success. After, however, the trick had been played for three more nights, he triumphed. Perhaps Madame de Bouillon had begun to find her experiment, which is said to have cost her 15,000 francs, the equivalent of five times as much to-day, somewhat too costly a one to be continued indefinitely; or possibly Racine, discovering the tactics of his opponents, had appealed to the King for protection, and the duchess had received a hint from his Majesty that such practices could not be permitted. Any way, the lady withdrew from the field, and, with her retirement, the two "Phèdres" speedily found their respective levels. Pradon's play, at best a very mediocre work, had to be withdrawn after fifteen or sixteen representations; while Racine's enjoyed a brilliant run, and will hold a foremost place in the classic répertoire of the Théâtre-Français for all time. Nevertheless, in spite of its ultimate success, Racine never forgot the mortification to which he had been subjected, which, there can be no doubt, contributed not a little to his decision to renounce writing for the stage. As for Pradon, he paid dearly for being the hero of a coterie which used him to wreak their spite on a great master of his art, by remaining the type of the worthless poet. However, he was not without talent, and his "Régulus," in which Baron achieved a great success, remained in the répertoire for many years.

CHAPTER XIII

Hortense and the Duc de Mazarin—Eccentricities of the duke—His jealousy and tyrannical treatment of his wife—He takes possession of her jewels—Temporary separation between them—They are reconciled, but quarrel anew—Hortense sent to the Abbey of Chelles and afterwards to the Couvent des Filles de Sainte-Marie—Sidonie de Lenoncourt, Marquise de Courcelles—Practical jokes played by the marchioness and Hortense upon the nuns—The "penitents" transferred to the Abbey of Chelles—Unsuccessful attempt of M. de Mazarin to seize his wife—The Cour des Enquêtes orders the duchess to be set at liberty—M. de Mazarin appeals to the Grande Chambre—Hortense leaves Paris and flies to Lorraine—Disgrace of her lover, the Chevalier de Rohan—Madame de Mazarin arrives at Milan.

FAR less happy in her married life than her youngest sister was Hortense, though never did any one embark upon it under apparently more favourable auspices. Nature and Fortune had lavished upon her their richest gifts. She was one of the most beautiful women of her time.

> Hortense eût du ciel en partage
> La grâce, la beauté, l'esprit,

sang La Fontaine. She had inherited the bulk of her uncle's vast wealth, and had for her residence the finest part of that wonderful Palais-Mazarin, filled with priceless pictures and the rarest marbles, and which surpassed the Louvre itself in the richness of its interior. She was a duchess, their Majesty's cousin, courted and adulated by all. Finally, she was married to a man who loved her passionately, and for whom, at the time of her marriage at least, she appears to have entertained a strong liking. Her life ought, then, to have been one of the happiest ; the very reverse was the case.

For this unfortunate state of affairs Hortense herself was, in a great measure, to blame. Her coquetry, incurable frivolity, foolishness, and complete absence of moral sense, were not calculated to please even the most complacent of husbands; but, in justice to her, it should be added that even a paragon of virtue would have found it difficult to live on amicable terms with the Duc de Mazarin.

Armand de la Porte, Duc de Mazarin, was of singularly unprepossessing countenance ("He bore on his face the justification of his wife's conduct," wrote Madame de Sévigné) ; but, in other respects, he seemed likely to make an excellent husband. His life, in a licentious age, had been beyond reproach ; he was well educated, open-handed, a charming companion, and distinguished for his courtly manners. But some latent germ of insanity there must have been lurking in his temperament, which, under the influence of conjugal jealousy and religious fervour, changed him, before he had been married many months,[1] into one of the most ridiculous and, at the same time, the most tyrannical of husbands to be met with outside the domain of fiction,

---

[1] Only a few weeks after their marriage, a very compromising note from Hortense to the Chevalier de Rohan was intercepted by M. de Mazarin, à propos of which we find Louis XIV writing to the Bishop of Fréjus :

"FONTAINEBLEAU, 21 *April* 1661.

"I have already done in advance all that you tell me is necessary. I ought to be very displeased at what has occurred ; but I wish to hope that the person of whom you speak will conduct herself better in the future than she has in the past. I am already aware of all the scandal that there has been, and I confess to you that what causes me the most pain, is the thought that a person who bears the name of so great a man should give occasion for every one to laugh."

only not mad enough to be shut up, because Louis XIV found his inexhaustible purse too convenient to borrow from.[1]

" He was the Alceste of good morals, but the devotees by whom he was surrounded made of him an Orgon." He threw himself into the most extravagant devotion ; he became a seer of visions, a dreamer of dreams. One day, he sought an audience of the King, and gravely told him that he had been informed by the Angel Gabriel that some terrible misfortune would befall his Majesty, if he did not immediately break off his connection with Louise de la Vallière.[2] He conceived the most unheard of scruples, and did not hesitate to give practical expression to them. The magnificent collection of statues and paintings in the Palais-Mazarin shocked his views, nor did he content himself, like Tartuffe, with throwing his handkerchief over the Michelangelos and Titians which offended him by an improper nudity ; but, with a hammer in one hand and a paint-pot in the other, made a tour of the galleries, demolishing the statues and smearing over the pictures.

The King, hearing of what was going on, deputed Colbert to endeavour to stop the destruction, and one can imagine the despair of Mazarin's former intendant, who knew almost to a sol what the offending masterpieces had

---

[1] Under date 13 September 1661, we find Louis XIV writing to the duke : " My Cousin, after having caused the Surintendant des Finances (Fouquet) to be arrested, of which fact you are aware, I am in need of the two million livres which you offered to lend me." In a second letter, the King thanks M. de Mazarin for having foreseen his request by despatching a gentleman, etc. Another time, his Majesty thanks him for the present he has made him of a superb Spanish horse ; and, in a fourth letter, dated 17 November, 1663, expresses his thanks for the assistance he has offered towards bringing water to Versailles. Letters cited by Amédée Renée, " Les Nièces de Mazarin."

[2] " Mémoires de l'Abbé de Choisy."

cost his patron, at the sight which met his eyes on entering the galleries and finding the duke in the midst of his
operations. His remonstrances were ill received; but
eventually he succeeded in prevailing upon the madman
to desist, though not before the collection had suffered
severely from the piety of its owner. Louis XIV, for
the reasons of which we have already spoken, contented
himself with mildly expressing his regret at M. de
Mazarin's proceedings. Visiting the Louvre one day
and noticing a hammer, he remarked to Perrault: "There
is the weapon which M. de Mazarin makes so much
use of."

A taste for lawsuits was another of this nobleman's
peculiarities; he is said to have had three hundred, and
to have lost nearly all of them. "I am very pleased,"
he observed, "for actions to be brought against me in
regard to the possessions which I have received from the
Cardinal. I believe them all wrongly acquired; and
when I have a judgment given in my favour, I regard it
as a title to the property, and my conscience is at rest."

"He used to cast lots for his servants," says Saint-
Simon, "in such a way that the cook became his
intendant and the floor-scrubber his secretary. The lot,
according to him, indicated the will of God." The same
chronicler relates that once, when a fire broke out at one
of his country-seats, he refused to allow the servants to
extinguish it, declaring that to do so would be to interfere with the intentions of the Almighty.

But it was his unfortunate young wife who had to
bear the brunt of his vagaries. If we are to believe only
half of what she tells us in her "Mémoires," he must have
led her a truly terrible life. He began by conceiving a
violent jealousy of the attentions paid her by the King,
and, in order to shield her from this supposed danger,

kept her in a state of perpetual locomotion. "As he feared for me to remain in Paris," she writes, "he continually marched me about to his estates and governments. During the first three or four years of our marriage, I made three or four journeys into Alsace and as many into Brittany, besides several others to Nevers, Maine, Bourbon, Sedan, and other places. He has often made me undertake a journey of two hundred leagues when I was enceinte and very near my confinement. My relations and friends were apprehensive of the dangers to which he exposed my health, and endeavoured to make him sensible of them, but for a long time in vain."[1] These continual journeys, however, were, after all, only a small part of what the lady had to suffer at his hands, and, "as she had no greater pleasure than that of seeing him," she assures us that she might have endured them, had it not been for the tyranny of his proceedings. He was jealous of every one who addressed or approached her, high or low, man or woman. "I could not speak to a servant, but he was dismissed the next day. I could not receive two visits in succession from the same man, but he was forbidden the house. If I showed any preference for one of my maids, she was at once taken away from me. He would have liked me to see no one in the world, except himself. Above all, he could not endure that I should see either his relations or my own—the latter, because they had begun to take my part, his own, because they no more approved of his conduct than did mine."

He would not even suffer her to sleep in peace. "No sooner were the beautiful eyes of his companion closed," says the duchess's friend Saint-Évremond, "than this amiable husband, to whose black imagination the devil

---

[1] "Mémoires de la Duchesse de Mazarin."

was always present, awoke her to make her share his nocturnal visions. They lighted torches, they searched everywhere ; but the only devil whom Madame de Mazarin found was the one who was with her in bed."[1]

He found fault with everything she did. "The innocence of my recreations occasioned him as much annoyance as if they had been criminal. Sometimes he said it was a sin to play with my servants at cock-all. At other times he said it was a heinous crime to go to bed late. He often declared that one could not in conscience go to Court, and much less to the play ; sometimes my devotions were too short. In fine, his peevishness upon my account was such that I verily believe, if any one had seriously asked him how and in what manner he desired me to live, he would not have been able to agree with himself about the matter."[2]

Hortense, according to her own account, bore her husband's eccentricities with the most exemplary patience ; but when, "not content with making her pass the best years of her life in unparalleled slavery," the duke began to squander her property in all directions, and "she saw that, by his incredible profuseness, her son, who might have been the richest gentleman in France, was in danger of becoming the poorest," her fortitude was exhausted. The crisis came when, on returning home one night from some Court function, she found that her husband had taken advantage of her absence to seize upon her jewellery. She demanded the reason of his conduct, and was told that she was of such a liberal and generous disposition that he feared that, if she were

---

[1] Saint-Évremond relates several other instances of M. de Mazarin's eccentricities, and accuses him of abominable vices, for which, he says, he was wont to declare that he had found justification in Holy Scripture. Saint-Évremond, however, was not, in this case, an impartial witness.

[2] "Mémoires de la Duchesse de Mazarin."

allowed to retain possession of her jewels, she might be
tempted to give some of them away, and that he, therefore,
considered it advisable to take them into his own keeping.
Hortense angrily insisted on their immediate restoration ; and, on the duke's refusal, left the room and went
to consult her brother, the Duc de Nevers, whose hotel,
as we have mentioned, adjoined the Palais-Mazarin, of
which it had originally formed part. Here she found
the Duchesse de Bouillon, who told her that " she was
well served, since she had suffered so much already without complaint," and despatched a Madame de Balenzane,
who happened to be with her, to remonstrate with M.
de Mazarin. The duke, however, refused to see her, presumably being of opinion that to receive a visit from a
lady at so late an hour would be a highly improper proceeding, and sent word that he intended leaving for
Saint-Germain on the morrow.

Hortense spent the night at the Hôtel de Bouillon,
where, next morning, a family council was held, which
deputed the Comtesse de Soissons to bring the matter
to the notice of the King. Louis XIV, unwilling to
offend so useful a friend as the Duc de Mazarin, suggested a temporary separation between the parties, and
Hortense accordingly went to the Hôtel de Soissons,
where she remained for two months. At the end of
that time, the King ordered her to return to her husband, and she was obliged to obey, though her jewels
remained in M. de Mazarin's possession, and the only
concession she was able to obtain was the dismissal of
some waiting-women whom the duke had placed about
her for the purpose of spying upon her actions.

Scarcely, however, had the duchess set foot in the
Palais-Mazarin than she had a new and violent quarrel
with her husband, due, she tells us, to the duke having

retaliated for the dismissal of his spies by getting rid of one of her most trusted attendants. She attempted to escape from the house; M. de Mazarin hurried forward to bar her passage, but she brushed past him and ran into the courtyard. The duke rushed to a window and shouted to the servants to shut the gate, but, "seeing her in tears, no one dared to obey," and, hastening into the street, where a crowd of people, attracted by the uproar, had assembled, she made her way to the Hôtel de Nevers.

After a few days, the family again intervened, and a reconciliation was effected. It did not last long, however, and, after more grotesque scenes, Hortense consented to retire to the Abbey of Chelles, while M. de Mazarin set out for his government of Alsace, where he was at war with the intendant, for his governments resembled his household. Finding, on his return, that his wife was enjoying too much liberty at Chelles, where the abbess, although his own aunt, had warmly espoused her cause, he obtained permission from the King to remove her to the Couvent des Filles-de-Sainte-Marie, situated near the Bastille.

The luckless Hortense would no doubt have infinitely preferred the Bastille itself as a residence, for the convent in question was a most rigorous institution. However, she was fortunate enough to find there a companion in misfortune in the person of Sidonie de Lenoncourt, Marquise de Courcelles, who had been incarcerated there for somewhat similar reasons.

The history of Sidonie de Lenoncourt, who has been termed the Manon Lescaut of the seventeenth century, was a particularly sad one. Heiress of a wealthy and noble house, she had been very carefully brought up at the Couvent de Saint-Loup, at Orléans, of which

From an engraving after the painting by Mignard

ARMAND DE LA PORTE, DUC DE MAZARIN ET DE LA MEILLERAYE

her aunt was abbess. However, Colbert, wishing to
enrich and, at the same time, ennoble his family, conceived the idea of marrying her to his brother, and, by
order of the King, she was removed from the convent
and brought to the Hôtel de Soissons, to receive a very
different education, under the eye of the Princesse de
Carignan, Olympe Mancini's mother-in-law. Here the
beautiful and innocent young girl attracted the notice
of Louvois, who fell madly in love with her. As the
result of a shameful compact, it was arranged that the
Marquis de Courcelles, a needy and worthless man,
should have the lady's fortune, while Louvois was to be
granted every facility for pressing his dishonourable suit.
In this he was so far successful that Sidonie consented
to become his mistress; but he was never able to gain
her affection, which was bestowed on the Marquis de
Villeroi, Madame de Soissons's admirer. To this succeeded other attachments, and her unworthy husband,
who had only been waiting his opportunity to get full
control of her fortune, availed himself of this pretext
to have her shut up in the Couvent des Filles-de-Sainte-
Marie.

The two captives naturally became sworn friends, and
rumour asserted that they relieved the tedium of their
existence by turning the convent upside down and
perpetrating all sorts of practical jokes on their unfortunate guardians, though Hortense, in her " Mémoires,"
declares that they were shamefully maligned. " As
Madame de Courcelles was very amiable and very
entertaining," she writes, " I had the complacency to
join with her in some pleasantries which she played upon
the nuns. A hundred ridiculous tales about this were
carried to the King, who was told that we put ink in
the holy-water basin to bespatter the good ladies, that

we ran through the dormitories, accompanied by a pack
of dogs, shouting out 'Tayaut! Tayaut!' and such-
like things ; all of which were absurdly false or grossly
exaggerated. For example, having asked for some water
to wash our feet, the nuns disapproved and refused our
request, just as if we were there to observe the regula-
tions. It is true that we filled a large coffer which stood
in our dormitory with water, and, the boards of the
floor being very loosely joined together, the water which
overflowed leaked through this wretched floor and
wetted the beds of the good sisters. This accident was
talked about as if it had been something which we
had done of design."[1]

However that may be, the two penitents seem to
have led the poor daughters of Sainte-Marie such a
life that they petitioned the King for their removal, and,
much to the relief of all parties, the ladies were transferred to the Abbey of Chelles, with whose superior
Hortense had contrived to ingratiate herself during her
former residence there. This change was by no means
to the taste of M. de Mazarin, who, a few days later,
appeared before the convent, accompanied by a troop
of cavalry and armed with an authorisation from the
Archbishop of Paris to enter and seize his wife. The
abbess refused to admit him, and handed the keys of
the convent to Hortense, who appeared at the grill and
brandished them defiantly in the face of her discomfited
lord. M. de Mazarin withdrew, in a very ill humour,
uttering terrible threats ; but, the following morning,
Hortense espied from her window a large body of
horse advancing towards the abbey. Believing that
it was her Bluebeard returning with reinforcements
and his friend the archbishop's authority to force an

[1] " Mémoires de la Duchesse de Mazarin."

entry, she was overcome with fear and hid herself in
the chimney of her room, where she stuck fast, and
was nearly suffocated by the soot. With considerable
difficulty she was rescued, to find, to her joy, that the
horsemen whose appearance had so alarmed her were
a party of friends, headed by the Duc and Duchesse de
Bouillon and the Comte de Soissons, who, having learned
of M. de Mazarin's proceedings, were hastening to her
succour.

In the meantime, Hortense had brought an action
against her husband before the Cour des Enquêtes of the
Parliament of Paris. This court, "composed," says the
duchess, "almost exclusively of young men, not one of
whom but was eager to serve me," decreed that she
should be set at liberty and reinstated in the Palais-
Mazarin, while her husband was to reside at the Arsenal,
the official residence of the Grand Master of the Artillery.
The duke, however, refused to accept this decree and
immediately appealed to the Grande Chambre, which,
Hortense tells us, being composed for the most part of
elderly counsellors, would be naturally more inclined to
favour the husband than the wife. From which it would
appear that the lady had not a very high opinion of the
judges of her time.

Foreseeing that the appeal was likely to go against her,
the duchess resolved to await the decision of the court
with her sister, the Constabless Colonna, at Rome. Her
brother, the Duc de Nevers, signified his approval of her
resolution, and her devoted admirer, the Chevalier de
Rohan,[1] promised her his assistance. Accordingly, one
night, at the end of June 1668, Hortense, disguised as
a man and accompanied by one of her waiting-women,

[1] Louis de Rohan, younger son of Louis VII, Duc de Rohan, Prince
de Guéménée.

similarly attired, and an equerry of the chevalier named Couberville, left Paris on horseback, and rode without drawing rein, except to change horses, to Nancy. Here she was well received by Charles IV of Lorraine, who, ever the slave of the fair, naturally sympathised with her misfortunes, and gave her a troop of his guards to escort her as far as Geneva.

A few hours after she had left Paris, M. de Mazarin was informed of her flight, upon which he rushed off to the Louvre, and, although it was then three o'clock in the morning, insisted on awakening the King, to demand that he would cause the duchess to be pursued and brought back. But his Majesty declined to interfere, and is said to have expressed some surprise that the Angel Gabriel, who had been so solicitous concerning himself and La Vallière, should have omitted to warn the duke of his wife's intentions.

M. de Mazarin, however, derived some consolation from the fact that the Grande Chambre shortly afterwards passed a decree authorising him to apprehend his wife in whatever place she might happen to be, encouraged by which he next brought an action against the Duc de Nevers and the Chevalier de Rohan as accomplices of her flight. In this he failed, but Hortense, having had the imprudence to write a very tender letter to Rohan, in which she spoke of the happiness which would follow their reunion, it was intercepted by her husband; and Louis XIV, happening to be in one of those austere moods in which he sought to atone for the laxity of his own morals by extreme severity towards other backsliders, deemed it his duty to disgrace the chevalier and deprive him of all his offices. The unfortunate Rohan, already overwhelmed by debt, found himself almost ruined. To better his fortunes he, some years later, entered into treasonable negotiations with the Dutch, but was detected, brought to trial, and beheaded in front of the Bastille, on 27 November 1674.

In the meanwhile, Hortense, still escorted by Couberville, of whom we shall have a good deal to say presently, continued her flight, crossed the Alps in safety, and at the beginning of July arrived at Milan, where she found Marie and the Constable, who had travelled thither to meet her.

T

CHAPTER XIV

Marie and the Constable Colonna—Happiness of their early married
life—Eccentric conduct of the Constabless—Probable explanation—
Birth of a son—A sumptuous bed—Birth of two other sons—Separation *di letto* between the Constable and his wife—*Liaison* of Colonna
with the Marchesa Paleotto—Arrival of the Duchesse de Mazarin in
Italy—The " Chevalier " de Couberville—Quarrel between the Duc
de Nevers and Hortense—Scene between Marie and Couberville—The
"chevalier" is arrested and imprisoned in a fortress—Hortense enters
a convent—An embarrassing situation—Escape of Madame de Mazarin
from the convent—Her lovers—She returns to France with her
brother—M. de Mazarin endeavours to have her arrested at Nevers—
Intervention of the King—The Duchess accepts a pension and returns
to Italy.

AND what of Marie during the seven years which had
passed since her arrival in Italy ?

For the first five years of her married life, Marie had
lived very happily with the Constable. Colonna, who
seems to have fallen passionately in love with his wife at
first sight, proved the kindest and most indulgent of
husbands. He allowed her the fullest liberty to live *à la
Française*, that is to say, to visit and receive whomever
and whenever it pleased her, to the great displeasure of
the Roman nobles, who deemed it a very bad example for
their wives, whom they kept shut up in their palaces and
guarded with the most jealous care. He overwhelmed
her with attentions and presents, anticipated her slightest
wish, and was perpetually inventing some new entertainment for her diversion. Marie, who was naturally of
an affectionate disposition, did not long remain insensible

to her husband's devotion and began to feel for him the warmest regard. "Although Italian customs were but little to my taste," she writes, "the inclination that I had begun to entertain for the Constable rendered them more endurable to me ; for, to be brief, he neglected nothing which could give me pleasure ; it would be impossible to describe his attentions and kindness, and, finally, I may say that I am the one whom he loved the most and the longest." [1]

Unhappily for Marie, since her arrival in Italy, she was much changed from the girl whom we have seen at the Court of France. Then, it is true, she had been headstrong and self-willed, though, perhaps, not more so than many of her countrywomen. Now, however, she gradually began to develop eccentricities which became a source of grave uneasiness to her husband and those about her. In the autumn of 1662, she became enceinte, to the great delight of the Constable, who was intensely anxious for an heir. Marie was no less anxious to gratify his wish ; but, instead of obeying the instructions of her physicians and taking the precautions usual in such circumstances, she indulged in all kinds of forbidden amusements, and on several occasions, in spite of the remonstrances of her husband, insisted on following the chase and remained in the saddle nearly the entire day. The result was a miscarriage, followed by an attack of fever, and it was some weeks ere she was able to leave her bed.

"The conduct of the Constabless under such grave circumstances," writes Lucien Perey, "would be impossible to explain, if one did not trace these vagaries to their source. In our opinion, it is certain that the brain-fever, accompanied by convulsions, by which she was

[1] "La Vérité dans son jour."

attacked during her journey to Italy, caused brain-trouble, of which she kept the trace all her life. We do not mean that she was insane in the fullest extent of the word, but undoubtedly her mind was deranged on some points, and persons at her house remarked, when observing her closely, that she seemed in a state of continual uneasiness and agitation."[1] The most common form which her affection took was an inability to reside in any one spot for more than a few weeks at a time. Although her husband was required to pass the greater part of each year in Rome, she wished to be perpetually travelling, no matter in what condition of health she might happen to be, now to their country-seats at Marino and Sisterna, now to Naples or Venice, anon to Milan or some other town, at which she had no sooner arrived than she wished to be on the move again. The Constable was so devoted to his wife that he bore the inconvenience and expense—for he invariably insisted on her travelling in semi-royal state—attendant upon these continual peregrinations without murmuring. But alas! this feverish restlessness was ere long to be followed by other and graver eccentricities, which, as her biographer suggests, were no doubt attributable to the effects of the illness which had so nearly cost her her life at Loretto.

Nevertheless, as has been said, the first years of her married life were happy. On 7 April 1664, she consoled her husband for his previous disappointment by bearing him a son, who was named Filippo, and bore the title of Principe di Palliano. Great was the joy of the Constable and his relatives at this auspicious event, and Marie found herself overwhelmed with costly presents and congratulations. According to custom, the members

---

[1] "Une Princesse romaine au xvii° siècle: Marie Mancini Colonna."

of the Sacred College and all the Roman nobility called at the Casa Colonna to felicitate the princess, and were received by her reclining on a sumptuous bed, "the novelty no less than the magnificence of which filled every one with admiration." "It was," she writes, "a species of shell, which seemed to float in the midst of a sea artistically represented, and which served as its foundation. The posts stood on the cruppers of four seahorses, mounted by sirens, so admirably sculptured and with their material so brilliantly gilded that they seemed to be made of the precious metal itself. Ten or twelve little Cupids served as clasps for the curtains, which were of a very rich golden brocade and were permitted to hang loosely, so as not to conceal anything which deserved to be seen in this sumptuous ornament."[1]

The birth of Marie's first son was followed by that of two others, baptized respectively Marco Antonio and Carlo, whose advent was welcomed by Lorenzo Colonna with scarcely less pleasure than he had shown at the birth of his heir, and the princess's happiness seemed complete, when, on a sudden, she announced to her husband her intention to live no longer with him as his wife.

Marie, in her "Mémoires," written, we must remember, while her husband was still alive, gives the following reason for her decision :—

"But having given birth to this child [her third son] to the apparent danger of my life, I took a resolution to avoid for the future all occasion of exposing myself to the like by giving birth to another. The Constable's consent being necessary to make valid a resolution of this nature, I pressed him for it and obtained it, and have ever since found him, in this particular, a man of his word."[2]

[1] "La Vérité dans son jour."
[2] *Ibid.*

The scandal-loving gazettes of the time, which do not fail to mention the *separazione di letto* between the Prince and Princess Colonna, attribute the latter's resolution to a more unusual cause, namely, to the prediction of an astrologer (Marie, like her father and mother, and, in a lesser degree, the Cardinal, was a firm believer in astrology, and was wont to attribute all her troubles to the malign influence of the stars),[1] who had predicted that the birth of a fourth child would be followed by her own death.

The real reason, however, was very different. It appears that shortly after her third son was born, Marie received an anonymous letter, informing her that the Constable was very far from being the faithful husband she imagined him to be, and that, some time before, he had become the father of a little girl. The name of the mother does not seem to be known, but the child was brought up with great care in a convent at Rome, where she died, in 1750, at the age of eighty-four.[2]

From what we already know of the pride and violence of Marie's character, it is easy to conceive the anger which must have possessed her on the discovery of her husband's infidelity. The idea of sharing his affection with another woman was intolerable to her, and she immediately informed him that henceforth they must live as friends only. Colonna, who adored his wife, did not acquiesce at all readily in this arrangement, and strove by every possible argument to shake her resolution ; but Marie was inexorable.

It was not long before she had cause to regret the

---

[1] Between 1670 and 1672, Marie published three curious volumes, containing a number of strange predictions, anagrams and calculations based on the influence of the stars.

[2] Lucien Perey, " Une Princesse romaine au xvii⁰ siècle : Marie Mancini Colonna."

hasty decision to which her wounded pride had urged her, for Colonna, who was of an exceedingly ardent temperament, "did not neglect to find compensation elsewhere for what our agreement had caused him to lose," and Marie confesses that his very marked attentions to a certain Marchesa Paleotto, whom they met at Venice during the Carnival of 1665, occasioned her "a secret displeasure."

However, she was too proud to allow the Constable to perceive her feelings, and when they returned to Rome, the lady and her husband accompanied them, and, at the invitation of the prince, installed themselves in a vacant suite of apartments at the Casa Colonna. The complacent husband only remained in Rome a short time, "for the sake of decorum," and then departed for Ancona, where he had received some military appointment; but the Marchioness stayed on, and her *liaison* with the Constable was soon the talk of Rome.

The relations between the latter and Marie were amiable, though somewhat distant. Colonna continued to allow his wife full liberty to pass her time as she felt disposed, and to keep open house for her friends and foreign visitors. The Roman ladies envied her, their husbands blamed her, and both declared themselves convinced that she must have a lover. However, they were quite unable to agree as to the identity of this fortunate individual, the fact being that Marie, although her desire to please was often mistaken for coquetry, was almost unrivalled in the difficult art of keeping adorers at a respectful distance.

Such was the state of affairs when Hortense arrived in Italy.

Marie was, of course, overjoyed to see her sister once more. "The affection which I had always felt for her," she writes, "made me undertake the journey to Milan with incredible pleasure, and I neglected nothing to induce the Constable to make it. He, on his side, did everything he could to dissuade me, but at length, having consented with the air of one who does something for which he has an extreme repugnance, we set out, in the month of July 1668, accompanied by the Marchesa Paleotto, and arrived six days later at Milan, where the Marquis Spinola de los Balbases, my brother-in-law, was the governor *par intérim*."

To Marie's intense disappointment, Hortense, "whose beauty surpassed all imagination, and in whom one discovered each time one saw her new charms," greeted her somewhat coldly, and rallied the Marchesa Paleotto and herself, because they were not attired in obedience to the dictates of the latest Paris mode, for, coming from France, "she judged people only by their exterior and esteemed them only in proportion to their being well dressed." Moreover, she appeared to have conceived a singular dislike to society, and remained in the apartments which had been allotted her nearly all day, "always *en déshabillé*, but always more charming," seeing no one but Marie and her own attendants. The reason she gave her sister for thus secluding herself, was that she was suffering from an injury sustained by a fall from her horse while crossing the Alps. A few weeks later, however, the Duc de Nevers arrived at Milan, and soon discovered the real cause of Madame de Mazarin's taste for solitude. She had, it transpired, conceived a violent fancy for Couberville, the equerry whom the Chevalier de Rohan had given her to escort her to Italy, and who had gained such ascendency over her that she even denied herself to her brother and sister when he happened to be with her. Soon this affair had become the talk of the city, and people made ribald verses about it, to the intense mortification of the duchess's relatives, who felt compelled, in consequence, to cut short their visit to Milan and remove to Sienna.

Here, soon after their arrival, there was a violent dispute between Hortense and the Duc de Nevers on the subject of Couberville. This worthy, whom the duchess persisted in addressing as "Monsieur le Chevalier," although he had no right whatever to that title, was so puffed up by his *bonne fortune* that he gave himself all the airs of a gentleman of quality, and treated M. de Nevers as if he were that nobleman's equal. The duke bitterly reproached his sister with her conduct, and threatened to throw the pretended chevalier out of the window, if he did not speedily mend his manners. Hortense flew into a passion, and angrily denied that there were any grounds whatever for the supposition of the duke, who thereupon left Sienna and went to Venice.

Soon after his departure, the Colonnas and Madame de Mazarin returned to Rome for the festival of All Saints' Day. But Hortense continued to show the same liking for solitude as she had evinced at Milan and Sienna, and her hosts enjoyed very little of her society. Marie now determined to interfere in her turn, and, after vainly remonstrating with her sister, sent for Couberville and gave him a piece of her mind. "This gentleman, far from seeking to excuse himself," she writes, "answered me rather impertinently, and, as he spoke of my brother in discourteous and far from respectful terms, I told him to leave the room immediately, and that he would find some one below to teach him how to behave himself, and to have for persons of my brother's quality the veneration that he ought to feel. He obeyed and quitted the room in a great anger."

Highly indignant at the way in which her lover had been treated, Hortense left the Casa Colonna and went to live with her aunt, Signora Martinozzi, where she remained for some weeks, "shut up like a prisoner," amusing herself by playing the guitar. As for Couberville, he deemed it prudent to leave Italy, and made his way to Civita Vecchia, with the intention of embarking for France. Here, however, the Constable Colonna caused him to be arrested, on some pretext, and imprisoned in a fortress, " to soften his haughty temper." After a confinement of some months, he was released, through the intercession of Francesco Rospigliosi, the Pope's nephew, whom Madame de Mazarin had contrived to interest in his favour, and disappears from our history.

In the meanwhile, the Duc de Mazarin, learning that his wife was no longer under the protection of the Colonnas, petitioned the Pope to have her sent to a convent. Hortense, however, anticipated him by retiring to the Convent of Campo-Marzo, of which another of her aunts was the superior, and where she could reckon on being permitted to do pretty much as she pleased. She had not been there long, however, when she fell into " a state of profound melancholy," and confessed to Marie, who visited her nearly every day, that an interesting event, in which M. de Mazarin had certainly no concern, was pending. The situation was most embarrassing, as Hortense could not leave the convent without the consent of her husband or the Pope ; and they were at a loss what to do. Eventually, however, Marie solved the problem by aiding her sister to escape and bearing her off in her coach, before the eyes of the indignant nuns,[1] to the Palazzo Mancini, which had been be-

---

[1] " My poor old aunt [the abbess]," writes Hortense, " took the matter so much to heart that she died a few days later, of the grief which my escape had occasioned her."

queathed by Mazarin to the Duc de Nevers, though their uncle, Cardinal Mancini, was at present residing there.

The unfortunate termination to her affair with M. Couberville does not appear to have had a very chastening effect upon the volatile duchess, who, to the mortification of her friends, declined to make the least attempt to conceal her condition, went frequently into society, and "appeared extremely pleased with herself." At the fêtes which followed the election of Cardinal Rospigliosi (Clement X) as Pope, in the spring of 1670, she was among the gayest of the gay, and was perpetually surrounded by a crowd of adorers. Among those whom she most favoured was a certain Jacques de Belbeuf, son of a counsellor of the Parliament of Normandy, a handsome young man, who had come to Rome to put the finishing touches to his education. Hortense presented him with her portrait, and we find the proud youth writing to his mother as follows :—

"There is also in the bag I have spoken of a little silver box, on one side of which is Madame de Mazarin's portrait and on the other my own. As the said lady has been pleased to give it me, I wish to place it by the side of mine, and feel obliged to keep them for ever. If you desire to see the said portrait, and even to show it, I beg you to make what use of it you think fit, but it is most important not to let it out of your keeping, and do not allow people to finger it. Also be careful who has access to it, as perhaps persons might wish to copy it, which would be most displeasing to me." [1]

Madame de Belbeuf was no doubt much gratified by so striking a tribute to her son's fascinations. Nowadays, we are inclined to think, mothers would be less complacent.

[1] Letter published by Amédée Renée, " Les Nièces de Mazarin." The duchess's portrait is still in the possession of the Belbeuf family.

The handsome young Norman, however, was not the only adorer to be thus honoured by the duchess, for an Italian correspondent of the *Gazette d'Amsterdam* of April 1670, informs the readers of that journal that "the Constable Colonna had just had to reconcile Don Dominico Gusman and Don Augustin Chigi, who had quarrelled over a portrait of Madame de Mazarin which one of them had received, and were about to settle their differences at the point of the sword." Nor did M. de Belbeuf long retain the post of honour in the lady's affection, being replaced by the Marquis del Grillo, who, in his turn, was succeeded by the Comte de Marsan, lately arrived in Rome with his brother, the notorious Chevalier de Lorraine, whom *Madame* had persuaded Louis XIV to banish from France. The Marquis del Grillo, to whom the duchess appears to have been under certain financial obligations, did not accept his dismissal with at all a good grace, and a second duel was with difficulty prevented by the efforts of Madame de Mazarin's relatives. Altogether, the Constable and Marie must have found the fair Hortense a pretty handful.

In the autumn, the Duc de Nevers, who had been residing in Rome since the previous winter and was now reconciled to his sister, set out for France to marry the beautiful Diane de Thianges, niece of Madame de Montespan. Hortense, who was perhaps beginning to find the welcome which her friends had at first extended to her growing a trifle cold, and was besides in need of money—she had been, she tells us, "reduced to pawn her jewels for the means of subsistence"—decided to accompany him and "throw herself at M. de Mazarin's feet." But her career at Rome, rumours of which had not failed to reach Paris, had been scarcely calculated to promote a reconciliation, and, on reaching Nevers, an official of the Grande Chambre presented himself with a warrant for her arrest, and a small army, composed of M. de Mazarin's guards and a brigade of archers, under the command of the Grand Provost of the Bourbonnais, wherewith to enforce it. The municipal authorities, however, held a consultation, as the result of which they decided to take the duchess under their protection, and called upon the citizens to defend her. Matters now began to assume a very serious aspect, and it seemed as if bloodshed must ensue, when a courier arrived from the King, commanding M. de Mazarin to sign a truce with his wife. The duke obeyed, weeping with rage, and Hortense continued her journey to Paris unmolested.

On her arrival, she had an audience of the King, in Madame de Montespan's apartments. His Majesty received her very graciously, and offered to order M. de Mazarin to pay her a pension of twenty-four thousand livres, with liberty to reside in Rome, if she preferred exile to returning to her husband. An income of twenty-four thousand livres seemed a miserable pittance to a woman who had inherited so many millions—("You will spend it at the first inn you stop at," remarked the Duc de Lauzun to her.) But even that seemed to her preferable to a *tête-à-tête* with M. de Mazarin, and she, accordingly, answered the King that "she felt that it would be impossible for her to return to M. de Mazarin, after all the endeavours he had made to ruin her reputation, and that she accepted the pension with a humble and heartfelt acknowledgment of his Majesty's great favour therein."[1]

At the beginning of the following spring, she returned to Rome, after an absence of nine months.

[1] "Mémoires de la Duchesse de Mazarin."

CHAPTER XV

Estrangement between the Constable Colonna and his wife—Growing desire of Marie to return to France—She has a dangerous illness—And believes herself the victim of an attempt at poisoning—A suspicious letter—Marie confides her fears to the Chevalier de Lorraine—They urge *Monsieur* to obtain Louis XIV's protection for the Constabless—Recall of the Chevalier de Lorraine to France—He informs the King of the danger which threatens Marie—Louis XIV promises the Constabless an asylum in France—Marie persuades the Duchesse de Mazarin to accompany her—Flight of the two sisters—Their perilous journey—Their arrival at Marseilles.

FOR two or three years after the separation *di letto* between Marie and the Constable Colonna, of which we have spoken in the preceding chapter, their relations appear to have been amicable enough ; but this state of affairs did not last. Whether it was that Colonna had his suspicions that what was denied him by his wife was accorded to others—Marie has been accused by some writers, though apparently on very untrustworthy evidence, of tender relations with both Cardinal Chigi and the Chevalier de Lorraine[1]—or that he was beginning to grow weary of the caprices and feverish activity which he had endured cheerfully enough so long as he possessed her affection, his manner towards her underwent

---

[1] If we are to place any faith in Marie's apocryphal memoirs, already mentioned, the Constable was particularly annoyed by a report that his wife had posed *pour l'ensemble* to the chevalier—who was by way of being an amateur painter—one day, while bathing in the Tiber. The lady, the writer adds, indignantly repudiated the charge, calling her waiting-women to witness that she never entered the river, unless attired in a *robe de gaze* which reached to her heels.

a change. "We passed the autumn [of 1670] in the country and the Carnival at the Operas," writes Marie, "but with less satisfaction to me, since, for some time past, I had remarked that the Constable had no longer for me the same kindness and affection which he had hitherto shown. He had no more regard for or confidence in me ; he rarely addressed me, and, if he did, it was in a way which made me prefer his silence to his words. The Principe di Sonnino [the Constable's brother, formerly known as the Abbate Colonna], who by his kindness has often appeased the secret troubles of his family, and by his prudence has frequently prevented them from being made public, will bear witness to what I had to endure."

The Principe di Sonnino did not, however, succeed, in this instance, in his task of peacemaker, or even in keeping the matter secret, and all Rome was soon discussing the differences between the Constable and his wife ; while the correspondents of the scandal-loving gazettes printed in Holland spread the news all over Europe.[1] The Roman ladies, who had never pardoned the Constabless for enjoying a liberty which their husbands denied to them, and had often been wounded by the haughtiness with which she treated them, did not fail to avenge themselves by circulating the most scandalous stories about both parties ; the wretched old Archbishop of Amasia was continually whispering malicious innuendoes regarding the Constable's conduct into his niece's ear, adding that he had warned her from the very beginning that the marriage could not fail to

[1] "The bad feeling which exists between them is known to every one. It is believed that his Excellency the Marquis d'Astorga, Viceroy of Naples, will discuss the matter previous to his departure for Naples, and endeavour to bring about a reconciliation" (*Gazette de Leyden*, 22 December 1670, cited by Lucien Perey).

prove an unhappy one ; and the breach grew wider and wider.

During the first years of her married life, the love and attentions of the Constable and the brilliant position she had occupied at Rome had aided Marie in her endeavours to forget the golden dreams of her youth, when even the throne of France had not seemed too high a position for her to attain. But from the moment she was assured of her husband's infidelity, the ghosts of the past refused any longer to be laid, and now that she felt that she had lost not only his affection, but his esteem, her thoughts turned towards France, and the prince who had once loved her so dearly, with a passionate longing. She was, of course, aware that her place in his Majesty's heart had long since been given to others, and that its present occupant was one of whom, if report spoke truly, the King was deeply enamoured. But when she recollected his intense chagrin at her departure, his tender adieux, his promise "to give her proofs of his esteem and attachment wherever she might be," his anxious solicitude during her illness at Loretto, she could not bring herself to believe that his feelings towards her could have changed so far as not to assure her a cordial welcome whenever she might choose to return ; and soon the desire to see France again became a fixed idea, to which all others were subordinated.

A few days after the return of the Duchesse de Mazarin to Rome, Marie was attacked by " so terrible a colic, that had its violence continued a little longer, it would have infallibly made an end of her." " My illness," she continues, " which was enough to move the most insensible heart to compassion, made no impression on that of the Constable, at least in appearance, since he listened to my complaints for an entire night with the utmost tranquillity."

At this epoch, the crime of poisoning was still rampant in Italy, as, a few years later, it became in France, though, fortunately, only for a comparatively brief period and over a limited area, and every one took infinite precautions on the slightest suspicion. Rightly or wrongly, Marie became convinced that she had been the victim of such an attempt, and that her husband had been its instigator ; and this opinion appears to have been shared by several of her friends. How far her suspicions were justified is difficult to say ; but since Colonna had obviously become weary of his wife, and was, moreover, a man of a peculiarly vindictive temper, who, it was common knowledge, had caused more than one person who had been so unfortunate as to offend him to be assassinated,[1] they ought certainly not to be dismissed as the hallucinations of a disordered brain. An incident which occurred during her convalescence increased her fears.

A letter addressed to the Constable was intercepted by Moréna, a Moorish waiting-maid whom Marie had brought with her from France, and carried by her to her mistress. Marie, to whose character nothing was more foreign than espionage of this kind, ordered it to be forwarded to its destination ; but the girl begged her so hard to open it that at last, though very reluctantly, she consented. The letter advised Colonna that the writer was in a position to arrange a very advantageous match

---

[1] At the time of the Constable's death, in April 1689, the Duc d'Estrées, French Ambassador at Rome, wrote to Louis XIV : " The Pope has shown himself extremely grieved at the death of the Constable Colonna. Notwithstanding his violence and his irregularities, and *even several assassinations,* for which the Pope testified so much horror at the beginning of his pontificate, he had become a kind of favourite."

U

for him, in the event of his happening to become a
widower, but added that, unless he were very speedily
able to avail himself of the offer, the hand of the heiress
in question would be bestowed elsewhere.

Deeming the letter capable of only one interpretation,
the princess, in great alarm, sent immediately for her
friend the Chevalier de Lorraine, to whom she confided
all her fears. The chevalier, grateful to Marie for the
kindness she had shown his brother and himself during
their stay in Rome, when almost every door had been
closed against them, readily promised her all the assistance in his power ; and it was decided that both of them
should write to *Monsieur*, to acquaint him with the
situation and beg him to secure the King's protection
for the Constabless.

Monsieur, who had always been much attached to
Marie, and had recently presented her, through the
Chevalier de Lorraine, with "a hunting equipage which
had cost a thousand pistoles, ornamented with a quantity
of the most beautiful and the richest ribbons to be found
in Paris," lost no time in laying the two letters before
Louis XIV, who, on learning of the danger which was
believed to threaten his former inamorata, appeared
much distressed. He refused, however, to take any
definite steps in the matter until he was in possession of
further information, which he promised to procure without delay. Soon afterwards, it was announced that,
through the intercession of the Abbate Oliva, the
General of the Jesuits, the Chevalier de Lorraine and
the Comte de Marsan had been pardoned and recalled
to Court.

The two brothers arrived in Paris in March 1672,
and the chevalier was immediately granted an audience
of the King, in which he did not fail to depict the fears

and sufferings of Marie in the most vivid colours; declared his conviction that her illness of the previous year had not been due to natural causes, and impressed upon Louis the necessity of protecting her from any further attempts upon her life.

His Majesty, more moved than he cared to appear, inquired what measures M. de Lorraine recommended to save the Constabless from the perils which surrounded . her; to which the chevalier answered that the only possible means of assuring her safety was for her to fly from her husband and seek an asylum in France.

The King at once decided to follow his counsel, directed him to assure the Constabless of his protection and support, and next day sent a letter for him to transmit to Marie, wherein he promised her a passport and an escort to accompany her the moment she set foot in France, and charged her to inform him of the port at which it was her intention to land.

Marie's joy and relief on receiving the King's letter were intense. Since the departure of the Chevalier de Lorraine and his brother from Rome, the relations between the Constable and herself had become more strained than ever, and the former now made so little effort to conceal the aversion and contempt he had begun to feel for his wife, even in the presence of her relatives, that the Duc de Nevers, who was, as usual, spending the winter in Rome, warned his sister to be very circumspect in her conduct, since otherwise he feared that some fine day she might find herself shut up in Palliano, a castle belonging to the Constable on the borders of the Ecclesiastical States and the kingdom of Naples.

The moment she was assured of the protection of Louis XIV, Marie hastened to make her preparations for flight.[1]   She said nothing, however, of her project to the Duc de Nevers, fearing that he might deem it his duty to inform his brother-in-law, but took Hortense into her confidence and begged her to accompany her. The duchess tells us that she employed every conceivable argument to dissuade her sister, but to no purpose, "for the same stars, or their influences, which drew her into Italy, drew her into France." Finally, she yielded, because, as she explains, "she had no mind to remain at Rome without her, and believed that she might be able to lessen the dangers she would have to incur by sharing them with her."[2]

Under cover to the Chevalier de Lorraine, Marie now wrote to Louis XIV, expressing her gratitude for his assurance of protection, and begging him to send to the intendant of the galleys at Marseilles the passports and the necessary papers for her and her sister, the latter being still in dread of the pursuit of her husband. She also requested permission to take up her residence in Paris, at the Hôtel de Nevers, with her brother, who, she had no doubt, would approve of her flight, although he might have refused to connive at it.

This done, she despatched Pelletier, an intelligent and devoted *valet de chambre* in the service of the Duchesse

---

[1] In her "Mémoires," Marie gives the following reasons for her flight. It will be observed that she only hints at the chief cause of her resolution, namely, the fear that her life was in danger : "The violent conduct of the Constable, joined to the aversion I entertained for Italian customs, and for the manner of life at Rome, where dissimulation and hatred between families are more in vogue than at other Courts, hastened my putting into execution the design I had formed to return to France, the place of my education, the residence of the majority of my relatives, and the centre of my genius, since I had an inclination for the novelties to be found there, the free and joyous humour of the people, and the warlike air and brave deportment of the men, rather than for life in a quiet spot and under a peaceable Government."

[2] "Mémoires de la Duchesse de Mazarin."

de Mazarin, to Naples, where he arranged with the master of a felucca which lay there to convey them to France. It was agreed that the felucca should proceed to Civita Vecchia, and that the fugitives should embark there.

On learning of the result of Pelletier's mission, the sisters resolved to make their escape without loss of time. Marie took with her the string of pearls, formerly the property of Queen Henrietta Maria, which Louis XIV had given her just before her departure for La Rochelle, a little valise containing some clothes, and about 700 pistoles. The remainder of her jewellery, the greater part of which were presents from the Constable and his relatives, she left behind, with a letter requesting that it should be equally divided between her three sons. Then, on 29 May 1672, taking advantage of the absence of the Constable, who had gone to visit a stud-farm belonging to him at some little distance from Rome, and was not expected to return until the following day, she left the Casa Colonna, accompanied by her Moorish waiting-maid Moréna, and proceeded to the Palazzo Mancini. Here she found a coach in readiness, at the door of which was Hortense, with whom were a waiting-woman named Nanon, Pelletier, and a footman.

But let us allow Marie to give her own account of their adventure :—

"In a few moments we entered my sister's coach. On leaving the house we cried to the coachman, 'To Frascati,' in order to deceive a throng of people who were at the gate of the Palazzo Mazarini. But when we had turned the corner of the street, Pelletier, my sister's *valet de chambre*, who had arranged for the felucca of Naples to be at Civita Vecchia, ordered the coachman to drive straight to the latter place. The coachman obeyed, and we arrived on the outskirts of Civita

Vecchia as night closed in. Pelletier had arranged with the sailors to take us on board four miles from the port. We sent him to announce our coming, after the footman, whom we had despatched for that purpose and awaited with extreme impatience, had failed to return.

"The delay occasioned us a little uneasiness. However, in spite of all our anxiety to conceal ourselves and our fears of being overtaken, Madame de Mazarin and I quitted the coach, penetrated into a very thick wood near the sea, and composed ourselves to sleep, which we did so soundly for two hours that Nanon, my sister's maid, and Moréna, who was with me, and mounted guard over us, were astonished to the last degree to see us sleeping so tranquilly.

"On awakening, towards morning, we perceived the *valet de chambre*, who told us that he had failed to find the vessel, and that the footman, after getting intoxicated, had remained in an inn to sleep off the effects of the wine he had imbibed, so that we judged it expedient to re-enter the coach and advance a little further, along a by-path, for fear of being overtaken, if we were pursued along the high road. But our horses were so tired that they were scarcely able to stand, which caused my sister to say that it would be better to send them back with the coach to the inn opposite Civita Vecchia, and give the coachman orders to say, if any one came in search of us, that he had seen us embark, in order that they might not pursue us further."

After having proceeded for a considerable distance along a dusty road and under a scorching sun, they retired into the depths of a wood and sent Pelletier once more in search of the felucca, telling him that, in the event of his still being unable to find that elusive vessel, he must charter another.

" The heat of the sun," continues Marie, "which had been beating on our heads for the space of five hours and which was then at its height, a fast of four-and-twenty hours, and the disappointment of hearing no news of the vessel, threw us into a despair which made me say to my sister that I wished to return, and that it would be preferable to die at Rome, in whatever manner I must, than to die of hunger where we were. But my sister, who is the most patient and the most cheerful woman in the world, encouraged me by her arguments, finally adding that, if in the course of the next half-hour we received no favourable news, we could still return. I resolved then to wait for that time, and scarcely had a quarter passed when we heard the sound of a horse approaching at full gallop in our direction. Thereupon the fear of being overtaken, joined to the other agitations of my mind, threw me into the greatest consternation conceivable. But my sister, who had at that moment two pistols in her hand, perceiving that it was the little La Roche (the name of the postilion, who had gone to look for the vessel, without saying anything to us about it), reassured me altogether, and my sorrow was on the instant converted into joy by the news that he gave us, which was that, so far as he could gather, our vessel was awaiting us four miles from the place in which we were. He forthwith took charge of our valises, which were neither heavy nor numerous. Nevertheless, we walked in front, on foot, in the full heat of the sun and through a flat country, in which we saw a number of vipers gliding about.

" The indefatigable Madame de Mazarin constituted herself our advance guard, and continued to walk so fast that, to keep up with her, I was forced to rest from time to time. Hunger, thirst, weariness, and the heat had

deprived me of strength to such a degree that I was
compelled to ask a man who was engaged in ploughing
to carry me only some hundred paces towards the sea,
telling him that I had lost my people while out hunting
(my sister and I having changed our clothes in the
coach).   At first, he refused, but when I added some
pistoles to my request, he finally allowed himself to be
persuaded.   He then lifted me up in his arms, and in
this manner I joined my sister.   Almost immediately
afterwards, Pelletier arrived and told us that he had
chartered another vessel for the sum of one thousand
crowns, but that, to tell the truth, he did not like the
appearance of the master or the sailors, who looked to
him thorough rascals.   We answered that Fortune had
decided otherwise, having permitted the little La Roche
to find the first, and that he had gone to meet her.

"Pelletier was no less delighted than ourselves at this
happy adventure, for he had a very good opinion of the
master of the latter vessel.   At length, partly on foot,
partly with the assistance of the labourer, I reached the
seashore, where, soon afterwards, our maids came to
rejoin us ; but, finding neither the first nor the second
vessel, and seeing our hopes so cruelly frustrated, I
abandoned myself to despair.   My sister was not less
disconsolate than myself at this counter-stroke.   However, she concealed her anxiety for fear of augmenting
mine.   The only recourse we had in this predicament
was, after throwing ourselves on a little straw that we
found in a cabin, to send Pelletier a second time to look
for the vessel, the while, for my part, I begged the
labourer to go and procure me a little water.

"At the end of a quarter of an hour, Pelletier returned, and, with a troubled air and in a very frightened
tone, told us that we were pursued, and that we were

lost. My weakness had rendered me so indifferent that I heard this intelligence almost without emotion. But my sister, pressing him to tell her if it were true, and eventually perceiving, by the manner in which he assured her of it, that it was nothing, told him angrily to speak seriously ; and when he replied that it was not the case, and that he had intended to frighten us by way of pleasantry, rebuked him sharply and told him that he had chosen his time for jesting very ill.

"We then made our way to the place where the vessel awaited us, and where, unfortunately, we found also the second, the master and the sailors of which urged us strongly to enter it. But Pelletier, having given me a more favourable account of the master of the first, I promptly entered it, without paying any attention to the importunities of the people in the other. My sister and our maids did the same, but had scarcely done so when the other crew began to threaten us and to endeavour to prevent our putting out to sea, so that I was obliged to give them some money to secure their good-will and free us from the difficulty.

"I was scarcely out at sea than I began to feel the effects of it, and yet was more sensible of the new proposition that our master made us of more money for our passage than the sum he had agreed to accept from our *valet de chambre*. He grounded his demand on the danger to which he had exposed himself in serving us. Pelletier, who did not want for courage, was enraged to find himself deceived in the good opinion of our master, who, contrary to his promise, demanded more than was his due, and, in great wrath, would have made him stand to his bargain. But the master had force on his side, and to his arguments, good or bad, added the threat to throw us overboard or set us ashore on some deserted island, so that I ordered Pelletier to desist, and, by adding one hundred pistoles to the sum previously agreed upon, silenced the master, assuring him of further recompense on his landing us in France, which he promised to do." [1]

In the meanwhile, in Rome, the greatest excitement prevailed at both the Casa Colonna and the Palazzo Mancini. When night fell, and the two ladies did not return, their respective households became very uneasy. When morning came, and there were still no signs of the absent ones, their anxiety gave way to consternation, and a servant on horseback was despatched to inform the Constable. Colonna at once returned to Rome, and sent off mounted messengers in all directions to gather news of the fugitives, but without any result. Towards evening, however, Madame de Mazarin's coachman arrived, with the news that the two ladies had embarked on a ship near Civita Vecchia, upon which the enraged Constable despatched a courier to the Marquis d'Astorga, Governor of Naples, begging him to send galleys in pursuit of his wife in the direction of Marseilles, a request with which that official hastened to comply.

The Constable did not doubt that the fugitives would make for France, and he had a shrewd suspicion that Louis XIV was a consenting party to his wife's escape, if he had not actually instigated it. He accordingly called upon the French Ambassador to the Vatican, Cardinal d'Estrées, who professed himself greatly shocked at the conduct of the Constabless, and promised to write to the Bishop of Marseilles and to Colbert, and also, at Colonna's special request, to the Queen, to beg her Majesty to do everything possible to prevent

[1] " La Vérité dans son jour."

the lady having an interview with the King.[1] Louis XIV, it should be mentioned, was then with the army in Holland ; but the Constable was well aware that his wife, in her present temper, would be quite capable of pursuing him from one end of Europe to the other.

Let us, however, leave the Constable, fuming with indignation, and return to the adventurous sisters, voyaging in their little felucca, at the mercy of a crew of rascally Neapolitans, who were probably only deterred from throwing them overboard and seizing on all they possessed by the thought of the reward which had been promised them on the safe arrival of their passengers on French soil, and through seas swarming with Turkish corsairs.

"We had the wind very favourable for the first six hours," continues Marie, "after which there fell a great calm, and we made scarcely any progress. At sunrise we sighted a brigantine, and, the master fearing that it was a Turkish vessel, we headed for some rocks on the coast of Tuscany, where he pointed out to us a place where we might land and conceal ourselves, in case he were attacked. Then, under cover of the same rocks, he proceeded to reconnoitre the vessel, and, having finally inquired and learned that she was a Genoese, we continued our voyage in the same calm weather so far as Monaco, where my sister was much incommoded by the sea, which became so rough under the influence of a

[1] Cardinal d'Estrées also wrote to Pomponne, then Minister for Foreign Affairs. His letter is interesting, since it shows that in well-informed circles Marie's flight was attributed to its true cause : "After the thousand conjectures that have been made about this escape, so far as regards the Constabless, it is thought that the most probable is that she was in dread of being poisoned. The Constable and she voluntarily ceased to live together as husband and wife three years since."

very high wind, that we should have been wrecked, had not our master been so skilful.

"As we were unable to disembark for want of a certificate of health, having come from Civita Vecchia, in the environs of which the plague then was, we landed at Monaco, where we secured false ones, which we made use of at Ciotat, our master being unwilling to land at Marseilles, owing to some differences which he had with the people of that port. This proved a rather fortunate circumstance for us, since it enabled us to escape the feluccas and galleys which the Constable had sent in pursuit of us, and which, failing to find us at sea, by reason of the unusual course which our master, a very shrewd man, had kept, made for Marseilles and the other ports, where we should undoubtedly have been captured, had we possessed certificates of health to enable us to land there.

"At length, after a voyage of nine days, we arrived safely at Ciotat, where, having rested about four hours, we mounted some horses which we had hired, and, travelling all night, reached Marseilles at a somewhat early hour, where I first inquired for M. Arnoux, intendant of the galleys, in the hope that he would have the passport for me which I had requested of the King, in the letter I had written his Majesty ere leaving Rome."

The intendant handed the Constabless a packet containing the passport and a letter from Louis XIV for herself, and another from Pomponne, the Minister for Foreign Affairs, to the Comte de Grignan, Madame de Sévigné's son-in-law, the King's lieutenant in Provence, recommending him to receive the lady at Aix and give her all the assistance she might require. Armed with these papers, Marie returned to the inn where she

and her sister had put up and went to bed, exhausted
with fatigue, to be speedily awakened, however, to hear
that a certain Meneghini, or Manechini, a swashbuck-
ling gentleman in the Constable's service, who had apparently arrived by one of the galleys which had been
sent in pursuit of them, desired to speak with her. In
great alarm, for she believed that Meneghini's object
was to carry her off or perhaps assassinate her, the
princess despatched a messenger to inform the intendant,
who sent some of his guards to protect her, and begged
her to remove to his own house for greater security.
However, Meneghini had come with pacific intentions,
his orders being to beg her to return to Rome, or at
least to postpone the continuance of her journey "until
the arrival of a suite more in accordance with her rank,"
both of which propositions the lady declined.

The sisters spent the night at the intendant's house,
" where the kind reception and the good cheer that was
provided for us, and the comfortable beds we found
there, repaired in some degree the evils we had suffered
on the vessel." On the morrow, the Comte de Grignan,
to whom they had forwarded the letter of the Minister
for Foreign Affairs, sent an escort of his guards to conduct them to Aix, where they were lodged in the house
of a M. de Moriès, a gentleman in the service of the
Duc de Nevers, who treated them " in the most magnificent and most obliging manner conceivable."

CHAPTER XVI

Sensation aroused in Paris by Marie's adventure—The Constable Colonna
writes to Louis XIV—Marie sends the *valet de chambre* Pelletier
with a letter to the King—The Constable despatches an agent to
Paris—Hortense goes to Turin and the Constabless to Grenoble—The
Queen forbids Marie to continue her journey—Interview between the
Duc de Nevers and his sister—Brief of Clement X to Louis XIV on
behalf of the Constable—Letter of Maria Theresa to the King—Louis
XIV leaves the army and returns to France—Second brief of the
Pope—Embarrassing position of the King—He advises the Con-
stabless to enter a convent—She ignores the orders of the Queen and
sets out for Paris—The King sends La Gilbertière to order her to
return to Grenoble—Her interview with the Duc de Créqui—Louis
XIV accedes to her request to enter the Abbey of Lys and sends her
a thousand pistoles—Her sojourn at Lys—Reply of the King to the
Pope's brief—He becomes more favourably disposed towards the
Constabless—Imprudent letter of Marie to Colbert—Louis XIV sends
her to the Abbey of Avenay—She is permitted to reside with her
brother at Nevers—She resolves to go to Turin.

THE news of the arrival of our two heroines in
Provence created a great sensation in Paris, and
Madame de Sévigné, to whom Madame de Grignan did
not fail to send early intelligence of the matter, wrote
to her daughter :—

"In the midst of our chagrins, the description that you
have sent me of Madame de Colonna and her sister is a
delightful incident; it is an admirable picture. The
Comtesse de Soissons and Duchesse de Bouillon are
furious against these madcaps, and say that they ought
to be shut up; they declare themselves strongly opposed
to this strange escapade. It is not thought that the

King will care to offend the Constable, who is assuredly
the most powerful nobleman in Rome. In the meanwhile,
we shall see them arrive like Mlle. de l'Étoile :[1] the
comparison is excellent."[2]

In the meantime, the Constable Colonna was moving
heaven and earth to recover his fugitive wife. He
appealed to the Pope ; he enlisted the good office of the
Pope's nephew, Cardinal Altieri, who governed the aged
Clement X and was bitterly antagonistic to Louis XIV;
he sent for the Duc de Nevers, who was at Venice, and
extracted from him a promise to use all his influence
with his sister to induce her to return ; and he wrote to
the King a letter in which he characterized the charges
which his wife appeared to have brought against him as
" imaginary pretexts to excuse her culpable departure";
dwelt upon the dishonour which her conduct had brought
upon him and his House ; implored his Majesty " to
make use of his lofty wisdom and to cut the thread of
scandal greater still than those of which this regrettable
imprudence had already been the cause," and ended by
expressing his opinion that, " thanks to his authority
and his great wisdom, his Majesty would not fail to
find means to bring back Madame to a sense of her
duties, and, at the same time, deliver him [the Constable]
from a grief as painful as it was undeserved, and which
occasioned him such cruel agitation of mind."[3]

Nor did he neglect other means, since he despatched
one Saint-Simon, a very resourceful individual in the
service of his friend Cardinal Altieri, to France, with
orders to endeavour to induce the Constabless to return

---

[1] One of the characters in the " Roman comique " of Scarron.
[2] Letter of 29 June 1672.
[3] Letter of 21 June 1672, Archives des Affaires Etrangères, published by Lucien Perey, " Marie Mancini Colonna."

to Rome; and, should he fail in this, which seemed almost certain, to proceed to Paris and do everything possible to persuade the King that a guilty passion for the Chevalier de Lorraine was the true motive of the lady's appearance in France.

On her side, Marie, foreseeing the influences which would be brought to bear upon the King, was not idle, and lost no time in sending the faithful Pelletier to Holland, where, as we have said, Louis XIV then was, with a letter for his Majesty, begging him to grant her permission to come to Paris. Pelletier, however, was waylaid by a troop of Italian bandits, who attacked him and left him half-dead by the roadside; nor was it until three weeks later that the Constabless learned of the fate of her envoy, and, in the meantime, suffered torments of anxiety at the non-arrival of the expected reply. There is some reason to believe that the attack upon Pelletier had been instigated by Saint-Simon, in order to prevent the Constabless communicating with the King. About the same time, news arrived that Saint-Simon had reached Paris and had appealed to the Queen and the Ministers, giving out that he was authorised to speak on behalf of the Vatican, in virtue of his connection with Cardinal Altieri. Thereupon Marie quitted Aix, with the intention of proceeding to Paris, accompanied by her sister and escorted by the Chevalier de Mirabeau, over whom Hortense appears to have cast her spells, and some of M. de Grignan's guards; but, on reaching Pont-Saint-Esprit, they learned that the Duc de Mazarin's chief myrmidon, Polastron, and a party of soldiers were approaching to arrest the duchess, against whom the decree of the Grande Chambre, authorising her husband to seize her person wherever he might find her, was still in force.

This alarming intelligence obliged them to quit the high road and seek refuge in a neighbouring château, and the same night Hortense took the road for Savoy, whose ruler, Charles Emmanuel II, it will be remembered, had once been a suitor for her hand, and had treated her, she tells us, with so much courtesy when she passed through Turin on her way to Italy the previous year, that she had resolved to take up her residence in his territories, if ever she quitted Rome.[1]

Madame de Mazarin's reception at Turin exceeded her fondest anticipations. The Duke, delighted to see her, not only promised her his protection, but even went so far as to offer her the ducal château of Chambéry as a residence, and to give orders for it to be immediately prepared for her reception. However, she only remained, for the present, a very short time in Savoy, as on learning that Marie was awaiting her at Grenoble, she at once set out for that town. During her journey through Charles Emmanuel's territories, every imaginable honour was paid her, and the various officials received orders to report every incident of her progress to their sovereign.

On her arrival at Grenoble, Marie had been very courteously received by the Duc de Lesdiguières, the Governor of Dauphiné, who begged her to take up her quarters at his hotel, or, if she preferred, at the Arsenal, which latter offer she accepted. But alas! a rather unpleasant surprise was in store for her, since, three days later, she received a letter from Maria Theresa—whom Louis XIV, during his absence in Holland, had appointed Regent of the kingdom—commanding her, "in the most courteous manner conceivable," not to proceed beyond the place where her Majesty's letter might happen to

[1] " Mémoires de la Duchesse de Mazarin."

x

find her, and adding "that she had no doubt that such was the intention of the King."

The Constabless had, of course, no alternative but to obey, and informed the royal messenger that she had no intention of going further, and would render implicit obedience to the Queen's commands. Although much annoyed at being thus prevented from continuing her journey to Paris, she consoled herself by the reflection that some opposition from the Queen was, after all, only to be expected, and that, in all probability, the King's "intention" in regard to her was very different from that which his jealous consort chose to imagine. But, as we shall presently see, the opposition of Maria Theresa did not stop here.

Madame de Mazarin reached Grenoble a few days later, and, almost immediately afterwards, the Duc de Nevers arrived from Italy. Faithful to the promise he had given the Constable at Rome, he urged Marie very strongly to return to her husband, pointing out the serious obstacles which stood in the way of her being permitted to reside in France, particularly the enmity of the Queen and Madame de Montespan, whom he made no doubt were both equally determined to keep her and the King apart. He expressed his conviction that circumstances would be too strong for her, and that the egotistical monarch would not hesitate to sacrifice her to the jealousy of his wife and mistress ; while, even if he declined to yield to their importunities, it was hardly possible that he could turn a deaf ear to the urgent representations which the Vatican would be certain to make on behalf of the Constable Colonna. Marie replied that she had not taken a resolution of such importance to stop half-way, but that she had no wish to compromise any member of her family. To which her brother, who valued his own peace and comfort above all things, rejoined that he entirely declined to be made a party to her escapade; and they separated on far from cordial terms.

The Duc de Nevers did not exaggerate the hostile influences which would be brought to bear upon Louis XIV. The Nuncio at the French Court kept Cardinal Altieri fully informed of all that was happening in France, and, on learning from him that Pelletier, now recovered from his injuries, had passed through Paris, on his way to the King in Holland, the Cardinal despatched to his Majesty a brief which he had extracted from the Pope, wherein his Holiness informed the Most Christian King that he took very much to heart the affair which concerned his beloved son, the noble Constable Colonna, and that it was "his sincere desire that his Majesty would lend a benevolent ear to the Constable's representations and assure him of his protection." Altieri himself wrote to the King in more precise terms. "I take advantage of the brief of his Holiness," he writes, "to represent also to your Majesty my grief at an incident so prejudicial to the family of the Constable, and to beg your Majesty to facilitate the reunion of the fugitive and her husband, by his royal authority and by every means which may appear opportune to his lofty wisdom."

About the same time that these epistles reached him, Louis XIV received a letter from the Queen which would appear to have been inspired by the Constable's crafty emissary Saint-Simon, wherein she assured him that the fears which had prompted Marie to fly from Rome were purely imaginary, and that her true motive in wishing to establish herself in France was to enjoy the society of the Chevalier de Lorraine, about whose conduct in the affair she expressed herself very strongly.

She insisted, also, on the difficulties and embarrassments, both political and domestic, which the open protection which his Majesty seemed resolved to accord the lady must inevitably entail, and made no attempt to conceal the anxiety and pain which the presence of the Constabless in Paris would occasion her.

It is highly probable that Madame de Montespan, who, on 20 June of that year, had presented her royal lover with a third pledge of her affection in the shape of a son (afterwards the Comte de Vexin), also wrote to his Majesty to much the same effect, and we can well believe that the arguments of his mistress would have at least as much influence with Louis as those of the Queen.

However, the King was disinclined to take any further steps in so delicate a matter until his return from Holland, and it would seem that Maria Theresa was acting entirely on her own responsibility when she sent orders forbidding Marie to continue her journey to Paris.

Finding that his demands for the return of his wife and her expulsion from France did not seem to be productive of any result, the Constable Colonna's suspicions that there was a secret understanding between Marie and Louis XIV gave way to conviction, upon which the tone he had hitherto adopted underwent a complete change, and what he had demanded as a right he now sought as a favour, promising that, if the Court of France would but employ its good offices to induce the princess to return to Italy, the past should be forgotten, and she should be treated with every possible consideration. At the same time, it is evident, from the correspondence of Cardinal Altieri with the Nuncio in Paris, that the Constable's intentions differed very widely from these professions, and that he was fully resolved, when once

he had got his truant wife into his hands, that a convent, either in Rome or in some other part of Italy, and
not the Casa Colonna, should be her residence.

Towards the end of July, Louis XIV quitted the army
and returned to Saint-Germain, where the Court then was.
The Nuncio at once pressed for an answer to the representations which the Vatican had made on behalf of its
" beloved son"; but Le Tellier, to whom he applied,
answered that the war and other important matters had
so occupied his Majesty's mind that he as yet had had
no leisure to attend to the affair in question. The
Nuncio, very dissatisfied with this evasive reply, thereupon resolved to have recourse to a second papal brief,
which Altieri had sent him, with instructions not to
make use of it, unless other arguments failed ; and
accordingly handed it to Le Tellier to transmit to the
King. It was as follows :—

Pope Clement X to Louis XIV.

" Very dear son in Christ, greeting, etc.

" It is with great sorrow that we have learned of the
sudden departure of our dear daughter in Jesus Christ,
the noble Constabless Colonna, since we are animated by
the kindliest sentiments towards that illustrious family,
and all matters which concern it affect us keenly. Now,
we have recently learned that the said beloved daughter
in Jesus Christ has set out for France, which, in truth,
occasions us a lively joy, since your Majesty will act in
conformity with the compassion which is innate in him,
in employing his royal authority to send her back as
speedily as possible to her husband. The venerable
brother Francesco (N),[1] Archbishop of Florence, will
explain our intentions more fully to your Majesty, on

[1] The Nuncio, Francesco Nerli.

whom we confer, in the meanwhile, our Apostolic bene-
diction.

"Given at Rome, the XII July MDCLXXII, the
third year of our Pontificate."[1]

Beset, on one side, by the representations of the
Constable and the Holy See, and, on the other, by the
importunities of the Queen and Madame de Montespan
and the solicitations of Colbert and Louvois, who, aware
of Marie's taste for politics, were terrified at the prospect
of her resuming her influence over the King's mind,
Louis XIV found himself in a most embarrassing position. He had promised his old love his protection, and
his honour, no less than the remains of the affection he
had once entertained for her, forbade him to go back on
his word. But, even if the fears for her personal safety
which had prompted her to take refuge in France were
well founded, and not a mere figment of an excited
imagination or a pretext for leaving a husband whom
she disliked, about which he had begun to have some
doubts, the security she sought had been attained so soon
as she had set foot in his dominions, and by no means
necessitated her residing in Paris. To permit her to do
this, in the face of the representations of the Constable,
the Nuncio, Cardinal Altieri, and even the Pope, would,
he felt, be a most impolitic step, and one capable of a
very sinister interpretation. Moreover, he valued his
tranquillity too highly to hazard it lightly, and signs
were not wanting that the advent of the Constabless in
Paris would be the signal for trouble in more than one
quarter of the Court. He, therefore, resolved to adopt
a middle course: he would refuse to surrender the lady
to her husband, though he would use every possible

[1] Published by Lucien Perey, "Marie Mancini Colonna."

After the painting by Mignard

MARIE MANCINI COLONNA, PRINCIPESSA DI PALLIANO

persuasion to induce her to return to him; but, at the same time, he would set his face sternly against her residing in Paris or approaching the Court.

Meanwhile the Constabless, at Grenoble, was impatiently awaiting the return of the faithful Pelletier with the King's answer. At last, the letter arrived, and we can imagine the eagerness with which she took it and broke the seal. But a bitter disappointment was in store for her, since, instead of according her the permission to come to Paris which she so ardently desired, the King advised her to retire to a convent, "in order to close the mouths of the slanderers who were placing sinister interpretations on her retirement from Rome."

The Constabless, deeply chagrined at the contents of the letter, so very different from the kind and sympathetic one she had received at Marseilles, felt convinced that, by some means, his Majesty's mind had been prejudiced against her. She had been expressly forbidden to proceed beyond Grenoble, and was, moreover, short of money; but she was not the woman to recoil before difficulties, and, believing that if she could only obtain an audience of the King, all might yet be well, immediately resolved to ignore the orders of Maria Theresa and set out for Paris. "I was so little satisfied with this letter," she writes, "that I determined to go straight to Paris and throw myself at his Majesty's feet, and communicated my intention to my sister. We started in a litter, without saying a word about our journey to any one, from fear that the governor would stop us, and travelled together to Lyons, where we separated, she to return to Chambéry, while I continued my journey to Paris, accompanied by a courier whom I had known at Rome, named Marguien, a trustworthy and intelligent man, whom I engaged to come with me, and who charged himself with all the expenses of the journey. I travelled post, in a *calèche*, and Moréna and he followed on horseback.

On arriving at Nevers, the Constabless learned, to her dismay, that a gentleman had forbidden the post, in the King's name, to furnish any one with horses without his permission, and that similar orders had been given to all the postmasters along the road to Paris. She was also informed that the gentleman in question, a certain M. de la Gilbertière, was awaiting her at the bridge over the Loire, a little further on, and entertained no doubt that he was the bearer of a message from the King, forbidding her to come to Paris. However, by dint of bribery and coaxing, she succeeded in obtaining post-horses, and, by making a détour through some by-streets, escaped the King's messenger and hastened on towards the capital. She travelled all night, and at such speed that her carriage was twice overturned; but at Montargis her maid Moréna was taken ill, and this necessitated a delay, which enabled La Gilbertière, who had been following in hot pursuit, to come up with them at Fontainebleau.

La Gilbertière lost no time in seeking an interview with the Constabless and communicating to her his instructions. "He desired to suggest to me," writes Marie, "that my wisest course would be to return to the Constable, as in France matters were not taking a very favourable turn for me, the King having been given to understand that I flattered myself that I possessed great influence over his mind. To this he added that the King was much annoyed at having accorded me his protection under frivolous pretexts, and for reasons which had no other foundation than my caprice; and he concluded by informing me that, in the event of my being resolved not to return to my home, I should go back to Grenoble and enter the Abbey of Montfleuri. These were the exact terms of his embassy.

"I replied that I had not quitted my home to return there so soon ; that frivolous pretexts had not caused me to take this resolution, but good and solid reasons, which, however, I could and would explain only to the King, and that I hoped for justice from him ; that, provided I could speak to him once, which was all I demanded, he would be easily disabused of all the bad impressions that had been given him of me ; that I was very far from flattering myself that I possessed the supposed empire over him of which he had just spoken to me; that I possessed neither sufficient merit nor sufficient capacity to take any part whatever in the management of his affairs ; that all I asked for was to withdraw to Paris, and that I limited my ambition to the extent of a cloister, where I begged his Majesty to suffer me to dwell among my relatives, as the Grand Duchess of Tuscany and the Princesse de Chalais were at present living, and as had a thousand other ladies, either widows or separated from their husbands. As for returning to Grenoble, I found myself too fatigued to undertake another journey ; and, besides, I awaited his Majesty's answer in regard to the steps I should take."

So saying, she turned her back upon the King's emissary, and taking up a guitar which stood in a corner of the room, began to play upon it, as a signal that the interview was at an end. Louis XIV had refused even to grant an audience to the woman who, twelve years before, had reigned at his Court almost like a queen. Her disappointment and mortification were intense, but she derived some little comfort from the reflection that La Gilbertière's mission must be the work of Maria Theresa rather than of the King.

Some days later, the Constabless received a visit from the Duc de Créqui, First Gentleman of the Chamber to Louis XIV, whom his Majesty had sent to reply to the propositions she had made to La Gilbertière. The duke found her lodged in a wretched *auberge*,[1] stretched on a pallet, and was unable to prevent himself from expressing his compassion at a spectacle which contrasted so strangely with the pomp and grandeur of the Casa Colonna where he had last seen her. The princess, however, cut short his " lamentations," by begging him to come at once to the point, upon which he told her, in the most courteous terms at his command, that the King did not wish her to enter Paris or to speak to him, since he had given his word to the Nuncio and the Constable, for reasons of which she could not be ignorant, that he would not do so, and that her only alternative, if she did not prefer to return to Rome, which was the wisest and the most honourable course to take, was to go back to Grenoble.

The lady rejoined that she was desolated by the King's refusal to allow her the honour of seeing him and to enter Paris ; but that she felt sure that he was too kind-hearted to compel her to make the return journey to Grenoble in the state in which she then was, prostrated by the heat and the rapidity with which she had travelled thither, and accordingly begged him to permit her to enter the Abbey of Lys, a convent situated near Melun, about two hours' journey from Fontainebleau.

M. de Créqui suggested that she should write a note to the King to that effect, promising to deliver it immediately on his return. He kept his word, and the following morning one of the royal pages arrived at Fontaine-

---

[1] This wretched *auberge* seems to have been chosen for the sake of effect, as the Duke of Modena, who had a palace at Fontainebleau, had placed it at her disposal ; but the offer had been declined.

bleau, bearing the permission the Constabless had requested, and an order to the Abbess of Lys to receive her. La Gilbertière, who had arrived at the same time as the page, was charged to escort her to the convent.

Soon afterwards, came a messenger from Colbert, bringing her " two purses of five hundred pistoles each, on behalf of the King, which his Majesty had given orders to send her, and this sum he continued to pay every six months during the time that I remained under his protection."[1]

The Constabless saw in these attentions of the King, and particularly in the permission to reside at Lys, so near to Fontainebleau, signs of a disposition on his part to relax the severity he had lately shown towards her ; and she was, in consequence, extremely mortified at finding on her arrival at Lys that she was to be treated like a prisoner of State, that she was to be kept under the strictest surveillance, and that no one was to be allowed to visit or communicate with her, save her sisters, Mesdames de Soissons and de Bouillon, and their husbands, unless by special permission.

However, the abbess and the nuns showed her the greatest consideration, and did everything possible to mitigate the rigour of her imprisonment. Both her sisters came to see her and overwhelmed her with presents and caresses, the Comtesse de Soissons, who appears to have forgotten their former rivalry in her hatred of the La Vallières and Montespans, sending her a sumptuous bed, ornamented with tapestries, and other costly articles of furniture, to relieve the bareness of her

---

[1] Madame de Scudéry wrote to Bussy-Rabutin : " She [the Constabless] replied playfully to M. de Créqui that she had often heard of people who gave money to ladies in order to see them, but never not to see them."

cell. However, poor Marie was very far from happy, and the abbess, who had received instructions from Colbert to furnish him with the minutest details concerning her charge, informs the Minister, in one of her letters, that the Constabless "has always appeared very gay since she has been here, but, in reality, we believe that she is very wretched."[1]

While the Constabless was fretting behind the walls of her convent, the Nuncio in Paris continued to press for a definite answer to the demands which Clement X and Cardinal Altieri had addressed to Louis XIV. But the King, true to the middle course which he had resolved to adopt, showed no disposition to surrender the lady to her husband, and the Nuncio invariably received the same assurance, namely, that, while the King was prepared to use every possible persuasion to induce the Constabless to return, he would not force her to do so or even refuse her an asylum in his dominions. At length, at the end of August, Louis XIV decided to return a positive answer to the representations of the Vatican, and wrote Clement X a very cold letter, wherein he presumed that "his Holiness had been informed by the Nuncio of all the reasons which had prevented him replying earlier to his brief of 22 June touching the retreat of the Constabless Colonna into his realm," and that "his Holiness had seen, from all the orders that he had issued relative to the affair, that he had an equal desire with his Holiness to contribute in every possible way to re-establish that confidence which had at first existed between two persons who ought to be so closely united."

[1] Letter of 27 August 1672, published by Amédée Renée, " Les Nièces de Mazarin."

After this very plain hint, the Vatican declined to take any further steps on behalf of the Constable, and though Colonna called upon the French Ambassador at Rome to protest against the conduct of the King, he got little consolation in that quarter, and the Ambassador wrote to the Minister for Foreign Affairs that he was of opinion that the Constable was more moved by the scandal which his wife's flight had aroused than by a sentiment of the heart, "which," he added, "is sufficiently diverted by other amusements." Evidently, Cardinal d'Estrées was quite *au courant* with the gossip of the Eternal City.

It would appear that Louis XIV sympathised far more deeply with the troubles of his old love than that lady had any idea. The curt messages he had sent her by La Gilbertière and the Duc de Créqui had been provoked by her unexpected arrival at Fontainebleau and her evident determination to ignore the wishes he had expressed in the letter which she had received at Grenoble. But his anger did not last long, and, on the return of the Comtesse de Soissons from her visit to Lys, the King sent for her to ask news of her sister, and also requested Colbert to submit to him the reports which he received from the abbess; and, on learning how irksome Marie found the restraint to which she was subjected, gave orders that she was to be allowed to take walks in the Forest of Fontainebleau, though always well accompanied.

The Constabless, however, was of course unaware of the more favourable disposition of his Majesty towards her, or of the reply which he had made to the demands of the Vatican for her surrender, and, as time went on, she became more and more incensed against the King, who, after countenancing her flight, now treated it as a crime, and had transformed the asylum he had promised her into a prison. An incident which occurred towards the end of September put the finishing touch to her resentment.

Colbert, to whom Louis had entrusted the entire direction of the princess's affairs, took upon himself to inform her that she would be expected to defray the cost of the maintenance of herself and her attendants at the convent out of the money which the King had sent her at Fontainebleau. As the Constabless had already expended the greater part of that sum in replenishing her wardrobe and in repaying the courier Marguien for the money he had disbursed on her behalf during the journey from Grenoble, she was extremely indignant, and, under the impression that the order had emanated from the King himself, wrote to the Minister "a very imprudent letter, complaining of the little consideration that his Majesty had for her, to which, she added, that, since he was unwilling to give her liberty to go to Paris, he should at least accord her that of going anywhere else she might wish."[1]

The tone of this letter deeply offended the King, and the enemies of the Constabless did not fail to profit by the occasion to persuade him that she was too near Paris, and that, one fine day, she would escape and make her appearance there. Louis XIV, fearful of such an event, which would be sure to provoke a grave scandal, thereupon directed Colbert to inform Marie, on his behalf, that she must choose a convent sixty leagues distant from Paris, and that, after the letter she had just written, she was no longer deserving of his protection.

[1] "La Vérité dans son jour."

This new disgrace threw the poor lady into the depths of despair, and she wrote imploring Colbert to intercede for her with the King and obtain his pardon, protesting that she had regretted what she had written " so soon as she had recovered her self-possession." Colbert replied that his Majesty had been graciously pleased to accept her excuses, but that he persisted in his resolution to send her sixty leagues from Paris, and begged her to notify him without delay what convent she had selected. The Constabless informed the Minister that she would repair to whatever convent his Majesty might be pleased to name, and she added : " Only tell the King that I ask to speak to him once more before I go. That will be for the last time in my life, and I shall return to Paris no more. Grant me this favour, I implore you, Monsieur, and, after that, I promise him that I will go even further, if he desires it, being always very disposed to obey him."

To this touching letter Louis XIV replied himself, though not until after an interval of several days, which leads us to suppose that Colbert very probably had not deemed it advisable to show it him.

Louis XIV to the Constabless Colonna.

" Versailles, 29 September 1672.

" MY COUSIN,—Being desirous of giving you a convenient abbey to which you may retire and dwell in full security during the time you remain in my realm, I have found that the one most likely to be in accordance with your wishes is that of Saint-Pierre, of my town of Rheims, of which the Dame d'Orvel is abbess; and for that purpose, so soon as I receive your final response to this letter, I will send the Sieur Goberti[1] to conduct you

---

[1] Presumably, La Gilbertière. The Abbess of Lys, in a letter to Colbert, speaks of him as La Giberti.

thither. On this, I pray God that he will have you, my cousin, in his holy and worthy keeping."[1]

"And that," writes poor Marie, "was all the reply that I received to my letter."

Four or five days later, La Gilbertière arrived with a coach and an order to the Abbess of Lys for the Constabless to leave her convent, and escorted her, together with the faithful Moréna and three other waiting-women—whom the Constable, anxious, in spite of his indignation against his wife, that she should maintain a suite in accordance with her rank, had sent from Rome —to the Abbey of Avenay, three leagues from Rheims and thirty from Paris. The King had thus diminished by half the distance of her exile.

This abbey, which had been chosen by Louis XIV, at the last moment, in place of that mentioned in his letter to Marie, was a noble chapter, which served as a retreat for ladies of very high rank. Its superior was Madame Brulart de Sillery, grand-daughter of Henri IV's Chancellor of that name, who "received her with every mark of esteem and kindness that it was possible to desire."

Notwithstanding the efforts of the good abbess, the poor lady seems to have been profoundly miserable, as the convent was too far from Paris to permit of the visits of her relatives, and there was, therefore, nothing to relieve the tedium of her existence. However, after she had been there about three months, she received a visit from her brother, the Duc de Nevers, whom she had not seen since they parted on such unfriendly terms at Grenoble. Struck by his sister's melancholy, the duke judged the moment favourable to make a last

---

[1] Bibliothèque Nationale MSS. cited by Chantelauze, "Louis XIV et Marie Mancini."

effort to bring about a reconciliation between her and her husband, or, failing that, to induce her to leave France, and accordingly told her that it was perfectly hopeless for her to expect any amelioration of her lot so long as she remained in France, as the Queen and Madame de Montespan would be certain to check any inclination towards clemency that the King might show. Marie replied angrily that the King was grievously mistaken if he imagined that the severity with which he had thought fit to treat her would have the effect of inducing her to return to the Constable, and that rather than do so, she would leave France and seek " a more hospitable country."

This was exactly what her brother, who appears to have been acting in concert with Louis XIV and also with the Constable, wanted ; but since he feared some fresh scandal, unless he first succeeded in calming the state of exasperation in which she then was, he promised to ask permission of the King for her to remove from Avenay to his house at Nevers. A few days later, he returned with the desired permission, and Marie joyfully quitted the abbey, but not before her brother had extracted from her a promise that, in the event of anything occurring to oblige him to leave Nevers, she would at once enter another convent.

After the Constabless had passed a very pleasant week at Nevers, where her charming sister-in-law, *née* Diane de Thianges, overwhelmed her with kindness, the duke suddenly announced that important business called him to Venice, and reminded her of her promise. Marie, though in despair at being separated from the duchess, thereupon made the round of the convents in the town, but, not finding one to her liking, suggested that she should accompany her brother as far as Lyons, where

Y

the convents were more commodious than those at
Nevers. The duke acquiesced readily enough, for, as
we have said, it was his object, if he could not prevail
upon his sister to return to her husband, at any rate to
induce her to leave France, and at Lyons she would be
within a short journey of the frontier.

On reaching Lyons, where they were received by the
Marquis de Villeroi, in the absence of his father, the
duke of that name, who was governor of the province,
the Constabless visited several convents, and had almost
decided to enter that of Sainte-Marie de la Visitation,
situated on an eminence which commanded a view of the
whole city, when " destiny, ever the enemy of her happiness, inspired the Marquis de Villeroi and her brother
to dissuade her, and they succeeded so well in exaggerat-
ing the sufferings which she had endured in France, and
the ill-treatment which she had received from the King,
that she took the resolution to leave it and withdraw
into Italy, without, however, informing them of the part
to which it was her intention to proceed."[1] This, as
will be anticipated, was Savoy, where her sister Hortense
had already found an asylum.

Foreseeing that his wife was not unlikely to take this
resolution sooner or later, the Constable Colonna had,
some weeks previously, begged Cardinal d'Estrées, the
French Ambassador at Rome, to communicate with the
Duke of Savoy, in order to ascertain whether he would
be willing to admit the princess into his realm, in the
event of her desiring to come thither. The Constable
was, above all things, anxious to get his wife out of
France and out of reach of Louis XIV, and, since he was
on friendly terms with Charles Emmanuel, he did not
doubt that that prince would do everything possible to

[1] " La Vérité dans son jour."

persuade his wife to return to him, and, if she refused, very probably consent to surrender her into his hands.

To the cardinal's letter the Duke sent a very favourable reply, promising not only to receive the Constabless, should she demand his protection, but " to make use of the greatest diligence to dispose her, by the good offices that he might judge most efficacious, to lend ear to an agreement so proper and so laudable (i.e. a reconciliation with her husband)."

And so it came about that when Marie wrote to Charles Emmanuel to solicit his protection and permission to enter some convent in Savoy or Piedmont, she received in reply a very courteous letter, readily granting her request and inviting her to Turin.

CHAPTER XVII

Cordial reception of the Constabless by Charles Emmanuel II of Savoy—
She enters the Convent of the Visitation at Turin—A touching in-
cident—Kindness of the Duke of Savoy to Marie—His reply to the
representations of the Vatican—He falls in love with the Constabless
—Don Maurizio di Bologna and the bravoes—Visit of the Marchesa
Paleotto to Marie—Alarm of the latter—She goes to visit the
Duchesse de Mazarin at Chambéry—Selfish conduct of Hortense—
Return of Marie to Turin—Arrival of the Marchese di Borgomainero
—Treaty between the Constabless and her husband—Marie goes to
reside with the Prince de Carignan—Irritation of the Constable—
Louis XIV, at his solicitation, orders the Prince de Carignan to send
the Constabless away—Charles Emmanuel invites her to La Vénerie
—Her dazzling position—Nature of her relations with the Duke of
Savoy considered—She quarrels with Charles Emmanuel—Vain
attempts of the Duke to effect a reconciliation—Louis XIV refuses
the Constabless permission to enter a convent in France—She sets out
for Flanders with Borgomainero.

MARIE arrived in Piedmont at the end of January
1673, and was met at Rivoli by a gentleman of
the Duke's household, with one of the royal carriages
and an escort of guards, who conducted her to Turin.
Some distance from the city she was met by Charles
Emmanuel himself, accompanied by a number of gentlemen on horseback, all eager to behold this beautiful
Constabless, whose adventures had been for the past few
months the talk of Europe.

The Duke received his fair guest most cordially,
begged her to enter his own coach, and seemed so much
impressed by the charms which had come so near to up-
setting all Mazarin's carefully-laid schemes that he could

hardly take his eyes from her face, until the lady, in some embarrassment, lowered her veil. In the meanwhile, they had entered Turin and arrived at the Convent of the Visitation, where his Highness had given orders for the best apartment to be prepared for the reception of the Constabless. The Archbishop of Turin was at the gate to receive them, and, while Marie went to her apartment to make some change in her dress, the Duke, who had received the archbishop's authorisation to enter the convent with her, waited in the garden. Presently the lady joined him, and, notwithstanding the cold, they paced the garden together for two hours, conversing with great animation. Before leaving, the prince, in the most delicate manner conceivable, begged his companion to regard him as her treasurer, if ever she happened to be in need of money. "This is all I possess," answered Marie, and, quickly unclasping the top of her corsage, she showed him a superb string of pearls which she wore round her neck. "It is the necklace which the King gave me when I left for Brouage," she added, in a tone of deep emotion. "It shall never leave me."

The Duke subsequently related this incident to M. de Gomont, the plenipotentiary whom Louis XIV had sent, at his request, to arrange terms of peace between Savoy and Genoa. Gomont duly informed his master, and the King, touched by this souvenir of the past, promptly remitted to the Constabless a further sum of one thousand pistoles, although this pension had originally been promised her only so long as she remained in France.

Turin was at this period one of the gayest and most brilliant Courts in Europe. The Duke and Duchess,[1]

[1] Marie Jeanne de Savoie-Nemours, only daughter of the Duc de Nemours.

both young and fond of pleasure—the former rather too much so, from all accounts, though his numerous gallantries do not seem to have lessened the affection he had always felt for his wife—neglected nothing to attract to their Court foreigners of distinction and the wealthiest and most magnificent of their own nobility. Splendid receptions, balls, fêtes, ballets, tournaments, horse-races in summer and sleigh-races in winter, followed one another in rapid succession, and scarcely a day passed without the courtiers being called upon to assist at one or more of these diversions. Poor Marie, shut up in her convent, was of course precluded from participating in any of the gaieties which were going on around her; but the good-natured and gallant Duke, pitying the loneliness and monotony of her life, visited her frequently, and, on one occasion, gave orders that the start for a sleigh-race should take place under the convent walls, in order to afford her some amusement.

The Constable Colonna, who was duly informed of this incident by the Nuncio at Turin, was highly indignant. In his eyes, the Convent of the Visitation ought to be a prison, of which the Duke of Savoy would be the gaoler, and here was the prince evidently bent on doing everything in his power to relieve the tedium of his wife's existence ! Nor did the reports which reached him of the frequent visits which the Duke paid to the convent tend to promote a more amiable frame of mind, and he accordingly spurred on the Vatican to make the same demands to Charles Emmanuel as it had previously to Louis XIV. Cardinal Altieri extracted another brief from the aged Pontiff, who must have been by this time heartily tired of hearing the name of his " beloved daughter," the Constabless Colonna ; and the Nuncio was instructed to make strong representations to the

Duke on the subject; but all to no purpose. Charles Emmanuel replied that he had already urged the lady to be reconciled to her husband in such "severe" terms that he had caused her to shed tears; but that he had given her his word that he would not permit any violence to be employed against her, and that he would accord her his protection whether she decided to remain at Turin or to go elsewhere. The Nuncio protested; the Duke declared that nothing could induce him to go back on his word, and the diplomatist sorrowfully informed the Vatican that "he greatly feared that it would be impossible to obtain anything from him."

Gradually the restrictions to which the Constabless had at first been subjected were removed. The Nuncio, at bottom a kind-hearted man, petitioned the Vatican to allow the devoted Moréna, who, on account of her religion, had been excluded from the convent, to join her mistress, and the request was acceded to. Next, the Archbishop of Turin granted her permission to receive as many visitors as she pleased in her little apartment, and Gomont and the French Ambassador, Servien, visited her two or three times a week. Finally, she was even allowed to take walks outside the convent walls, which was altogether contrary to the rules of Italian convents, far more rigorous than those of France.

For these concessions Marie was no doubt indebted to the good offices of Charles Emmanuel. The Duke was falling more and more under the spell of his guest's charms, and "paid her interminable visits," which soon became the chief topic of conversation in both Court and town; and it was whispered that the Constabless had established as complete an empire over the mind and heart of his Highness as she had formerly exercised over Louis XIV's.

These reports duly reached the Constable Colonna, who thereupon despatched one of his confidants, a certain Don Maurizio di Bologna, ostensibly on a visit of courtesy to his wife, but in reality to spy upon her actions and keep him informed of all that concerned her. About the same time, a band of bravoes arrived in the neighbourhood, and the Constabless was convinced that they had been sent by her husband to carry her off, if she were indiscreet enough to venture far from the convent. Don Maurizio pretended that they were in the pay of the Governor of Milan, and had come in search of a man who, having committed an assassination in that city, had fled to Turin ; but, in order to reassure the princess, the Duke of Savoy caused them to be expelled promptly from his dominions.

Soon after this incident, Marie received a visit from her husband's former enchantress, the Marchesa Paleotto. This lady, who had long since been abandoned by Colonna for fresh conquests, but had never pardoned his defection, sought to persuade the Constabless that it was commonly believed at Rome that, if her husband ever succeeded in getting her into his power again, he would certainly cause her to be made away with, and darkly hinted that the object of Don Maurizio in coming to Turin was to bribe one of her waiting-women to poison her. She succeeded in alarming the Constabless to such an extent that she had an attack of fever, which greatly disturbed the Duke, who sent his own physicians to visit her three times a day and wrote her numerous letters of sympathy with his own hand.

On her recovery, the princess confided to Charles Emmanuel the fears which oppressed her, and though the Duke offered to send her her meals every day from his own table, under the pretext that the doctors had prescribed for her a special diet, nothing would satisfy her but to leave Turin and take refuge with her sister Hortense at Chambéry. The Duke, who had tried every possible means to dissuade her, was, of course, in despair at the prospect of her departure, but she consoled him by a promise that she would not be absent more than a month. She set out for Chambéry at the beginning of April 1673,[1] in one of the prince's carriages and escorted by some of his guards, while, to render her still more secure, Charles Emmanuel gave orders that, for that day, horses were not to be furnished to any one, save the courier of the French Embassy; and when Don Maurizio demanded horses in order to follow her, they were refused him. The greatest secrecy as to her destination had been preserved, and it was the belief in Turin that she was on her way to England, where Charles II, whom she had met frequently at the French Court during his days of exile, had instructed Lord Montague, the English Minister to Savoy, to offer her an asylum.

During the weary months which poor Marie, wounded to the heart by the severity of Louis XIV and tormented by the persecutions of her husband, had been spending in convents at Lys, Avenay, and Turin, Hortense, installed in the ducal château at Chambéry, had been leading a very different kind of life. The generosity of Charles Emmanuel enabled her to maintain a semi-royal state, and to gather around her a little Court, composed of the nobility and the high officials of the province; and we may presume that she had no lack of adorers, without whom she would have found even the most sumptuous

---

[1] M. Chantelauze says that she "escaped" from the convent, but this is incorrect.

existence difficult to endure.   The Duke invited her to
his hunting parties, entertained her magnificently at his
country residences, and occasionally came to pay her
homage at Chambéry.   As for her husband, she troubled
very little about him, except to apply to him for the payment of the pension of 24,000 livres which Louis XIV
had promised her, and which seems to have been occasionally in arrears, since, in September 1672, we find her
writing to the King, begging him to command M. de
Mazarin to disgorge without further delay, and "not
to reduce her to the extremity of not knowing where
to lay her head."

On receiving the letter announcing that her sister
was on her way to visit her, Hortense was anything but
delighted.   Beneath an appearance of good nature and
a readiness to oblige in small things, the beautiful
duchess concealed a thoroughly selfish heart, and now,
forgetting the obligations under which Marie had
placed her, in the fear that she might compromise her
own interests with Louis XIV, and perhaps forfeit her
pension by extending to her her hospitality, she suddenly remembered a vow which she had made to Saint-
Francis of Sales, and the accomplishment of which
would not permit of a moment's further delay, and
hastily quitted Chambéry without saying a word as to
her destination.

Marie was naturally much incensed at the conduct of
her sister, and after remaining a few days at Saint-Inno-
cent, as the guest of the bishop, returned to Turin,
where she had the additional mortification of learning
that Louis XIV, at the solicitation of her husband, who
appears to have been under the impression that France
had been her objective, had issued the most stringent
injunctions to the officials of the frontier provinces to

From an engraving by G. Vallet

CHARLES EMMANUEL II, DUKE OF SAVOY

prevent her entering his realm. However, the Duke of Savoy showed himself so delighted at her return, and paid her such delicate attentions, that she soon recovered her spirits, and profited by the permission which she had obtained to leave the convent once a week to attend several hunting-parties and other entertainments which Charles Emmanuel gave at his country-seat of La Vénerie.

Having tasted the sweets of liberty once more, the Constabless began to find the restrictions of convent life more irksome than ever, and she implored the Duke to permit her to leave her cloister. The prince, only too anxious to have greater facilities for enjoying the society of the lady to whom he had now completely lost his heart, communicated with the Constable, who despatched an envoy to Turin in the person of Don Carlo d'Este, Marchese di Borgomainero.[1] Between this nobleman and the Prime Minister of Savoy, the Marchese di San Tommasso, interminable *pourparlers* took place, until the latter declared that no affair of State had ever occasioned him such trouble and annoyance. At length, a kind of treaty was drawn up, whereby it was arranged that the Constabless was to be permitted to remain at large for the space of four months, but on the condition that she should not quit the dominions of the Duke of Savoy, who, on his side, undertook to prevent her departure. If, on the expiration of the four months, the lady still declined to return to her husband, she must then select a convent (those in the Ecclesiastical States and all States subject to the Spanish Crown excepted), and remain there during the Constable's good pleasure.

Marie now quitted her convent and accepted the invitation of the Prince de Carignan, brother of the

---

[1] He was the second son of Filippo Francesco d'Este and Margherita, legitimated daughter of Charles Emmanuel I, Duke of Savoy.

Comte de Soissons, to take up her residence at his palace. Here she was so hospitably entertained that the Constable, informed by his agents, Don Maurizio and Borgomainero, of the minutest details concerning his wife, became exceedingly angry, and wrote a very discourteous letter to the prince, complaining that the hospitality which his wife was receiving at his palace was the principal motive of her persistent refusal to return to Rome, and accusing him of encouraging her in her contumacy.

M. de Carignan informed the Prime Minister, and the lady's affairs had by this time assumed so much importance that a Council of State was held to consider what course to pursue. In the meantime, however, the irate Constable had appealed to Louis XIV, who, anxious to avoid any appearance of supporting the Constabless against her husband, wrote to the Prince de Carignan, who was a French subject, ordering him to send her away. The prince, in great distress, informed his guest of the receipt of the King's letter, which, he said, left him no alternative but to obey, and Marie, in high dudgeon, at once quitted the palace, without even taking leave of her host, and hurried to La Vénerie, where Charles Emmanuel then was, to inform him of the manner in which she was being treated. The chivalrous Duke immediately offered her the hospitality of La Vénerie, and a few days later, the Constable Colonna had the mortification of learning that his wife was installed in one of the finest suites of apartments in the ducal residence.

The position now occupied by the adventurous princess was in many respects similar to that which she had enjoyed at the French Court during the two years which had preceded her exile to La Rochelle. It was in her honour that all the hunting-parties, fêtes, and ballets

were arranged; every day she received in her apartments
the foreign Ministers and the principal personages of
the Court, and she exercised over the Duke the most
absolute empire, for the Duchess of Savoy was the
most complacent and unsuspicious of consorts, and there
was no Mazarin to interfere. What was the exact nature
of that empire is difficult to determine ; the Duke was
certainly of a very ardent temperament, and his conquests,
or what he flattered himself were conquests, were innumerable. But, on the other hand, the Constabless had
hitherto shown herself as discreet in affairs of the heart
as she was rash and impetuous in other matters ; and
we are, therefore, inclined to think that his Highness
remained a *soupirant*, "*toujours affligé, jamais désespéré*," as
that most ingenious of literary forgers, La Beaumelle,
makes Madame de Maintenon say of Louis XIV.

One cloud alone obscured the brightness of the princess's horizon : the thought that, in a few short weeks, she
would have to choose between a reconciliation with her
now detested husband and a return to the solitude and
monotony of convent life. Marie, however, was never
one of those who take thought for the morrow, and the
knowledge that this delightful existence must so soon
come to an end caused her to plunge with an added zest
into the pleasures of the moment.

But, ever unfortunate, her evil star was soon in the
ascendant again. She quarrelled with the Duke and
quitted his realm, to fall into a succession of misfortunes
far greater than those which she had hitherto experienced.
Let us listen to her own account of the matter :—

"My happiness was too great. Fortune, which de-
lighted in tormenting me, took care not to permit it to last.
To interrupt, accordingly, its course, she inspired his
Royal Highness with political sentiments, and impelled

him one day to propose to me to return to Rome, pointing out that I should be much happier there than in a
cloister, and that, if there were any obstacle to my return,
besides the ill-feeling existing between the Constable and
myself, he would be the guarantor of our reunion.

"This proposal, joined to other things that he said to
me at La Vénerie, shocked me so much that, following
the impulse of my hasty temper, I determined to set out
immediately to return to the convent.   And this I did,
although the Duchess of Savoy hindered my departure
and kept me a week longer, at the expiration of which
time they both accompanied me to the convent." [1]

According to Lucien Perey and Marie and Hortense's
Italian biographer, Signor Domenico Perrero,[2] the Constabless, in her "Mémoires," has told us only a portion of
the truth.   The real facts were as follows :—

The Duchess of Savoy, although as we have mentioned, one of the most complacent and unsuspicious of
consorts, was beginning to be somewhat alarmed at the
assiduous attentions paid by the Duke to their beautiful
guest, and the influence which the latter exercised over
her husband.   The prince, perceiving this, proposed one
day to Marie that, in order to allay any suspicions which
might have arisen in his consort's mind, it would perhaps
be as well if, now and again, he were to insist, in the
Duchess's presence, on the advisability of a reconciliation
between the Constabless and her husband.   Unhappily
for herself, Marie appears to have misunderstood him,
and when, shortly afterwards, his Highness proceeded
to put his little plan into execution, she flew into a
violent passion, brusquely quitted the room, and, the

---

[1] "La Vérité dans son jour."

[2] Lucien Perey, "Marie Mancini Colonna." Perrero, "La Duchessa
Ortensia Mazzarino, la Principesse Maria Colonna, et il duca Carlo
Emanuele II di Savoia."

same evening, announced her intention of immediately returning to the convent.

At the request of the Duchess, Marie, as she has told us, consented to remain another week at La Vénerie, during which the Duke attempted to heal the breach between them; but to no purpose. However, he did not abandon hope, and, after the Constabless's return to the convent, sent the Prime Minister, San Tommasso, to endeavour to bring the lady to a more reasonable frame of mind. But his efforts were equally fruitless, and Marie directed him to inform his Highness that she had determined to relieve him of the burden of her presence so soon as the four months mentioned in the agreement with the Constable had expired, and that nothing could alter her resolution.

Still hankering after her beloved France, the Constabless wrote to Louis XIV, begging him to permit her to enter some convent within his realm and informing him of the agreement which she had entered into with her husband, whereby she had solemnly engaged not to leave whatever religious house she might decide to enter without his express permission. This, she imagined, would relieve his Majesty's mind of all fears of her suddenly descending upon him at Versailles or Fontainebleau. She also wrote to Colbert and to other Ministers, entreating them to intercede for her with the King.

Louis XIV, as might have been foreseen, refused to accede to her request—or rather, he ignored it; but he directed Colbert to send her a further sum of a thousand pistoles, since he did not wish it to be supposed that his refusal had been prompted by motives of economy.

Marie now resolved upon a most fatal step. The Constable Colonna, who had of late adopted a much more conciliatory tone towards his wife, even going so

far as to second her request to Louis XIV to allow her
to re-enter France—he had, of course, previously taken
care to ascertain that there was not the remotest likelihood of such a request being granted—now suggested
that, since France was closed to her and she did not
wish to remain in Savoy, she should enter some convent
in Flanders, whither he would send his friend the Marchese di Borgomainero to escort her.　The Constabless
had at first entertained the most profound distrust of
this personage, whom she regarded as the creature of
her husband; but he was a handsome man of insinuating
manners, and he ended by gaining her entire confidence
and in convincing her of his own and the Constable's
good faith.　And so, notwithstanding the warnings of
the French plenipotentiary Gomont, who entertained a
warm regard for the Constabless, and entreated her not
to trust Borgomainero, Marie resolved to proceed to
Brussels, and, on 15 October 1673, left Turin, in company with the marquis and a certain Abbate Oliva, whom
the Constable had sent from Rome to act as her chaplain.

Charles Emmanuel, to whom, the lady tells us, she
went to bid adieu, "more from motives of courtesy
than of inclination," overwhelmed her with reproaches,
and appeared deeply grieved by her determination to
leave his realm, "imploring her earnestly to tell him
whither she was bound, and assuring her that in no
country would she find a prince more devoted to her, or
one who would accord her more powerful protection."
"I listened," she adds, "to his reproaches and his offers
with great attention, and, in taking leave of him,
thanked him for the latter, which my resolution to quit
his State left me no longer room to accept. He gave
me his hand and conducted me to the coach in which
we departed."

CHAPTER XVIII

A comedy of errors—The Constabless is warned by the French plenipotentiaries at Cologne not to enter Flanders—She is lodged in the
citadel of Antwerp, and finds herself a prisoner—She obtains permission to enter a convent at Brussels—But, at the last moment,
changes her mind, and takes sanctuary in a church—She returns to
Antwerp—Letter from the Duke of Savoy—The Constable Colonna
gives his consent to her entering a convent in Madrid—She embarks
for Spain with Don Ferdinando Colonna—Her arrival in Spain—
The Admiral of Castile—Marie's stay at his house—She enters the
Convent of San Domingo-el-Real—Permission to leave it refused her
—She escapes, but is induced to return—Her letter to Charles II
of England— Publication of Marie's apocryphal Memoirs — Her
genuine Memoirs—Recall of Don Juan of Austria to Madrid—
Second escape of the Constabless—She is compelled to return—The
Council deliberate on her case—She flies to Ballecas, but is again
brought back—The Constable Colonna, appointed Viceroy of
Aragon, arrives in Madrid—His interview with his wife—Entry of
the young Queen, Marie Louise d'Orléans, into Madrid—The
Constabless takes refuge at the French Embassy—Severe orders of
Carlos II in regard to her—The Queen takes her part—She is
forcibly carried off and imprisoned in the Alcazar of Segovia—She
promises to become a nun, and enters the Convent of the Conception
at Madrid—Brief of Innocent XI—Marie declines to carry out her
promise, and scandalises the nuns—She is set at liberty.

THE Constabless, accompanied by Borgomainero,
the Abbate Oliva, the faithful Moréna, and a
valet de chambre, took the St. Bernard route, but the
rest of her suite, with the greater part of her baggage,
travelled by way of the Milanese, intending to rejoin
their mistress at Mayence. And this division of their
forces resulted in an amusing little comedy. The Constable Colonna, who, in spite of his assurances to the

z

337

contrary, had not the smallest intention of keeping faith
with his wife, had no sooner been informed of her intention to leave Turin than he sent a courier to the
Duque d'Ossuna, the Governor of the Milanese, with
whom he was on intimate terms, begging him to arrest
his wife and keep her until further instructions from
him. He apparently, however, neglected to inform
Borgomainero of his intentions, so that the only prison-
ers whom the governor secured were Marie's waiting-
women, one of whom, called Nanette, being a very
handsome and distinguished-looking young woman, was
mistaken by the officer in command of the soldiers sent
to arrest them for her mistress, and treated with every
imaginable honour ; nor was it until she had been in a
very luxurious kind of captivity at Ancona for nearly
a week that the mistake was discovered, and she and her
companions permitted to resume their journey. The
Constable, on hearing of what had occurred, hastened to
disavow the governor's action ; nevertheless, it seems
scarcely credible that Marie should still have persisted
in her belief in his good faith, and that, when she
arrived at Cologne, where the abortive Congress was
then sitting, she should have refused to listen to the
warnings of the French plenipotentiaries, Courtin and
Barillon, who begged her not to venture into Flanders,
as, from information they had received, they had not the
least doubt that she would be arrested the moment she
set foot on Spanish territory. On arriving at Malines,
she was received with great courtesy by the governor of
the town, but informed that he had orders from the
Comte de Monterey, the Governor of Flanders, not to
allow her to proceed to Brussels, where she had decided
to enter the Couvent de Barlemont, until everything was
ready for her reception. A few days later, Monterey

sent one of his suite to request the princess to proceed
to Antwerp, whither instructions had been sent to prepare apartments for her reception in the citadel. Here
she was again received with great respect, and conducted
to the fortress by the governor himself and an escort of
nobles. But when, a day or two later, she expressed a
wish to take a drive into the town, she was informed
that it could not be permitted, and, going to the door of
her apartment, found an officer and two guards stationed
there.

From that day she was treated like a State criminal,
prohibited from receiving visitors, and even from communicating with her friends. However, having pressed
the Comte de Monterey to permit her to enter a convent
at Brussels, her request was eventually acceded to, and
Borgomainero was charged to prepare an apartment for
her in the Couvent des Anglaises in that city. She set
out for Brussels, accompanied by the captain of the
governor's guards, but, ascertaining in the course of
the journey that the Couvent des Anglaises was little
better than a prison, and that every imaginable precaution had been taken to guard against any possibility of
her escape, she resolved that nothing should induce her
to enter it, and took sanctuary in an adjoining church,
" under the pretext of making her devotions," which
she absolutely refused to quit, unless the governor would
promise her permission to enter some convent of her
own selection.

The captain of the guards sent for the governor,
who, finding entreaties and threats equally unavailing,
sent, in his turn, for the Nuncio and the Archbishop
of Brussels, to obtain their authorisation to enter the
church and remove the lady by force. The ecclesiastics,
however, anxious to avoid scandal, counselled patience,

and Monterey, having posted a guard at the door of
the church, withdrew. The princess, on her side, had
resolved to spend all night in the church, when a
worthy citizen named Bruneau, with whom she had
some slight acquaintance, entered and begged her to
leave the church and enter his house hard by, warning
her that the governor had only desisted from employing
force for fear of scandal, and that, so soon as night fell,
the soldiers had orders to tear her from her sanctuary.
The lady consented, and repaired to M. Bruneau's
house, around which the soldiers immediately posted
themselves, and rendered it "more secure than the
tower of Danae."

After "sobs and tears" had failed to procure any
mitigation of her lot from the stony-hearted governor,
the Constabless implored him to allow her to proceed to
Madrid and enter a convent there. Overjoyed at the
prospect of being relieved of his troublesome charge,
the Comte de Monterey wrote to the Constable, urging
him to give her the desired permission. In the meantime, as he found himself obliged to proceed to Antwerp
and to withdraw his guards, he begged the princess to
return to the citadel, promising that she should be
treated with less rigour, and that he would even permit
her an occasional drive, under the escort of the lieutenant of the fortress. And, having first insisted on
his signing a sort of treaty embodying these conditions,
she consented. Here a letter full of expressions of
tenderness and devotion from the Duke of Savoy was
smuggled into the fortress by the faithful Moréna, and,
we are assured, produced on the wounded feelings of
her mistress "the effect of a sovereign balm." From
that time a regular correspondence was established between Marie and Charles Emmanuel, which continued

until the latter's untimely death in the following June ; but unfortunately none of these letters have come down to us.

A few weeks later, Don Ferdinando Colonna, a natural brother of the Constable, arrived at Antwerp and informed Marie that her husband had given his consent to her removing to Madrid, and had charged him to escort her thither. Marie, thereupon, wrote to the Duque de Medina de Rio Secco, Admiral of Castile, who was a friend of her husband, to beg him to receive her on her arrival in Madrid, and to the Queen-Dowager[1] to request permission to enter a convent there, and without waiting for an answer, she and Don Ferdinando travelled to Ostend and embarked on an English vessel, which, in nine days, landed them at San-Sebastian. Here they waited a week, when, having received no reply either from the Queen-Dowager or the Admiral, they continued their journey until they reached Alcobendas, a village three leagues from Madrid, where a courier met them with the expected letters, both containing favourable answers. A little further on, they saw approaching at a gallop two handsome but unwieldy carriages, each drawn by six magnificent mules. They contained the Admiral of Castile, the Duque d'Albuquerque, the Marqués d'Alcagnicas, his second son, and the wives of the two last noblemen, who had come to receive their guest and conduct her to a beautiful pleasure-house belonging to the Admiral in the environs of Madrid, "splendidly furnished and ornamented with the richest paintings in Europe."

[1] Maria Anna of Austria, daughter of the Emperor Ferdinand and the Infanta Donna Maria. She governed Spain during the minority of her son, Charles II, from 1665–1675.

The Admiral of Castile, although more than fifty years of age, was one of the handsomest as well as one of the wealthiest grandees in Spain, a great patron of art and letters and an amateur poet of some distinction. His love for the arts, however, was not his chief passion, and he is said to have kept as many as sixteen mistresses in his immense palace in Madrid, without, however, in any way incommoding the duchess, who complacently ignored their presence. With the beautiful Constabless he fell deeply in love at first sight; but the lady does not appear to have responded to his advances.

The life now led by Marie was in pleasing contrast to the rigorous confinement to which she had been subjected at Antwerp and Brussels. She was splendidly lodged and "treated like a queen" by her host, who did everything possible to please and divert her, visited by the greatest families of the capital, the Nuncio and the foreign Ministers, and received by the Queen-Dowager. She was still, however, in a state of honourable captivity, and the Abbate Don Ferdinando Colonna watched over her with jealous care, and was terribly alarmed when, one day, accompanied by Moréna, and without saying a word to any one, she went for a drive along the promenade by the river. This proceeding, the Nuncio Marescotti informs Cardinal Altieri, had greatly shocked the Court and society generally, as it was not the custom in Madrid for ladies of quality to frequent the public promenades, and he feared that, after this escapade, no *grande dame* would care to visit her. However, her friends excused the Constabless's conduct on the ground of her ignorance of Spanish etiquette, and the wrath of the fashionable world was appeased.

After remaining for some three months in the

Admiral's delightful residence, Marie, unwilling to be at any further expense to her host, requested permission of the Queen-Dowager to allow her to enter the convent of San Domingo-el-Real. It was contrary to the rules of Spanish convents to take pensioners, and the nuns refused to receive her, until the Queen-Dowager had declared, by a royal decree, that this favour would not be considered a precedent. The princess entered the convent at the beginning of September 1674, escorted thither by the Admiral and the Nuncio. In order to enjoy greater liberty, she was given a house adjoining the monastery, precautions having first been taken to make it secure, One half she occupied herself; while the Abbate Colonna and her domestics were installed in the other. Don Pedro of Aragon, whom she had known during his Viceroyalty at Naples, from 1666 to 1672, furnished it from top to bottom with tapestries of great value.

Perhaps the Constabless might have resigned herself to pass the remainder of her days in the convent of San Domingo-el-Real, where the abbess, Donna Vittoria Porcia Oroseo, and the nuns did all in their power to render her stay as pleasant as possible, if, as she had been fully led to expect, permission had been granted her, as at Turin, to go out once a week to visit her friends at the Court. But, on the express demand of her husband, this privilege was refused her, and, in great indignation at what she considered an unpardonable breach of faith on the part of the Court, Marie now demanded permission to return to Flanders and make her home with her second son Don Marco Colonna, who, although only a boy of thirteen, had recently, at her request, received the command of two companies of Spanish cavalry stationed there. The Queen-Dowager and the Admiral both wrote to the Constable to obtain his consent ; but Colonna replied that he preferred to know that his wife was in security in Madrid rather than at liberty elsewhere.

Soon after this, the Marqués de los Balbases, who had never forgiven the Constabless for the manner in which she had treated him on the occasion of their first meeting fourteen years before, when, it will be remembered, he had pretended to be her husband, wrote to Rome, warning the Constable that it was his wife's intention to fly from Spain, as the result of which the unfortunate lady was kept under the strictest surveillance, and even the liberty which she had heretofore enjoyed to go wherever she pleased within the convent was curtailed. Her patience was now exhausted, and, at the beginning of November, taking advantage of the absence of the watchful Don Ferdinando, she effected her escape and took refuge at the house of one of her friends, from whence she wrote to the Admiral and other Ministers, to inform them that her intention was not to fly to France or England, as her enemies had falsely asserted, but only to reside in the house in which she then was, and begging them to assist her to obtain this concession. However, neither the Admiral nor his colleagues seemed disposed to assist her, and, after a week of comparative liberty, through the efforts of the Nuncio Mellini and the Admiral, the Constabless consented to return to her convent. Here a new difficulty presented itself, as the nuns refused to receive a lady who had caused such a scandal, and it was not until the Nuncio threatened them with excommunication that they finally yielded.

The Nuncio promised the Constabless to write to her husband and endeavour to prevail upon him to consent to her leaving the convent, begging her, at the same time, to give him her word that until his reply was received she would make no further attempt to escape. Marie declined, however, and, shortly afterwards, a second scandal was only prevented by the vigilance of Don Ferdinando.

During the next two years, the life of the Constabless was uneventful ; she remained in her convent, chafing under the restraints to which she was subjected, and continually petitioning the Queen-Dowager and the Ministers to accord her her liberty ; but, since her husband absolutely refused to give his consent to her leaving her prison, her prayers were unproductive of any result. In March 1676, we find her writing to Charles II of England, who, during her stay at Turin, had, as we have seen, offered her an asylum in his realm. She makes no definite request, save that of retaining his friendship, but she no doubt hoped that he would interest himself on her behalf.

The Constabless to King Charles II of England.

"Madrid, 26 March 1676.

" I should have given myself the honour of writing to your Majesty, if I had been able to hope that my letters would have been conveyed to him with all the secrecy that I wished. My desire to retain the kindly sentiments which your Majesty expressed for me, while I was at Turin, and my fear that you have been prejudiced against me, impels me to ask you for their confirmation. Send it me, I entreat you, since I could receive nothing more opportune or more agreeable in the state in which I find myself. But let your Majesty accompany it with secrecy, since there is nothing of more importance, and since the good or ill success of my affairs depends upon it absolutely, as I depend upon your Majesty ; being all my life his most humble and very obedient servant." [1]

About the same time, appeared a pamphlet entitled "Les Mémoires de M.L.P.M.M. [Madame la Princesse Marie Mancini] Colonne, G. Connétable du Royaume de Naples." This little work, a tissue of gross false-hoods, took the same form as the "Mémoires" which the Duchesse de Mazarin had just published in collaboration with Saint-Réal, and this gave it a false appearance of authenticity, and caused it to command a ready sale. It had been, as a matter of fact, inspired, if not actually written, by Marie's enemy, the Marqués de los Balbases, with the intention of injuring the poor lady still further in public estimation. [2] A copy fell into the hands of the Constabless, who, in high indignation, at once set to work on the compilation of her genuine Memoirs, which appeared under the title of " La Vérité dans son jour.' The publication of this work, which, unfortunately, does not go beyond the year 1677, assisted by the version of it which Brémont published in Belgium, called the " Apologie ou les Véritables Mémoires de Marie de Mancini, Connétable Colonne," did much to counteract the evil effect of the apocryphal Memoirs ; but unhappily the latter had a considerable start, and continued to be accepted by many persons as from the Constabless's own pen.

[1] British Museum MSS.
[2] This is the opinion of the latest and best-informed of Marie's French biographers, Lucien Perey; but M. Chantelauze, though acknowledging that the first part is undoubtedly spurious, expresses his belief in the authenticity of the second, which, however, he thinks was never intended for publication, and owed its appearance to some person to whom the Constabless had been so indiscreet as to lend the manuscript.

At the beginning of the year 1677, Carlos II decided to recall his half-brother, Don Juan of Austria, from his exile at Saragossa, to which the jealousy of the Queen-Dowager had relegated him, to entrust him with the chief share in the government of his kingdom. "It was at this moment," writes the Constabless, "that I saw appear a ray of hope, and remembering that Padre Ventimiglia, whose capabilities and rare talents had rendered him as illustrious as the nobility of his birth, had told me an infinitude of times that my liberty must be the work of this prince, and that his return would undoubtedly give it me, I considered seriously about taking advantage of an event so favourable, not doubting that it would produce the effect for which I had been led to hope."

In the belief that her unhappy lot could not fail to appeal to the generous and chivalrous Don Juan, notwithstanding the way in which she had treated his jester Capitor, during the prince's visit to the French Court in 1659, the Constabless could not bring herself to await his arrival in Madrid, and no sooner was she informed that he had quitted Saragossa, than she resolved to go and meet him. Accordingly, one fine day, she succeeded in effecting her escape, for the second time, and made her way to the house of the Marquesa de Mortara, sister-in-law of the abbess of the convent which she had just quitted. The marchioness, overcome with astonishment at this visit, received her unwelcome guest very courteously, but lost no time in writing to inform Don Garcia de Ledra, the President of the Council of Castile, of what had occurred; while, on her side, Marie wrote to several grandees, begging them to assist her to carry out her intention. Two days later, the Nuncio, the Admiral, and the President of the Council

came to visit her, bearing the King's order for her to
return to the convent. The Constabless angrily refused,
upon which her visitors gravely informed her that they
were authorised to employ force, if necessary; and the
Marquesa de Mortara, adding her entreaties to their
persuasions, the Constabless "condescended to return."
This return was not easy, and the intervention of the
Nuncio and a peremptory order from the King were required to compel the now exasperated nuns to receive
their penitent.

A week later, Don Juan arrived in Madrid, and the
Constabless lost no time in addressing to him a memorial
reciting her woes and imploring him to redress them.
Don Juan was about to grant her petition, when the
King received a letter from Colonna, complaining of the
recent flight of his wife, and begging that, for greater
security, she should be imprisoned in a fortress. Don
Juan thereupon laid both the memorial and the letter
before the Council, which finally decided that Marie
should be set at liberty and allowed to take up her residence in a house suitable to her rank. As, however,
the King judged it best to suspend the decree of the
Council until he had received an answer to a letter
which he had addressed to the Constable, the lady lost
patience, made her escape from the convent for the
third time, and proceeded to Ballecas, a village a league
from Madrid. The Nuncio and Don Ferdinando pursued her, and persuaded her to return to the capital;
but, though she was not sent back to the cloister, the
Council decided that, instead of being allowed to occupy
a house of her own, she must reside in one with Don
Ferdinando.

Six months later, the Constable Colonna was appointed
Viceroy of Aragon by Don Juan, who had need of his

influence and that of his friends in his struggle against the party of the Queen-Dowager. To please the Constable, who had been much irritated by the permission accorded his wife to leave her convent, and in the hope of reconciling them, the prince begged Marie to return to her cloister, in order that her husband might find her there on his arrival at Madrid. She consented, declaring, at the same time, that she would not remain there more than three months. However, it was not until the beginning of November 1678, that Colonna reached Madrid, accompanied by his three sons and a party of his household. On the day of his arrival, he visited the convent of San Domingo-el-Real, where he and his wife, according to the *Gazeta de Madrid*, "exchanged the most lively demonstrations of joy and reciprocal affection, which caused one to hope more and more for their approaching reunion."

How far these demonstrations of affection were sincere is difficult to say, but it would appear that, thanks to the efforts of the Nuncio, Marie was now better disposed towards her husband than she had been for a long time. She refused, however, to live with him or accompany him back to Rome when he returned thither, but consented to follow him to Saragossa and enter a convent there, on the distinct understanding, however, that she was to be allowed to go out two or three times a week.

However, the Pope, who had been appealed to, declined to grant her this permission, and, learning, about the same time, that her husband had brought with him to Saragossa a desperate character named Restà, who had fled from Rome to escape the punishment of his crimes, she became convinced that the Constable intended to employ this person to carry her off to Italy and perhaps assassinate her on the way, and absolutely refused to leave Madrid.

The death of Don Juan of Austria, on 17 December 1679, removed a friend upon whose powerful protection she had always been able to rely. But the marriage of Charles II with Marie Louise d'Orléans, daughter of *Monsieur* and Henrietta of England, inspired her with fresh hope, since she could not doubt that the daughter of a prince who, thanks to the Chevalier de Lorraine, had always defended her interests, would sympathise with her misfortunes.

The young Queen made her entry into Madrid on 13 January 1680, with all the pomp usual in such circumstances.

"The Queen-Mother," writes Madame d'Aulnoy, "went in the morning to Buen-Retiro, which she left, some time later, in company with the King. They went together to see all the streets through which the Queen was to make her progress, and took up their position at the house of the Condesa de Oñate, in a balcony made for the purpose, and having a lattice-window gilded all over. About eleven, the Queen, mounted on horseback, and those who were to precede her began to march, and passed through a marble gate, which had been but lately erected. The kettledrummers and the trumpeters of the city, habited in the costumes usually worn in these ceremonies, led the procession; after them came the Alcaldes, the nobility, and the knights of the three military Orders (St. James, Calatrava, and Alcantara), the gentlemen of the King's Household, the high officials of the Queen's, and the grandees of Spain, followed by a great number of lackeys, whose different liveries, gallooned with gold and silver, made an agreeable diversity. The Queen's equerries marched on foot

before her, the Conde de Villa Mayana, her chief
gentleman-usher, was on her right hand, and she was
surrounded by her gentlemen-in-waiting and her
pages (When she walked on foot, she always leaned on
one of these). The Duquesa de Terranova and Doña
Laura de Alagon followed her, both of them mounted
on their mules and in their widow's weeds, which somewhat resemble the costume of nuns, except that, when
on horseback, they wear enormous hats, which are not
less unsightly than the rest of their garb. Next, we
saw the Queen's maids-of-honour, all very beautiful and
richly dressed ; they were on horseback, and each was
escorted by her relations, in the midst of whom she
rode ; then came several beautiful horses, led by grooms
in rich liveries. In the Prado, which is one of the most
agreeable walks in Madrid, by reason of the fountains
which water it, a gallery open on every side had been
erected, with one-and-twenty arches, to which were
affixed the Arms of the several kingdoms under the
dominion of Spain. The Queen found, at the end of
the gallery, a triumphal arch, very magnificent and well
designed, through which she entered the city. The
Corrigidors and the Rigidors, apparelled in scarlet and
gold brocade such as the Castilians wear, presented her
with the keys of the city, and with a canopy, which
they carried over her head during the procession. The
streets were adorned with the richest tapestries, and the
precious stones that were to be seen in the Goldsmiths'
Row were valued at eleven million.[1]

---

[1] Another account says: "On each side of the street was a row of
great angels made of pure silver. One saw there shields of gold, on
which were inscribed the names of the King and Queen, with the Arms
formed of pearls, rubies, diamonds, and other precious stones, of such
richness and beauty that the connoisseurs declared that they were worth
more than twelve million."

" It would take too much time to describe all the magnificence of that day, and I shall therefore confine myself to saying that the Queen was mounted on a fine Andalusian horse, which, in this noble march, seemed proud to carry so beautiful and great a princess. Her gown was so covered with embroidery that its material was completely hidden ; she wore on her head white plumes blended with red, and a pearl called there the 'Peregrina,' which is as big as a small Catherine pear and is of inestimable value, hung below a clasp of diamonds which decorated her hat. She wore on her finger the great diamond of the King, which, so they assert, surpasses in beauty anything that was ever set in a ring. But the graceful deportment of the Queen in all her actions, and particularly in the management of her horse, and the charm of her person made a greater lustre than all the precious stones she wore, although it is certain that people were well-nigh dazzled by the glitter of them. She halted below the balcony of the Condesa de Oñate to salute the King and Queen-Mother. They opened the lattice about four fingers' breadth, in order to see her, and the King, taking his handkerchief in his hand, carried it several times to his lips, his eyes, and his heart, which is the most gallant action that a Spaniard can perform. The Queen continued her way, and the King and the Queen-Mother received her in the court of the Palace. He assisted her to alight, while the other, taking her by the hand, conducted her to her apartments, where she embraced her repeatedly, telling her that she was but too happy to have such an amiable daughter-in-law."[1]

Before the departure of the Constable for Saragossa, Marie had expressed a desire to leave her convent

[1] " Memoires de la Cour d'Espagne."

From an engraving by L'Armessin

MARIE LOUISE D'ORLEANS, QUEEN OF SPAIN

and spend a few days at the house of his brother-in-law, the Marqués de los Balbases, in order to witness this pageant. The Constable, somewhat to her surprise, did not raise the least objection, and she was still more puzzled at the warmth of the welcome which awaited her at Balbases's house. Finding herself so well received, she resolved to remain there until the return of her husband from Saragossa. But, two days before the entry of the Queen, she received warning, from one of her friends, that Balbases had arranged with Colonna to have her seized and carried off to Saragossa. On learning this, she asked for a coach in order to go for a drive, and, on its arrival, directed the coachman to take her to the French Embassy.

"Yesterday, at ten o'clock in the morning," writes the Ambassador's wife, Madame de Villars, "we saw enter our room a *tapada*,[1] followed by another, who appeared to be her attendant. I made a sign to M. de Villars that it was for him to do the honours; the attendant retired. The other signified her desire that some persons who were in the ante-chamber should retire also; she went to a window with M. de Villars, at the same time making a sign to me to approach. She raised her cloak; but I was but little the wiser, though I had some recollection of a person who resembled her. M. de Villars exclaimed: 'It is the Constabless Colonna,' upon which I paid her some compliments. She wept and besought us to have pity upon her. To describe her appearance in a few words, her shape is one of the most beautiful; her corsage *à l'Espagnole*, which does not conceal her shoulders either too much or two little. Two long tresses of black hair tied with a beautiful flame-coloured ribbon;

[1] A woman who conceals her face with a mantilla or a veil.

2 A

the rest of her hair in disorder and badly combed; very beautiful pearls round her neck;[1] an agitated manner, which would not become any one else, but which, for her, seemed rather natural; beautiful teeth."

The Ambassador, in great embarrassment, for the lady had announced her intention of remaining at the Embassy until she was forcibly ejected, started off for Balbases's house "to find some way out of the difficulty." It was suggested that the Constabless should retire to her convent; but the nuns absolutely refused to receive her, and the other convents followed suit. "I was obliged," writes M. de Villars to Louis XIV, "to summon the Nuncio and some ladies among her friends, and, after a long and difficult negotiation, which lasted until midnight, we have brought her back with her own consent to the marquis's house."

A few days later, by order of the King, the Constabless was sent to a convent of Franciscan nuns at Cien-Puzuales, some five leagues from Madrid. Here she remained for a month, when Colonna returned to the capital, and she was brought back and installed in her external apartment at the Convent of San Domingo-el-Real, "where the Constable went every day to converse with her in her parlour, and to pay her attentions such as a lover might pay to his mistress."[2]

These attentions on the part of the Constable were not without an ulterior object. He desired to obtain his wife's consent to transfer part of the dowry which Mazarin had given her to their eldest son Filippo, Principe di Palliano, for whom he desired to arrange a marriage with the daughter of the Spanish Prime Minister, the Duque de Medina Coeli. After some

---

[1] Presumably, the pearls given her by Louis XIV.
[2] Madame d'Aulnoy, "Mémoires de la Cour d'Espagne."

hesitation, Marie agreed to what was demanded of her, thanks to which the marriage was decided on, and the Constabless quitted the convent and went to reside at her husband's palace, each of them occupying a separate floor.

For the first time for several years, Marie now enjoyed the fullest liberty, visiting and receiving whom she pleased, and going regularly to pay her court to the Queen, who treated her with the utmost kindness. In September 1680, the Constable returned to Saragossa, leaving his wife in his palace at Madrid. Soon afterwards, she was officially informed that the King had decided to interfere no more in her affairs, and that nothing remained for her but to obey her husband and go wherever he might desire her, whether to Italy or elsewhere. The next day, she was forbidden to leave the house, the following one, to receive any visitors. Beside herself with fear, for the sinister figure of the Constable's myrmidon Restà was for ever before her eyes, she besought his Majesty to shut her up in the most austere convent in Madrid rather than deliver her to the tender mercies of her husband. But her petition was ignored, although, thanks to the intercession of the young Queen, the King's orders were not immediately executed.

In the meanwhile, the Constabless declared that she would refuse to sign the contract by which a considerable part of her fortune was to be assured to the Principe di Palliano, and would make the hospitals of the city her heirs. This sudden resolution greatly alarmed the Duque de Medina Coeli and his family; they appealed to the Nuncio, who had great influence over Marie, promising that the King should continue to afford her his protection, and that she should be treated with every

possible consideration, if she would but renounce the
decision at which she had just arrived. The princess
eventually yielded, but, in return for this concession,
obtained an audience of the Queen, who, in response
to her appeal, exacted from the Duque de Medina Coeli
his word of honour that during her absence at the
Escurial, for which she was about to set out, no
violence should be employed against the Constabless.
A few days, however, after the Queen's departure, the
duke and Balbases, thinking the opportunity too good
a one to be lost, obtained an order from the Junta,
whom Carlos II had ordered to decide upon the differences between the Constabless and her husband, to have
the lady shut up in a fortress.

One night, Marie, reassured by the promise which
had been made her, was sleeping peacefully, when she
was awakened by a loud knocking at the door, and the
voice of Don Garcia de Medrano, Councillor of the
Royal Council, informed her that he had come with an
order from the King to convey her to the Alcazar of
Segovia. She declined to open to him, upon which the
councillor ordered the officers who accompanied him
to force the door, which speedily yielded to their
assault upon it. One of the invaders roughly seized
the Constabless and prepared to tie her arms with a
cord. Marie resisted desperately, and, snatching up a
little knife which lay upon a table hard by, gave him a
cut in the hand. Upon which, the rest of the company
"fell upon her with barbarous fury, and dragged her by
the hair of her head, half naked as she was, like one of
the most abandoned of her sex," to a coach in which sat
Don Ferdinando Colonna, who had not dared himself to
assist in the outrage, and carried her off to the Alcazar
of Segovia.

In the Alcazar of Segovia the unfortunate lady remained for nearly four months, in the closest confinement, seeing no one but the Queen's confessor and the kind-hearted Nuncio. To add to her misfortunes, the winter was an extremely severe one, and, in her bare and draughty room, the Constabless suffered terribly from the cold ; while the food served to her was of the poorest quality and abominably cooked.

In the meanwhile, however, the miserable condition of the princess, of which the Queen's confessor and the Nuncio did not fail to bring back a faithful report to the capital, had begun to excite the greatest indignation in Madrid ; the Queen sent a vigorous remonstrance to the Constable, and the latter, finding the opinion of the Court against him, proceeded to make to his wife the most extraordinary proposition. He would consent, he informed her, to her returning to some convent in Madrid, but on condition that, on the very day on which she entered it, she should assume the dress of a novice, and, three months later, take the vows. He, on his side, also engaged to enter Orders and become a monk.

As the Constabless had not the least inclination for the religious life, every one was persuaded that she would refuse even to consider such an offer. But, anxious at any price to escape from Segovia, she accepted it, though she was absolutely determined to die rather than make profession. She returned to Madrid on 15 February 1681, and entered at once the Convent of the Conception, in a state of the most profound dejection. She declined to see her husband, but had an interview with her sons, to whom she said that "she esteemed herself the most unfortunate person in the world, and that she was about to take a step which would ruin the rest of her life, and the consequences of which

she regarded with terror, but that, since she had passed
her word, she was resolved upon it."

"The Constabless Colonna," writes Madame de
Villars, "arrived early on Saturday. She entered the
convent ; the nuns received her at the door with tapers
and all the ceremonial which is usual on such occasions ;
then she was conducted to the choir, where she assumed
the dress [of a novice] with a very modest demeanour
. . . the dress is pretty and rather coquettish, the
convent commodious."[1]

A few days later, a brief arrived from Innocent XI,
whereby his Holiness permitted "Lorenzo Onofrio
Colonna, Grand Constable of the kingdom of Naples,
and Marie Mancini Colonna, Duchessa di Tagliacozzo,
in order to appease the controversies and discussions
which existed between them, and to enable them to pass
the rest of their lives more tranquilly, and to assure the
salvation of their souls, to embrace both of them by
common accord and mutual consent the religious life ;
she in some monastery of the town of Madrid, and he in
one of the religious orders of the Hospital of St. John
of Jerusalem." And his Holiness further permitted the
said Marie Mancini Colonna, in consideration of her
being of mature years and having already spent long
years in convents, the "privilege" of abridging her
novitiate.

To Lorenzo Colonna the obliging Pontiff also granted
certain privileges, permitting him to dispense with the
usual vows of chastity and poverty and the obligation
of making pilgrimages to the Holy Land, so that all the
religious profession of the Constable consisted in wearing the Grand Cross of his Order.

Marie, needless to say, did not avail herself of his

[1] Letter of February 1681.

Holiness's gracious permission to abridge her novitiate; indeed, she absolutely refused to take the vows, and finally declined even to appear in her religious costume, "but wore petticoats of gold and silver brocade under her woollen robe, threw aside her veil, and arranged her hair *à l'Espagnole* with ribbons of all colours. Sometimes it happened that she was summoned to an observance which she was compelled to attend. Then she resumed her robe over her ribbons and hair, which fell in curls over her shoulders; this had a very pleasing effect." [1]

But the effect upon the good Sisters of the Convent of the Conception was the very reverse of pleasing. They were unutterably shocked; but to complain was useless. The Queen had conceived the greatest affection for the Constabless, and visited her constantly; the King was entirely under his consort's influence; the Nuncio was Marie's devoted friend. As for the Constable, he had played his last card and lost; he ignored his wife— if a monk can be said to have a wife—and troubled her no longer.

Unheard of privileges were granted to the lady, who was still nominally supposed to be preparing herself to become the bride of Heaven. She went for long drives in carriages sent her by the Queen; she received all manner of people; she visited the Court, where she was welcomed most graciously by Carlos II, who seemed anxious to atone to her for the severity with which she had been treated in his name.

At length, however, the long-suffering nuns revolted; and, in the early spring of 1686, the Constabless's old enemy Balbases succeeded in so disquieting the conscience of the good abbess that, one day when her novice had left the convent to attend a magnificent fête

[1] Madame d'Aulnoy, " Mémoires de la Cour d'Espagne."

given by the Admiral of Castile to the King and the two queens, she refused to permit her to return, and informed her that, since she appeared to find the wicked world so pleasant a place, she had better remain in it.

"Deeply offended by this refusal, which was very galling for a person of her quality and merit," says Madame d'Aulnoy, "she set her friends to employ their influence with the King, who sent orders to the abbess to open her doors to the Constabless. The abbess and all the nuns persisted in their refusal, announced that they intended to present their reasons to his Majesty, and were coming to demand an audience of him." When Carlos II was informed of this, he burst out laughing and exclaimed : ' I shall be very much amused to see this procession of nuns who should come chanting—

Libera nos, Domine, de la Condestabile.'

The nuns did not come, however, but decided to obey his Majesty's orders."[1]

The Marqués de los Balbases did not fail to inform the Vatican of this incident, representing that force had been employed to compel the reluctant nuns to receive the Constabless. But, to his intense mortification, the only result of his interference was that the Pope, wisely concluding that the most effectual means to put a stop to such scandals was to set the lady at liberty, ordered her to leave the convent and forbade her to enter another. Shortly afterwards, the Constable, who knew that there was no likelihood of the King consenting to a second sojourn of his wife in the Alcazar of Segovia, decided to make a virtue of necessity, and consented to her being accorded complete liberty, a decision which

[1] Madame d'Aulnoy, " Mémoires de la Cour d'Espagne."

greatly pleased every one concerned, with the exception of the malignant Balbases, who could not forgive himself for having been the involuntary cause of the Constabless's restoration to freedom.

But let us leave Marie in the enjoyment of her hardly won liberty, and see what had become of her two sisters who had remained at the Court of France.

CHAPTER XIX

The Poison Trials in France—The Duchesse de Bouillon and the Comtesse de Soissons compromised—The magician Lesage accuses Madame de Bouillon of attempting to get rid of her husband—Her trial—She is acquitted, but exiled to Nérac—The Comtesse de Soissons and la Voisin—Louvois and Madame de Montespan conspire to ruin the countess—Louis XIV connives at her escape from justice—Her last evening in Paris—She flies to Flanders—Letter of Louvois to the President of the Chambre Ardente—Hostile reception which Madame de Soissons meets with in Flanders—An extraordinary story—She takes up her residence in Brussels—Marriage of her eldest son to Mlle. de la Cropte-Beauvais—Early life of Eugène de Savoie.

FOR six years after Marie's second departure from France the lives of Olympe and Marianne were comparatively uneventful. In 1673, the former lost her husband, who died rather suddenly in Champagne, while on his way to join the army under Turenne in Germany. M. de Soissons's death gave rise to sinister rumours, and the countess's enemies—and she had many and powerful ones—did not hesitate to ascribe it to poison administered by an agent of his wife. But, since the count had always been the most devoted and, at the same time, the most complacent of husbands, and her accusers were unable to attribute any satisfactory reason for such a crime, the charge would appear to have been entirely without foundation, even in view of the facts which we shall presently relate.

In March 1679, the countess was requested by Louis XIV to resign her post of Superintendent of the

Queen's Household, which was bestowed upon Madame de Montespan. This has been represented by some writers as a kind of disgrace ; but, as a matter of fact, it had no such significance. Madame de Montespan had endeavoured to prevail upon the King to appoint her to the office in question some years before ; but Louis had had sufficient consideration for his unfortunate consort to spare her this last humiliation. When, however, early in 1679, his Majesty transferred his affections to Mlle. de Fontanges, and his illicit connection with the marchioness terminated, the former objections disappeared, and, with the idea of tempering the wind to the shorn lamb, and, at the same time, proclaiming to the world that all was at an end between them, he resolved to gratify her ambition. "On Wednesday [21 March]," writes Bussy-Rabutin, "the Comtesse de Soissons received the King's command to resign her post [as Superintendent of the Queen's Household]. The princess in question was at Chaillot, in a little house which she has there. M. Colbert was continually passing to and fro. In the evening, she spoke to the King in the Queen's apartments, and he complimented her highly upon the satisfaction which she had given her Majesty. She replied with all the respect imaginable, and, finally, she has accepted 200,000 écus ;[1] and Madame de Montespan has in this way become Superintendent of the Queen's Household, and is no longer mistress.[2]

Of the Duchesse de Bouillon during this period we hear little. In 1675, the duke's family persuaded him

---

[1] Presumably *petits écus* of 3 livres, which, as Mazarin had given 250,000 livres for this office in 1660, would represent a very handsome profit.

[2] Correspondance de Bussy-Rabutin IV., 354.

to send his wife to the Couvent de Montreuil, "to give her an opportunity for salutary reflections." It would appear that the too pronounced encouragement given by the lady to the advances of the handsome Comte de Louvigny, younger son of the marshal of that name, which had occasioned a good deal of scandal and some piquant couplets, was the cause of this retirement. However, her exile only lasted a very short time, and she returned to Court with spirits unaffected by conventual life and more amused than any one at her misadventure. She resumed her former rôle of patroness of the poets, and became an assiduous frequenter of the Hôtel de Vendôme and the Temple, where the duke (afterwards the famous marshal) and the Grand Prieur de Vendôme, sons of her eldest sister Laure, held high revel with their intendant the Abbé de Chaulieu. The two brothers, particularly the elder, seem to have cherished for their charming aunt feelings a good deal warmer than their relationship warranted, and though happily this passion did not terminate in a tragedy as that of the Chevalier de Soissons, youngest son of Olympe, for his aunt Hortense,[1] if any reliance is to be placed in the evidence given before the Chambre Ardente, of which we are now about to speak, it was certainly not the fault of the duchess.

So far back as the year 1673, the penitentiaries of Notre-Dame—without, of course, mentioning any names—had warned the police that the majority of women who had confessed to them for some time past accused themselves of poisoning some one. This warning, strange to say, does not appear to have made much impression upon the authorities, and even the famous case of

[1] See p. 398 infra.

Madame de Brinvilliers, in 1677, the prelude to the grisly drama which was about to send a thrill of horror through Europe, left them still unmoved. Apparently, they inclined to the belief that the crimes of this fiendish woman were merely such as occur from time to time even in the best-regulated communities, and were not to be regarded as in any way typical of the state of public morality.

However, towards the close of 1678, the authorities, roused at last from their lethargy by the discovery of a supposed plot to poison the King and the Dauphin, and led by the able and fearless Gabriel Nicolas de la Reynie, Lieutenant of Police, became exceedingly active; and some indiscreet words dropped by a woman called Marie Bosse led to her arrest and that of another woman named Vigoureux. On 10 January 1679, an Order in Council was issued, directing La Reynie to proceed against these women and their accomplices; and, two months later, the police effected the arrest of the abominable monster la Voisin, one of the greatest criminals known to history.

The state of affairs which the confession of this woman and her accomplices brought to light was the most appalling that the imagination can possibly conceive. "Human life is publicly trafficked in," wrote the Lieutenant of Police. "Death (by poison) is almost the only remedy employed in family embarrassments; impieties, sacrileges, abominations are common practices in Paris, in the surrounding country, in the provinces."

The consternation of the authorities on discovering that such frightful crimes were rampant in their midst was unbounded. Louis XIV shared the general horror and indignation, and gave orders that no stone should be left unturned to bring the offenders to justice; and, with the view of avoiding the cumbersome proceedings of the ordinary courts, and, at the same time, of ensuring greater secrecy, a special commission was appointed, composed of the élite of the Councillors of State, presided over by Louis Boucherat, afterwards Chancellor, with La Reynie and Bazin de Bezons, of the Academy, as examining commissioners.

This court was called the Chambre Ardente, not, as some writers have supposed, because it had power to condemn persons to the stake, though that was among its prerogatives and was exercised in the case of la Voisin, but because, in former days, tribunals specially constituted to deal with extraordinary crimes sat in a chamber hung with black and lighted by torches and candles.[1]

The Chambre Ardente met for the first time in the hall of the Arsenal on 10 April 1609, and on 15 May sentenced to death Madame Philbert, wife of the fashionable flutist of that name, convicted of having made away with her first husband, a wealthy wholesale tradesman named Brunet, with poison procured from Marie Bosse. The hope, however, aroused in the breasts of lovers of justice by this rigorous sentence was not, unhappily, destined to be realised, and disgraceful miscarriages of justice occurred in the cases of Madame Dreux, the wife of a *maître des requêtes*, a lady of great beauty and of "infinite charm and distinction," who was convicted of having poisoned at least three persons, and of having offered la Voisin " 2,000 écus, a ring, and a diamond cross to make away with her husband"; and of Madame Leféron, found guilty of having poisoned her husband, the President of the first *Cour des Enquêtes*, in order to enable her to marry a worthless adventurer named

---

[1] "Le Mercure Galant," 1679, p. 336.

de Prade, for whom she had conceived a violent passion.[1]
Soon the affair began to assume alarming proportions.
The operations of the sorceresses and poisoners had
been by no means confined to the *bourgeoisie* and the
professional classes; the Court was equally besmirched;
members of the noblest families in France were implicated, and, among them, were the Duchesse de Bouillon
and her sister, the Comtesse de Soissons.

One of the principal accomplices of la Voisin[2] was a
man who called himself Lesage; his real name was
Adam Cœuret, and he appears to have been at one time
a wool merchant, a calling which, however, he soon
abandoned for the more profitable one of a magician.
He had a remarkable talent for jugglery, by means of
which he duped not only the people who came to avail
themselves of his art, but even the witches with whom
he worked. One of his favourite tricks was to make
his clients write requests to the "Spirit"—as the devil
was called—in notes, which he then enclosed in balls of
wax and pretended to throw into the fire. Some days
later, he would give them back their notes, saying that
the "Spirit," who had received them through the flames,
had returned them.

In his examination before the commissioners on
28 October 1679, Lesage stated that he had met the
Duchesse de Bouillon at la Voisin's house, and that
"that lady, having told him that she was aware that he
could ensure the success of anything that she might
desire," after some conversation, he told her to write
down her requests, which she did, and he saw that she

---

[1] Ravaisson, "Archives de la Bastille," VI.

[2] La Voisin, when questioned about her relations with Madame de
Bouillon, brought no charge against her, merely stating that the duchess
had visited her house out of curiosity.

demanded the death of the Duc de Bouillon, her husband, and to marry the Duc de Vendôme, who was with her at the time she wrote the note. After this, Madame de Bouillon and M. de Vendôme obliged him to come to the Hôtel de Bouillon, where he pretended to throw a second note into the fire, as he had done the first; and the lady, "wishing to engage him still further to do what she demanded in regard to her husband, brought a bag, containing a number of gold pieces, which she tried to induce him to accept." But he refused to take more than four pistoles, and, though the duchess had come several times to see him, he had always avoided her, "not wishing to have any dealings with her."

This charge sounds puerile enough to us, though it was not so regarded at that time, when belief in magic and witchcraft was almost universal, and even such men as Bossuet were firmly persuaded of the efficacy of sorcery. But, in a second examination, Lesage made a far graver accusation against the duchess. This was to the effect that Madame de Bouillon had only had recourse to his magic after other means had failed, since la Vigoureux had told him that the lady had applied to her for poison to get rid of her husband; but that, as the dose with which she had supplied her had failed to take effect, she had advised her to consult Lesage.

The evidence against the Duchess of Bouillon was considered so serious that the Chambre Ardente, which had no power to arrest any one on its own authority, applied for a *lettre de cachet* for her apprehension, which was granted by the King, and, after being kept under arrest at her own house for some weeks, the duchess was brought to trial on 29 January 1680. Perhaps fortunately for her, la Vigoureux—who would, of course, have been the principal witness against her—had died under torture some time before Lesage's examination, and the knowledge of this fact no doubt accounted for the haughty tone which the lady thought fit to assume towards her judges.

Madame de Bouillon proceeded to the Arsenal, supported, on one side, by the Duc de Vendôme, and, on the other, by the husband, against whose life she was accused of conspiring, while a crowd of the nobility followed to show their sympathy. She entered the court "like a little queen," sat down on a chair that had been placed for her, and, instead of replying to the first question, asked to be allowed to enter a formal protest against the authority of the Chambre, declaring that "she had only attended out of deference to the King's command, and not for that of the court, which she did not recognise, as she declined to allow any derogation to the ducal privilege.[1] She refused to answer any questions until this had been taken down by the clerk of the court. Then she removed her glove and "disclosed a very beautiful hand," and the examination began.

"Do you know la Vigoureux?"

"No."

"Do you know la Voisin?"

"Yes."

"Why did you want to do away with your husband?"

"I do away with my husband! Why, you have only to ask him if he thinks so! He gave me his hand to this very door!"

"But why did you go so often to la Voisin's house?"

"I wanted to see the Sibyls and prophetesses she promised to show me. Such a company would have been well worth all my journeys."

---

[1] The ducal privilege consisted in being tried by all the courts united in the Parliament.

Then, after denying that she had ever shown la Voisin a bag full of money, she inquired with a mocking and disdainful air :

" Well, Messieurs, is that all you have to say to me ?"

" Yes, Madame," was the reply : upon which the duchess rose and left the court, remarking as she did so : " Really, I should never have believed that men of sense could ask so many foolish questions."

Such is the amusing account given of Madame de Bouillon's examination by Madame de Sévigné.[1] But the records of the court show that the accused was subjected to a very close examination in regard to her dealings with Lesage. She confirmed what that worthy had stated about his interview with her at la Voisin's house and his visit to the Hôtel de Bouillon ; but absolutely denied that she had asked him to assist her to get rid of her husband, or that she had given him a note to burn containing such demands. However, this charge was of small importance in comparison with her alleged dealings with the poisoner la Vigoureux, and, as no further evidence was forthcoming in regard to that matter, the duchess was acquitted. She did not, however, escape altogether, as Louis XIV, hearing that she had had the temerity to boast of having baffled the judges, exiled her to Nérac ; nor was she allowed to return to Paris for some considerable time.

Far less fortunate than the Duchesse de Bouillon was

[1] Letter of 31 January 1680. Voltaire, in his "Siècle de Louis XIV," relates an amusing passage of arms between the duchess and La Reynie, in which the latter got decidedly the worst of the encounter. "Did you ever see the devil at la Voisin's house, since you went there to meet him ?" inquired the Lieutenant of Police. "Monsieur," replied the lady, "I see him here at this very moment. He is disguised as a judge, and very ugly and villainous he looks." The questioner proceeded no further.

her elder sister Madame de Soissons. After a confession made by la Voisin on 9 October 1679, the examining commissioners, La Reynie and Bazin de Bezons, drew up the following report :—

"She [la Voisin] declared to us that the Comtesse de Soissons, feeling somewhat aggrieved because the King had neglected her and no longer appeared to have any kindness for her, was one day at her house, in company with Madame de la Ferté and Mlle. du Fouilloux,[1] who appeared to have not long recovered from the small-pox ; and the Comtesse de Soissons, without saying who she was, made her [Voisin] go into her garden, where the lady gave her her hand to look at, after examining which, she told her that she saw there a solar line, which was strongly defined, and showed that she must have been loved by a great prince. Upon that, the Comtesse de Soissons asked her abruptly if that would not return. She replied that it might possibly return ; but the lady rejoined that it was very necessary that it returned, and that she absolutely declined to be made a dupe of, and spoke to her on the subject of La Vallière as being the cause of the aversion which the King appeared to have for her, *and demanded the means of getting rid of Mlle. de la Vallière.*

"And when she [la Voisin] told her that that would be a very difficult matter, the lady replied passionately

---

[1] As la Voisin never seems able to remember dates, it is often very difficult to fix even approximately the time at which the events she speaks of occurred. But she gives du Fouilloux the title of demoiselle, so that the visit of that lady and the Comtesse de Soissons to her house must have occurred previous to January 1667, when the former became the wife of the Marquis d'Alluye. Moreover, the countess expresses herself in her interview with la Voisin with an indignation which would appear to indicate a comparatively recent grievance, and we shall therefore probably not be far wrong in dating the incident during the early years of La Vallière's "reign," probably after the failure of the Spanish letter plot.

that she would certainly find a means, and that, if she were unable to avenge herself, she would carry her vengeance further and would spare nothing. But, on that, she [la Voisin] told her that it was necessary to bide her time for the satisfaction which she desired, and not to do anything inopportunely. And she was not aware until after the conversation, and when the lady was going away, that it was the Comtesse de Soissons to whom she had spoken; and it was Mlle. du Fouilloux who informed her of the fact, at the time when Mesdames de la Ferté and du Fouilloux were leaving her house. She believed herself obliged to say also that she was not aware if the Comtesse de Soissons persevered or not in her design, and that she did not see her, except on that one occasion."

On 16 January 1680, la Voisin was interrogated, by La Reynie and Bazin de Bezons, at Vincennes, in regard to her relations with the Comtesse de Soissons, when she confirmed the statements she had made in her confession.

Asked if the Comtesse de Soissons did not tell her the means she proposed to employ to avenge the wrong she had suffered, she replied that the lady only declared that "she would destroy both [the King and La Vallière]."

Asked if it were true that she had had constant relations with Madame de Soissons, and had visited her at her hôtel, she replied that she had never seen the countess, save on the occasion mentioned.

Questioned as to whether Madame de Soissons had applied to any one else to further her designs, she answered that, so far as she was aware, she had not.[1]

"The examinations to which la Voisin was subjected," says M. Funck-Brentano, in his admirable work on the

[1] "Archives de la Bastille, VI : Interrogatoire de la Voisin."

Poison Trials, "were very numerous. They brought out innumerable details on a multitude of crimes, in which a very large number of persons were implicated. The declarations of the terrible sorceress were submitted to careful investigation by examining magistrates like Nicolas de la Reynie. *All her declarations were found to be accurate.*[1]

That Madame de Soissons did, therefore, visit la Voisin, indulge in threats against the King and La Vallière, and demand " means to get rid of " the latter is practically certain ; that she ever obtained the "means" she sought, either from la Voisin or any one else, much less actually attempted to put her criminal design into execution, is highly improbable.

However that may be, the admissions of la Voisin brought the countess's career at the French Court to a sudden and sensational termination. She had, as we have mentioned, powerful enemies. Madame de Montespan, not yet herself implicated in this terrible affair,[2] hated her, as she had hated every one for whom the King had shown any predilection. Louvois hated her, too, because she was the friend of Colbert, and also, if the lady herself is to be believed, because she had refused to give her daughter in marriage to his son. The two conspired together to ruin her, as, ten years before, they had conspired to ruin the Duc de Lauzun ; and they succeeded.

But Louis XIV did not wish the countess to be proceeded against. This reluctance was due less probably to consideration for the woman who had been the play-

---

[1] " Le Drame des Poisons."

[2] For a full account of Madame de Montespan's connection with the poisoners, see M. Funck-Brentano's " Le Drame des Poisons " and the author's " Madame de Montespan " (London : Harpers ; New York : Scribners, 1903).

mate of his childhood and the mistress of his youth, than to the fear that his own dignity might be compromised by a trial which would have involved the public discussion of royal frailties which would not bear the light. When, therefore, the Chambre, urged on by Louvois, demanded her arrest—together with that of her friend and confidante, Madame d'Alluye—we have mentioned that the Court had no power to arrest any one on its own authority—the King delayed sending the necessary warrant for three days, and, in the meanwhile, despatched her brother-in-law, the Duc de Bouillon, to the Hôtel de Soissons to offer the countess her choice between the Bastille and exile.

"On Wednesday she was playing at bassette,"[1] writes Madame de Sévigné; "M. de Bouillon entered; he begged her to step into her cabinet, and told her she must leave France or go to the Bastille. She did not hesitate; she made the Marquise d'Alluye leave the card-table, and they did not reappear. The hour for supper arrived. It was said that the countess was supping in town. Every one went away, persuaded that something extraordinary was happening. In the meantime, a great deal of packing went on. They took money and jewellery; the lackeys and coachmen received orders to put on their grey *justaucorps*; eight horses were harnessed to her coach. She made the

---

[1] Madame de Soissons was a great gambler. During the campaign of 1678, when the Court accompanied the army to Flanders, Colbert de Saint-Pouange, one of Louvois's agents, wrote from Lille to the War Minister: "The day before yesterday M. de Langlée, who kept the bank, lost 2,700 pistoles, of which Madame de Montespan and the Comtesse de Soissons won a considerable part." The countess's exploits in this direction were, however, mere bagatelles in comparison with those of Madame de Montespan, who was one of the greatest gamblers who ever lived, and was accustomed to win or lose hundreds of thousands of livres at a single sitting.

Marquise d'Alluye,—who, it is said, did not wish to go
—enter it with her, and two waiting-women took their
seats in front. She told her people not to distress
themselves on her account, as she was innocent; but
that it had suited those scoundrelly women [la Voisin
and her accomplices] to mention her name. She was in
tears. She made her way to Madame de Carignan's
hôtel, and left Paris at three o'clock in the morning."[1]

On 24 January, the day after the countess's flight,
Louvois wrote to Boucherat, the President of the
Chambre Ardente :—

"The King has sent two officers of his guard to
arrest Madame la Comtesse[2] and Madame d'Alluye ;
they have orders to render an account to you of what
they may do, and the Chancellor has desired that one
adds to their instructions that, in the event of their not
finding these two ladies, they should inform you of it
and return with the ushers whom you will give them to
make a formal report of their search for these ladies,
after which the Chambre will be able to commence the
proceedings against them for contumacy which it may
judge proper. These same officers have instructions to
leave some of the King's guards in the houses of these
ladies, if you deem that necessary."[3]

This letter was, of course, merely a piece of minis-
terial diplomacy which deceived no one, either in the
Chambre or at the Court ; but Louvois considered it
necessary, in order to conceal from the general public
the share which the King had taken in the escape of the
two ladies.

[1] Letter of 30 January 1680.

[2] This, as we have said elsewhere, was the official title of the Comtesse
de Soissons, just as the wife of *Monsieur* was called *Madame* and the
wife of the Prince de Condé, *Madame la Princesse*.

[3] "Archives de la Bastille," VI.

Madame de Soissons having crossed the Flemish frontier, wrote to the King, offering to return and stand her trial, provided that she was not subjected to the indignity of imprisonment in the Bastille or at Vincennes before her case was adjudicated upon. The condition was refused ; her trial was the very last thing which Louis XIV desired.

She continued her journey towards Brussels, but the news of the charges against her had preceded her, and the principal inns in the towns and villages through which she passed refused to receive her ; and on more than one occasion she was compelled to sleep on straw and suffer the insults of the populace, which reviled her as sorceress and poisoner.[1] "We are assured," writes Madame de Sévigné, " that the gates of Namur, Antwerp, and other towns have been closed against the countess, the people crying out : ' We want no poisoners here.' Henceforth, in foreign countries, a Frenchman and a poisoner will be the same thing."[2]

At Brussels, the capital of the Spanish Netherlands, the municipal authorities did not dare to shut their gates against a princess connected by marriage with the Court of Madrid, and the Comte de Monterey took her under his protection. Nevertheless, her sojourn there was, at first, far from a pleasant one, and every time she ventured out she was assailed by the vilest insults. Madame de Sévigné relates an extraordinary story, which she had from the Duc de la Rochefoucauld, the son of the author of the " Maximes."

---

[1] According to Choisy, Louvois had despatched an agent to Flanders, who distributed money among the people to stir them up against the countess, and she was one day forced to spend the night in a shop where she had gone to buy lace, as a howling mob had assembled outside, threatening to tear her to pieces.

[2] Letter of 21 February 1680.

" One day, soon after her arrival at Brussels, Madame de Soissons went to church. As she was entering the building, she was recognised, whereupon a number of people rushed out, collected all the black cats they could find, tied their tails together, and brought them howling and spitting into the porch, crying out that they were devils who were following the countess."[1]

Madame de Soissons, however, remained at Brussels, and gradually the storm which had been raised against her subsided. A little court gathered about her, and as, in spite of her forty-two years, she was still very attractive, she did not lack for admirers, prominent among whom was the Prince of Parma, who, towards the close of the year 1680, succeeded the Comte de Monterey as Governor of the Netherlands.

Two years after her flight from France, Olympe learned of the marriage of her eldest son, the young Comte de Soissons ; he had espoused Mademoiselle de la Cropte-Beauvais, one of the second *Madame's* (Princess Palatine) maids-of-honour, whom Saint-Simon describes as " beautiful as the most beautiful day,"[2] and who had had the distinction of having repulsed the advances of Louis XIV.[3]

The Comtesse de Soissons and her mother-in-law, the old Princesse de Carignan, were furious at this misal-

---

[1] Letter of 20 February 1680.

[2] She was the natural daughter of an equerry of the Prince de Condé. According to Saint-Simon, when her father lay on his death-bed, the Prince went to visit him and entreated him to marry the mother, " representing the position in which, in default of this marriage, he would leave so beautiful a creature as his daughter "; but Beauvais refused.

[3] The Princess Palatine writes : " I had a *fille d'honneur* named Beauvais. She was a very honest creature. The King became enamoured of her, but she remained firm. Then he turned his attention to the Fontanges girl, who was also very pretty, but without any intelligence." " The Fontanges girl," as all the world knows, did not long remain obdurate.

liance, and both promptly disinherited the poor youth.
Louis XIV, however, showed himself more indulgent
towards the marriage, and gave the count a pension of
20,000 livres, which, though sufficient to keep him from
want, was quite inadequate to enable him to support
his position as a Prince of the Blood. A brave soldier,
like his father, he might, under ordinary circumstances,
have hoped for advancement in his profession. But
Louvois, who hated him, for his mother's sake, refused
him promotion, and at length, in disgust, he entered the
service of the Emperor, and was soon afterwards killed
in battle against the Turks. His wife retired for a time
to a convent in Savoy, and afterwards returned to Paris,
where she died in middle life, "still beautiful as the
day," according to Saint-Simon. She had several
children, all of whom died young.

Olympe's second son, Philippe de Savoie, who is
described by the Princess Palatine as "a great fool,
ugly, awkward, and always with a wild look about him,
with a hawk-like nose, a large mouth, and hollow
cheeks," and her third son, called the Chevalier de
Savoie, both died at a comparatively early age—the one
from small-pox, the other through an accident. Of the
youngest, called the Chevalier de Soissons, we shall have
something to say in our next chapter.

The fourth of the countess's five sons, Eugène
Maurice, amply atoned to her for the misfortunes of his
elder brothers, and left behind him a name which will
endure for all time. It was the custom in noble families,
where there were several sons, for one of them to take
Orders, and as Eugène's physique—he was very short,
very slight, and a little crooked—seemed to unfit him
for a military career, his mother insisted on his entering
the Church, and he was given three abbeys, one in

France and two in Piedmont. However, the youth, though he appears to have been an intelligent and industrious student, soon discovered that he had no inclination whatever for an ecclesiastical career, and applied to Louvois for a commission in the army. His request was harshly refused, and Louis XIV, when appealed to, declined to interfere, and spoke of him disdainfully as "the little abbé."

After the peace of Nimeguen, in 1678, some young noblemen, the Prince de Conti, son of Anne Marie Martinozzi among them, went to serve as volunteers with the Austrians against the Turks, and Eugène joined them. Certain letters addressed by one of their number to a friend at Court, in which his Majesty was referred to in far from respectful terms,[1] were brought to the notice of the King, who sent a peremptory order to the party to return. Eugène, however, declined to obey, and sent word that he had decided to renounce France and enter the service of the Emperor. "*Ne trouvez-vous pas que j'aie fait là une grande perte?*" observed Louis, with a contemptuous smile, to those about him, when he received the news. Little did he suspect how bitterly he would live to regret his contemptuous rejection of a sword which, had it been on his side, instead of against him, might have enabled him to remain the arbiter of Europe to the end of his life! But the subsequent career of Eugène de Savoie is too well known to need recapitulation here.

[1] One of these letters contained the following passage: "Quand il [Louis XIV] faut representer, c'est un roi de théâtre; quand il faut combattre, c'est un roi d'échecs."

CHAPTER XX

Madame de Soissons leaves Brussels and takes up her residence in Madrid —Her relations with her sister Marie—Her intimacy with the Queen —Antipathy of Carlos II to her—Correspondence between the Comte de Rebenac, French Ambassador in Madrid, and Louis XIV in regard to the countess—Carlos II convinced that Madame de Soissons has bewitched both him and the Queen—He is warned that it is intended to poison the latter—Sudden death of Marie Louise —Suspicions of poisoning—Letter of Rebenac to Louis XIV— Opinions of other contemporaries—Saint-Simon accuses Madame de Soissons of having poisoned the Queen in a glass of milk—Considera- tion of this charge—The countess is ordered to leave Madrid, and goes to Portugal—She returns to Brussels—Her later years and death.

AFTER spending some time in Flanders, the Com- tesse de Soissons appears to have visited Hamburg and other parts of western Germany; but eventually returned to Brussels, where she remained until the spring of 1686. She made great efforts to obtain per- mission to return to France; but Louvois had treated her too badly to lend himself to her recall; while Madame de Maintenon was hardly more favourably disposed towards her than Madame de Montespan had been; and so she remained in exile. Early in 1686, she determined to leave Brussels and take up her resi- dence in Madrid, and in March embarked for Spain. Her reasons for this step are somewhat doubtful; but, since, during her residence in Flanders, she had estab- lished friendly relations with several noble Spanish families, it was the general belief that her object was to arrange an advantageous marriage for Eugène, who accompanied her, and for whom she obtained the rank of a grandee of Spain.

The Constabless Colonna, who soon after the countess's arrival regained her liberty, expressed at first great pleasure at seeing her sister, and there was some talk of their living together in the same house. But the unpleasant side of Olympe's character soon began to assert itself, and Marie, discovering that she was engaged in political intrigues, and frequented the society of several persons of whom she strongly disapproved, went to live in a house adjoining a convent, and communicating with it by means of a private entrance, which permitted her to retire thither whenever she felt disposed.

Madame de Soissons, however, was well received by the Queen, with whom she had been on intimate terms previous to the latter's marriage, and neglected nothing to ingratiate herself with her Majesty. She succeeded, for Marie Louise clung to everything which reminded her of the France which she had never ceased to regret, though the superstitious Carlos II, who strongly disapproved of the intimacy between his beloved consort and a lady who had been the associate of sorceresses, did everything possible to combat the Queen's inclination for the countess.

Two years passed, and then Madame de Soissons found herself threatened with expulsion from Spain. Under date 7 October 1688, the Comte de Rebenac, the French Ambassador at Madrid, writes to Louis XIV:—

"The Comtesse de Soissons has been the cause during the last fortnight of an intrigue of considerable importance at this Court. The King of Spain was warned against her ; he accused her of sorcery, and I learn that, some days ago, he conceived the idea that, had it not been for a spell which she had cast over him, he would have had children. This idea, Sire, troubled him extremely, and he made a brawl which had taken place between the Spaniards and Madame de Soissons's servants the pretext of intimating to her, through the Constabless Colonna, that it would be well for her to retire to Flanders, where she would be given the enjoyment of the estate of Terveuren for life. She did not wish to defer to this counsel, and it was believed that the taking of Belgrade, the first news of which has been brought here by a gentleman of the Chevalier de Savoie, will cause some change in this order. Nevertheless, the Marqués de los Balbases was charged to confirm it. Upon that, she went to find the Queen, having no doubt that she would be able to persuade her to espouse her cause ; but that princess counselled her, on the contrary, to accommodate herself to the wish of the King."[1]

The countess, however, found two powerful allies in the Graf von Mansfeld, the Austrian Ambassador, and the Prime Minister, the Conde de Oropesa, a warm friend of Austria, whom, says Rebenac, she succeeded in persuading that the Queen had obtained the order for her expulsion at the instance of Louis XIV, and through their intercession she was permitted to remain in Madrid.

From the correspondence between the Comte de Rebenac and Louis XIV, it is evident that both regarded the presence of Madame de Soissons in Madrid with the gravest suspicion. At the time of which we are speaking, the Court of Spain was divided into two

---

[1] "Archives des Affaires Etrangères," published by Amédée Renée, "Les Nièces de Mazarin."

factions, the French and the Austrian ; and the young
Queen, who had gained a great ascendency over her
feeble husband, was striving her utmost to detach him
from the league formed on all sides against Louis XIV.
Her task was a difficult one ; she had against her the
Queen-Mother, Mansfeld, the Prime Minister, and the
majority of the Council ; and Louis XIV did not doubt
that the Comtesse de Soissons, burning with resentment
as she must be against France and its King, and on
intimate terms with the Ambassador of the Emperor
and the head of the Austrian party in the Council,
would do all in her power to persuade Marie Louise of
the hopelessness of her efforts on his behalf. The
Comte de Rebenac received instructions to keep the
closest watch upon the actions of the countess, and to
do everything possible to checkmate her influence, and
here is the picture which he gives of her life in Madrid—
a cruel contrast indeed to the salon of the Hôtel de
Soissons of other days :—

"The life of the Comtesse de Soissons consists in
receiving at her house all persons who desire to come
there from four o'clock in the evening up to two or
three hours after midnight. She keeps a table of from
ten to twelve covers, of which five or six are taken
possession of by as many professional gormandizers
[*goinfres*], who come there every evening without fail,
neither play nor talk, and do nothing but stuff themselves with food, there being no nation so sober as
the Spanish at home nor so gluttonous ; it is a thing
one experiences every day in this country. The rest of
the company is formed of a score of persons of no consideration, who conduct themselves with so little respect
that they enter, their hair tied behind, their bucklers
on their arms, and wearing their long swords and

poniards. There is, Sire, everything which can convey an air of familiarity and contempt for the house of a woman of quality. Moreover, no great nobleman appears there, or very seldom.

"Your Majesty will have the goodness to pardon these details. I only give them because I believe it to be my duty to him to furnish an exact account of the manner in which the Comtesse de Soissons lives here. . . . It is, moreover, certain that the Comtesse de Soissons's intelligence, if she wishes to use it, would enable her to ascertain many things which one could not discover oneself. I shall observe her very closely, and will do my utmost to oppose the confidence which the Queen of Spain might perhaps one day repose in her again."[1]

To this letter the King replied :—

"I approve the resolution that you have arrived at not to hold any communication with the Comtesse de Soissons. It would certainly appear that the manner in which she conducts herself will not give her much influence in the place where you are, and that will do more to compel her to withdraw than all that you can do to send her away. Endeavour, notwithstanding, to keep yourself always well informed of her intrigues,

[1] Rebenac to Louis XIV, 7 October 1688. In the same despatch, the Ambassador refers to Marie in these terms : "As for the Constabless, she is here in a little convent, which she leaves whenever she feels disposed. She does not meddle in any intrigues ; she has many influential friends, and, although she has not quarrelled with her sister, the Comtesse de Soissons, no one was so much rejoiced as was she at the order that had been given the latter to withdraw."

In subsequent despatches, the Ambassador speaks frequently to the King of a "person" devoted to the interests of France, whom he often consults, but whose name he does not mention. And, in one dated 16 January 1689, he states that he has given a portrait of the King set with diamonds "to the person for whom your Majesty intended it," and that it has been received "with respect and gratitude." In the opinion of Lucien Perey, there can be no question that this mysterious person was the Constabless Colonna.

From a contemporary print

OLYMPE MANCINI, COMTESSE DE SOISSONS

in order to give on this subject to the Queen the counsel most conformable to her interests."[1]

The resentment which Marie Louise's refusal to intercede for her with Carlos II had occasioned Madame de Soissons did not last long, and, on 22 October, Rebenac informs Louis XIV that the " Comtesse de Soissons is reconciled to the Queen, and has expressed her great regret for having unjustly accused her of having had any share in the events which have recently taken place."

Although Carlos II had allowed himself to be prevailed upon to withdraw his order to Madame de Soissons, he remained convinced that the countess was a sorceress of a peculiarly dangerous type, and that the non-arrival of the long-awaited heir to his throne was due to a spell which she had cast over his consort and himself. All his efforts were now directed to the raising of this supposed charm, and after pilgrimages to various shrines and other religious exercises recommended in such cases had proved of no avail, he had recourse to the services of a Dominican monk, who professed to have the power of exorcising evil spirits. " The ceremony was horrible," writes Rebenac to Louis XIV, after many apologies for shocking his Majesty's modesty, " *car, Sire, le roy et la reyne devoient estre déshabillés tout nuds.*" On its conclusion, it appeared that the physicians of the Court were called in, and the unfortunate Queen had to submit to a medical examination, in the presence of the monk, " in order to discover if the charm had been removed." The Ambassador expresses the opinion that this affair had been concerted by the Prime Minister, the Conde de Oropesa, and the Austrian faction, with the object of

---

[1] Letter of 23 October 1688.

persuading his Majesty that the Queen had been be-witched *previous* to her marriage, and obtaining its dissolution.[1]

But alas! a far worse fate than sterility was in store for poor Marie Louise. For some time past, Carlos II had received repeated warnings that it was intended to poison the Queen, and, if Madame de la Fayette is to be believed, Marie Louise herself was convinced that such would be her fate, and had written to that effect to *Monsieur*, who sent her an antidote. The antidote, however, arrived too late. On 9 February the Queen was taken suddenly ill, and three days later, in spite of all the efforts of her physicians, she expired.

Her death gave rise to the same terrible suspicions as had that of her mother, the ill-fated Henrietta of England, nineteen years before; but whereas the latter's end is now generally believed to have been due to natural causes,[2] Marie Louise's is capable of no such explanation, and the belief that she was a victim of her private or, more probably, her political enemies— the latter had certainly strong reasons for desiring her removal—is the opinion of nearly all the best-informed of her contemporaries. Let us listen, however, to the account of the affair sent by Rebenac to Louis XIV :

"The courier bears to your Majesty the most sad and deplorable of all news. The Queen of Spain has just expired, after three days of colic and continual vomiting. God alone, Sire, knows the cause of so tragical an event. Your Majesty will have been made aware, by several of my letters, of the sad forebodings I entertained in regard to it.

---

[1] Despatch of 23 December 1688.

[2] See on this question M. Funck-Brentano's admirable study in his "Drames des Poisons."

"I saw the Queen some hours before her death. The King, her husband, had twice refused me this favour; she asked for me herself with so much insistence that they permitted me to enter. I found, Sire, that she had all the signs of death; she recognised them and was not affrighted. She was like a saint as regards God, and like a hero as regards the world. She commanded me to assure you that she was, in dying, as she had been throughout her life, the most faithful friend and servant that your Majesty could have."

According to the Ambassador, the conduct of the Queen's chief physician, Francini, was highly suspicious. "Since the death," he continues, "he has avoided me, and I have not seen him till the third day, although I had sent several times to seek him. I know further that he told one of his friends that it was true that at the autopsy, and during the progress of the malady, he had remarked extraordinary symptoms; but that he would lose his life if he spoke of them.

"The public is at present persuaded that she was poisoned, and has no doubt about it; but the malignity of this people is such that many persons view it with approbation, because they say the Queen had no children, and they regard the crime as a *coup d'État* which has their approval.

"I demanded to be present at the autopsy, or at least that they would permit me to send physicians and surgeons to attend it; but I was refused. . . . When I saw that the Queen was in the last extremity, I left the surgeons and other persons at the doors of her apartment, in order that they might take advantage of the confusion which ordinarily prevails on occasions of this kind, to enter and see if there were any sign on the countenance of the Queen ; but every precaution was taken to prevent any one from entering. . . .

" People coming from Portugal encountered a number of couriers on the way before even the Queen was believed to be in any danger ; this circumstance would indicate communications between the Conde de Oropesa and Portugal.

" At the commencement of the malady there was a great effort made to circulate reports that the Queen had sustained a fall from horseback and had ruptured a vein in the body ; and that she had partaken of a prodigious quantity of oysters, lemons, and iced milk ; and a number of the same people were very busy in circulating these rumours. However, I have made inquiries and found them false. It is not true that she sustained a fall from horseback, or that she partook of anything unusual. And it is true, Sire, that she died in a very horrible manner."

Rebenac goes on to inform the King that he strongly suspects the Prime Minister, Oropesa, and Don Emanuel de Lira, another leader of the Austrian faction, as the authors of the crime, and that the Queen-Mother was privy to it. " The Duquesa d'Albuquerque, lady-of-honour to the Queen," he writes, " has behaved in so suspicious a manner and testified such joy, at the moment even of the Queen's death, that I cannot but regard her with horror ; and she is the devoted creature of the Queen-Mother.[1]

Louville, who succeeded Rebenac as French Ambas-

---

[1] If we are to believe Dangeau, the most reliable, if the dullest, of all contemporary choniclers, Louis XIV seems to have been firmly convinced that his niece had died from the effects of posion. " The King said at supper : ' The Queen of Spain has been poisoned, in an eel-pie, and the Comtesse de Pernitz and the maids-of-honour, Zapada and Nina, who partook of it after her, are dead of the same poison.' "

sador at Madrid two months later, is of the same
opinion, as are the Princess Palatine, *Monsieur's* second
wife, Mademoiselle de Montpensier, and Madame de la
Fayette, one of the most intimate friends of the family.
But neither Rebenac nor any of the writers mentioned
say a single word to inculpate Madame de Soissons ;
and it was left to Saint-Simon, who went as Ambassador
to Madrid thirty years later, to attribute the supposed
crime to the countess, and here is, in brief, what he says :

"The Comte de Mansfeld was the Ambassador of
the Emperor at Madrid, and the Comtesse de Soissons
was on intimate terms with him from the moment of
her arrival. The Queen, who longed only for France,
had a great desire to see the Comtesse de Soissons.
The King of Spain, who had heard her talked about, and
who, for some time past, had been the recipient of
numberless warnings that it was intended to poison the
Queen, raised every conceivable objection before consenting to it. It appears that in the end the countess
came occasionally after dinner to the Queen's apartments,
by a secret staircase, and saw her only in the King's
presence. These visits redoubled, and always with
repugnance on the part of the King. He had asked of
the Queen, as a favour, never to taste anything that
he had not eaten or drunk first, because he was well
aware that it was intended to poison her. The weather
was hot ; milk is scarce in Madrid. The Queen expressed a desire for some, and the countess, who had
gradually usurped brief *tête-à-têtes* with her, boasted of
some that was excellent, which she promised to bring her
in a glass. It is asserted that it was prepared at the
Comte de Mansfeld's house. The Comtesse de Soissons
brought it to the Queen, who swallowed it at a draught,
and died shortly afterwards."

Saint-Simon adds that the countess, for whose flight preparations had been made, quitted the palace the moment the Queen had drunk the milk, and succeeded in effecting her escape from Spain.

Now, what reliance are we to place in this accusation of Saint-Simon ? We are inclined to think little or none. If any real suspicion had attached to the countess, we should certainly find mention of it in the despatches of Rebenac or in the memoirs of the chroniclers we have spoken of : all persons in a position to learn all that was to be learned about the tragedy. Moreover, the fact is now well established that Saint-Simon never hesitated to impute all kinds of crimes to those whom he disliked on the flimsiest of evidence, and not infrequently, we suspect, without evidence at all, and that his memoirs teem with the grossest in-accuracies.

And what had the countess to gain by such a crime ? It may be argued that the death of the Queen would be a severe blow to French interests at Madrid, and would thus avenge her disgrace. That is true ; but it is by no means certain that Olympe had abandoned all hope of returning to France, and in the support of Marie Louise lay her best, almost her only, chance of being recalled. As for the supposition that she rendered this service to Austria in order to further the interests of her son Eugène, that merits scant consideration. Eugène's reputation was already too firmly established to stand in need of any such aid.

However that may be, one part of Saint-Simon's narrative is entirely false. Madame de Soissons did not, as he avers, fly from Spain before even the Queen's death. She remained in Madrid until the following May, when she received orders to depart within a week,

and went to Portugal, where she remained for a year.
That such an order implied a belief on the part of
Carlos II that the countess had been in some way concerned in his wife's death is quite conceivable, though,
if such were the case, it is strange that no objection
should subsequently have been raised to her return to
Flanders ; but it is more likely to have proceeded from
his dread of her powers as a sorceress.

From Portugal Olympe seems to have gone to
Germany ; but, two years later, we find her again in
Brussels, where she resumed the life which she had
lived during her former residence in that city, visiting
and receiving all the most notable residents and distinguished foreigners, like the Elector of Bavaria, whose
intimacy with her is in itself a repudiation of Saint-
Simon's accusation. Of her later years, however, we
know very little. Saint-Simon declares that all the
French of distinction who visited the city were strictly
forbidden to visit her ; but, if such were the case, it is
somewhat singular to find the Maréchal de Villeroi calling upon her and presenting his son, and the sister
of Madame de Coulanges inviting her to supper.[1] The
same veracious chronicler further declares that her
famous son Eugène only visited her on one occasion,
and that she died " in a species of opprobrium." But
let us listen to a Brussels journal of the time, *Les
Relations véritables:*—

" Brussels, 10 July 1690.

" At noon of the same day (6 July), the Prince
Eugène de Savoie, accompanied by Major - General
Cadogan and travelling post, passed by this town on his
way to the camp of Assche, where he held a council of

[1] " Lettres de Madame de Coulanges."

war with the Prince and the Duke of Marlborough ;
and the 7th, about five o'clock in the evening, he came
to this town and alighted at the house of her Highness
the Comtesse de Soissons, his mother, where he received
the compliments of the Ministers and the nobles, and
left again the following morning for the army."

Three months later, the same journal announces the
death of the countess.

"Brussels, 7 October 1690.

"Tuesday morning, the 9th of this month, her
Highness the Comtesse-dowager de Soissons died in
this town, after an illness of some weeks : her good
qualities, her virtues, and especially her charity towards
the poor, render her worthy of praise and cause her to
be regretted by all the world."[1]

Of the seven nieces of Mazarin, Olympe was the
one who most nearly resembled him. She resembled
him in her ambition, in her ostentation, in her un-
scrupulousness, and in her love of intrigue ; but she
had none of his discretion, none of his foresight, and
she was vindictive, which the Cardinal certainly was
not. Hence she failed, and spent the last years of her
life in well-merited exile.

[1] Cited by Amédée Renée, " Les Nièces de Mazarin."

CHAPTER XXI

The Duchesse de Mazarin leaves Savoy and takes up her residence in England—Her reception by Charles II—He makes her a pension, and gives her apartments in St. James's Palace—His answer to her husband's representations—Saint-Évremond's account of her life in England—His devotion to her—His description of her charms— She frequents the society of wits and men of letters—Fatal duel between her nephew, the Chevalier de Soissons, and her lover, the Baron de Banier—Her despair—She resolves to enter a convent in Madrid, but is dissuaded by Saint-Évremond—Her passion for bassette—Remonstrances of Saint-Évremond—Visit of the Duchesse de Bouillon to England—The Revolution of 1688 occurs during her visit—She is sent back to France in William of Orange's yacht— Hortense's pension reduced by the new King—Her last years—She dies at Chelsea in July 1699—Saint-Évremond's eulogy of her—M. de Mazarin's treatment of her remains—Her children—Visit of the Duchesse de Bouillon to Rome—Her quarrel with the Duchess of Hanover—Saint-Simon's opinion of her—Her sons.

IN recounting the adventures of her three sisters, we have somewhat neglected Hortense, whom we last saw, in February 1674, making a diplomatic pilgrimage to the shrine of Saint-François de Sales, to avoid the compromising visit of her sister Marie. After the departure of the Constabless for Flanders, Charles Emmanuel would appear to have sought consolation for his loss in frequent visits to Chambéry, which aroused the jealousy and resentment of the Duchess of Savoy, so complacent where the elder sister had been concerned. The result was that soon after the Duke's death, in the summer of 1675, Madame de Mazarin received an intimation from his widow that she must look elsewhere for an asylum. Hortense, accordingly, quitted Chambéry, travelled through Switzerland, Germany, and Holland "on horseback, and wearing a plumed hat and a peruke," according to her former ally the Marquis de Courcelles, and reached Amsterdam, where she embarked for England.

It has been pretended that this journey had a political end. Louise de Kéroualles, Duchess of Portsmouth, was at this time in possession of the lion's share of Charles II's heart, and using all her influence to keep that estimable monarch in the path marked out for him by his paymaster at Versailles ; and the leaders of the country-party are supposed to have invited the woman whom rumour credited with being the most beautiful of her time to England, in order to oppose her to the reigning siren. It would, however, appear more probable that the fact that the Duchess of York was her cousin,[1] and that she was, in consequence, sure of a welcome at Whitehall, had been Hortense's principal reason for choosing England.

However that may be, Charles II received the duchess with open arms—in the literal as well as the figurative sense of the expression—installed her at once as one of his subordinate sultanas, and gave her a pension of £4000, while Waller hastened to chant her praises :

> "When through the world fair Mazarine had run,
> Bright as her fellow-traveller, the sun ;
> Hither at length the Roman eagle flies,
> As the last triumph of her conquering eyes."

Soon the star of Louise de Kéroualles began to pale before the "conquering eyes" of the beautiful exile,

[1] Marie Beatrix d'Este, daughter of the Duke of Modena and Laure Martinozzi.

and the joy of her enemies, private and political, knew
no bounds, when, on a sudden, the capricious Hortense
dashed all their hopes by transferring her affections to
the Prince de Monaco, one of her friends of Savoy.
The King, in high dudgeon, stopped the pension and
treated the lady with marked coldness; but his anger
did not last long, and, after a few weeks, he not only
restored the pension, but gave her apartments in St.
James's Palace. The Duc de Mazarin, highly indignant
at his Majesty's generosity, and evidently under the
impression that the pension was in the form of a loan
for which he himself might be made responsible,
despatched an emissary to England to represent to the
King that his wife's receipts were valueless, to which
Charles replied, laughing, that it was a matter which
troubled him not at all, since he never took any.[1] He
remained the duchess's friend, and perhaps an inter-
mittent lover, to the end of his life; and John Evelyn
relates that he saw him "toying with her" at Whitehall, only a week before his death.[2]

In her apartments at St. James's, Hortense led a very
agreeable existence, and "found herself surrounded by
all the noblest and most witty persons whom England
possessed." One of the habitués of this little Court,
Saint-Évremond, has left us the following picture of it:

---

[1] "Œuvres de Saint-Évremond," vol. V.

[2] "Diary and Correspondence of John Evelyn," vol. II, 210: "I
can never forget the expressible luxury and profaneness, gaming, and all
dissoluteness, and, as it were, total forgetfulness of God, which this day
se'nnight I was witness of: the King sitting and toying with his concu-
bines, Portsmouth, Cleveland, *Mazarin*, etc., a French boy singing love
songs, in that glorious gallery, while about twenty of the great courtiers
and other dissolute persons were at Basset, round a large table, a bank of
at least two hundred in gold before them; upon which two gentlemen who
were with me made reflections with astonishment. Six days after, all was
in the dust."

"Freedom and discretion are equally to be found there. Every one is made more at home than in his own house, and treated with more respect than at Court. It is true that there are frequent disputes there, but they are those of knowledge, not of anger. There is play there, but it is inconsiderable and only practised for the sake of amusement. You discover in no countenance the fear of losing, nor concern for what is lost. Play is followed by the most excellent repasts in the world. There you will find whatever delicacy is brought from France and whatever is curious from the Indies. Even the commonest meals have the rarest relish imparted to them. There is neither a plenty which gives a notion of extravagance, nor a frugality that discovers penury or meanness."

Saint-Évremond, banished from the Court of France, had been living some fourteen years in England when Madame de Mazarin came to reside there. His admiration for the beautiful duchess was boundless,[1] though it would appear to have been of the platonic order, such as Chateaubriand cherished for Madame Récamier. He visited her every day, became her poet, her advocate, and her secretary, and remained to the end of her life her most devout worshipper. It is in his writings that we must seek for details of Madame de Mazarin's life in England ; but his devotion rendered

[1] Saint-Évremond has left a description of the duchess's charms, which sounds almost fabulous :

"She is one of those Roman beauties who in no way resemble your dolls of France . . . the colour of her eyes has no name ; it is neither blue, nor grey, nor altogether black, but a combination of all the three ; they have the sweetness of blue, the gaiety of grey, and, above all, the fire of the black . . . there are none in the world so sweet . . . there are none in the world so serious and so grave when her thoughts are occupied with any serious subject . . . they are large, well-set, full of fire and intelligence . . . all the movements of her mouth are full of charm,

him so blind to her failings that it is as well to accept some of his statements concerning her with considerable reserve.[1]

Among Hortense's other friends were Charles, Lord Buckhurst, afterwards Earl of Dorset, poet, philanthropist, and wit, the most malicious of writers, and the most kind-hearted of men, of whom Rochester cleverly said :

> For pointed satire I would Buckhurst chuse,
> The best good man with the worst natured muse.

Dr. Vossius, canon of Windsor ; the Protestant refugee, Justel ; Saint-Réal, whom she had first met in Savoy and in collaboration with whom she wrote her memoirs, and the poet Waller.

It will thus be seen that the duchess had begun to form a decided taste for intellectual pleasures ; but this did not prevent her from indulging in numerous gallantries, one of which had a most tragic termination. Some years after her arrival in England, she was visited by her nephew, the Chevalier de Soissons, Olympe's youngest son. The chevalier "breathed the contagious air of the house," and conceived for his aunt, who, though

and the strangest grimaces become her wonderfully, when she imitates those who make them. Her smiles would soften the hardest heart and ease the most profound depression of mind ; they almost entirely change her expression, which is naturally haughty, and spread over it a certain tincture of sweetness and kindness, which reassures those hearts whom her charms have alarmed. Her nose, which without doubt is incomparably well-turned and perfectly proportioned, gives a noble and lofty air to her whole physiognomy. The tone of her voice is so harmonious and agreeable that none can hear her speak without being sensibly moved. Her complexion is so delicately clear that I cannot believe that anyone who examined it closely can deny it to be whiter than the driven snow. Her hair is of a glossy black, with nothing harsh about it. To see how naturally it curls as soon as it is let loose, one would say it rejoiced to shade so lovely a head ; she has the finest turned countenance that a painter ever imagined."

[1] As, for example, when he writes that "with the beauty of ancient Greece, Madame de Mazarin combined the virtue of ancient Rome."

approaching her fortieth year and already a grandmother, was still almost as beautiful as ever, a most violent passion. Hortense, however, repulsed him with horror, her heart being fully occupied by a fascinating Swedish nobleman, the Baron de Banier, son of the general of that name who had distinguished himself under Gustavus Adolphus. Transported with jealousy, the Chevalier challenged the baron to a duel, and wounded him so severely that he died a few days later.

This affair caused a terrible scandal, and M. de Soissons was arrested and had to stand his trial for man-slaughter.[1] Poor Hortense was in despair ; she denied herself to nearly all her friends, draped her rooms in black, and spoke of withdrawing to Spain and joining Marie in her convent. Saint-Évremond sought to dissuade her. "When the ugly and the imbecile," wrote he to her, "throw themselves into convents, it is a divine inspiration which causes them to quit a world where they only appear to disgrace the authors of their being. On your part, Madame, it is a veritable tempta-tion of the devil.

". . . Perhaps you hope to find consolation in con-versing with the Constabless ; but, if I am not mistaken, that consolation will soon come to an end. After having talked for three or four days about France and Italy; after having spoken of the passion of the King (i.e. Louis XIV's passion for Marie), and the timidity of your uncle (Mazarin), of that which you intended to be and that which you have become ; after having exhausted the recollections of your stay in the Constabless's house, of your departure from Rome, and of the ill success of your journeys, you will find yourself shut up in a con-

---

[1] "I could not have believed," wrote Madame de Sévigné, "that the eyes of a grandmother could work such havoc."

vent. There you will experience all the hardships of the
nuns, and will not find that Spouse which consoles them.
All spouses are odious to you, whether in a convent or
in the world. . . ."

Hortense's desire for a conventual life did not last
long, and was replaced by a violent passion for play, and
in particular for the fascinating game of bassette. A
certain professional gamester named Morin, compelled
to fly from France, established himself in London, and
succeeded in insinuating himself into the duchess's
apartments at St. James's, where the game quickly became
the rage. Having no longer any thought in her pretty
head but bassette, Hortense neglected the pleasures of
the mind and the wits and men of letters who had
formerly found so warm a welcome there, to the great
sorrow of Saint-Évremond, who took upon himself to
remonstrate with her in the following verses :—

> "Qui sert à ces messieurs leur illustre science ?
> A peine leur fait-on la simple revérénce
> Et les pauvres savants, interdits et confus,
> Regardent Mazarin, qui ne les connait plus.
>
> Hortense joue à la bassette,
> Aussi longtemps que veut Morin,
> Vous veillez jusqu'au lendemain ;
> Plus de l'opéra, plus de musique
> De morale, de politique. . . .
>
> Beau yeux, quel est votre destin !
> Périrez-vous, beau yeux, à regarder Morin ? "

In July 1687, the Duchesse de Bouillon came to
England on a visit to her sister. Marianne had fallen
into fresh disgrace with the King, for what cause is uncertain, and Paris and the Court had been interdicted
her. The duchess had always been fond of play, but
she was fonder still of intellectual pleasures, and with

her arrival Hortense's apartments at St. James's became once more the rendezvous of wits and men of letters.

Madame de Bouillon's visit was made the occasion of a kind of joust, between Marianne's favourite poet, La Fontaine, and the old and witty cavalier of Madame de Mazarin ; but each was magnanimous enough to chant the praises of his rival's idol as well as those of his own ; and it was now that La Fontaine wrote those charming verses, the first lines of which we have already had occasion to quote :

> "Hortense eût du ciel en partage
> La grâce, la beauté, l'esprit, ce n'est pas tout :
> Les qualités du cœur ; ce n'est pas tout encore :
> Pour mille autres appas le monde entier l'adore
> Depuis l'un jusqu'à l'autre bout.
> L'Angleterre en ce point le dispute à la France,
> Votre héroïne rend nos deux peuples rivaux."

In praising the *esprit* of Hortense, La Fontaine was not, as some may suppose, merely availing himself of the licence enjoyed by poets of all ages of attributing all manner of moral as well as physical perfections to the ladies in whose honour they tuned their lyres. The duchess, though in her youth frivolous and giddy, was never an insipid beauty. She had all the quick intelligence of her family, and, though her life with M. de Mazarin was hardly calculated to develop her faculties, the society she met at Rome, that of Saint-Réal in Savoy, and later the friends whom she drew around her in London, all exercised a beneficial influence upon her mind. Bayle, who, though he never himself was under her spell, was well acquainted with several of those who were, declared that " there were surprising charms in her mind and manners, that she loved study, and took pleasure in the conversation of learned men :" [1]

---

[1] Cited by Amédée Renée, " Les Nièces de Mazarin."

The Revolution of 1688 surprised the two sisters in England, and Madame de Bouillon found herself the prisoner of William of Orange. It was at first believed that he would not allow her to depart, but the austere Dutchman treated her with the greatest courtesy, and gave orders for her to be conveyed to France in his own yacht. Hortense, as the relative of James II's queen, naturally found herself regarded with suspicion by the triumphant party, which demanded her expulsion. However, her friends were sufficiently influential to interest the new king in her favour, and not only to obtain for her permission to remain in England, but also a new pension ; for the one which she had received from Charles II, and which had been continued by his brother, had, of course, ceased with the fallen dynasty. However, William III, being neither a lover nor a relative by marriage, did not feel himself justified in allowing the lady more than half the sum which she had hitherto been receiving, and although Hortense succeeded in continuing to the end the appearance of a princely existence, it was only by the aid of confiding tradesmen. At length, however, some of her creditors became so pressing that she was forced to appeal for assistance to M. de Mazarin, who, while piously dissipating her millions, left her unprovided for. The duke declined to assist her, and advised her to become bankrupt, a step which, said he, she might quite legitimately take, since her creditors were all heretics. He, however, magnanimously invited her to return to the conjugal domicile where she had passed so many unhappy days ; but Hortense invariably replied with the old battle-cry of the Fronde : *Point de Mazarin ! Point de Mazarin !*

During the last years of her life, she seems to have

2 D

become rather too much addicted to the pleasures of the table, particularly in the matter of wine ; and the rhyming epistles which Saint-Évremond addressed to her contain certain counsels of temperance which are for us distinctly unpleasing revelations.

> " Beauté des models chérie,
>   Et de moi plus que ma vie !
>   Moins d'eaux fortes, de vins blancs
>   Vous irez jusqu'a cent ans.
>
>   Mais que le ciel vous envoie
>   Double rate et double foie,
>   L'eau de Madame Huet
>   Vous les séchera tout net
>   Contre eau d'anis, eau d'absinthe
>   *Qu'on boit en tasse de pinte*
>   Vos poumons ne tiendront pas
>
>   Et votre cœur doux et tendre,
>   Qu'ont fait les dieux pour se rendre
>   Au service des amants,
>   Périra par vos vins blancs."

These excesses no doubt hastened the duchess's end, and it would indeed have needed a constitution of iron to have long withstood " *absinthe en tasse de pinte*," and, in the spring of 1699, she fell seriously ill. Hoping that the air and repose of the country might afford her relief, she removed to a house which she had at Chelsea —then, of course, only a village—where she usually spent the summer, but she grew rapidly worse, and we hear of her as " living only on brandy."[1]   Her son, the Duc de la Meilleraye, and the Duchesse de Bouillon, who had been summoned at the beginning of her illness, arrived just before the end, which took place on 2 July 1699, at the age of fifty-three.

[1] Letter of the Abbé Viguier to Monsieur d'Aubigny, cited by Amédée Renée.

The inconsolable Saint-Évremond wrote to a friend :
"She had been the most beautiful woman in the world,
and her beauty preserved its splendour up to the last
moment of her life. She had been the greatest heiress
in Europe, and magnificent, though poor, she had lived
more honourably than the most opulent could do. *Elle
est mort serieusement, avec un indifference chrétien pour la vie.*"

The best, we think, that can be said for poor Hortense, is that she was the victim of circumstance. Married
very young to a half-lunatic husband, and surrounded by
all the temptations of a dissolute society, she would have
needed more than the average share of moral stamina to
have lived a life free from reproach, whereas she was by
nature frivolous and self-willed, greedy for pleasure, and
vain of admiration. She possessed, however, in a very
marked degree the art of endearing herself to those with
whom she came in contact, and in her friendships, as
distinguished from her love-affairs, she appears to have
been singularly faithful, which perhaps accounts for the
extremely lenient judgment passed upon her by Madame
de Sévigné and others of her contemporaries.

In death, Hortense fell into the hands of the husband
whose pursuit she had so successfully evaded during
life. "M. de Mazarin," wrote Saint-Simon, "so long
separated from her, caused her body to be brought back,
and marched it about with him from place to place.
On one occasion, he deposited it at Notre-Dame-de-
Liesse, where the worthy inhabitants prayed to it as
to a saint and touched it with their chaplets."

Madame de Mazarin had four children ; a son Paul
Jules, Duc de Mazarin et de la Meilleraye (1687–
1731), and three daughters, Marie Charlotte (1662–
1729), married to the Marquis de Richelieu, who had
carried her off; Marie Anne (1663–1720), who took

the veil and became Abbess of Lys, where her aunt
Marie had once been imprisoned, and Marie Olympe,
born in 1665, who married the Marquis de Belle-
fonds.

Paul Jules had a son, Gui Paul Jules, Duc de
Mazarin et de la Meilleraye, on whose death, in 1738,
the male branch of the family became extinct, and a
daughter, Armande Félicité, who married Louis de
Mailly, Marquis de Nesle, and became the mother of
the four celebrated sisters, the Comtesse de Mailly, the
Comtesse de Vintimille, the Duchesse de Lauraguais, and
the Marquise de la Tournelle (better known under the
title of Duchesse de Châteauroux), who were succes-
sively the favourites of Louis XV.

After her departure from England, Madame de
Bouillon, to whom Paris and the Court were still forbidden ground, took up her residence at the beautiful
Château de Navarre, two leagues from Évreux, which
her husband had constructed on the site of an old
pleasure-house of Queen Jeanne of Navarre.[1] She
did not, however, remain there long, as having had for
some time a great desire to visit Italy, she set out from
Rome to join her brother, the Duc de Nevers. Here,
they appear to have led a very festive kind of existence, keeping open house and giving the most
sumptuous entertainments. One of their favourite
diversions was to parade the streets of the city, on
moonlight nights, "in an open chariot, having with
them the Signora Faustina, one of the most beautiful
voices in Rome, and the instruments necessary to accompany her." On one occasion, they made her sing

---

[1] It was to this château, which had been presented to her by
Napoleon, that the Empress Josephine retired after her divorce in 1810

under the windows of the Spanish Ambassador, "who the moment Faustina had ceased, did not fail to respond from a balcony by the Signora Georgina, his mistress, whom he had carried off from the Duke of Mantua, who, having a voice not less beautiful than that of Faustina, had also partisans." This kind of competition, the chronicler adds, continued for several nights and attracted a numerous company, "who formed themselves into two rival factions, and raised shouts of ' *Viva Fraucia ! Viva Espano !* ' which could be heard in the most remote quarters of the city."[1]

The latter part of Madame de Bouillon's life was uneventful, the only incident out of the common which is recorded of her being a violent dispute with the Duchess of Hanover over a question of precedence. The sequel to the quarrel was that, a few days later, when the German princess was on her way to the p[l] y, she was met by Madame de Bouillon and several of her relatives, at the head of a small army of retainers, who fell upon the unfortunate foreigners and, having put them to flight, cut the traces of the horses and nearly demolished the coach.

She died in 1714, preserving, according to Saint-Simon, her beauty and charm to the last. "She was the Queen of Paris and of all places to which she was exiled ; husband, children, the whole Bouillon family, the Prince de Conti, the Duc de Bourbon, who did not budge, while at Paris, from her house, all were more lowly than the grass before her. She only very rarely visited any one . . . and preserved an air of superiority over every one, which she knew how to apportion and to season with much skill according to the rank of those with whom she came in contact. Her house was open

1 "Mémoires de Coulanges."

from the morning . . . . morning and evening she kept
a splendid table ; high play went on there, and of all
kinds at the same time.   Never did woman occupy herself less with her toilette; never had beautiful and
singular features like hers less need of the resources of
art.   She was intelligent, spoke well, argued freely, and
always went to the heart of anything.   Intelligence and
beauty sustained her, and the world accustomed itself to
be governed by her." [1]

Madame de Bouillon had four sons, who all embraced
the profession of arms, and the eldest, the Prince de
Turenne, would have been celebrated, had not the
memory of his achievements been unfortunately merged
in that of the illustrious captain whose name he bore.
In 1679, he accompanied the Prince de Conti and
Eugène de Savoie to Hungary, and distinguished himself at the battles of Grau and Neuhausel.   Whether he
was actually the author of the compromising letter we
have spoken of elsewhere is uncertain ; but, any way, he
had no sooner returned to France than he received a
lettre de cachet ordering him to repass the frontier.   He
went to Venice and took service, as a volunteer, under
the Republic, then disputing with the Turks possession
of the Morea and Greece.   His military talents, and
still more his reckless courage, so delighted the Venetians
that, on his return, the Republic presented him with a
sword encrusted with diamonds, charged their Ambassador in Paris to compliment his family, and offered
him the rank of lieutenant-general.   But the young
prince, unlike his cousin Eugène, had no wish to renounce his country and preferred to remain a volunteer.
Soon afterwards, he was permitted to return to France,
but did not long survive his recall.

[1] " Mémoires de Saint-Simon."

The duchess's second son, the Duc d'Albret, was Grand Chamberlain to the King and Governor of Auvergne; a third was a Knight of Malta; the youngest, a colonel-general of light cavalry, married the daughter of a wealthy financier, who was called by Madame de Bouillon, "her little ingot of gold." The family became extinct on the death of Godefroy Charles Henri de la Tour d'Auvergne, in 1791.

CHAPTER XXII

Death of the Constable Colonna—On his death-bed and in his will he
asks pardon of his wife and recommends her to the care of their sons—
Visit of Don Carlo Colonna to Madrid—Meeting between Marie and
the Duc de Nevers at Toulouse—The Constabless goes to Rome, but
decides to return to Spain—On her way from Genoa to Marseilles,
she is captured by a corsair—But is released by the Governor of
Finale—Consideration which she enjoys at Madrid—Her intimacy
with the new Queen, Maria Anna of Neuburg—She follows her to
Toledo, on her banishmeut thither in January 1702—Her interview
with Philip V—She leaves Spain and visits various towns in the south
of France—Receives permission to come to Paris, and goes to live at
Passy—She declines Louis XIV's invitation to Court—Departure for
Rome—Her last years—She dies at Pisa, in May 1715—Her epitaph.

MARIE survived all her sisters, though, like theirs,
her later years were comparatively uneventful.
On 15 April 1689, the Constable Colonna died at
Rome. Since 1684, when he had had a serious illness,
he had lived for the most part in retirement, and latterly
had become very devout. Five priests assisted him in
his last hours, and afterwards drew up and signed a
Relatione of his repentance, evidently intended to cause
people to forget the decidedly unedifying life which the
prince had lived. On his death-bed, he expressed the
tenderest sentiments towards his wife, and his regret
for the harshness with which he had treated her, and
summoning his eldest son, the Principe di Palliano, recommended to his care and that of his brothers their
"excellent mother."[1] In a codicil to his will, he
"demanded pardon of his wife, and, for fear that appear-

[1] Lucien Perey, "Marie Mancini Colonna."

408

ances might leave to his children some resentment against their mother, he took the blame upon himself, and did not inspire them with anything for her, save respect, gratitude, and esteem." [1]

Marie received the news of her husband's death with the most profound grief. Always generous, she forgot her wrongs and reproached herself bitterly with having doubted his good faith when, three years before, he had begged her, for the last time, to return to him. She shut herself up in her house and refused to receive any one, save her sister-in-law, the Marquesa de los Balbases, until her youngest and favourite son, Don Carlo Colonna, who had taken Orders, arrived in Madrid, to acquaint her with particulars of his father's death and to bring her the Constable's betrothal ring, which he had bequeathed to her.

Don Carlo endeavoured to persuade his mother to return with him to Rome and make her home there ; and he and his brothers, shortly afterwards, gave her a pension of 12,000 crowns, besides offering to place apartments in the Casa Colonna and in whichever of the numerous country-seats of the family she might prefer at her disposal. However, she elected to remain for the present in Madrid, and it was not until the end of the year 1691 that she set out for Rome. She travelled by way of Bayonne and Toulouse, Louis XIV having granted her a passport, notwithstanding the fact that France and Spain had been at war since the summer of 1689 ; and at the latter town was met by her brother the Duc de Nevers, whom she had not seen for eighteen years. The object of their meeting seems to have been to discuss the project of a marriage between Don Marco Colonna, Marie's second son, and the duke's eldest

---

[1] " Œeuvres de Saint-Évremond."

daughter,[1] who was then about fifteen years of age; but the Duchesse de Nevers and her relatives the Morte-marts were opposed to the young girl leaving France, and nothing came of their *pourparlers*. The Constabless then continued her journey to Rome, where, however, she only remained until May 1692, when she decided to return to Madrid. Nor is this decision a matter of surprise. Her long residence in the Spanish capital had accustomed her to the ways of the country, and enabled her to speak the language fluently, while she had many influential friends and was in high favour at Court. On the other hand, she had always entertained a strong distaste for the customs of her native land, and found that during her absence of nearly twenty years Roman society seemed to have forgotten her, and that there was little chance of her being able to resume the rôle which she had once played in it.

On her return journey, she passed some months at Genoa, and then embarked on a little felucca bound for Marseilles. This proved an unfortunate step, as she had not been many hours at sea when the felucca was attacked and captured by a corsair of Finale, which carried off both the vessel and its distinguished pas-senger into that port. The governor of the city, how-ever, having learned of the Constabless's plight, sent soldiers to liberate her and to arrest the captain of the corsair, whom he threw into prison. Matters would no

---

[1] The Duc de Nevers, who died in May 1707, had four sons and two daughters: 1. Éloi, who died young; 2. Gabriel, Duc de Donzi, died in 1683; 3. Philippe Jules François, Prince de Vergagne, Duc de Nevers, who attained the age of ninety-three, and was the father of the amiable and accomplished Duc de Nivernais, whom Lord Chesterfield holds up to his son as a model for him to form himself upon; 4. Jacques Hippolyte, Marquis de Mancini, who inherited his father's property in Italy; 5. Diane Gabrielle Victoire, who married the Prince de Chimay; 6. Adélaïde Philippe, who became the wife of Louis Antoine, Duc d'Estrées.

doubt have gone hardly with the audacious pirate, had not Marie, probably thinking, as one of her biographers suggests, that the poor man had been sufficiently punished by being compelled to surrender so beautiful a prize as herself, obtained his pardon from the governor, after which she resumed her interrupted voyage and reached Marseilles without further adventures.[1]

On her return to Madrid, Marie seems to have occupied a very enviable position, her house being the rendezvous of the foreign Ambassadors and all the most notable persons of the Court ; while, notwithstanding her pronounced French sympathies, she was on terms of the closest intimacy with the new Queen, Maria Anna of Neuburg. When, on the death of Carlos II, Louis XIV's grandson, the Duc d'Anjou, became King of Spain, under the title of Philip V, Maria Anna was exiled to Toledo (January 1702). The Constabless, however, remained faithful to her royal friend, accompanied her in her exile, and did everything possible to bring about a reconciliation between her and the new king. Chiefly, it would appear, through her efforts, Philip made a journey to Toledo and had an interview with the Queen-Dowager. The Constabless was present on this occasion, and was very graciously received by his Majesty, who conversed with her for some time ; while she, on her part, was no doubt charmed by the strong resemblance which he bore to his grandfather. However, the outbreak of the War of the Spanish Succession precluded any hope of Maria Anna being allowed to return to Madrid, and, in the autumn of that year, the Constabless received a friendly hint from the Marquis de Louville, the French Ambassador at Madrid, that, by her advocacy of the Queen-Dowager's cause, she had

[1] Lucien Perey, "Marie Mancini Colonna."

somewhat compromised herself with the new Court, and that it would be advisable for her to retire to Barcelona.

At the end of January 1703, the Constabless, finding that Madrid was likely to remain prohibited ground to her for some time to come, decided to visit France, to which Louis XIV had accorded her permission to return whenever she pleased. After spending some time at Lyons, a town endeared to her by the souvenirs of the happy past, she passed on to Avignon, where we hear of her driving about "in a coach and six accompanied by two equerries." While at Avignon, she narrowly escaped being made the victim of an impudent impostor, a young man named Morandi, who pretended to be a connection of the Mazarin family, and whose fraud was only discovered on the eve of his receiving a considerable sum of money from the Constabless and other members of the family, whom she had asked to assist him.

This incident seems to have disgusted Marie with Avignon, which she shortly afterwards quitted, and after spending some time at Marseilles and other towns in the south of France, she determined to visit Paris. Nothing had been said about Paris in the permission which she had received to enter France ; but, when she wrote to the Minister Barbézieux, leave was immediately accorded her. She arrived at the beginning of September 1703, but did not reside in the city itself, preferring to take up her quarters in a house at Passy, which belonged to the Duc de Nevers. She was accompanied by two waiting-women, two equerries, and about a dozen men-servants.

Saint-Simon, with his customary inaccuracy where the Mancini are concerned, states that Marie only received permission to reside at Passy, "on condition that she should not set foot in Paris, much less in the

Court." But, as a matter of fact, Louis XIV sent the Duc d'Harcourt to pay her "a thousand compliments," and to invite her to Versailles. The invitation, however, was courteously declined, for what reason is uncertain, though, as the Marquise d'Huxelles, who saw her at this time, states that she was "*fort détruite de sa personne*," it is not improbable that feminine pride rendered her reluctant to reveal to the lover of her youth the ravages which time had wrought. She, however, visited Paris, which had been improved out of all knowledge since she had last seen it in 1661, and wrote to her son Don Carlo that the changes seemed to her incredible.[1]

The Constabless remained at Passy until the middle of October, when she left for the South, and, after spending some weeks at Lyons and Nevers, at the beginning of January 1704, quitted France, for the last time, and returned to Rome.

Until recently, nothing was known of Marie's last years, and even the place and date of her death were matters of conjecture. Thanks, however, to the indefatigable researches of Lucien Perey, it now appears that they were passed entirely in Italy, where she divided her time between Rome, Florence, and Venice, and devoted herself with much solicitude to all that concerned the welfare of the Colonna family. Of her three sons, Filippo succeeded his father as Grand Constable of Naples; Don Carlo, a great favourite at the Vatican, was made a cardinal in May 1706; while Marco Antonio married Diana Paleotto di Bologna, a daughter of Lorenzo Colonna's former mistress.

The death of the Constabless's sister Marianne, followed closely by that of her eldest son, the Constable, who died in her arms in November 1714, affected

---

[1] Lucien Perey, "Marie Mancini Colonna."

her deeply, and she became convinced that her own end was at hand. Though she had had little religion in her youth, in her old age she had become very devout, and, in May 1715, went to Pisa to consult a certain Spanish monk Padre Ascanio Salvatore, whom she had taken for her confessor during her visits to that city, about certain changes in her will, which the death of her eldest son had rendered necessary. One day, while visiting him, at the Priory of the Holy Sepulchre, she was seized with an attack of apoplexy, and died early on the following morning, without recovering consciousness, on the humble pallet of her confessor, to which she had been carried.

In her will, the Constabless had left directions that she was to be buried in the place where she died, and she was accordingly interred in the Church of the Holy Sepulchre at Pisa, where the simple inscription

"MARIE MANCINI COLONNA
ASHES AND DUST."

marks the spot where she lies.

"Marie Mancini," says Saint-Simon, "was the best of the Mancini and the most foolish"; and with this dictum few who have read these pages will be inclined to disagree. She had many noble qualities; she was high-minded, generous, sincere, and affectionate; but she was headstrong and impetuous, and subordinated everything to her desires and her passions, though how far the escapades of her middle life were due to her natural impulses and how far to the effects of the illness from which she had suffered at Loretto in 1661 is difficult to say. However that may be, there can be no question that her influence over Louis XIV was, as we have said elsewhere, in its early phases at least, a most salutary one, and that is perhaps her best claim to be remembered.

INDEX

A

Aiguillon, Duchesse d', 49

Alençon, Mlle. d', 199

Alluye, Madame d', 101, 141, 371 and note, 372, 374, 375

Altieri, Cardinal, 303, 307, 308, 309, 310, 320, 342

Angelelli, Marchese de, 221, 235, 237

Anjou, Philippe, Duc d'. *See* Orléans, Philippe, Duc d'

Anne of Austria, Queen of France, her reception of Mazarin's nieces, 4–6; her relations with Mazarin considered, 6–14; rebuffs the Marquis de Jarzé, 18, 19; libelled by the Frondeurs, 21 note; her correspondence with Mazarin during his exile at Brühl, 25–28; her tender letter to him, 33; accompanies Louis XIV to Lyons, 85–95; alarmed at Louis XIV's passion for Marie Mancini, 101–103; endeavours to dissuade the King from marrying Marie, 111, 112; her touching interview with her son, 116, 117; accused by him of embittering the Cardinal against his niece, 127; Mazarin's letter to her from Cadillac, 129, 130; and from Saint-Jean-de-Luz, 139–141; her interview with Marie Mancini and her sisters at Saint-Jean-d'Angely, 143–145; Mazarin's diplomatic letter to her, 158, 159; her aversion to Marie Mancini, 180, 181; her interview with Philip IV of Spain, 197, 198; Mazarin's treatment of her during his last illness, 223, 224; opposed to Marie Mancini remaining in France, 234; also mentioned, 63, 65, 68, 104, 107, 109, 110, 113, 118, 128, 130, 141, 142, 146, 159, 187, 199, 204, 210, 217, 235

B

Astorga, Marques d' (Viceroy of Naples), 287 note, 298

Aulnoy, Madame d' (cited), 350–352, 359, 360

Banier, Baron de (lover of Madame de Mazarin), 398

Barberini, Cardinal, 16

Barine, Arvède (cited), 72, 112, 201

Bartet (confidential agent of Mazarin), 175, 176, 179, 226

Beaufort, Duc de, 4 note, 18, 22, 24

Beauvais, Madame de, 19, 66, 216, 217

Beauvau, Marquis de (cited), 206, 207

Belbeuf, Jacques (lover of Madame de Mazarin), 283, 284

Benedetti, Abbé (cited), 236, 237

Benedetti, Elphideo, 12

Blouin (*valet de chambre* to Louis XIV), 129, 177

Bologna, Don Maurizio, 328, 329

Borgomainero, Marchese di, 331 and note, 336, 337

Bouillon, Duc de (husband of Marianne Mancini), 253, 254, 255, 258, 363, 364, 367–370, 405

Bouillon, Duchesse de (Marianne Mancini), brought to France, 52; Mazarin's practical joke at her expense, 53; sent with her sisters, Marie and Hortense, to La Rochelle, 118; accompanies them to meet the Court at Saint-Jean-d'Angely, 142–145; her letters to the Cardinal, 140 note, 148, 174, 189; Mazarin's bequest to her, 232; married to the Duc de Bouillon, 253, 254; her patronage of La Fontaine, 255–258; her intrigues against Racine's "Phèdre," 259, 260; sent to a convent, 364; compromised in the Poison Trials, 367, 368; her trial

before the Chambre Ardente, 369, 370; exiled to Nérac, 370; visits the Duchesse de Mazarin in England, 399, 400; returns to France, 401; visits her brother in Rome, 404, 405; her quarrel with the Duchess of Hanover, 405; her death, 405; Saint-Simon's eulogy of her, 405, 406; her children, 406, 407; also mentioned, 260, 267, 271, 302, 315
Brienne, Madame de, 8, 9
Brinvilliers, Marquise de, 365

C

Candale, Duc de, 16, 17 and note, 40
Capitor (jester of Don Juan of Austria), 103
Carignan, Princesse de, 29, 60, 61, 62
Carignan, Prince Thomas de, 32, 60
Chantelauze, M. (cited), 110, 201, 329, 346 note
Charles II of England, 225-227, 329, 345, 346, 394, 395 and note, 401
Charles IV, Duke of Lorraine, 178, 205-209, 216, 272
Charles Emmanuel II, Duke of Savoy, 84 and note, 88 and note, 91, 92 and note, 93, 225, 322, 323, 324-336, 340, 341
Charles of Lorraine, Prince, 178, 183, 190, 191, 200-202, 205, 206, 209, 210, 212, 216, 233, 234
Cheruel, M. (cited), 11, 12, 110
Chigi, Cardinal, 286
Chigi, Don Augustin (lover of Madame de Mazarin), 284
Choisy, Abbé de, 200; (cited), 158 note, 376 note
Christina, Queen of Sweden, 63, 71
Christine of France, Duchess of Savoy, 83, 84, 88-95
Clement X, Pope, 303, 307, 309, 310, 326
Colbert, 77, 121, 125, 129, 157, 162, 177 note, 205, 218, 224, 231, 268, 318, 319, 347, 348, 355, 359, 360, 373, 381, 382
Colbert de Terron (Governor of La Rochelle), 121, 165, 177
Colbert, Madame, 187
Colonna, Carlo, 277, 409, 410, 413
Colonna, Lorenzo Onofrio, Constable (husband of Marie Mancini), 178, 182, 183, 216, 223, 234, 235, 236, 237-242, 274-280, 282, 284, 296-297, 298, 301, 303, 307, 308, 309, 310, 321, 322, 323, 326, 328, 331, 332, 335, 336, 337, 338, 341, 342, 343, 348-350, 352, 353, 354, 357, 353, 359, 408, 409
Colonna, Constabless (Marie Mancini), her childhood, 35-37; brought to France, 37, 38; sent to the Couvent de la Visitation, 44; her remarkable intelligence, 45; her letters to Mazarin, 46-48; her hand refused by the Marquis de la Meilleraye, 49, 50; harshly treated by her mother, 53, 54; becomes one of the most cultured women of her time, 55, 56; beginning of her friendship with Louis XIV, 56; her personal appearance, 69; her increasing intimacy with the King, 69, 70; her beneficial influence over his mind, 70-71; her grief during his illness at Calais, 78; Louis XIV's attentions to her at Fontainebleau, 79-81; accompanies the Court to Lyons, 85-88; dissuades the King from marrying Princess Margherita of Savoy, 91 and note; resolved to become Queen of France, 96, 98; constantly in the King's company, 96, 97; growing passion of Louis XIV for her, 100-104; secures the dismissal of Don Juan of Austria's jester, 104; her influence over the King alarms Mazarin and Anne of Austria, 107-109; Louis XIV determined to marry her, 109; ordered to leave the Court, 112; her interview with the King, 114; presented by him with the pearls of Queen Henrietta Maria, 115, 116; her departure for La Rochelle, 117, 118; falls ill at Notre-Dame-de-Cléry, 119, 120; receives "very long and very tender letters" from the King, 120, 121; arrives at La Rochelle, 124; her interview with Louis XIV at Saint-Jean-d'Angely, 142-145; pretends to submit to the Cardinal's wishes, 146, 147; breaks off her correspondence with Louis XIV, 162-166; declines to reply to the King's letters, 168-171; writes to Mazarin, 171, 172; goes to Brouage, 172, 173; in despair at the resumption of the King's relations with the Comtesse de Soissons, 180-182; refuses the hand of the Constable Colonna, 182, 183; returns to Paris, 184-187; receives a letter from the King, 187, 188; attentions paid to her by Prince Charles of Lorraine, 190, 191; anxious to marry the prince, 200-

203 ; Charles IV, Duke of Lorraine, proposes for her hand, 205–209 ; her icy reception by Louis XIV at Fontainebleau, 211–215 ; pressed by Mazarin to marry the Constable Colonna, 216 ; witnesses the entry of Maria Theresa into Paris, 217–222 ; promises to marry the Constable Colonna, 223 ; her remark on learning of Mazarin's death, 230 ; her painful interview with Louis XIV, 233, 234 ; refuses to break with the Constable Colonna, 234 ; her marriage, by procuration, with the Constable, 235 ; her journey to Italy, 235–237 ; her meeting with her husband, 238 ; her dangerous illness at Loretto, 240, 241 ; arrives in Rome, 241, 242 ; her early married life, 274–277 ; separation di letto between her and her husband, 277–279 ; goes to Milan to meet her sister Hortense, 280 ; assists Hortense to escape from the Convent of Campo-Marzo, 282 ; estrangement between her and the Constable, 286, 287 ; believes that her husband intends to poison her, 288–290 ; promised an asylum in France by Louis XIV, 290, 291 ; her flight to France, 293–301 ; sends a message to Louis XIV, 304 ; forbidden by the Queen to come to Paris, 305 ; her interview with her brother at Grenoble, 306 ; her journey to Fontainebleau, 312, 313 ; enters the Abbey of Lys, 314, 315 ; her imprudent letter to Colbert, 318 ; sent to the Abbey of Avenay, 324 ; goes to Turin, 324 ; her life there, 324–333 ; her relations with Charles Emmanuel II considered, 334 ; quarrels with the Duke, 334, 335 ; refused an asylum in France, 335 ; sets out for Flanders, 336–338 ; imprisoned at Antwerp, 339, 340 ; goes to Madrid, 341, 342 ; enters a convent, 343 ; escapes, but is brought back, 344 ; writes to Charles II of England, 345 ; publication of her apocryphal and her genuine memoirs, 346 ; second attempt at escape, 347, 348 ; visited by her husband, 348, 349 ; takes refuge at the French Embassy, 353, 354 ; goes to reside in her husband's palace, 355 ; imprisoned in the Alcazar of Segovia, 356, 357 ; promises to become a nun and enters the Convent of the Conception, 357, 358 ; refuses to carry out her promise, 359, 360 ; set at liberty, 360, 361 ; coldness between her and the Comtesse de Soissons, 381 ; her grief on learning of her husband's death, 409 ; visits Rome, 410 ; returns to Madrid, 411 ; accompanies Maria Anne of Neuburg to Toledo, 411 ; visits France, 412 ; declines Louis XIV's invitation to Court, 413 ; her last years and death, 413, 414

Colonna, Ferdinando, 341, 342, 343, 345, 348, 356

Colonna, Filippo, 276, 277, 354, 355, 413, 414

Colonna, Marco Antonio, 277, 343, 413

Condé, Prince de, 19, 20, 23, 30, 32, 145, 377 note

Conti, Prince de, 20, 38–42, 197

Conti, Princesse de (Anne Marie Martinozzi), 3–6, 38–42, 143, 197

Cosnac, Daniel de (cited), 17, 58, 59

Couberville, "Chevalier" de (lover of Madame de Mazarin), 272, 280–283

Coulanges, Marquise de, 391

Courtenay, Prince de, 227

Créqui, Duc de, 197, 314, 315 and note, 317

Créqui, Duchesse de, 187

D

Deshoulières, Madame, 254, 258

Du Fouilloux, M., 141, 142, 145

Du Fouilloux, Mlle. See Alluye, Madame

Du Saussois (physician), 77

E

Épernon, Duc d', 87

Épernon, Duchesse d', 67

Estrées, Cardinal d' (French Ambassador in Rome), 298, 299 and note, 317, 322

Estrées, Duc d', 289

Evelyn, John (cited), 395 and note

F

Fontanges, Mlle. (mistress of Louis XIV), 235 note, 243, 377 note

Fouquet, Nicolas, 224

Francesco I, Duke of Modena, 51

Francesco II, Duke of Modena, 51, 314 note

G

Gazette de France (cited), 61, 221
Gazette de Leyden (cited), 287 note
Gomont, M. de, 325, 327
Gramont, Chevalier de, 219 note, 248, 249
Grignan, Comte de, 300, 301
Grignan, Comtesse de, 258 and note, 302
Grillo, Marchese del (lover of Madame de Mazarin), 284
Gusman, Don Domenico, 284

H

Haro, Don Luis de (Prime Minister of Spain), 108, 136, 198
Henrietta Anne of England. *See* Orléans, Henrietta Anne, Duchesse d'
Henrietta Maria, Queen of England, 115, 186, 217, 293
Hocquincourt, Maréchal, 21, 29, 30
Hôpital, Maréchal de l', 186
Hôpital, Maréchale de l', 74
Huxelles, Marquise d' (cited), 413

I

Innocent X, Pope, 13, 14
Innocent XI, Pope, 358, 360

J

Jarzé, Marquis de, 18–20
Juan of Austria, Don, 103, 104, 347, 348, 350

K

Kéroualles, Louise de, 394, 395 note

L

La Fayette, Madame de la (cited), 109, 214, 389
Lafesnestre, M. Georges (cited), 256
La Fontaine, 148, 255–258, 400
La Gilbertière, 312, 313, 314, 315, 317, 319 and note
La Grande Mademoiselle. See Montpensier, Mlle. de
Lamoignon, Mère Élisabeth de, 44
La Motte d'Argencourt, Mlle. de, 65, 66
La Motte-Houdancourt, Mlle. de, 75, 101 note, 102
La Rochefoucauld, Duc de, 55
La Vallière, Louise de, 42, 235 note, 242, 245, 371
Le Camus, Abbé, 105
Le Fare, Marquis de (cited), 244, 250
Lesage (magician), 367, 368, 370

Lionne, Hugues de, 106, 107, 237 note
Livet, M. Charles (cited), 110
Loiseleur, M. Jules (cited), 11–14
Loret, Jean, 148; (cited), 185
Lorraine, Chevalier de, 284, 287 note, 290–292, 307
Los Balbases, Marques de, 238, 280, 353, 356, 359, 360, 382
Los Balbases, Marquesa de, 409
Louis XIV, goes to meet Mazarin on his return from his second exile, 33; beginning of the friendship between him and Marie Mancini, 56; "dancing with grace and majesty," 57; his intimacy with Olympe Mancini, 62–64; his early *galanteries*, 65, 66; growing attachment between him and Marie Mancini, 68–70; her beneficial influence over him, 71, 72; has a passing fancy for Mlle. de la Motte-Houdancourt, 75, 76; falls dangerously ill at Calais, 76–78; his attentions to Marie Mancini at Fontainebleau, 79–81; Mazarin's matrimonial projects for him, 82–84; his journey to Lyons to meet the Princess Margherita of Savoy, 82–99; his passion for Marie Mancini increasing, 101, 102; dismisses Don Juan's jester from Court, 104; scandalizes the Spanish envoy, 107; openly braves the Queen, 107, 108; demands Mazarin's permission to marry Marie Mancini, 109; flies into a violent passion with Anne of Austria, 113; refused by the Cardinal his niece's hand, 113; attempts to console Marie Mancini, 114; touching interview with his mother, 116, 117; Mazarin's letters to him relative to his passion for Marie, 122, 126–129, 130–138, 143–145, 150–157; declines to accept Marie's refusal to write to him, 167, 168; has no heart for the gaieties of the Court, 175; resumes his relations with the Comtesse de Soissons, 179; his marriage with the Infanta Maria Theresa, 192–200; his entry with the Queen into Paris, 217–221; his letter to Madame de Venel, 239; and to the Constable Colonna, 241, 242; takes no pleasure in the society of the Queen, 243, 244; abandons the Comtesse de Soissons for Louise de la Vallière, 244, 245; exiles the Comtesse de Soissons, 252; under financial obligations to the Duc de Mazarin, 263 and note; finds himself in an embarrassing position in regard

to the Constabless Colonna, 310; annoyed at her imprudent letter to Colbert, 318; his letter to her, 319, 320; sends her a thousand pistoles, 325; orders the Prince de Carignan to send her away from his house, 332; ignores her request to be allowed to return to France, 335; banishes the Duchesse de Bouillon, 370; connives at the escape of Madame de Soissons from justice, 374, 375; his correspondence with the Comte de Rebenac, French Ambassador in Madrid, 383–388; gives the Constabless Colonna permission to return to France, 409; invites her to Court, 412, 413. See also Anne of Austria; Colonna, Constabless; Mazarin, Cardinal

Louvois, 267, 373, 375

M

Madame. See Orleans, Henrietta Anne, Duchess d'

Maintenon, Madame de, 216, 217, 336, 380; (cited), 217–220

Mancini, Alphonse, 52, 73

Mancini, Hortense. See Mazarin, Duchesse de

Mancini, Laure. See Mercœur, Duchesse de

Mancini, Lorenzo, 2, 55, 56

Mancini, Marianne. See Bouillon, Duchesse de

Mancini, Marie. See Colonna, Constabless

Mancini, Olympe. See Soissons, Comtesse de

Mancini, Paul, 3, 6, 28, 30, 31

Mancini, Philippe. See Nevers, Duc de

Mancini, Signora, 2, 3, 35–38, 53, 54, 56, 57

Mansfeld, Graf von (Austrian Ambassador in Madrid), 382, 383, 385, 389

Maria Anne of Neuburg, Queen of Spain, 411, 412

Marie Beatrice of Modena, Queen of England, 51, 394, 401

Maria Theresa of Austria, Queen of France

Marie de' Medici, Queen of France, 19

Marie Louise d'Orléans, Queen of Spain, 381, 382, 383, 385, 386, 387, 388, 389, 390, 391

Margherita of Savoy, Princess, 84, 85, 86, 88–95

Marsan, Comte de, 284, 290

Martinozzi, Laure. See Modena, Duchess of Modena

Martinozzi, Anne Marie. See Conti, Princess de

Martinozzi, Signora, 2, 3, 51, 282

Mazarin, Cardinal, his misplaced kindness to his brother Michele, 1, 2; summons the first detachment of his nieces and nephews to France, 3, 4; his coolness towards them, 4, 5; his relations with Anne of Austria considered, 6–14; sends his nieces to Val-de-Grâce, 15; his plans for their establishment in life, 16, 17; affiances Laure Mancini to the Duc de Mercœur, 17, 18; goes into exile, 20; burned in effigy, 20 note; his sojourn at Brühl, 22–24; his correspondence with Anne of Austria, 25, 26; returns to France, 26–28; his grief at the death of his nephew Paul Mancini, 30, 31; shamefully libelled, 31, 32; goes into exile for the second time, 32; returns in triumph to Paris, 33, 34; summons a second detachment of his relations to France, 35, 36; marries Anne Marie Martinozzi to the Prince de Conti, 38–41; marries Laure Martinozzi to Francesco d' Este of Modena, 50, 51; summons Alphonse and Marianne Mancini to France, 52; present at the Duchesse de Mercœur's death, 59; marries Olympe Mancini to the Comte de Soissons, 60, 61; his dislike of Philippe Mancini, 73, 74; does not interfere with the intimacy between the King and Marie Mancini, 80; his matrimonial projects for Louis XIV, 82–85; regards Marie Mancini as a useful factor in his plans, 85, 86; announces to Anne of Austria the arrival of the Spanish envoy, Pimentel, 90; regards Pimentel's mission with suspicion, 91; refuses Hortense Mancini's hand to the Duke of Savoy, 92; his interview with the Duchess of Savoy, 93; fears for the virtue of Marie Mancini, 97, 98; alarmed at her growing influence over the King, 102, 107; his conduct in the matter considered, 109–111; resolves to send Marie to La Rochelle, 112; refuses Louis XIV's demand for her hand, 114; sets out for the Pyrenees, 118; his letters to Louis XIV and Anne of Austria relative to Marie Mancini, 122, 126, 127, 128, 129–141, 150–157, 158–161; learns that Marie has resolved to renounce the King, 162–170; sends his agent Bartet to

Bordeaux, 175; discovers the treachery of the Governor of La Rochelle, 176, 177; determines to find a husband for Marie, 177, 178; sends the Bishop of Fréjus to Brouage, 182; sends his nieces back to Paris, 184–187; greatly alarmed at Louis XIV's visit to Brouage and La Rochelle, 203–205; intrigues to awaken the jealousy of the King, 209–214; urges Marie to wed the Constable Colonna, 216; magnificence of his household, 218, 219; his last illness, 223, 224; his death, 229, 230; his fortune, 230, 231; his will, 231, 232. *See also* Anne of Austria; Bouillon, Duchesse de; Colonna, Constabless; Louis XIV; Mazarin, Duchesse de; Soissons, Comtesse de

Mazarin, Duc de, 49, 50, 64, 227, 228, 229, 261–71, 272, 273, 282, 284, 285, 305, 330, 395, 401, 403

Mazarin, Duchesse de (Hortense Mancini), brought to France, 37; sent to the Couvent de la Visitation, 44; her letters to Mazarin, 45–48; passion which she arouses in the Marquis de la Meilleraye, 49, 50; accompanies the Court to Lyons, 85; Charles Emmanuel II of Savoy, a suitor for her hand, 92; "taking the same road as Marie," 140; accompanies her sister to Saint-Jean-d'Angely, 142–145; goes to Brouage, 170; returns to Paris, 184, 185; her suitors, 225–228; her marriage, 228, 229; inherits the bulk of the Cardinal's fortune, 232; her unhappy married life, 261–271; flies to Italy, 271–273; her *liaison* with the "Chevalier" de Couberville, 280–282; escape from the Convent of Campo-Marzo, 282; her lovers, 283, 284; returns to France, 284; attempt of her husband to have her arrested, 284, 285; returns to Rome, 285; shares her sister Marie's flight to France, 292–301; goes to Savoy, 305; rejoins her sister at Grenoble, 305; goes to reside at Chambéry, 311; her life there, 329, 330; her diplomatic conduct in regard to Marie, 330; leaves Savoy and takes up her residence in England, 393–394; her relations with Charles II, 394, 395 and note; Saint-Évremond's description of her charms, 396 note; her life in England, 396–399; visited by the Duchesse de Bouillon, 399,

400; her last years and death, 400–403; fate of her remains, 403; her children, 403, 404

Medina Cœli, Duque de, 354, 355, 356

Medina de Rio Seco, Duque de, 341, 342, 344

Mercœur, Duc de, 18, 23 and note, 24, 59

Mercœur (Laure Mancini), Duchesse de, brought to France, 3; her personal appearance, 3; her reception at Court, 4–6; sent to Val-de-Grâce, 15; Mazarin's plans for her establishment in life, 16, 17; betrothed to the Duc de Mercœur, 18; her marriage opposed by Condé, 18; accompanies Mazarin to Brühl, 21, 22; married to the Duc de Mercœur, 23 and note; returns to Paris, 23, 24; takes charge of her sister Hortense, 54; her death, 57, 59; her children, 59

Modena, Duchess of (Laure Martinozzi), 35–38, 50–52

Monaco, Prince de, 395

Moréna (*femme de chambre* to Marie Mancini), 289, 293, 294, 312, 320, 327, 337

Monsieur. See Orléans, Philippe, Duc d'

Monterey, Comte de (Governor of Flanders), 338, 339, 340

Montespan, Marquise de, 235 note, 243, 285, 306, 310, 315, 321, 363, 380

Montpensier, Mlle. de, 30, 67, 85, 87, 88, 97, 98, 103, 104; (cited), 67, 68, 79, 87, 88–90, 91, 94, 99, 104, 197, 200, 389

Motteville, Marquise de, 64, 96 note, 110; (cited), 1, 3, 57, 63, 66, 70, 92 note, 109, 116, 196, 229

N

Navailles, Duc de, 219, 249, 250

Navailles, Duchesse de, 249, 250

Nevers, Duc de, 37, 38, 43, 104, 105, 106, 204, 230, 231, 271, 272, 281, 284, 306, 307, 321, 322, 404, 405, 409, 410 and note

Nevers, Duchesse de, 284, 321, 410

Noailles, Duc de, 52

Noailles, Duchesse de, 52

O

Ondedei, Bishop of Fréjus, 162, 182, 183, 227, 228 and note, 254

Orléans, Gaston, Duc d', 20, 26, 27 and note, 206

Orléans, Charlotte Elizabeth, Duchesse d' (cited), 10 note, 377 note, 389
Orléans, Henrietta Anne, Duchesse d', 217, 226, 245, 250–252, 259, 386
Orléans, Philippe, Duc d', 6, 78, 97, 103, 104, 110, 199, 219, 226, 245, 290, 350
Oropesa, Conde de (Prime Minister of Spain), 382, 388
Ossuna, Duque d' (Governor of the Milanese), 338

P

Palatine, Princess (Anne de Gonzague), 86
Palatine, Princess. See Orléans, Charlotte Elizabeth, Duchesse d'
Paleotto, Marchesa, 279, 280, 328, 413
Parma, Duke of, 95
Pedro II, King of Portugal, 225
Pelletier (valet de chambre to Madame de Mazarin), 292–297, 304, 311
Perey, Lucien, 413; (cited), 85, 110, 159, 172, 213, 221, 275, 276, 333, 346 note
Perkins, Mr. J. B. (cited), 9, 110, 111
Perrault, 264
Philip IV, King of Spain, 85, 95, 192, 197–199
Philip V, King of Spain, 411
Pimentel (Spanish envoy to France), 90 and note, 91 note, 93, 103, 106, 133
Pomponne, Marquis de, 299 note, 300
Pradon (poet), 148, 259, 260

R

Racine, 258–260
Rebenac, Comte de (French Ambassador in Madrid), 381, 382, 383, 384 and note
Renée, M. Amédée (cited), 110, 257, 258.
Retz, Cardinal de (cited), 24
Richelieu, Cardinal de, 4 note, 6, 7
Rohan, Chevalier de (lover of Madame de Mazarin), 262 note, 271 note, 272, 273

S

Saint-Évremond, 55, 395, 396, 398, 403; (cited), 265, 266 and note, 396 and note, 399, 402
Saint-Réal, 397, 400
Saint-Simon, Duc de (cited), 230, 377 and note, 389, 390, 414

San Tommasso, Marchese di (Prime Minister of Savoy), 331, 335
Sarrazin (poet), 39 and note, 40, 41 and note
Savoie, Eugène de, 378, 379, 381, 392, 393
Savoie, Philippe de, 378
Scudéry, Mlle. (cited), 315 note
Sévigné, Madame de, 300; (cited), 303, 312, 374, 376, 398 note
Soissons, Chevalier de, 378, 397, 398
Soissons, Comte de, 60–62, 247, 362
Soissons (Olympe Mancini), Comtesse de, brought to France, 3; her personal appearance, 3; her reception at Court, 4–6; sent to Val-de-Grâce, 15; accompanies Mazarin to Brühl, 21, 22; returns to Paris, 23, 24; marries the Comte de Soissons, 60–62; her intimacy with Louis XIV, 62–64; her strange behaviour to la Grande Mademoiselle, 67, 68; flaunts her intimacy with the King, 74, 75; her indifference during Louis XIV's illness at Calais, 78, 79; the King ceases to visit her, 81; accompanies the Court to Lyons, 85; in disgrace with Louis XIV, 87; endeavours to do her sister Marie an ill turn, 143; misrepresents the latter's conduct to Mazarin, 147; advised by the Cardinal to behave " with more prudence and moderation," 148; endeavours to recover her influence over Louis XIV, 175; resumes her former intimacy with him, 179, 181; intrigues with Mazarin against Marie and the King, 210; her spiteful remark to Marie, 213; Mazarin's bequest to her, 231, 232; "visited daily by the King," 234; discarded by him for Louise de la Vallière, 247–251; mistress of the Marquis de Vardes, 245–247; intrigues against La Vallière, 247–250; exiled to Champagne, 250–252; recalled to Court, 252; visits her sister Marie at the Abbey of Lys, 315, 316; loses her husband, 362; resigns her post of Superintendent of the Queen's Household, 362, 363 and note; compromised in the Poison Trials, 371–373; escapes to Flanders, 374, 375; her adventures there, 376 and note, 377; settles in Brussels, 377; her sons, 377–379; goes to Madrid, 380; suspected by Carlos II of sorcery, 381, 382; her life in Madrid, 383, 384; charged by Saint-Simon with having poisoned

the Queen of Spain, 389, 390 ; her last years and death, 391, 392 ; her character, 392

T

Thianges, Diane de. *See* Nevers, Duchesse de
Turenne, Maréchal de, 29, 30, 76, 137, 227, 253, 254

V

Vallot (first physician to Louis XIV), 77, 148, 150
Valois, Mlle., 199
Vardes, Marquis de, 219 and note, 245-252
Villars, Duc de, 353, 354
Villars, Duchesse de, 353, 354 ; (cited) 358, 370
Villeroi, Maréchal de, 27, 391
Vendôme, Louis Joseph, Duc de, 59, 364, 368, 369

Vendôme, Philippe, Grand Prieur de, 59, 364
Venel, Madame de (*gouvernante* of Marie, Hortense, and Marianne Mancini), 98, 102, 103, 112, 135, 121, 122 note, 125, 138, 141, 142 and note, 146, 147, 148, 152, 163, 168, 170, 171, 173, 174, 177, 188, 190, 191, 201, 202, 209, 221, 222, 234, 235, 239, 240 and note.
Victor Amadeus I, Duke of Savoy, 83
Vigoureux, la (poisoner), 365, 368, 369, 370, 371 and note, 372
Voisin, la (poisoner), 365, 366, 367 and note, 369
Voltaire (cited), 205
Vossius, Dr., 397

W

Waller (poet), 397 ; (cited) 394
William III, King of England, 401

PLYMOUTH
WILLIAM BRENDON AND SON, LIMITED
PRINTERS

www.ingramcontent.com/pod-product-compliance
Lightning Source LLC
Chambersburg PA
CBHW020922020726
47495CB00002B/307